The Thing filled his mind. It was too powerful to push away. Sean felt like he was drowning in a sea of writhing tentacles. It was reptilian and evil . . . and ancient. It was incredibly, unbelievably ancient. All he was aware of was the presence that threatened to consume him. The Thing was a monstrous weight in his head that was pushing him deeper and deeper toward oblivion.

Sean's tongue was hanging from his mouth and he was panting like a dog as he struggled to get away from the presence that was burying him. From some far corner of his mind that still remained his own, a voice called out to him urgently, "If you ever sense anything like that again, run as fast as you can." Sean tried to make sense out of the words, but they seemed to be in a foreign language. "Run, Sean. Run as fast as you can." Again the warning voice, weaker now. Sean felt himself slipping closer to the abyss that yawned hungrily, waiting for him.

"Run . . . run, Sean. Run!"

DICK BARRETT

LYNX BOOKS
New York

TIME DOUBLE

ISBN: 1-55802-379-8

First Printing/June 1989

This book is published by Lynx Books, a division of Lynx Communications, Inc., 41 Madison Avenue, New York, New York, 10010. The name "Lynx" and the logo consisting of a stylized head of a lynx are trademarks of Lynx Communications, Inc.

Printed in the United States of America

0 9 8 7 6 5 4 3 2 1

To the real Marilyn, who thought
it was a good story, this
book is affectionately dedicated.

PROLOGUE

The End . . . 1985

It was a perfect afternoon for a flight. The sky was cloudless, the visibility limitless, the air calm. It was the kind of weather pilots refer to as "Severe Clear." The southern Ohio landscape floating under his wings was a panorama worthy of an Ansel Adams photograph, but it brought no pleasure to Peter Marston, who glared at the fuel indicator in his Cessna Skyhawk. The offending instrument insisted he had a fuel shortage. Peter knew better. He had left Meadows Field with full tanks less than half an hour before. The gauge had to be malfunctioning. Peter sighed and wondered if he could afford to replace the instrument with his next paycheck. Probably not. The rule of thumb for estimating the cost of aircraft replacement parts involves picking a dollar amount fifty percent higher than is reasonable, squaring that figure, and adding four percent sales tax. The thought crossed Peter's mind—and not for the first time—that if man was intended to fly he'd be born with more money.

There are people who go through life seemingly without difficulty or effort, very much the favored pet of some cosmic teacher. There is a second group that experiences a mix of luck both good and bad. Those born into this second group frequently point out to those less fortunate that "You get out of life what you put into it," and the even more profound, "Life is what you make it."

There is also a third group, which included Peter. Members of this group move from one mishap to the next with a consistency bordering on the uncanny.

Peter's troubles began even before he entered the world.
His genetic blueprint was plainly the creation of genes
with a sense of humor. To begin with, Peter was short. It
is very difficult to go through life in a world where six feet
is average and you stand five foot four.

It could be argued that being short is not so terrible.
Many short people have achieved success, recognition, and
fame. Julius Caesar was short and he did all right for himself. Napoleon Bonaparte lacked stature but certainly not
status. If Peter's genes had been content to make him short
and then called it a day and adjourned for a beer, all might
still have been well. Instead, at least one of those pesky
little devils gave him a tendency to overeat. Another,
caught up in the spirit of the game, made him slightly my-
opic.

People seeing Peter for the first time were often reminded of a very large wardrobe packed into a very small,
bespectacled overnight bag.

As if to cushion the effect of these less than awesome
characteristics, Peter had entered the world with a com-
placent, good-humored disposition that seldom degener-
ated into anger or irritation. Those who got to know him
quickly found themselves thinking of a lovable overnight
bag.

Peter saw the blue of Lake Hammer appear in the distance and knew he had drifted slightly to the east. He took
a chart from the seat beside him and unfolded it awkwardly in the cramped cabin. He scanned the map for
several minutes while he steadied the yoke with his knee.
Satisfied at last, he refolded the map and banked gently to
a corrected course that would bring him to Brookline Field.

Peter Marston passed through childhood and adoles-
cence quietly and without fanfare. He was an adequate, if
not inspired, student who after high school got his teaching credentials and became an adequate, if not inspired,
teacher. His days were now spent lecturing uninterested
high school seniors about important people and events of

the past, and his evenings were spent dreaming of himself one day becoming an important person.

The airplane coughed absently as it winged through the sky. Peter felt a surge of adrenaline as he scanned the instruments fearfully. Everything looked okay except for that damned fuel gauge. There was no way he could be out of fuel.

The preflight procedure for a Cessna Skyhawk involves a series of inspections. There are five separate and independent fuel checks, beginning with the gauge in the cockpit, followed by a manual drain of fuel from the bottom of both tanks to ensure the absence of contamination. Finally, the gas caps on both wings are removed and visual confirmation of the fuel level is made. Peter had left Meadows with nineteen gallons of usable fuel in each of his tanks. At his five-thousand-foot altitude that was enough to keep him flying for at least two and a half hours. He checked his watch and calculated that he had been in the air for roughly twenty-five minutes. Peter frowned again at the troublesome indicator and wished the needle wasn't bouncing gently above the "E."

Flying became Peter's solution to the problem of becoming an important person. Two years earlier he had gotten his license after experiencing the thrill of flying and a new image of himself as a steely-eyed professional aviator. If his instructors had found him a slow student during training and only a mediocre pilot at completion, they had been kind enough to keep this knowledge from him.

The bad luck that seemed to follow Peter like a devoted puppy dog had been very much in evidence during his flight training. His first instructor, after bringing him almost to the point of solo, had left the business, citing long hours, low pay, frustrating students, and multiple family problems. He had subsequently accepted a minimum-wage position as a security guard in one of the rougher areas of Columbus. This left Peter looking for another instructor and starting all over again. His second choice, a morose old-timer who could have learned his trade from the Wright brothers, lasted twelve lessons before developing a severe drinking problem that led to his hospitalization and the loss of his own license.

Peter's third choice was made of sterner stuff and had stayed with him right up to that magic day when an easygoing F.A.A. examiner signed Peter's ticket, making him, finally, a licensed aviator. None of Peter's three instructors, if they thought of him at all, ever confused him with a steely-eyed, professional anything. The image Peter presented to the world was difficult to reconcile with his own view of himself as a dapper flying ace. A dapper teddy bear, perhaps, but nothing more. It may be hard to imagine a teddy bear battling a disabled DC-10 to the ground and saving hundreds of lives, but this was indeed Peter's favorite, if secret, daydream.

The Muskingum River sparkled and glowed as it captured the reflection of the sun that was dropping below the mountains behind the plane. The river marked the boundary of the Brookline Traffic Control Area. Peter lifted the microphone and paused before depressing the call button. He began in his best steely-eyed, professional voice, "Brookline Field, Cessna Niner-Hotel-Niner, twenty-five miles north, northwest."

"Niner-Hotel-Niner, good evening. This is Brookline tower with five thousand scattered, visibility ten, wind calm, temperature seventy-nine, dew point six-nine, altimeter two niner six niner, ILS runway one seven left in use. Contact approach control at Brookline Hospital and advise you have foxtrot."

"Niner-Hotel-Niner."

Peter replaced the microphone contentedly. One of the great joys of flying was calling the tower and sounding professional.

The Cessna coughed twice and lurched. The engine smoothed briefly and then stopped.

For an instant Peter sat motionless while the enormity of the disaster swept over him in paralyzing waves. It's one thing to daydream about in-flight emergencies, but the reality is a completely different, totally devastating experience.

Peter's aviation skills might have charitably been called average. Certainly his instructors had despaired of ever making a first-rate pilot out of the rotund little history teacher. Perhaps there were times when they had doubts that he would qualify for a license at all. But these instructors would have to concede that Peter knew emergency procedures, having allowed him to solo in a sixty-five-thousand-dollar aircraft while risking his life and their own professional reputations on Peter's ability to bring the plane safely back to ground. Each had spent hour after weary hour drilling him again and again (as they did with each student to come under their tutelage) in procedures designed to extricate him from every emergency or malfunction their experienced minds could concoct. These hours of rote training now came to Peter's aid. With trembling fingers he set his radio frequency to 121.5 megahertz, keyed the mike twice, and began letting the world know he was in trouble.

"MAYDAY . . . MAYDAY . . . MAYDAY . . . CESSNA NINER-HOTEL-NINER . . . I HAVE ENGINE FAILURE AT FIVE THOUSAND FEET, HEADING TWO ZERO ZERO!"

Even as he was broadcasting, Peter was pulling the nose of Niner-Hotel up to an attitude that would slow the plane to sixty-five knots and provide for the longest possible glide path. He rotated the trim wheel on the floor beside his seat to maintain the controls in this position, then reached under his transceiver to a more specialized radio set below it on the instrument panel. Tuning this transponder to "7700," he depressed a small button to the left of the digital display.

Several things started to happen on the ground below.

Peter's initial distress call, limited only by line of sight, was heard at every airport, flight service facility, and control tower within a five-hundred-mile radius in all directions. As the source of the call was identified on radar, flight controllers prepared to divert any and every other craft from the emergency area. Telephone calls began radiating out from control towers that had received Peter's call to airport managers of smaller airports that lacked towers. A designated Flight Service Emergency Coordinator was contacted a hundred miles away in Columbus, and he prepared to move people and equipment if necessary, as the details of the emergency became known.

Peter's second signal on the transponder was received by every control tower and radar installation monitoring the sky within a two-hundred-mile radius. On radar screens across southern Ohio, the blip of light that was Cessna Niner-Hotel-Niner began to glow brightly and grow until it was several times larger and brighter than anything else on the screen. As the glow began fading back to normal, the numbers "7700" started blinking on and off below the spot of light. *"AIRCRAFT IN DISTRESS."* Peter Marston and his Cessna had just become the most important objects in the sky. From this moment until his plane was back on the ground no expense or inconvenience would be spared to ensure his safe return to earth.

"Cessna Niner-Hotel-Niner, Brookline Control, say altitude."

"Brookline Control, Niner-Hotel, four eight hundred."

"How many persons on board, sir?"

"Just me. My name is Peter Marston."

"What type of aircraft, sir?"

"Cessna 172."

"What color is the plane?"

"Eh . . . blue . . . blue and white." Peter had a sudden picture of search and rescue planes hunting for blue wreckage and tried to put the thought from his mind.

"Mr. Marston, we have you on radar. Will you please change frequency to 122.7?"

"Niner-Hotel-Niner." Peter keyed the mike then dropped it into his lap before switching to the requested frequency.

The tower supervisor at Brookline nodded without looking up as an air controller hurried over with performance charts for Cessna 172s. As he waited for Niner-Hotel to change frequencies, the supervisor began looking at these charts and jotting notes on a pad.

"Niner-Hotel, say altitude."

"Four six hundred."

"Have you tried to restart your engine?"

"I've got carb heat on. It turns over but won't catch."

"How about fuel?"

"Gauge says empty but I just left Meadows about thirty minutes ago and both tanks were full. I thought the gauge was defective."

"Okay, for now we'll assume you're out of fuel. At your present altitude without power you have a range of seven, maybe eight miles. Do you see any possible landing sites?"

Peter had been scanning the ground below in the fading light for the past several minutes without success. To his left was a forested area with no meadows or fields within range of Niner-Hotel. On his right and in front of him, the landscape was built up and semi-industrial without any clearing large enough to tuck an airplane into.

"I'm looking, Brookline. Nothing yet."

While he continued anxiously searching the ground below, Peter began preparing his craft for a forced landing. The lessons of years before returned like a nursery rhyme of survival: mixture control to idle . . . shut off the fuel selector valve . . . turn off the ignition switch . . . master switch off. No—wait. That would be later. Just before touchdown. Or impact.

Peter glanced at the fuel gauge and saw himself forty-five minutes earlier, balancing precariously on a wing strut, struggling with a misplaced center of gravity as he tried to peer into the gas tank. That was when he got the phone call. An instructor with the flight school had trotted up to Peter and told him he had a telephone call inside. Peter had clambered awkwardly to the ground and returned to the FBO only to find the telephone line silent and dead.

No, the caller had not left a name. Yes, he had asked for Peter Marston. No, no one had any idea who it might have been.

Peter returned to his plane and . . . and . . .

And suddenly, Peter knew what had happened. There was nothing wrong with the fuel indicator. He was out of gas. His beautiful airplane was going to turn into an ugly crumpled wreck and he was going to be killed just because he had forgotten to put the gas cap back. Peter groaned and knew that even if he brought Niner-Hotel to ground in one piece he was still likely to die of acute and painful embarrassment.

Every fixed-wing aircraft flies by producing a low pressure area over the wings that pulls the craft up. A Cessna Skyhawk has fuel tanks in the wings that are filled from the top. Without a gas cap, the fuel in both tanks is sucked out by the same low pressure area that's lifting the plane.

"Niner-Hotel." The radio crackled to life. "Turn right, heading two seven zero."

"Niner-Hotel," Peter acknowledged and banked gently to the right, rolling out of his turn on a due west course.

"Say altitude."

"Three eight hundred." Peter's throat constricted and he did his best to stay calm as he watched the needle on his altimeter ticking off the distance between himself and the ground below.

"Niner-Hotel, just about five miles in front of your nose you should be able to see Tracy Field. It's an uncontrolled airport, two-thousand-foot runway, not too well maintained but it should be within your range. Have you got it?"

"Looking." Peter searched frantically in front of the plane for an airstrip and at first saw nothing. The land below him was totally industrial now with railroads and warehouses taking up every available bit of land. A patch of gray suddenly appeared in the distance in front of him and a little to his left.

"Brookline, I've got it. I can see the field."

"Is it within your range?"

"I know I can make it, Brookline. It's going to be close but I'm sure I can make it. I'm going to make it!"

"Take it easy, sir. Calm down and concentrate on flying the airplane. There will be emergency equipment on the field when you touch down. Is there anyone we can call for you?"

"Negative, Brookline," Peter said. He heard his voice cracking and tears of relief formed in his eyes as survival began to seem possible. For once Peter Marston didn't care if he sounded professional or not. "I'm going to make it."

"Yes, sir. Stay on this frequency until you're on the ground. We'll be keeping it clear for you. Good luck, Mr. Marston."

"Thank you, Brookline." Unable to think of any other words to say and not certain he could manage to say them if he could think of them, Peter dropped the microphone into his lap while he turned his attention to the runway ahead of him and to safety.

While Peter was guiding Niner-Hotel to the end of the runway, Willie Ketzbeck and his sister were climbing aboard a Piper Tomahawk on the flight line at Tracy. Willie had been a licensed pilot for almost four hours now, and Melinda Ketzbeck wasn't sure how she felt about being her brother's first passenger. Still . . . she had promised.

Although Tracy Field was an uncontrolled airfield and there was no tower to clear him for takeoff, the field was assigned a frequency that arriving and departing aircraft used to alert other traffic of their intentions. Willie tuned the radio to 123.0 and depressed the call button on the mike.

"Piper Five-Seven-Two-November, taxi for takeoff, runway two seven."

As Willie and his sister taxied toward the runway, the roar of the Piper's four-cylinder Lycoming engine prevented them from hearing the wail of sirens converging on Tracy Field.

Peter could see fire trucks entering the airfield from his seven-hundred-foot altitude. He lined up with runway two seven with altitude to spare. After lowering twenty degrees of flap to increase his rate of descent, he flipped off the master switch, killing all electrical power to the craft. Peter tried to ignore the hard knot in his stomach and the trembling of his limbs as the Cessna floated, silent and dark, toward the end of the runway.

Wild Willie had finished his run-up and the last of his instrument checks before he saw the fire trucks moving onto the taxiway at the other end of the airport. For a moment he wondered what they were doing there and then decided they didn't concern him.

"Last chance to chicken out, Lin." He turned to his sister.

"I guess insanity runs in the family. Let's go, Willie."

Wild Willie pushed the throttle all the way in and pulled on to runway two seven directly in front of Cessna Niner-Hotel-Niner.

Peter was pulling Niner-Hotel's nose into a landing flair when a Piper Tomahawk suddenly appeared in front of him. With a knee-jerk reaction that ignored all the training he had ever received, he slammed the yoke all the way back to the stop. The Cessna's nose, which had been pointed to the horizon, suddenly bounced skyward. The stall warning blared raucously for a moment and then fell silent as Niner-Hotel stopped flying. The plane's left wing dipped, almost touching the ground, and then continued around as the Cessna flipped over in the air. Peter Marston screamed once before he and his airplane smashed upside down into the runway.

PART ONE

Going Around

"In the time when Dendid created all things,
He created the sun,
And the sun is born, and dies, and comes again."

African song,
Anonymous

CHAPTER ONE

1950

Blackness covered and soothed him. There was no pain. There was no sensation. Nothingness persisted for an eternity and then there were dreams. Misty apparitions seemed to float close to perception only to fade again to blackness. There was light that wasn't light, a blue glow that never penetrated the blackness but lingered almost in memory as a retinal afterimage. Peter drifted without pain, awareness, or fear in a place that alternated between nothingness and blackness . . . and the ethereal, almost dreams.

There was only the soothing dark . . . and peace.

How long he drifted in this place couldn't be measured. Peter existed outside of time and space in a dimension unconnected with reality.

So gradually as to be almost unnoticed, there was a perception. Self existed. As the realization of self consumed him it brought with it a calm joy that lasted for moments . . . or centuries. Peter basked in the awareness, content to let wave after wave of self wash over him.

Memories returned. They came slowly at first and then with a rush: memories of airplanes and students, of childhood and animals and Coca-Cola and classrooms. They were sanitized fragments lacking cohesion and emotion but existing and appearing much as the earlier dreams. And always, spaced between periods of self, misty dreams and unreal, phantom memories were the embracing periods of nothing . . . more profound than sleep . . . more soothing than a mother's arms, restoring him, rebuilding him.

There was sound. Beginning so softly and growing so

slowly that Peter, or the thing that had been Peter, was unaware for several eternities of the rhythmic ebb-and-flow murmurings, seeming like nothing so much as a large ocean, powerful and loving, enclosing and caring for him. Then came an awareness of limbs, extremities somehow attached to him but not yet under his control.

And finally came the yearning. It started as a tiny unease and grew to a definite sense of purpose. It was a need to . . . to what? The Self that had been Peter didn't know. He tried to retreat to the blackness but the blackness, the earlier total all-embracing blackness, wouldn't return. He struggled harder and sought refuge in the soothing nothingness he had known but there was no longer a refuge to be found. The periods of restorative nothingness had become rarer and finally ceased altogether, leaving Peter, or the thing he had become, with only long periods of sleep to comfort him. With sleep came more dreams, more definite and less misty now.

The feeling of arms and legs existing somewhere persisted and grew. Then there was a moment when Peter began to control those extremities. First, just a twitch, barely discernible, then larger movements until one . . . one what? A day, a night, a time, a kick . . . a stretch . . . a new sensation . . . MOVEMENT.

Marilyn Jeffries carefully swung her feet out of bed and winced as the pain came again. Easing her bulk upright, she considered waking Jason but decided she could get dressed and pack a bag a lot easier without a hysterical husband underfoot. Mugs, their gray-and-white terrier, looked up sleepily from his place at the foot of the bed and, apparently deciding the situation required his expertise, hopped to the floor and followed Marilyn to the closet. Moving slowly and with obvious effort, Marilyn removed the suitcase and opened it on the dresser. After putting in a nightgown, a change of clothing, and various toilet articles from the bathroom, she began dressing herself.

"You okay, honey?" Jason sat up in bed.

"I think it's time."

Jason kicked the covers off and moved to his wife's side. "Why didn't you call me, you dummy? Here, I'll get that. You go in the living room and sit down."

"That's why I didn't call you." Marilyn laughed at her husband. "You get dressed and I'll go call the hospital. I'm okay, really."

Nine minutes later Jason was pulling their old Studebaker out of the driveway and fighting a losing battle with several thousand butterflies in his stomach.

Marilyn watched her husband fumbling with the shift, nervously trying to put the car into first gear, and had to smile in spite of her discomfort.

She had met Jason on a blind date three years before, when he was in his second year at McGeorge School of Law in Sacramento and she was a junior at Sacramento State College. She had thought the tall law student was brash, arrogant, and opinionated. He dropped her off in front of her dorm at the end of the evening and she never expected, nor wanted, to hear from him again.

She was surprised when she received a single rose and a card the next day. She was even more surprised when he phoned that afternoon to ask her out again.

But what surprised her the most was how quickly she accepted.

It was only after she began to see the boy inside the man that her opinion of Jason began to change. What she had taken for arrogance she began to realize was just a refusal to accept any idea or philosophy until he had thought it through from all sides. If he was brash, he was also gentle. By their fourth date, Marilyn knew she was in love.

They were married a year later, just three days after he took the California bar exam.

The yearning could no longer be ignored. Peter struggled and moved again. The comforting darkness had

*changed character. It was constricting and . . . frighten-
ing. The thing that was Peter felt anxiety. He kicked out
as powerful muscles closed over him, crushing and pressing him forward. The pressure eased slightly and then came
again, pushing him, stifling him, urging him along. He
screamed without sound as monstrous forces he didn't understand battered and moved him toward their own private
goal.*

Jason Jeffries lit another cigarette then stubbed it out
after a few quick puffs. Unable to sit still, he paced back
and forth in the tiny waiting room to the amusement of
the room's other occupant: a veteran of four children over
the previous six years.

"You may as well relax, my friend. If anything happens
they're gonna tell you. In the meantime you may be waiting here for hours."

"Women have children every day," Jason said, more
for his own benefit than for the other expectant father's.
"I don't know why I'm so jumpy."

"Believe me, I know the feeling." The other man
waited until Jason's orbit brought him within social distance and then stuck out a hand. "I'm Charlie Wade. This
your first?"

"Jason Jeffries. Yes. First and last. I can't picture going
through this again."

"Seems to me your wife is doing most of the hard
work."

"That's debatable. At least she's in there doing something about it. I can't think of very much that's harder than
waiting out here and not knowing what's going on."

"That's probably because you've never had a baby."
Charlie smiled thoughtfully. "I was like that the first couple of times. If it helps any, you get used to it."

"Oh, God." Jason slapped his forehead in mock dismay. "I don't want to get used to it."

Charlie laughed out loud. "Just don't make any rash

decisions about no more kids till the baby gets here. You may feel different then. What kind of work do you do?''

"I'm a lawyer. We just moved here from Elk Grove a month ago and I'm actually still looking for a job.''

"Why Los Angeles?''

"Well, my wife Marilyn has relatives in the area and it seemed like there would be more job opportunities in southern California than in Elk Grove . . .''

For the next two hours, Jason was able to forget his panic as he and Charlie Wade swapped life stories in a shared intimacy common to cell mates in prison, police officers in patrol cars, and expectant fathers in waiting rooms.

At three-thirty in the morning Charlie left the hospital, the sleepy father of a fifth daughter, but it wasn't until almost seven that a nurse collected Jason and led him to see his wife and new son.

Marilyn looked radiant and exhausted as she smiled up at him. Nestled in her arms, looking just a bit disgruntled at the indignities that had been heaped upon him, Jason's son slept peacefully. Jason wondered in amazement whether he could be harboring an incredible bias without realizing it, or if his son was, in fact, the most beautiful baby he had ever seen.

The visit was too brief. It seemed to Jason that he had been in the room only a minute before a no-nonsense head nurse was insisting that the new father let his wife get some rest. Jason kissed his wife and son and left the hospital in a happy daze. Arriving home, he telephoned his and Marilyn's parents with the joyous news before finally collapsing into an exhausted and dreamless sleep.

At the hospital, Sean Jeffries was moved to the glassed-in ward for newborns, where everyone who saw him commented on what a beautiful baby he was.

CHAPTER TWO

1958

Jason pulled the Cadillac into his parking stall and enjoyed the new-car smell that still lingered after a month. He scooped his briefcase and several loose files from the seat beside him, locked the car, and sprinted for the closing doors of the elevator. The boyish-looking attorney was regarded in legal circles as a young man on the way up. When Jason realized he wouldn't make it to the elevator doors before they closed, he bounded up the stairs, taking them two at a time. Pausing on the third floor landing to straighten his tie and catch his breath, he felt a rush of pride as he saw the freshly painted letters on the door of his office, SUTTON AND JEFFRIES, and below that in slightly smaller lettering, LAW OFFICES.

Al Sutton had taken a chance on Jason eight years earlier, just one month after the birth of the young lawyer's son. Jason had proven himself hardworking and thorough. He had a knack for seeing two, three, or a dozen sides to an issue and was seldom taken by surprise in the courtroom. This talent for anticipating the legal maneuvering of counsel for the other side had more than once saved the day for his client. He quickly gained a reputation as a competent and resourceful attorney, and with the reputation came referrals. Al Sutton watched with amazement as the practice he had spent twenty-five years building doubled in size over the first four years of Jason's association with the firm. Now in his sixties, Al was content to pass more and more of the load to his younger colleague and finally, just one week before, he had given Jason a full partnership.

"Hi, Jason." His secretary put her hand over the telephone mouthpiece and greeted him. "Your messages are on your desk and Mrs. Meyers is here for her two o'clock appointment." There was the barest hint of reproach in her voice as she nodded toward a heavyset older woman sitting nervously under a wall clock that said it was ten after three.

"Sorry, Margaret. I should have called." Jason gave his secretary an apologetic grin before turning to his waiting client.

"Anita, forgive me." He approached the older woman and extended a hand cordially. "I had a one o'clock hearing in Los Angeles and the traffic coming back was murder. How are you feeling today?" As he spoke Jason herded the older woman gently into his private office and indicated a chair. "Just give me another minute to clear some of this mess away and I'll be right with you." Jason scooped a handful of messages from the center of his desk and sorted quickly through them. Satisfied there was nothing that demanded his immediate attention, he dropped them into his basket to handle later. He took a legal pad from his briefcase and withdrew a mechanical pencil from his shirt pocket. "Al tells me you want to change your will again. Is that right?"

"That's right." The woman's lower lip trembled and Jason prepared for the worst.

Anita Meyers was Al's client. Her husband had been a wealthy contractor before his death six years earlier, and he had set up a trust that Sutton and Jeffries managed for the benefit of his widow. All four of Anita's children lived in the area and all four spent as much time with their mother as their schedules and lives permitted, but the sixty-eight-year-old widow was convinced her children no longer had time for her. At regular three- or four-month intervals Anita would call the office and make an appointment to discuss rewriting her will in order to exclude whichever offspring was currently in disfavor. Al and Jason both cared about the lonely old woman and endured her quarterly demands on their time without complaint and without ever billing her, even though the maintenance fees on the trust were negligible.

". . . And I certainly don't think a daughter who's too busy to drive two miles to see her mother should get my money when something happens to me. Don't you agree?" Mrs. Meyers faced Jason with righteous indignation.

"Anita, that's not my decision to make. We're just here to do whatever we can to make sure that everything is divided according to your wishes. You're saying that you want to leave Lisa out of your will?"

"Absolutely. I want to leave all of them out of my will."

"All of them?" Jason looked blankly at the old woman.

"That's right. I don't want any of them getting any of my money." Anita fumbled in her purse for a Kleenex, and Jason realized wearily that the conference was entering phase two. "I want Precious to get my money."

Jason considered his next move and reluctantly asked the question, "Anita, who is Precious?"

"Precious is my cat. The dear thing loves me and deserves to be provided for, unlike some ungrateful children I could name." The old woman was crying openly now. "I've given the best years of my life to those children and now when I need them they toss me aside like a worn-out pair of shoes."

"Now, Anita, I'm sure no one is tossing you aside like an old pair of shoes." Jason was distracted by a commotion in the outer office and forced his mind back to the sobbing woman across from him. "The biggest problem that I see right now is that you're upset. I think you ought to give this a few days to consider what you want to do. Maybe you could call your daughter and talk about it. This is a big decision and you shouldn't jump into anything until you've examined all the consequences."

"You think I'm being too hasty, don't you?"

"Well, perhaps just a little." Jason heard an angry male

voice through the closed door and again had to force his attention back to Anita Meyers. "Why don't you just relax and tell me what's been happening and maybe together we can decide the best thing to do about—"

There was a crash from the outer office and Jason rose from his chair. "Anita, Margaret has some kind of a problem out there. Would you excuse me for just a minute?" Without waiting for a reply, Jason moved around his desk and out of the office, closing the door behind him.

The source of the disturbance was a thin, gray-haired man who stood facing Margaret with his back to Jason.

"Listen, missy, I want to see your boss and I want to see him now, so you just go get him and tell him that George Braun is waiting for him!" The man slapped his open hand on the front of Margaret's desk and again Jason heard the sound he had thought was a crash.

"What the hell is going on out here?"

George Braun turned a rage-contorted face to the young attorney.

"The name's Braun. George Braun. I want to know what this means. It's got your name on it."

"I don't care what you want. The first thing you're going to do is stop shouting. This is an office, not a barroom." The anger in Jason's voice almost matched Braun's and the older man seemed to calm a bit.

"Just tell me what this is all about," Braun demanded. Jason took the letter the older man thrust in his direction and glanced at it quickly. As he read, keeping one eye on the glaring Braun, Jason remembered why the man's name was familiar. Al was handling the Johnson matter but they had talked about it briefly and Jason had a pretty good idea of the problem. He handed the letter back to Braun and spoke in level tones.

"What I really ought to do is have you locked up for disturbing the peace, but I am going to give you three minutes. Come in here." Jason opened the door to Al's office and waited while Braun walked ahead of him into

the room. Before closing the door behind them he turned
to Margaret and winked at her.

"How about going in and holding Anita's hand for a
few minutes. I'll get right back to her."

Margaret nodded and gave Jason a quick smile of gratitude for the rescue. Jason smiled back in acknowledg-
ment, then closed the door of Al's office.

"And now let's see about your problem." The face
Jason turned to George Braun was unsmiling and hard.

"I want to know what you mean by this." Braun waved
the letter he still clutched in his hand.

"That should be obvious to you. The letter is from my
partner and is our notification to you of our intention to
appear in Department Twelve of Municipal Court tomorrow morning at ten o'clock. We're going to secure a re-
straining order enjoining you from having any contact with
Dr. William Johnson or any member of his family. You
will be ordered to remain off his property and out of his
life. Should you violate this order, if you continue harassing our client and vandalizing his property, then you will
be hauled off to jail. The letter you have explains all of
this very clearly."

"Why are you doing this? What kind of man sells out
his own race? Just because that black sonofabitch has a
few bucks you gonna help him walk all over decent white
folks?"

Jason ignored the first two rejoinders that sprang to
mind, opting instead for a more reasonable if less satisfying approach. "Mr. Braun, you seem to be the only one
in this situation who insists on walking all over decent
people. Since my partner has been handling this I'm not
completely familiar with all the details, but I understand
that you've waged quite a campaign against our client.
This letter and our appearance in court tomorrow is our
way of telling you that the campaign is over. You lose."

Braun's tone was calmer than before, but his expression
remained hostile. "The missus and me, we been in our
house for four years now. We paid eighteen-thousand dol-

lars for it. Maybe it ain't much. It ain't anything big and fancy like yours probably is, but it's still our home. I didn't work all my life just to have some damn spear-chucker move in next door to me and destroy everything I've worked for.''

"And that brings us back to the fact that you're the only one doing any destroying or harassing. You seem to be overlooking the fact that the kind of conduct you've engaged in carries criminal as well as civil penalties. You're getting off a lot easier than you deserve.''

"You can say that because you don't know how they work. It starts with one. Before long a couple more of them move in. First thing you know the whole neighborhood is nigger and yours is the only white face around. Once they get their foot in the door they take over.''

"Braun, I have neither the interest nor the time to debate the issue with you. You got the explanation you were after. Good day.'' Jason opened the door and stepped back to let Braun precede him out of the office.

"Well kiss a rat's ass.'' Braun looked shocked at the abrupt dismissal. Jason felt some of his own anger dissipate as he saw Braun's ears turn a brilliant red. He had never see such a dramatic reaction before and watched with interest as the color spread to the rest of the man's face. His own adrenaline began flowing as Braun's hands started to tremble violently. When he spoke the older man's voice was a threatening hiss.

"Well, I'm going to tell you something, Mr. Smart-ass lawyer. No one pushes George Braun around . . . NO ONE! I'll get that black sonofabitch and when I do he'll be only too happy to move back where he belongs. Just you be sure . . . I ain't forgettin' you either . . .'' Braun paused for breath and seemed to be choking on his own venom.

"I said, get the hell out of here.'' Jason took a step in the older man's direction. For a moment their eyes locked and neither man moved, then Braun half turned and stalked out of the office. A second later Jason heard the outer door slam. He took a deep breath and let the anger drain from him until his heartbeat and breathing almost returned to normal. Then he sat down behind his partner's desk and spread a sheet of legal notepaper in front of him. With firm, rapid strokes he wrote as close to a word-for-word account as he could recall of his meeting with George Braun. When this was completed he attached a brief note to Margaret, asking her to type it up and give a copy to Al in the morning, then took the transcript and laid it in the middle of her desk.

Three floors below, George Braun stormed through the main doors of the office building into the bright afternoon sunlight. He was quivering with rage. The sonofabitch had treated him like dirt, like he wasn't as good as some nigger with a few bucks. Nobody could get away with treating him like that. This was only the first round.

He strode to a dingy 1950 Hudson parked next to the curb and yanked the door open, then hesitated with one hand still on the door handle.

He had said he would be gone about an hour. Tom was expecting him back at the high school. Well, that was tough. Washington was just going to have to take care of the school by himself this afternoon.

A little calmer now, George settled into the driver's seat and slammed the door. Right now, what he needed was to smash something . . . or someone. Somebody had to pay.

Braun started the car and pulled into traffic. Highland Vista High School could wait. George was going to Hollywood.

When Jason opened the door of his own office he was startled to find Anita Meyers and Margaret conversing cheerfully.

"Sorry I took so long. I get the feeling you two had a pleasant chat."

"I was telling Margaret about my granddaughter, Eileen. I swear, that child understands every word I say.

Would you believe, she's only six months old and last week . . ."

Anita was fairly bubbling and Margaret gave Jason a smug look before excusing herself and returning to her desk. It took Jason almost fifteen minutes to steer the old woman back to the subject of her visit to the office.

"Then I guess you've decided to think a bit more about changing your will before making any firm decisions," Jason finally said, hoping it wouldn't sound like a non sequitur.

"My will . . . ?" Anita pulled her mind back from a detailed comparison of her grandson, Tommy, and her own son Robert at ages five and six. "Oh, yes, my will. Of course I'm not going to change my will. You know, that Tommy looks exactly like his grandfather. It's absolutely amazing . . ."

It was another twenty minutes before Jason was able to lead a smiling Anita Meyers to the office door. She departed finally, and Jason closed the door behind her before turning to Margaret with a rueful expression.

"I'm not sure I know which one was worse."

"From the conversation I just typed I know which one I'd pick."

"Maybe if you hadn't upset him so much before I got to him I could have brought a new client into the firm." Jason laughed and dropped into a chair across from Margaret as the tension of the afternoon began to ebb with the departure of the last client.

"I take it you don't want me to open a client file for Mr. Braun." Margaret seemed to share his mood.

"I think not. Just give Al the transcript and have his office fumigated. Let's hope the sonofabitch never finds out I live only about seven blocks away. All I need is a cross burning on my front lawn."

"Oh my God, I didn't know that. You don't think . . ." Margaret looked genuinely afraid.

"No, no . . . I was kidding. Even George Braun couldn't be that stupid."

"I hope not." Margaret still looked worried. "By the way, Marilyn called a few minutes ago and told me to remind you of the PTA meeting tonight at seven."

"Damn!" Jason glanced at his watch and made a face. Could it be quarter of five already? "You would have done me a favor if you'd forgotten to tell me. I have enough work backed up to keep me busy until midnight if I wanted to stay here that long."

"You know, boss, you spend so little time at home that if you dropped dead tomorrow, Marilyn would have to use dental records to identify you."

"Why am I fated to have a wife who doesn't nag and a secretary who does?" Jason smiled to take the sting from his words. "I'm spending all my time in court. When do I have time for the paperwork?"

"You and Al need to hire another associate to handle the routine stuff."

"You're probably right. Business has been good." His face grew thoughtful, almost as though he was considering the merits of adding an associate to the firm or perhaps recalling his own early days working with Al Sutton. Some secret memory triggered a smile that flickered briefly and then was gone. With all the enthusiasm of an errant schoolboy forced to go to the principal's office for some misdeed, he turned reluctantly to his office. "Hold my calls for me unless it's a new client. I'm going to try to straighten out some of the mess piled on my desk."

Three hours later, two-and-a-half hours after Margaret had left for the day, Jason was still absorbed, updating client files, returning phone calls, and preparing for a deposition scheduled for the next day. When he finally left the office at eight o'clock, the PTA meeting he had once again forgotten about was just ending.

Sean Jeffries and Mugs crouched in the bushes in front of Puerta Grande School and waited for Michael to call an "Ollee, Ollee, Oxen-in-Free." Mugs, in particular, was beginning to find the game a little boring and chose that moment to bite noisily at a flea that was goose-stepping on his tail.

"Shut up, Mugs. He'll hear you." Sean slapped at the little gray terrier and then contritely began scratching the dog's tail for him. "Just be quiet," he whispered.

"I see you in the bushes, Sean." Michael whooped and raced for the tetherball post that marked "home." Sean bolted from his hiding place and scrambled after his friend. Mugs gamboled next to him, barking happily at the exciting turn the game had taken. Michael touched the goal a split second before Sean, and both boys collapsed giggling and breathless on the ground.

"My turn to hide." Michael started to climb to his feet.

"Let's do something else instead."

"Like what?"

"Didja ever go up there?" Sean pointed to the hill called Red Mountain rising six hundred feet into the air behind the school.

"Noooo." Michael followed Sean's finger and considered the idea. "My dad says there are coyotes and things up there. We'll get killed if he finds out we were messing around behind the fence."

"How'll he ever find out?" The younger boy was excited now. "We'll only go a little way up and then we'll come back. Nobody's gonna catch us."

"I dunno." Michael frowned at his smaller friend. "What's up there, anyway?"

"How do I know, dumbhead. We gotta go up if we're gonna find out. Come on. You scared or somethin'? We'll just climb up part of the way and then we'll come back." Sean's face was animated.

"Course I'm not scared." Michael gave his friend an indignant look at this slight to his manhood and then looked nervously back at Red Mountain. He wavered for a moment and then relented. "All right, let's go."

Puerta Grande School was built on Canyon Drive at the northernmost point in Highland Vista, an unincorporated bedroom community of Pasadena. The land in the foothills had been cheap when the school was planned and the county had allocated twice as much acreage to the project as might have been necessary, both for aesthetic reasons and to provide a fire break: important protection in an area that experiences destructive biannual brushfires with regularity. The school was completed before most of the homes that now clustered on its south and west sides. The three single-story buildings that made up Puerta Grande nested in the center of twenty-five acres of manicured lawn that was bordered on the north and east by rugged foothills. One of these foothills was known by local residents as Red Mountain, a somewhat pompous designation for the little hill of chaparral that rose abruptly just beyond the playground fence. Covered with dusty buckthorn, sumac, sagebrush, and scrub oak, stunted by the short wet winters and long dry summers of southern California, Red Mountain and the hills rising beyond and above it made up a part of the San Gabriel mountain range. The eastern and northern boundaries of the school were closed off by an eight-foot chain-link fence meant to discourage young explorers from venturing out of the playground. The effectiveness of the barrier was less than hoped for. During the school year at lunchtimes and recess periods, two teachers acted as fence-monitors with only limited success. Each year the winter rains washed away channels of earth from beneath the fence, many of them large enough for small bodies to wriggle through. It was to one of these natural ditches that Sean now led Michael. The two boys squeezed under the fence with Mugs in the lead and began their climb of Red Mountain.

Neither Sean nor Michael noticed the boy who stood near the swings a hundred yards away and watched their progress up the hill. The boy, who looked eleven or twelve years old, could have been returning from a costume party. He was dressed in baggy gray knickers that came down several inches below his knees then narrowed to grip his calves snugly, barely covering the tops of his knee socks. The plain wool shirt he wore was buttoned all the way to the top despite the afternoon heat. A paperboy cap rested at a jaunty angle on the top of his head as he stood motionless next to the playground swings, his eyes locked on Sean and Michael.

The boys climbed for almost ten minutes before they stopped and looked down at the playground, which was now a hundred feet below them. By that time the boy in the old-fashioned clothes had disappeared.

Marilyn Jeffries pulled into the driveway, veering toward the left to avoid the two bicycles abandoned on the right.

"SEAN!" She looked across the street at Puerta Grande as she called out but she didn't see her son in the playground or hear him responding. She returned to the car and opened the passenger door. Lifting the groceries from the front seat, she struggled to reclose the door with her body and managed to get her burden to the service porch before setting down the bags and opening the screen door.

"Sean, are you home?" There was no reply from the empty house and Marilyn sighed in exasperation. The only way to keep track of an active eight-year-old was to tie him up and lock him in the closet. Marilyn had considered this option on several occasions with more than a passing affection. He and Mugs were probably next door with Michael.

She busied herself putting away the groceries and enjoyed the stillness of the empty house. When the last of the food was put away she set the table for dinner. The quiet of the house, unusual for this time of day, began to generate a vague uneasiness and Marilyn went to the phone and dialed her neighbor. She counted five rings and was about to hang up when Linda Taylor answered breathlessly.

"Linda, this is Marilyn."

"Oh, hi. I was out back taking clothes off the line when I heard the phone. Ed's been promising to fix the dryer for me. Now I just need to get him off the couch and away from the TV long enough. What's up?''

''Are the boys over there with you? I just got back from the market and seem to have misplaced my son.''

''No. Michael said he was going over to your house.''

''Well, don't worry. They must be over at the playground. I'll take a walk over there and bring them home.''

''Wait a minute and I'll walk over with you.'' Marilyn heard her own concern echo in her neighbor's voice. ''Be right over.''

Marilyn and Jason had purchased the home across from Puerta Grande Elementary School a year and a half earlier. Ed and Linda Taylor had appointed themselves the official welcoming committee and arrived uninvited at their door three hours after the moving van had driven off. Bringing a supply of pizza and beer with them, they cheerfully helped haul boxes and move furniture. Marilyn's embarrassment at the clutter and complete disarray evaporated quickly in the face of their neighbors' casual geniality, and the two families hit if off immediately. Before long, Linda and Marilyn were getting together for coffee in the morning after their husbands and sons had left for the day. Sean and Michael Taylor became inseparable, and when they weren't in school or asleep they were usually together. Despite the two-year difference in age, Sean usually decided what he and his older friend would be doing, which greatly amused both sets of parents. Linda and Marilyn filled in for each other as baby-sitters and both boys now felt equally at home in either house.

Ed was a child psychologist who spent half of his time at Puerta Grande and the other half at Highland Vista High School, three miles away. He was a quiet, soft-spoken man who inspired confidence. It was to Ed that Marilyn had mentioned her fears two months after she and Jason had moved into the house on Canyon Drive.

The families had eaten dinner together that evening. Jason had suggested ice cream cones for dessert—a proposal the boys had responded to enthusiastically. Linda had liked the idea, too, and the four of them had piled into Jason's car, leaving Marilyn to clean up the dishes with Ed's help. It was Ed who started the conversation.

"Have you ever watched the way the boys interact?" He was drying a saucepan and paused to look at Marilyn. "Even though Michael is nine and Sean just turned seven, Sean is definitely the dominant personality. You know you have a very unusual youngster. As a matter of fact, a couple of times when I've talked to him, I've forgotten he's only seven years old."

"Sometimes I forget, too, and I'm his mother." Marilyn laughed and turned from the sink to face her neighbor. "Tell me something, Ed. You're a professional at this kind of thing. Does Sean seem happy to you?"

"That's a strange question."

"I'm serious. Can you tell if something might be bothering him?"

"He seems completely normal to me. If there's a problem I certainly haven't noticed it. On the other hand, I've known him for only a couple of months and I'm not around him that much. Do you think he might have a problem?"

"I'm not sure. When he was five he started having nightmares. They weren't like typical kids' dreams. There weren't any monsters or people chasing him. In fact, he never could tell us much detail except that they all seemed to involve falling. As far as Jason and I know, he's never had an accident that involved a fall. But the dream kept coming back. We used to wake up a couple of times a week hearing him screaming at three or four in the morning. This went on for about six months and then the dreams stopped. We never learned what caused them and to this day we don't know why they stopped."

"Okay, he was going through something and now it's over. What's the problem?"

"A week after we moved in here the dream came back. He's had the nightmare at least five or six times and last week he started bed-wetting again." Marilyn's voice shook and tears welled in her eyes.

"Here, calm down." Ed took Marilyn's arm and led her from the sink to the table, where he gently offered her a seat. "I think you're getting a little more upset than seems justified by what you're telling me. Have you ever talked with a doctor about this?"

"No. You're the only one I've talked to. Even Jason doesn't know about the bed-wetting. I didn't want to worry him but I've got to admit, I'm a little worried myself."

"Think back to the time the dreams started. Can you remember if there was anything going on in your lives that might have been—" Ed paused, searching for the right word, "anything that might have been upsetting Sean?"

"I don't know of anything."

"Everything was normal? Was there possibly any change in your day-to-day routine that might have been stressful to him or to you?"

Marilyn thought about this. "It was a good time, really. We had just moved from a tiny apartment into a much larger house that we rented."

"So you moved from an apartment and Sean began having nightmares. You moved here and Sean again begins having nightmares. Do you see any connection?"

"Okay, I see what you're saying. But . . . why?"

Ed Taylor leaned back in his chair and looked over Marilyn's head at the kitchen wall with a serious expression on his face. "People have the wrong idea about psychology and psychiatry. The layman assumes we know a great deal more about human behavior than we really do and that what we know is far more immutable than it is. This is especially true in the area of child psychology and child development. There are a few things though that we can say with some degree of certainty. We know, for example, that the real bogeyman for small children is nothing more than a fear of abandonment. If a child is given a base to operate from that is secure and loving, and most important, a base that's permanent, that child will be able to develop into a healthy and well-functioning adult. A child that doesn't have this base will be insecure and unhappy and will grow up to be an insecure and unhappy adult.''

"Do you think Sean feels insecure?"

"I think he may be experiencing some stress as a result of the move to Highland Vista. Remember, I've never sat down with him on a professional level, but based on what I've seen of him and of you and Jason, I'm quite sure he knows he's loved and knows he can depend on you. As a matter of fact, I believe he's a very well-adjusted little boy in spite of what you've just told me. When a child faces a major change in his life that removes him from familiar surroundings and routines, it sometimes has a temporary effect on behavior. It can produce stress and cause nightmares and bed-wetting. The word I want to emphasize is *temporary*. I don't think you need to worry about it.''

Marilyn felt a gloom she had lived with for six weeks begin to lift.

"Is there anything we can do to . . . reinforce his sense of stability?"

"Just what you're doing. Give him lots of love and attention. On the other hand, don't spoil him rotten because he's having a little problem. Sometimes a kid gets more love out of a swat on the backside than from a kiss on the cheek. Keep in mind, you're dealing with only one problem. The nightmares are an attempt to express the problem in a way his mind will accept. The bed-wetting isn't really a problem; it's a symptom. Go to him when he hurts. Hold him and try to get him to talk about specific details in his dream. You say the dreams lasted six months the last time. I'll be willing to bet they'll disappear a lot sooner this time. Be patient with him and let him work it out. And since you're getting all this terrific professional advice after working hours, how about getting your friendly neighborhood shrink another cup of coffee.''

"Doctor Taylor, you can have a whole pot if you want it." Marilyn got to her feet, surprised at how buoyant and lightheaded she felt. "You have no idea how relieved I am."

"There is one other thing," Ed continued as Marilyn took a cup from the drainboard and poured his coffee, "bed-wetting can be a psychological or a pathological problem. If it continues beyond a few weeks, you might consider taking Sean to his regular doctor to be sure there isn't a physical cause that can be corrected with medication. In the meantime try to restrict his fluid intake after dinner. Also, keep in mind that he's not doing it on purpose. It's not something you should punish him for or embarrass him about. He's already embarrassed. Treat the whole thing matter-of-factly and let him know it's something you and he are going to work out together. The most important thing is to let him know that you love him and that he's not to blame for anything. Once he accepts that, the bed-wetting and the nightmares should end."

Marilyn felt a rush of affection for the soft-spoken psychologist who sat at her kitchen table waiting for his coffee. When Jason and Linda and the boys returned, stuffed with ice cream, she and Ed were sitting in the living room watching *The Honeymooners* on TV, and Marilyn was feeling better than she had in six weeks.

There were three more nightmares over as many weeks, and then, as suddenly as they had started, both the bed-wetting and the nightmares stopped. Sean remained either unable or unwilling to remember any of the details of his dream.

Linda was just walking up to the back door as Marilyn stepped out on the service porch.

"I just noticed the time. My gosh, the kids are usually home by now." Linda's voice held a subtle note of controlled panic that amused Marilyn and took some of the edge off her own concern. If Linda had one failing, it was her tendency to worry a great deal over minor things.

"Oh, they're okay. I'm sure they're just busy playing and have lost track of the time." Marilyn reassured her neighbor as they began walking across the street to the school.

"How can you be so calm? There's a maniac on the loose. I read in this morning's paper that they found another body in Hollywood. It was a little girl this time."

"My God, that's terrible."

"It's worse than terrible. I worry every time Michael is out of my sight. If I could, I'd make him stay in the house until they catch whoever's responsible and lock him away." Marilyn glanced quickly at Linda, surprised at the naked fear she could hear in the other woman's voice.

"At least all the murders have been in Hollywood. It's a terrible thing to say but at least none of the children have been from Highland Vista."

"Well, I still worry," Linda said.

There was no sign of the boys in front of Puerta Grande and Marilyn steered her neighbor around the administration building toward the playground. The area was deserted and Marilyn's concern was beginning to change to fear when Linda suddenly grabbed her arm.

"Look at that!" The anger in her voice couldn't conceal her relief. "Those little monsters know they're not suppose to be up there."

Marilyn followed her friend's gaze and saw nothing at first. "Where are you looking? I don't see them."

"Look on the hill."

Marilyn looked beyond the fence at Red Mountain and felt a surge of relief. Two very dirty little boys could be seen scrambling rapidly down the fire trail toward the playground and home.

The sun had moved quite a bit closer to the horizon in the two hours since the boys and dog had climbed under the playground fence.

"Hey, Sean, we gotta get back."

"I suppose so." Sean gazed down at the school and the houses spread below him, looking like toy scenery for a model railroad. "Isn't this neat? It's just like being in an airplane."

"How do you know? Have you ever been in an airplane?"

"Well, no, but I'll bet this is what it's like."

"Well I'll bet it's almost five o'clock and if we don't get back my mom's gonna kill us."

Sean was staring at the vista spread below him and appeared not to hear.

"Where's Mugs?" Michael cast about for the terrier. "Here, Mugsy, come on boy. Here, Mugs." Michael turned back to his friend as the little dog bounded from the brush to join them. "Come on, let's go."

Sean didn't move. He seemed transfixed by the scene below him.

"Well, I'm going home. You coming or not? Hey, Sean, what's the matter?"

Still no response. Sean's face had a dazed expression and he was panting rapidly. Michael punched his friend on the arm and peered at him anxiously. "Sean, you okay?"

Sean mumbled something Michael didn't understand and the dreamy look seemed to fade a little.

"Come on, we gotta go now." Michael tugged on the younger boy's sleeve and Sean half turned toward his friend. His mouth worked but no sound came out. Michael began to be afraid. He pulled Sean several steps down the fire trail and Sean followed meekly.

"What's wrong? Sean . . . Sean?"

A shudder passed through the smaller boy's body and he looked at Michael with a confused expression. "What did you say?"

"I said we've gotta go now. What's the matter with you? You sure look funny."

"Nothing's the matter with me. I was just lookin' at the houses and stuff down there."

"Well, you looked crazy."

Sean and Michael climbed down the trail in silence for

several minutes before Sean said anything. "It was kinda weird. It was like I was flying and all of a sudden everything got scary."

"You're nuts," Michael insisted. He had already dismissed the younger boy's lapse as a daydream and went back to the only important subject at hand. "Do you think we can get back home without getting caught?"

"Sure, it's still early." Sean was completely normal now. "Besides, no one told us we couldn't come up here."

"I guess not."

"Well, okay then. We don't—" Sean stopped in mid-sentence when he saw two familiar figures in the playground. "Look there."

The boys quickened their pace down the trail but only Mugs seemed pleased to see the grim-faced welcoming committee waiting behind the chain-link fence.

Marilyn said nothing to her son as she led him by the hand out of the playground and across the street. As they parted in front of their houses, Marilyn winked at Linda, who was leading Michael in a similar fashion. Still without a word she led Sean into the kitchen and to a chair at the table. Taking a seat opposite him, she faced her woebegone son.

"Will you please tell me why you left the playground?"

"We just went a little way up." Sean's voice quavered, and Marilyn wanted to give him a hug and tell him to forget about it but knew she couldn't do that.

"Whose idea was it to climb Red Mountain?"

"Michael wanted to go and . . . we thought . . . I guess it was sorta my idea . . . in a way."

"Don't you know that you're not supposed to leave the playground and climb around in those hills?"

"You never told me I couldn't."

"That wasn't my question. Did you know that you weren't supposed to go up there?"

"I guess so."

"Do you know why we don't want you going up there?"

"No."

"We have about a dozen reasons. There are trails up there that wander and twist for miles. Every year kids get lost on those trails and sometimes it takes days to find them. There are snakes in the brush and if you get bitten you would have to make it back here on your own before we could get help. What if Mugs got bitten by a snake? What if you fell and hurt yourself? Nobody would know where you were. What if there was a fire? You wouldn't have time to get down. You could be trapped."

"I'd be careful."

"Being careful won't change the biggest reason of all for staying in the playground and out of the hills. Daddy and I don't want you going up there. That should be reason enough."

"Not ever?"

Marilyn was surprised at the vehemence of her son's question. She realized sadly that her baby was growing up and she was going to have to begin, at least in small ways, letting him go. The age-old problem of every caring parent was made no easier by recognition. Marilyn was torn between a desire to protect her son and the knowledge that he needed room and space to grow.

"No, not 'not ever.' If you want to, then maybe you and I can go hiking together. I'm sure you can talk Daddy into going with you once in a while. I hate to tell you that you can go hiking alone when you're a big boy, because you're a big boy now, but I'm afraid you're going to have to be a little older and a little bigger before we're going to let you wander around in the hills by yourself."

"Can Michael come, too?" The excitement in her son's voice warned Marilyn that she was in danger of losing control of the conversation.

"We'll have to see what his mom and dad say about that. In the meantime, it should be enough for you to know that we don't want you hiking in the hills without an adult. I want your word that you won't do it again."

Sean barely hesitated. "I promise," he said with a grin.

"Okay then, the only thing we have left to do is decide the kind of punishment you deserve. Any ideas?"

"No." His grin faded, and his woebegone expression reappeared. "Maybe you should send me to my room . . . without any dinner . . . for all this week?" The quaver in his voice had also returned.

"That would hardly be fair." Marilyn feigned irritation. "Your dad and I like having you around and that would mean we wouldn't get to see you at mealtimes. Why should we be punished because you misbehaved? No. I think this is a case where the punishment should fit the crime. Look at your dog."

"Huh?" Sean looked around the room in surprise.

"He's under the table."

"Oh." Sean obediently looked under the table at Mugs.

"Do you see all those foxtails in his coat?"

"Uh-huh."

"Since you're the one responsible for them being there I think you should be the one to get them out. Go find his brush and comb and I want every tangle and foxtail off him before you turn on the TV. Do you think you can handle that?"

"Sure." Sean grinned at his mom again and then became serious. "I'm sorry, Mom, really. I won't go up there again."

Marilyn watched her son lead Mugs out of the kitchen to begin grooming him and she felt a warm glow of love for the boy.

Sean's odd behavior on Red Mountain went unreported. Michael never said anything about it to his mother. He believed Sean had merely been daydreaming. Sean never mentioned it either. In fact, he no longer remembered it.

Jason and Ed, Marilyn and Linda sat comfortably in lawn chairs around the barbecue and enjoyed the early evening breezes. The day had been clear and perfect with none of the smog that usually casts an unhealthy pall over southern California. Sean had nagged his father for weeks to take him hiking and today Jason and Ed had taken Michael and Sean back to Red Mountain. They climbed to the summit and returned five hours later, tired and ready for the meal that Linda and Marilyn had been preparing. After dinner, everyone pitched in to clear the dishes, and then the adults moved to the backyard, where lawn chairs had been set up.

On the lawn in front of the Jeffries' house, Michael and Sean were watching the cars arrive at the school across the street.

"Are those people voting to see who's gonna be president of the United States?" Sean had a dim memory of sitting on his father's lap two years earlier when he was six and being told that someone named Eisenhower had been re-elected as president of the whole country. "I thought Eisenhower was president."

"Nah." Michael replied scornfully at the younger boy's ignorance. "This is just a local election for Highland Vista."

"What are they voting for?"

Michael remembered a word his father had used. "They're voting on zoning stuff . . . things like that."

"Zoning stuff?"

"Yeah. You know . . . zoning stuff." Michael had no idea what "zoning stuff" meant but wasn't about to admit this to his friend. "They're also voting to see who's gonna be president of Highland Vista."

"Really?" Sean looked impressed.

"Yup. You'll learn all about stuff like that when you get to the fourth grade."

Mugs, who had been sleeping on the lawn next to Sean, sat up suddenly and barked.

"What's the matter, boy? You see a cat?"

At the sound of the magic word, Mugs came fully alert. He sniffed the air excitedly and barked again.

"Go get your toy, Mugs. Toy!"

Another magic work. Mugs ran in a circle searching the ground for his toy.

"Over there, Mugs." Sean could see the little dog's tennis ball by the front porch. He got up and walked over to it. Mugs was now dancing happily up and down, waiting for Sean to throw his toy.

"Go get it, Mugs." Sean threw the ball as hard as he could and watched the gray blur that was Mugs streak after his toy. The ball bounced once in the middle of the street and rebounded into the schoolyard. It bounced once more on the grass before Mugs snagged it on the roll. With his tail waving, he turned and trotted into the street on his way back to Sean and another game of Toy.

Sean saw the VW a split second after Mugs stepped into the road. There was no time to move or call out. He watched in horror as twelve hundred pounds of steel tossed thirteen pounds of terrier four feet into the air to come crashing down on the sidewalk at his feet.

Ed was rising to his feet to get another beer when they heard the commotion in front. The squeal of brakes was followed by a barely audible bump and the louder sound of breaking glass. The four adults were galvanized to action as the night air was suddenly rent by screams of terror and pain from human and animal throats.

Sean was not aware he was screaming. The world wavered and undulated around him as though a door in his mind that had never completely closed swung inexorably and fully open for the first time in his life. Forty years of memories flooded his brain, and mental circuit breakers began overloading and shutting down, one after another. With the memories came terror and then pain, red waves of agony that threatened to split his head open and spew thoughts, emotions, memories, and ideas all over the sidewalk.

Jason rounded the corner of the house at a gallop. It took a second for his mind to register the scene before him, and his first thought was that his son had been struck by the car. The boy was on his knees with his head thrown back, screaming in a piercing wail. As Jason got closer, Sean turned in his direction and the horrified father began to make out words . . . strange words that made no sense at all.

"MUGS . . . HE KILLED MY DOG . . . MUGSY . . . WHEREDIDTHATGODDAMNEDPIPERCOME FROM . . . MAYDAYMAYDAYCESSNANINERHO-TELNINER . . . MUGS . . . HEKILLEDMYDOG . . . IDONTWANTTODIE. . . ."

Jason had time to throw his arms around his son before the convulsions started.

CHAPTER THREE

Awakening

The wail of the siren added a nightmarish quality to the drive to the hospital. Jason narrowly missed running into the back of the ambulance as it slowed and made a left turn into the entrance of St. Mary's Hospital. It braked again and turned to the left, preparing to back up to the double emergency doors. Jason swung the car sharply to the right into a parking spot marked DOCTORS ONLY and came to a lurching stop. Marilyn had her door open before the car stopped moving and Jason had to sprint to catch up with her. Together they ran to the stretcher being rolled from the back of the ambulance. Jason's anguish was a physical pain as he saw his son struggling mindlessly against the straps that held him securely in place. The faces of the paramedics were somber as they raced the stretcher past the swinging doors into the hospital. Both parents entered the reception area just as Sean was being rolled through another set of doors marked EMERGENCY CARE NO ADMITTANCE BEYOND THIS POINT. Jason and Marilyn would have ignored the prohibition and followed the stretcher, but they were intercepted by a young nurse.

"If you'll come with me, please. We need to get a medical history on the patient."

Jason felt an irrational anger at the woman's impersonal tone but said nothing as they followed the nurse to the admitting desk.

Dr. Royce Alvarez was the staff physician on duty when Sean was brought into the emergency room. As he listened with one ear to the paramedic who was briefing him, he ran his hands over Sean's limbs, gently probing and searching. He noted the blood on Sean's mouth where the boy had either bitten his tongue or broken a tooth, and turned to the nurse standing next to him.

"Get a tongue blade inserted and start an IV of D5W."

The dextrose and water would do nothing for the patient by themselves but would provide a medium for getting other medication into the boy's system. Dr. Alvarez checked the boy's mouth and throat more closely and observed with satisfaction that his air passages were clear. "Start forty milligrams of phenobarbital. Here, get that arm secured."

"Doctor, I'm having trouble getting a vein."

"I'll do that." Alvarez took the needle and located a vein on his third attempt while he addressed a second nurse who was holding Sean's head still and inserting a steel plate into his mouth. "Do we have a history?"

"Not yet, Doctor. The parents are outside." The nurse answered without looking up.

Alvarez passed a small vial of blood to the nurse standing beside him. "Have it typed and order a CBC." As he connected the IV, the doctor observed that his patient's breathing was slow and deep. The boy's heart was beating rapidly and tonic seizures were continuing to rack his small body. Alvarez gripped the boy's head firmly with his left hand and with his right hand he gently pulled back the eyelids. Sean's pupils were dilated and locked to the right as if the boy were looking at something to the side. The doctor walked around the table and placed his fingers lightly on Sean's left wrist. He looked at his watch and began counting the rhythmic beat of the boy's pulse.

"What's his BP?"

"One sixty over one twenty."

Alvarez straightened and took a chart from the nurse. He wrote a number on it and looked back to his patient. In the next few minutes he would determine what approach to take. If the phenobarbital took effect, the seizures would stop and they could stabilize the patient. If there was no change, they would have to begin looking for a pathological cause, such as a brain tumor or an aneurysm.

At the end of a minute the boy's condition was unchanged. At the end of two minutes the convulsions appeared to abate slightly. After four minutes Sean was sleeping peacefully, looking frail and helpless and no longer struggling.

"I'm going to talk to the parents," Alvarez said. "I want four views of the skull and then admit him."

Jason and Marilyn had been joined in the waiting room by Ed and Linda and a white-faced Michael Taylor. They had rushed Mugs, who was still alive, to an animal hospital in Highland Vista and they had arrived at St. Mary's only moments before. Linda was crying softly on Ed's shoulder and Ed had a stricken look on his face as Royce Alvarez approached the group.

"I'm Doctor Alvarez. Which of you are the boy's parents?"

Jason took a step forward and automatically put out a hand. "We are, Doctor. How is he?" The two men shook hands and Alvarez noticed with clinical detachment that the taller man's hand trembled as he released it.

"The boy is asleep. We've got the convulsions under control and I've admitted him. Is there a history of seizures?"

"Not at all."

"Has he ever fainted . . . had periods of disorientation? Have you ever noticed anything like that?"

"Not that I know of. He's had the usual childhood things. He had chicken pox when he was four and the measles last year. Nothing else."

The doctor smiled reassuringly at Jason. "We'll keep an eye on him tonight. He should be okay."

"When can we take him home?" Marilyn asked in a weak voice.

"Anytime a patient is admitted with convulsions and

there isn't a history we like to do a complete work-up. There are some tests I want to run tomorrow. Right now, I want to let him sleep.''

"What kind of tests?" Marilyn looked confused and shaken. Alvarez made a mental note to prescribe something for her before she left.

"I want to do a lumbar puncture . . . a spinal tap. We take out a small quantity of spinal fluid and examine it for white blood cells or bacteria. We can also tell if there's unusual pressure in the fluid that could indicate a problem. We'll do an electroencephalogram on your son. That involves hooking him up to a machine that records his brain waves and gives us a picture of what's going on in his head. These tracings can tell us if there are any abnormalities in the pattern.''

"Could Sean have . . . could he have epilepsy?" Marilyn finally asked the question that had been tormenting her.

"There's no way to tell until we do these tests and get back the results. I wouldn't jump to conclusions if I were you. There are a lot of things besides epilepsy that can induce a seizure. After the lab results come back, I'll be able to tell you more. Keep in mind that we know a lot more about epilepsy today than we did twenty years ago. Now we can control it with medication. In any case, it's too early to say anything except that your son is comfortable and sleeping and should be able to go home again in a day or two.''

"May we see him?" Jason asked in a husky voice.

"Just for a minute. We'll be moving him to a room shortly and it will be better if he's not disturbed until he wakes up on his own.''

"I want to stay with him," Marilyn insisted. "I want to be there when he wakes up.''

"He's probably going to sleep through the night and when he wakes up he may be disoriented and confused. He might not even know who you are for a short time. You'll be doing us and yourself and your son a lot more good if you'll go home, get some sleep, and come back in the morning.''

Unable to hold them back any longer, Marilyn felt tears begin to run down her cheeks as she buried her face against Jason's chest and gave up the battle for control.

Seven blocks away from Puerta Grande, George and Mildred Braun parked their station wagon in the driveway of a small frame house on Las Flores. As they emerged from the car George heard, without noticing, a siren passing close by.

This election had been particularly unexciting with nothing of any substance on the ballot, but George voted in every election and insisted that his wife do the same. Even so, he remained convinced that his vote couldn't change things anyway. The country was run by kikes, niggers, and commies. Everyone knew that.

As George trudged gloomily to the front door with his wife chattering happily beside him, he wished, as he had almost every day for twenty-nine years, that she would shut up.

George and Mildred Braun were as unlike each other as two people could be. Their friends, actually her friends, often wondered how two such people could have found enough in common to go out on a date let alone exchange wedding vows.

Millie Braun was a petite, gray-haired woman with a pleasant, open face and laugh lines around her eyes. Her eyes were, in fact, her best feature, a startling gray that verged on blue. These, combined with her warm smile, gave her face a happy, alert expression. The appearence was deceptive. Millie could be described as warm and cheerful, but even her most charitable friends would have had trouble thinking of her as alert. Her reality only occasionally coincided with the real world other people inhabited.

In 1924 Mildred Hanson was twenty-one and a virgin when she first met George Braun. With both parents dead and no relatives willing or able to help her, Millie had

found a job as a seamstress in Minneapolis, where she eked
out enough piecemeal work to keep her rent current at
Mrs. Bowman's boarding house in nearby St. Paul. Her
attraction to the lanky twenty-five-year-old foreman was
an odd mix of excitement and fear, a combination very
similar to her feelings about her own father before his
death.

Apparently the attraction was mutual and when she
turned twenty-two she was no longer a virgin. In July of
1925 she became pregnant and George reluctantly heeded
the dictates of society and his conscience and made an
honest woman out of her. Their marriage ceremony was a
furtive ritual performed before paid witnesses with no relatives or friends in attendance. Millie quit her job and
moved into George's tiny bachelor flat in Minneapolis
where, six months later, George junior was born.

For the next four years the family did well. Those were
prosperous times and if George senior wasn't advancing
as quickly as Millie believed he should, he was at least
keeping food on the table and a roof over their heads. In
August of 1929 they became property owners with the
purchase of a small house in St. Paul. Millie had no reason
to doubt the future would be bright.

The stock market crash a month later seemed a remote
event that was to have no influence on their lives. They
owned no stock and certainly Covington Brothers ("Fine
Clothes for Discerning People") wouldn't be affected by
events happening hundreds of miles away in New York.

It was therefore a very shocked George Braun who came
home in December 1929 with news that he had been laid
off. To compound the problem, Millie was pregnant again.
George made the announcement matter-of-factly and then
went into the living room, where he brooded in silence
until three in the morning.

George discovered there were few jobs to be had and
none of the places he applied to seemed interested in hir-
ing him. He began drinking heavily. If it was the era of
Prohibition, it was also the age of speakeasys, bathtub gin,

and moonshine. Although George was unable to find work he seemed to have no trouble locating the whiskey that consoled him each night until he passed out. Feeling trapped in a marriage he never wanted with a young son he resented, George became withdrawn and irritable. Millie learned to stay out of his way during his drinking bouts. A casual word could lead to violent arguments and sometimes blows.

Millie never considered leaving him. She had been raised a Catholic and believed that marriage was forever. You pick a card and take your chances. If the luck of the draw was against you, that was unfortunate . . . and unchangeable.

One morning, barely three weeks after being laid off, George was sitting at the breakfast table nursing a hangover and trying to decide whether to spend the day looking for a job or looking for a drink. George junior was sitting across from him playing with his corn flakes that had become a soggy and unappetizing mound in the bowl. The boy had awakened cranky and irritable that morning and was whining petulantly at his mother. Millie was at the stove fixing her husband's breakfast and feeling slightly nauseous. The sound of a crash made her turn around.

The baby was laughing happily. Soggy cornflakes and broken bowl littered the floor at his feet.

"Can't you control that brat?" George glared at his wife then looked back at his son. "Shut up," he yelled furiously.

The boy's laughter changed to wails of terror. Millie started for the boy as George senior jumped to his feet, knocking his chair over behind him.

"If you can't keep him quiet then I can." He started for the baby but Millie was there first, blocking his path. In a move that was more instinctive than planned, she slapped her husband across the face.

George reacted instantly. Grabbing Millie by the throat, he hit her twice in the stomach. As her legs began to fold under her he held her upright long enough to hit her once

more in the mouth, hard enough to loosen a tooth before
releasing her and letting her collapse to the floor, retching
and bleeding. Without a word he slammed out the back
door.

It was after eight that night before he returned, drunk,
contrite, and tearful. Millie forgave him and held him and
put him to bed. At eleven that night the labor pains began.

They flushed the tiny fetus down the toilet. It would
have been a girl.

George found a job the following week at Waldorff Grain
and Feed unloading trucks and cleaning up around the
store at a salary that was slightly more than a third of what
he had been making at Covington Brothers.

For the next eight years George worked at the feed store
earning barely enough to survive. Their house was fore-
closed and they moved into a series of drab, rodent-infested
flats and apartments. George's frustration continued as did
his drinking. The bruises his wife and son endured were
evidence of the rage that was building in him.

The beatings and the drinking both stopped abruptly
when George junior was twelve years old.

George had spent the day unloading three freight cars
and arrived home in a foul mood. Millie had gone to the
market and the flat was silent as he let himself in through
the front door. He walked to the icebox and uncapped a
beer before going into the living room. His son's school
shoes and jacket were on the floor next to a pile of books
and George stared at the clothes angrily. Kiss a rat's ass!
That little bastard was going to learn to pick up after himself if it killed him and George was just the one to teach
him. He took a swallow of his beer and let the anger grow.

When Millie returned from the market, George had left
again on some errand of his own. She put away the meager
groceries their budget had allowed her to buy and went to
the living room, where her eye fell on the jacket and books
on the floor. She frowned in exasperation as she gathered
them up. Better put them away before George saw them.
She went to her son's bedroom and thought it odd that his

door was closed. She knocked softly before opening the door and entered the room to put the boy's things on his bed. There was a crash as her burden fell from her arms and a moment later she emerged, white-faced and trembling. She gagged and then vomited on the threadbare carpet.

The ceiling in George junior's room had several gaping holes where the plaster had fallen away, exposing the ceiling joists. The boy left no note before hanging himself with a length of lamp cord from one of those joists.

Death hadn't come quickly to the boy. His face, bloated and purple, bore silent testimony to the agony he endured before death released him. The boy's bladder and bowels had voided and the stench mixed with the odor of vomit as Millie held the wall for support and shuddered convulsively. A draft from the open door moved the body in a slow circle as the woman straightened and lurched drunkenly through the living room and out the front door, gasping and sobbing.

In the weeks following the boy's suicide, George became even more distant and withdrawn. At the feed store, his work that was marginal in the best of times, deteriorated still further. After a violent confrontation with Tom McCarthy—the manager of the store—during which George's nose was broken, he was fired and physically thrown off the property. At age thirty-seven George had reached rock bottom.

Millie also retreated into herself. Unable to cope in a world of death and pain, she created a world inside herself and peopled it with loving husbands and strong, healthy children. This became her reality and in it she was happy. George observed the change in his wife and didn't care. Never again would he touch the woman he had married, either in anger or in affection.

George decided to migrate to California. There was no work to be found in the Twin Cities of Minneapolis/St. Paul and he heard that the Depression was least felt in the Golden State. George watched Millie load their few belongings into the battered Ford that was their only significant possession. He rubbed his broken nose thoughtfully as the shabby fruits of seventeen years of labor were carried and stowed in the car. There remained only one thing to do.

The day before their departure, George left the house shortly before three in the afternoon. When he returned it was after midnight and he was humming cheerfully.

The Brauns were on the road by six and a hundred miles away when construction workers began arriving for work at a jobsite two blocks from Waldorff Grain and Feed. They were fifty miles farther before the body, hidden behind a stack of two-by-fours, was identified as Tom McCarthy. Identification was made difficult by the condition of the head, which had been battered repeatedly by some blunt instrument, possibly a steel pipe. Police never found a murder weapon and didn't make a connection between the incident and a certain former employee of the feed store. The body had no wallet and the motive for the murder was thought to be robbery. No suspect was ever apprehended.

For the next ten years George worked at a variety of jobs and as he got older he learned to conceal the rage burning inside him. In 1950, six months after the birth of a very unusual baby to a young Pasadena attorney and his wife, George got a job with Highland Vista High School as a custodian. The starting salary was more than he had ever made in his life and the Braun family's lot began to slowly improve. In 1952, George and Millie bought a small two-bedroom house in a new development in Highland Vista.

After eight years with the school district, George felt secure in his job and planned eventually to retire from the school with a pension that would keep them comfortable if not wealthy. The day that he finally kicked the dirt of Highland Vista High School from his shoes would be, he was convinced, the happiest day of his life.

He hated his job. He hated the people he worked for

and with. He despised the faculty and students at the school. In particular he resented the injustice of being forced to earn his daily bread by picking up after smart-assed kids and snooty teachers who didn't know one-tenth as much about life as he did. George knew that he could teach them a thing or two. Someday he would. Just like that asshole lawyer he had told off a month before. Just like that nigger who thought he could move next door as bold as you please.

George unlocked his front door and paused, looking across at the Johnson house. He frowned and entered his own house with Millie still chattering inanely behind him.

He felt the anger swelling inside his chest. It was a physical thing that gnawed at his innards like a voracious parasite. That Jeffries bastard was going to get his. He'd show that sonofabitch. No overpriced lawyer with his big house and his airs and certainly no nigger doctor was going to walk all over George Braun. George didn't know how and he didn't know when but he was certain that someday, somehow, he was going to get both of those sonsofbitches.

Sean Jeffries woke at five in the morning with no memory of events of the previous twenty-four hours. He remembered many other things instead. While his body slept, his mind had been busy cataloging, sorting, and integrating. With consciousness came vivid recollections of flying and classrooms . . . of students . . . of being fat and ungainly . . . and of dying.

Sean lay motionless and cautiously moved down mental corridors he had never explored before, into rooms that had been sealed up for years. It wasn't frightening. It was more like rediscovering treasures long packed away and forgotten. He wondered if he was still Sean Jeffries and knew immediately that he was. He still felt like himself, therefore he had to be himself. The problem was not who he was so much as what to do about it. There was still another, more urgent problem. Where was he? This was a hospital, of course, but how had he gotten here? What was wrong with him? Where were his mom and dad?

He stretched carefully and noticed that all his limbs seemed to be working. His mouth was sore as if he had bitten his cheek and he felt stiff all over, but otherwise he felt okay.

Sean became aware of another sound in the room and turned his head. There was another bed next to his and an older boy with a bandage on his head was sleeping there, breathing softly. He muttered something and rolled away from Sean as the younger boy watched him. There was something odd happening and Sean concentrated on identifying the source of the strangeness.

There it was. It wasn't so much a sound as a feeling. It was soft, barely within the limits of perception, but it was there. Sean had never felt anything like this mental buzzing sensation. As he tried to name the feeling he became aware that it was growing stronger. It seemed to be coming from outside the room. As he lay quietly waiting, Sean could feel fatigue and a sense of sadness.

A young nurse came into the room and moved to the side of his bed with starched efficiency.

"Well, I see you've decided to rejoin us." She spoke softly to avoid waking the other patient. "How do you feel this morning?"

Sean was so surprised he almost forgot to answer. As the nurse had moved next to his bed so had the feelings of sadness and fatigue. Sean realized they were coming from her.

"I'm fine. How are you?"

The nurse smiled at him and Sean felt warmth radiate from her. "The truth is I'm tired but I couldn't go off duty without checking on my newest patient." Again a flash of sadness, held in check but present, a gentle, controlled undercurrent.

"What am I doing here?"

"You had an accident and fainted. Your mom and dad brought you in so we could make sure you were okay."

She was lying. Sean knew it without wondering how he knew.

"Please tell me what happened."

This time Sean could feel the nurse weighing and choosing her words before replying.

"Do you know what a seizure is?"

Now it was Sean's turn to choose his words carefully. He almost answered that it was a series of involuntary muscle spasms usually accompanied by unconsciousness, but stopped himself in time. There was nothing to be gained by complicating the discussion unnecessarily. He settled on a one-word response.

"Convulsions?"

The nurse seemed to find this answer surprising.

"That's right. You had a small seizure last night and we just want to make sure you're okay. You're going to be fine."

"Why?"

"Why what?"

"Why did I have a seizure? What caused it?"

Sean could feel the nurse's confusion. He also felt a twinge of guilt at pressing her, but somehow it was very important to find out what had happened.

"I don't know, honey. Maybe the doctor can tell you when he gets here."

This time it felt like the truth and Sean settled back on the pillow to digest this new information. If he was going to be fine, then the curious feeling of sadness must be about something else.

"Hey, don't go back to sleep on me. Let's see what your temperature is this morning." She popped a thermometer under his tongue before he could protest and took his wrist with her fingers to check his pulse.

Her fingers were cool and gentle and Sean felt someone else's emotions flow through the conduit of flesh and muscle, filling his mind. Someone had died. Another patient in the ward. That was the sadness.

"Why the tears, honey? Do you hurt somewhere?" The nurse looked at him with a concerned expression.

"Uh . . . no. I don't hurt."

"Why are you crying? There's nothing to be afraid of."

"I du . . . du . . . don't know."

"Everything's going to be fine. You'll see. You're going to be back home in no time." The nurse released his wrist and brushed a stray lock of blond hair from his forehead. "My name is Joanne and I'll be going off duty in a little while, but the nurse on days is Sister Mary Agnes and she's going to take real good care of you. I'll be back tonight and I'll see you then if you're still here, okay?"

"Okay."

"That's better. Now, I'll bet your mom and dad will be coming to see you this morning and I know the doctor will be in to talk to you before long. Are you feeling better now?"

"Yes, ma'am," Sean answered truthfully. He felt better as soon as Joanne had let go of his wrist.

Even the combined memories and experiences of Sean Jeffries and Peter Marston had not prepared him for this latest shock. The tears he had cried belonged to her, not him.

Joanne moved to the other bed and woke the older boy while Sean again lay back against the pillow, beginning for the first time to feel a little frightened at these new things that were happening to him.

The sedative Alvarez gave Marilyn did its job superbly. She slept soundly through the night until shortly after seven in the morning. Jason tossed and turned, unable to banish the images from his mind. He was still awake to hear the clock strike four before sleep finally brought relief. When he awoke shortly before eight he was tired but fully alert. He got out of bed and dressed quickly before joining his wife in the kitchen.

Marilyn was hanging up the kitchen phone as Jason walked up behind her and kissed her on the back of the neck. She turned into his arms and buried her face in his shirt. They held each other silently for several minutes before she pulled away and looked up at him. Jason was surprised to see the hint of a smile on her lips.

"The doctor says he's awake, alert, and demanding his breakfast. We'll be able to see him at ten o'clock."

"We'll be able to see him anytime we damn well please, which is going to be in about thirty minutes when we get to the hospital," Jason corrected his wife.

"Sit down and let me get you some coffee. They're taking him upstairs for tests right now. That's why we have to wait until ten. He said we could probably take Sean home sometime after lunch."

Somewhat mollified, Jason sat down at the kitchen table and then took a sip of the coffee Marilyn handed him. "I called Al last night after you went to sleep. He's going to cover for me. Margaret will reschedule my appointments until . . ." Jason let the sentence trail off, uncertain how to finish it.

"He's going to be fine. I know it."

"How can we be sure of that?" Jason heard the fear in his voice. "We don't even know what caused the . . . the seizure. What's wrong with our son?"

"Sean is going to be fine. What's the alternative? I'm just not going to let myself believe anything else. He's got to be fine!" There was a determination in his wife's voice that Jason seldom heard. He knew that sometime during the night their roles had reversed.

Jason could act quickly and decisively in a crisis. While the world fell apart around him, Jason could rise above emotion and fear in order to protect his family. It was only when there was nothing left to do that Jason had a problem. Without the anesthetic of action Jason would begin to crumble. This was when Marilyn became the pillar he leaned on, that supported and buoyed him. He would wait until ten o'clock to see his son.

Marilyn turned to the sink and rinsed out her cup. She too was aware that it was her turn to be strong. She tried to force herself to feel the confidence she had expressed just seconds before but another thought kept intruding: Oh, God, don't let me break. Not yet. Please, God, don't let me break.

It was another sunny, cloudless day and Marilyn had opened the back door to let in the air and sunshine. The light rap on the screen caused both of them to jump. Before Marilyn could get to it, the door opened and Linda popped her head in.

"Hi. Any word yet?"

"He's fine now." Marilyn repeated the doctor's report to their friend. "We're hoping to pick him up after lunch."

"Thank God." Linda took the chair across from Jason at the table and lit a cigarette. "Ed will be across the street all day." She gestured toward Puerta Grande. "He said to call him as soon as I found out anything. If you need us for anything I'm going to stick close to home and he can leave anytime you call. We've both been so worried."

Jason felt a lump form in his throat. "You're a good friend, Linda. I hope you know how much we appreciate both of you," he said softly.

"Of course we do." Linda brushed his thanks aside with an embarrassed smile. "No, don't pour me any coffee, Marilyn. Michael is alone at home and I've got to get back before he tears something up. I just came over to find out how Sean was doing and to let you know we'll be here if you need us."

As her friend turned to leave Marilyn felt a ray of hope break through her fear. She wanted to say something, to express the gratitude she felt but, before she could speak, Linda paused and turned to face them again.

"Damn, I almost forgot. There was something else. I called Doctor Campeau this morning."

Marilyn and Jason exchanged blank looks.

"Doctor Campeau . . . the veterinarian . . . Highland Vista Animal Hospital . . ." Linda waited for a sign of comprehension before continuing.

"Oh, my Lord, that's right." Marilyn realized she hadn't thought of Mugs since the accident.

"Mugs is going to be okay. He's got a broken leg . . . the back one I think . . . and two cracked ribs. He's going to be in a cast for a couple of weeks but should be fine. That ought to help cheer up Sean when you tell him."

"That cheers all of us up. Believe me, we needed some good news. You're an angel, Linda."

"Remember, call if you need anything." Linda turned again to the door.

"We will. Thanks again, Linda." Jason was beginning to believe that life might soon return to normal, and his voice was almost cheerful.

After Linda had gone they decided to shower and go out for breakfast. Neither of them wanted anything to eat but it was a way of killing time before going to St. Mary's. As it was, they pulled into the visitor parking area of the hospital exactly ten minutes after ten.

St. Mary's Hospital was run by the Sisters of Mercy. As Jason and Marilyn approached the admissions desk, one of the sisters looked up from her work and beamed happily at them. Her face conjured images of cookies and milk after school and Jason warmed to her immediately.

"May I help you?" Her face revealed nothing of her age. She was small, almost tiny, and she could have been any age from forty to seventy.

"Our son was admitted last night. His name is Sean Jeffries."

"Oh, yes. I remember the name." The elderly sister ran her finger down a Kardex file on the wall next to her. "Here it is. He's in five-thirty-four. If you follow the blue line on the floor it will take you to the elevators." She leaned over the counter and pointed unnecessarily to a blue line painted on the floor. "Take the elevator to the fifth floor. Please check in with the nurses' station and I'm sure they will be able to help you."

"Thank you, Sister. We'll find it." Jason gave her a

friendly smile and the little nun went happily back to her work.

Following the sister's directions, they emerged from the elevator a few moments later on the fifth floor in front of a long counter with a sign that identified it as the pediatrics nurse's station. Jason was surprised to see a face he thought he recognized in earnest conversation with a mixed group of three nursing sisters and two civilian nurses. He waited until the tall black man finished his conversation and was beginning to walk away before striding up and extending his hand.

"Doctor Johnson, I don't know if you remember me. I'm Jason Jeffries."

The doctor turned and looked at Jason without recognition.

"I'm Al Sutton's partner. I met you once at the office."

The doctor's face broke into a smile. "Aha, so you're that Jeffries." He took Jason's hand and shook it vigorously. "Is that your boy down the hall?"

"Yes, it is. We brought him in last night."

"I know. I relieved Doctor Alvarez this morning. He comes in at night to work the emergency room. You folks didn't indicate a family doctor so I'm covering your boy's case." He turned to Marilyn with the same friendly smile. "And you must be Mrs. Jeffries. We spoke this morning."

"Yes, we did. Forgive my husband's manners." Marilyn returned the smile. "I'm Marilyn Jeffries. How's Sean doing?"

"Let me get his chart and we'll go to my office and chat." Dr. Johnson returned to the counter and spoke briefly with the nurse, who took a patient chart from a rack beside her and handed it to him. He turned back to Jason and Marilyn and motioned them to follow him. He led them to a cramped office at the end of the hall that could have served as a large broom closet but somehow managed to hold two desks and two visitors' chairs. There was a short delay while he cleared papers and books from one chair. The other was miraculously squeezed into a tiny open spot in front of the desk before he finally asked them to sit down.

"The good news and the bad news is that we can't find a thing wrong with him. All his tests are normal. His blood pressure is a little high but that's normal given his situation, being in a strange place with people doing things to him that he doesn't understand. The elevation isn't significant. We did an EEG and a lumbar puncture and the results were normal. He seems alert and normal in every respect we've tested."

"How is that bad news?"

"It's not bad news exactly. It's just unfortunate that we can't tell you what caused the episode last night. More accurately, it's unfortunate that we can't guarantee you it won't happen again."

"I see." Jason felt the ominous clouds of fear gathering again on the horizon. "Isn't there some kind of medication he could be taking?"

. "You misunderstand me," Dr. Johnson said kindly. "I didn't say he would have another episode. I said I couldn't guarantee that he won't. Your boy might never have another seizure as long as he lives. In light of the tests we've done and the results we've found, I don't personally believe he's going to have a problem. Only time will tell us for sure. I can hardly put him on any kind of maintenance medication when I have nothing to treat."

"So all we can do then is wait and hope for the best," Marilyn said.

"That's right. Wait, hope for the best, and watch him closely for the next few months. Look for any signs of disorientation, unusual behavior, temper tantrums, anything that doesn't square with his previous behavior. If you notice anything, bring him back and we'll run more tests until we find out what's causing the problem." Dr. Johnson paused and looked at Jason, perhaps seeing in him a greater need for reassurance. "Your boy is fine, counselor. His biggest problem right now is one hell of a headache."

"Headache?"

"It's an unfortunate side effect of a spinal tap. Some people react more than others. Your boy is one of those who develops the granddaddy of all headaches. I gave him a shot that knocked him out. He's asleep now and will probably be pretty groggy for the next five or six hours. This is actually for the best. When you get him home I want you to keep him quiet for the rest of the day. Keep him in bed if you can. I know it's hard with a boy that age, but the medication ought to help. I'm also going to give you some pills in case he has any discomfort when he wakes up. Do either of you have any questions? Is there anything else I can tell you?"

"If we don't notice any of the behavior changes you talked about can we assume there won't be a future problem?"

"That's correct."

"May we see him now?" Marilyn asked.

"You can see him and you can take him home if you'd like." Dr. Johnson rose from behind the desk and Jason and Marilyn stood up. "I'll get one of the nurses to help you get him dressed."

The heavy drapes in room 534 were pulled together and the room was dim and cool. Sean lay on his side with his eyes closed, one arm dangling over the side of the bed. A sister helped Jason and Marilyn dress the boy, who woke only once.

"Hi, Mom," he said weakly.

"Hello, baby. We're going home."

"That's nice." Sean seemed confused and his eyes focused on the nun bending over him in the white habit that distinguished her from the administration staff.

"Why do some of you wear white and some of you wear black?" The question seemed to come from nowhere.

The nun smiled at him and leaned over to whisper in his ear. "The ones in white are supposed to be the good guys."

Sean giggled and a minute later was asleep again.

Marilyn and the sister rolled Sean to the car in a wheelchair while Jason completed the paperwork for his discharge from the hospital. Marilyn stretched the sleeping youngster on the seat bed and then climbed into the back with him. A few minutes later they pulled out of the hospital parking lot. The twenty-minute drive home was completed in a relieved and comfortable silence.

Sean remained asleep until five that afternoon.

CHAPTER FOUR

Coming Home

It was good to wake up in his own bed. There was comfort in the familiar clutter of toys, books, and games strewn haphazardly about the room. Sean looked around and saw his bedroom through eyes that had aged a lifetime in the past twenty-four hours. He felt glad to be home.

The morning had been brutal. The discomfort of the poking and prodding he endured and the pain of the spinal tap had been bad enough. Even worse was the flood of emotion that had battered him as he was wheeled down corridors past rooms full of the frightened, the sick, and the dying. The most common emotion Sean discovered in the hospital was also the most unpleasant to eavesdrop on. He was white-faced and trembling when he was brought back to his room a little before ten o'clock. The massive headache he suffered was only in part due to the spinal tap and in part due to the waves and swells of other people's fear that had inundated him for almost three hours.

As Sean climbed out of bed he realized that he was famished. The house felt empty and he padded barefoot into the kitchen and poured himself a glass of milk before going to the open back door and looking through the screen.

His mom was on her hands and knees in her backyard garden, weeding with a pair of clippers and a pruning knife. Mugs was nowhere to be seen and Sean wondered where the little dog had wandered off to.

He didn't call out to his mom. He loved both his parents

but wanted a little more time alone to think before he faced them.

He took his milk into the living room and turned on the TV. *The Mickey Mouse Club* was on Channel 3 and Sean stared at the screen without seeing it.

What should he tell them about the things he remembered, the things he knew? How was he going to tell them? And would they believe him? Sean couldn't answer any of these questions. For a moment he felt a wave of self-pity wash over him. Why was this happening to him? Sean had a feeling that the wealth of memories and the knowledge that he had somehow acquired weren't the only changes to have taken place. His whole way of thinking seemed to be affected. The boy felt burdened. He tried to remember what it had been like just twenty-four hours before when the biggest worry facing him each day had been getting home in time for supper. Those earlier, simpler days began to seem like heaven.

He sensed his mother as she came through the house. Like his room with its familiar furnishings and toys, the feeling his mother radiated was comfortable and warm.

"Well, sleepyhead, you finally decided to wake up. How long have you been up?"

"Just a few minutes. Where's Mugs?"

"Oh, dear. You don't remember?" Marilyn hesitated and Sean detected an odd disappointment.

"Remember what?"

"Mugs was hit by a car last night." Marilyn saw the frightened look on her son's face and continued quickly. "He's going to be fine. His leg is broken and he's at the vet's. We can pick him up Saturday."

Sean tried to fight back the tears, but couldn't do it. Too much was being loaded on his shoulders. For a little while at least, he was a completely normal eight-year-old, crying in his mother's arms and missing his dog.

Jason went to the office after bringing Sean home from the hospital. For once he came back early, and Marilyn was setting the dining room table for dinner when Sean approached his father in the living room.

"Dad, can all three of us have a talk after dinner?"

Jason looked up from his newspaper in surprise. "Sure, I guess so. Is there anything special you want to talk about?"

"I'd rather wait till after dinner, okay?"

"Sure." Jason looked at his son. "Is something wrong?"

"Everything's okay. I just want to talk to you and Mom."

Dinner was a quiet affair. Sean, who was usually a chatterbox at mealtimes, was strangely silent and seemed preoccupied. Jason and Marilyn both thought uneasily of Doctor Johnson's caution to watch for any unusual behavior.

An hour after dinner, with the dishes washed and put away, the family gathered in the living room. Jason and Marilyn sat on the couch across from their obviously nervous child.

"We're listening whenever you're ready, son." Jason broke the silence that threatened to continue indefinitely.

"Dad, if I tell you something that's hard to believe, will you believe me?"

"If you told me something was true I would try very hard to believe you."

"What if the thing I told you was really impossible? Would you still try to believe me?"

Jason thought about this. His son was visibly troubled by something and he tried to find the words to convey an adult thought to an eight-year-old boy. "If you told me something was true that I knew was impossible, I would believe you were telling me the truth as you saw it. Maybe what you think is impossible isn't really impossible. Sean, what the dickens are we talking about?"

"Something's happened to me. All of a sudden I feel things."

Marilyn sagged against the couch. Jason looked at her

and then at the boy across from him. "You feel things," he repeated uncomprehendingly.

"Yeah, I feel things other people are feeling and I can remember things, too. It's like I know all kinds of stuff I didn't know before." Sean's voice began to sound happy and excited. "I don't feel like I'm the same person I was yesterday." He looked at his parents and misinterpreted what he saw on their faces. "But I am," he assured them quickly. Some of the excitement left his voice. "You believe me, don't you?" He looked first at his mother and then at Jason and knew that they didn't.

"It's like I said, Sean, I believe that you believe it."

Like a swimmer preparing to dive into a pool of ice water, Sean took a deep breath and then took the plunge.

"What you're saying is that my credibility may be intact but my sanity is now in some doubt."

The idea might have been possible to his son, but Jason knew the words were someone else's. He kept his voice level and tried to conceal his shock as he replied, "I don't think you're crazy, Sean."

"But you don't believe me." There was no excitement in the boy's voice now. Only a kind of sad resignation.

"I don't know what to believe. Okay, you say you remember things. Let's start with that. Tell me about the things you remember."

And Sean began talking. He talked about growing up fat and ungainly. He talked about people he had known and things he had done. He described flying and teaching . . . and dying. At times his voice took on a pedantic quality and he seemed to be lecturing an unseen classroom of students as he talked about Peter the Great of Russia and his attempt to travel incognito to England, about Wilson's Fourteen Points and the Treaty of Versailles, about the inevitability of World War II and the rise of America as a world power. He talked for more than an hour without stopping and without interruption. His parents, numb and shocked, listened. As the boy related one event, the telling triggered a dozen more memories, and his words, which had been slow and hesitant at first, began tumbling out in a rush. When the words finally stopped, Marilyn was crying softly and Jason wore a dazed expression.

"Do you believe me now?" Sean spoke quietly and sadly.

Neither parent answered for a moment. Jason was the first to recover sufficiently for speech.

"God help me," he croaked hoarsely. "I think I do believe you."

Sean looked from his father to his mother and sighed unhappily. This wasn't going the way he would have liked. The room seemed to vibrate with fear, and knowing it was coming from his parents made it even worse.

"I have a feeling I shouldn't have told you anything," Sean said at last. "Mom, please don't cry. Everything's okay." He tried to ignore the emotions that bathed him in a suffocating ocean of fear and an undertone of anger. "It's not something I did. It just happened. I couldn't help it."

Marilyn spoke for the first time. "Who are you? You look like my son but you're somebody else. What are you?" Her tone was empty, and Sean felt isolated and lonely.

"I'm your son now just like I was yesterday and the day before. There isn't any problem. What's happened is incredible. It's a good thing. It's not something to be afraid of. Can't you understand that?"

"So you think that you've somehow gained another person's memories." Jason looked at the boy sitting across from them and suddenly felt tired. "That's an awful lot for me to accept."

"I've told you the story. What do you think?"

"I think I need a drink." Jason rose from the couch and continued talking as he walked to the bar on the opposite side of the room. "You're saying that you're the same person you were with some kind of added dimension. Is that right?"

"Not exactly." Sean watched his father mixing a drink

and tried to find a way to explain what was inside his head. "I think I'm the same person I used to be with something missing."

Jason looked up in surprise.

"I think some kind of a barrier or a . . . a block was removed. Maybe everybody has other memories and other knowledge in his head and just isn't able to remember. I don't think I'm any different from anybody else. The only thing that sets me apart is that I do remember."

Marilyn was shaking her head. "I don't believe it. I don't believe any of this is happening."

Sean looked at his mother and wanted to travel back in time. If only he could turn the clock back. He wouldn't try to talk to his parents. They didn't understand. They would never understand. He sighed unhappily. "I've told you what happened. You can accept it or not. I have no control over what you choose to believe. The thing I don't understand is why you have this feeling that I've done something wrong. If this is really so terrible it seems to me I'm the victim, not you." He looked at his father again. "I can see it was a mistake to try to talk to you. I'm sorry."

"I don't think you're being fair with us, Sean." Jason's voice came out with a frustrated edge. "Nobody's mad at you. We're trying to understand what's happened. That's all. This isn't exactly the kind of thing you hear about every day. I'm not sure you understand what you're saying or what you feel."

It was Sean's turn to feel a stirring of anger.

"I know you're not mad at me. I told you before, I can feel what you're feeling." He gave his father an accusing look. "So don't believe me then. I don't care. Whether you believe it or not I can feel the fear all around me. You're afraid of me." The words hung in the air between them, unacknowledged and unchallenged. "My headache is back. May I please go to bed? We can talk tomorrow." He looked sadly from one parent to the other and added, ". . . if you want to."

When neither said a word the boy rose from his chair and walked slowly from the room.

"I don't think we should do anything yet." Jason turned from the bar, where he was pouring his fourth drink. "I just can't believe this is what Johnson was talking about when he warned us about behavior changes. This is too bizarre." Jason looked quickly around the room as though an answer to the whole problem might be lurking under the coffee table or behind the couch. "My God, I'm just about ready to believe that whatever happened to Sean was what caused the seizures instead of the other way around."

"Then you believe that someone else is living inside our son's body?" Marilyn shuddered.

"I don't know what I believe. Maybe it's . . ." Jason searched for an explanation. "Oh, hell, I don't know. One thing's for certain though, he sure didn't learn to talk that way from watching *Captain Kangaroo*." He took a swallow of bourbon and stared at his wife. "What do you think?"

"I don't know either. Jason, I'm frightened. Why is this happening to our son? What are we going to do?"

"I'm frightened too, honey. I have all the same questions you do and none of the answers." Jason set his drink on the bar and bowed his head in helpless resignation. "I don't think there's any more to talk about tonight. It's one o'clock in the morning and I still have to be in court at eight. The world is going to keep turning. Maybe there'll be answers tomorrow. Maybe there won't be. In any case, there isn't any more we can do right now." He walked to the couch and held his arms out to his wife.

Marilyn set her own drink on the coffee table and rose unsteadily to her feet. She and Jason clung to each other as they made their way to the bedroom.

Too much bourbon and too little sleep the night before had Jason snoring gently within minutes of getting into bed, but Marilyn remained wide awake, replaying her son's words again and again in her mind. "You're afraid of me." The accusation rang out, taunting her. She felt ashamed of her fear. He was her son and he needed her. Maybe he needed her now more than he ever had in his life. She choked back a sob. He was her baby and no matter what else he was, that fact would never change.

Marilyn got out of bed carefully to avoid waking Jason and moved through the darkened house. She went to her son's door and opened it quietly. The moonlight streaming through the window illuminated the small body that looked for all the world like a beautiful, untroubled little boy sleeping peacefully.

Sean wasn't sleeping. Like his mother, he was unable to stem the flow of thoughts that raced through his brain, all leading to the same conclusion. His parents were afraid of him. He was alone. Maybe he wasn't even Sean anymore. Maybe he was somebody else now, somebody frightening and bad. Maybe his parents would never love him again.

A thought came to him from another lifetime. Let it go. In a hundred years it will all be one. The boy held on to the thought and nurtured it. He tried to stop caring. In a hundred years it will all be one. What difference if he was alone today? There was tomorrow. And if he were alone tomorrow . . . why, what difference would it make in a hundred years? Let go of the hurt. Nothing matters.

He couldn't let go. He couldn't stop caring. His eyes were red and his pillow was damp when he felt his mother moving in his direction. He feigned sleep as he heard the door open.

The vision of her son blurred and disappeared as Marilyn's tears began in earnest. She stumbled blindly to the side of Sean's bed and put her arms around the still form.

"I love you, baby. Oh, God, I love you so much."

"I love you too, Mom."

Mother and son clung hungrily to each other, each crying and each needing the other. Twenty minutes had passed before Marilyn returned to her room and to bed. This time sleep came quickly and when she awoke the next morning Jason had already left for work.

The sun was still trying to break through low morning clouds as Jason guided his Cadillac south on the freeway to the federal courthouse. He drove mindlessly, disengaged from the task of negotiating his way through the other morning commuters. Traffic was light and he was exiting on Hill Street in downtown Los Angeles by seven forty-five. He turned left on Spring Street and moments later was taking the last available parking spot in the lot next to the court building.

Jason noted that his client hadn't arrived yet. He locked the car and walked slowly through the main entrance to the lot instead of going in the side door the way he usually did. A ragged woman with a vacant face and bare feet brushed past him, aimlessly pushing the accumulated flotsam and jetsam of her life before her in a shopping cart. As Jason approached the broad stairs leading to the ten main doors of the courthouse, he had to step around a sprawled wino, snoring and red faced. Jason looked grimly up and down the street and decided the population matched his mood. There was still no sign of his client and Jason lit a cigarette and sat down on a bus-stop bench to wait.

A patrol car pulled to the curb ten feet away and a young officer stepped from the car. He took his nightstick from his belt and prodded the sleeping wino roughly. The drunk stirred and opened bleary eyes. Jason watched the drama without interest. He felt old. You know you're over the hill, he thought to himself, when cops start looking like high school kids.

The drunk was struggling to get to his feet with the help of the young officer. Jason wondered what had brought the man to this state. Did he once have a family? Had he been successful? Had he owned a home? Did he have children somewhere? Did his eight-year-old son ever talk to him with the words of an adult and . . . no. Not now. I won't think about that now, Jason vowed.

It was eight-fifteen and the cop was struggling to maneuver the drunk into the backseat of the patrol car when Jason sighted a familiar figure coming around the corner. He forced a smile and stood to greet his client.

Dr. Thomas Venado was a recent dental school graduate whose bills had grown faster than his fledgling practice. Dr. Venado was an excellent dentist and a terrible businessman. He had come to Jason three months before with a briefcase full of bills and an empty bank account. Today he arrived with a nervous smile and a moist handshake.

"I feel like I'm going on trial. I don't think I got any sleep at all last night."

You think you've got problems, Jason thought while forcing himself to smile. "You'll be all right. Just relax. All the judge is going to do is review the assets you've listed and make sure we didn't forget anything. Just answer his questions honestly and don't worry. He's not going to try to trip you up. The whole thing shouldn't take more than fifteen minutes once we're called."

It took only ten minutes in front of the judge. Of course it took almost two-and-a-half hours for the judge to hear the sixteen petitioners ahead of Dr. Venado, and it was after eleven before Jason and his client stood again on the sidewalk in front of the courthouse.

"You mean that's all there is to it?" Venado sounded relieved.

"That's about it. There'll be one more hearing in a couple of months, but the second hearing is nothing to worry about. It's just a roll call of petitioners. When the court calls your name, you'll answer and the judge will tell you that you've been discharged in bankruptcy. It's a simple procedure designed to give people a second chance."

"I had no idea how easy it was."

"Well, just remember, you won't be able to do it again for seven years. Any debts you incur from this point on will have to be paid or you can be sued."

"Don't worry, once is enough. Listen, thank you, Jason. If you ever need a root canal I want you to come see me.''

"I'll remember that." Jason chuckled. He shook hands with the dentist and then walked rapidly back to the parking lot.

Traffic had picked up considerably as Jason drove slowly back to the freeway. He was able to keep his mind blank until Chinatown was behind him and then his wife's words came back suddenly to haunt him: "Then you believe there's someone else living inside our son's body?"

Someone . . . or something. Jason tried to remember what he knew about demonic possession. It was easy. He didn't know anything at all. He was neither superstitious nor religious. Before today he would have dismissed the idea of a demon taking over his son's body as insane, childish, and impossible. It was cut from the same cloth as a belief in vampires, bogeymen, and werewolves. It was the stuff you conjure up around a campfire to tell your children as the world shrinks to a small island of light in a black, threatening universe—the delicious horror that delights and titillates precisely because no one believes any of it. In the world of cars and freeways and bankruptcy hearings such things couldn't happen.

And eight-year-old boys didn't suddenly have somebody else's memories and knowledge. Possession was no less believable than the story Sean had told them.

When he got to the office back-to-back appointments helped take his mind off his son. He walked his last client to the exit at quarter-to-five, and told Margaret to hold his calls. He returned to his office and shut the door. There was one thing that ought to be easy enough to check.

Sean, or someone that was inside him, had mentioned flying a Cessna 172. Jason had never heard of the plane and took a phone book from his desk drawer. Looking under "Aircraft" in the Yellow Pages, he located a Cessna dealer and, feeling a little foolish, he dialed the number.

"Air West, good afternoon."

"Hello. My name is Bill Riley. I'm interested in buying a plane and wanted to talk to someone there about a one seventy-two."

"One moment, please." The line went dead and Jason waited for the call to be transferred.

"This is Scott Deschenaux. May I help you?"

"Yes, I hope so. I'm interested in buying a one seventy-two and wondered if they were still available. My name is Bill Riley and I do a lot of flying." Jason wondered if that sounded as stupid to Scott Deschenaux as it did to him.

"No problem, Mr. Riley. We have an inventory of twelve planes on the line right now and we can add any options you might be interested in from local stock. Do you want the plane equipped for IFR or are you a VFR pilot?"

"Oh, yes." Jason had no idea what IFR equipped might involve but knew that he couldn't very well ask. "I would want IFR."

"We have a really nice bird on the line right now." Scott lowered his voice as though sharing a secret. "The avionics alone will make you drool. Perhaps you'd like to come in and look over our stock?"

"How much do they run . . . er . . . fully equipped?"

"Well, it all depends of course on what you want in your instrument package but a plane certified for IFR should be in the area of twelve thousand. The plane I think you ought to see on our line is eleven seven-fifty list."

"I'm surprised you're still making them. A friend of mine swears by his one seventy-two that he bought back in . . ." Jason did some fast arithmetic. Sean was born in 1950 so allow a year. ". . . That he bought in 1949."

There was silence on the other end of the line. When he spoke again, Scott sounded confused.

"There must be some mistake. We weren't making one seventy-twos in 1949."

"Maybe I'm wrong about the date. How long have you been making them?"

"Mr. Riley, the one seventy-two is our newest airplane.

We introduced it three years ago. The first plane moved off the assembly line in 1955."

Jason hung up the phone and sat motionless, lost in thought.

Thirty minutes later when the attorney left his office, he noticed that Margaret had gone for the day. He was about to let himself out the door when he heard a noise in his partner's office. He knocked softly on Al's door before opening it and poking his head inside.

"You got time for a problem?"

"I've always got time for you, Jason." The older man was dressed in shorts and a floppy beach hat. "You know, I should have made you a partner a long time ago. Look at what I've missed." The old man grinned and then sobered as he saw the pain in his colleague's eyes. "Here, sit down. What's the problem?"

"It's not a client, Al. This is personal. I'm in the middle of a situation and I don't know how to cope. Maybe you can give me some guidance."

"That's what I'm here for, son. What's the problem?"

Jason told the story in a methodical fashion, beginning with the nightmares and bed-wetting that Marilyn wasn't aware he knew about. He talked about the accident and his own fears for his son as they had rushed him to the hospital. Finally he told Al about the conversation the night before. He omitted nothing, including his phone call to Cessna of thirty minutes earlier. He concluded with a dispassionate evaluation of the possibilities as he saw them. He found himself suggesting demonic possession in the same everyday tones he would use suggesting a motion to continue a difficult court case. When he finally ran out of words he felt drained and empty and somehow grateful not to have to carry the burden alone anymore.

Al Sutton had assumed his lawyer posture. This consisted of leaning back in his reclining chair, putting his fingers together tent fashion below his nose, and closing his eyes until they were mere slits in his face. Many a lawyer had learned to his chagrin that Al Sutton was not asleep when he assumed that look. Jason knew that he had heard and understood every word. He waited morosely for his partner's response to the story.

Al seemed lost in thought. A minute passed, then two. When he spoke, his words were casual and his voice held none of the doubt Jason had feared and half expected. "Who have you talked to about this?"

"You're it."

"Hmmm. It does sound as though you have a problem. Have you given any thought to the possibilities other than possessed versus reincarnated?"

"What are the other possibilities? Last night I wasn't talking to a boy. I was talking to an adult."

"Maybe so, maybe not. It seems to me you could consider a couple of other areas for possible answers. I heard one time that the mind never forgets anything it learns. I've heard of people being hypnotized and recalling how many telephone poles they pass on the way to work every day, or what they had for lunch on a given Tuesday three years before. Now I'll grant you, it's stretching the imagination a bit but certainly no farther than you're trying to go with your theories."

"Al, where would he have learned about flying an airplane or teaching a history class in high school? He didn't talk in general terms. He was specific. His story was coherent and even his words, his vocabulary . . ." Jason looked down at his hands and then almost defiantly back at his partner. "Damn it, he sounded like a teacher!"

"Maybe he saw a movie or read a story and he's putting himself in the place of one of the characters."

"His taste in movies is *Snow White* and *Lady and the Tramp*. He's supposed to start third grade in September, Al. They don't write stories like that for second and third graders. He's always been a bright kid but his reading level isn't much more than fourth grade. Correction: His reading level used to be fourth grade. God only knows what it is now."

"Okay, for the moment we'll rule that out. Let's approach this from a slightly different angle. Like the poet says, 'There are more things in heaven and earth than are dreamed of in your philosophy, Horatio.' Just for the sake of argument, what if the boy is exactly what he says he is?''

"What's that? Some middle-aged history teacher turned pilot who bought the farm over eight years ago in a plane that wasn't manufactured until last year? Does that make any logical sense to you?''

"The argument does have its weak points, granted. Could he be confused on that one point? In other words, can his story be substantially the truth?''

"He wasn't confused. He was nervous. He was excited and he was very specific. That was the frightening part of the whole thing. The things he was talking about, his tone of voice, the words he used. It was like he was telling us about something that happened last week or the day before yesterday. He was a completely different person. Whoever he was, he wasn't Sean.''

"Which doesn't answer my question. Could his story be substantially the truth?''

Jason shook his head impatiently. "I do not believe my son is the reincarnation of anybody!''

"Where does that leave you?''

"That leaves me wondering if the person, or the thing I talked to last night is my son . . . or something else.'' Jason kept his voice level despite the emotion churning in his gut.

Al didn't reply immediately and Jason's feeling of help-lessness increased as he realized his partner wasn't going to be able to come up with any miracle answers this time. This was a problem without a solution. It was a nightmare that wouldn't vanish when he opened his eyes. He rose from his chair and looked sadly at the older man. "Thanks for listening to me. I just don't see an answer, at least not one that makes any sense.''

"Sit down.'' The old man barked sharply and Jason sat

instantly, a look of surprise on his face. "You asked me for guidance and I'm going to give it to you." He looked angrily at Jason.

"We've known each other for some time now, son. You're a fine young man and a brilliant attorney. If I had a son I don't think I could be any fonder or prouder of him than I am of you. Which is why, when you start handing out bullshit, and even worse, believing it yourself, I'm going to tell you that you're acting like a horse's ass."

Jason started to protest but Al waved him to silence. "I said listen. Don't talk. You've talked enough already." Al took off his floppy beach hat and ran his hand through the thinning patches of gray that still remained. "I've been sitting here listening to you talk about your boy as though he were some kind of monster. I personally believe the only monster around here is the one you've created in your own mind." Al paused as if challenging the younger man to deny it. Jason remained silent.

"I want you to talk to somebody. Like I say, we've known each other for a long time now. You know I'm not a religious type. As far as I know, you aren't either. Neither one of us is qualified to talk about devils or demons from hell or Mars or wherever, coming down and taking over your boy's soul. Since we have to admit going into this that we don't know what we're talking about, we certainly have no right to convict Sean of being a monster or any other damned thing. Now do we?"

Jason considered this and had to admit that his partner was right. "No," he said in a low voice.

The old man wrote something on a memo pad then tore the sheet off and handed it to Jason.

"We had a case about two years ago. I don't think you were involved with it. A juvie in Los Angeles went joy-riding in someone else's car. LAPD pulled him over and the parents were on my doorstep when the office opened in the morning. The kid got probation but the point of the story is that his pastor, Father Cassidy, came in and talked to me, then wrote a letter to the court to try to help the kid out. I had met the man before and I think he's a pretty sharp guy. He's about my age and if anything, he's more pragmatic than I am.''

"You want me to talk to a priest?"

"Who's better qualified to talk about devils, real or imagined? Besides, I think you'll like him.'' Al reached for his floppy hat on the desk beside him and put it back on his head.

"Well, if you think it might be helpful.'' Jason looked at the paper uncertainly. "I suppose I could give him a call. I guess I've got nothing to lose.''

"That's right. There isn't anything to lose. And one more thing. I think you ought to keep an open mind about your son. If you turn away from him now and then find out that what's happening has a natural explanation, no matter how bizarre, you're going to have one hell of a burden to carry around for the rest of your life.''

Jason bowed his head, and Al walked to the door. He started to open it and then turned back to Jason. "If you need me anytime, day or night, just call. By the way, I forgot to mention that Father Cassidy got bit by the religion bug rather late in life. When I first met him he was a lawyer. We used to share an office years ago.'' The old man laughed at the look on his partner's face then turned and left the office.

Jason felt better when he left the building to go home. Al was right, of course. He had no business drawing conclusions in areas he knew nothing about, especially where his son's welfare was concerned. Suddenly, Jason knew that he had been avoiding going home. He was apprehensive about facing the stranger who looked like a child and spoke like an adult. Just as suddenly he knew that he wanted to see Sean. He wanted to take the boy on his lap and tell him a bedtime story. He wanted to be interrupted reading the paper by a breathless recap of the events of the day as seen through the eyes of an excited eight-year-old. Jason Jeffries wanted more than anything else in the world to have his son back.

Jason clutched the open door of the car for support. The dizziness passed but the ache remained. He relocked the car door and on unsteady legs climbed the three flights of stairs back to his office. He let himself in and went directly to his desk. He collapsed in his chair and buried his face in his hands. It was almost ten minutes before he slowly lifted his head and reached for the telephone with one hand while fumbling a folded piece of paper from his shirt pocket with the other. He unfolded the paper and dialed the number.

"St. Anthony's Rectory."

"My name is Jason Jeffries. May I speak to"—Jason checked the note on the desk in front of him—"Father John Cassidy, please?"

"I'm sorry. Father John isn't available right now. May I give him a message?"

"Do you have a way of reaching him? It's very impor-tant."

"Is this an emergency?"

"It is." Jason didn't hesitate. "Could you tell him that I'm Al Sutton's partner and I have to talk to him as soon as possible?"

"What was your name again?"

"My name is Jason Jeffries. I'm an attorney with Sutton and Jeffries. I'm Al Sutton's partner."

"Wait just a minute, please."

Jason waited for the housekeeper to find a pencil and felt his irritation growing as the wait stretched into several minutes and she still hadn't returned to the phone. He was about to hang up and call back when a rich baritone voice came on the line.

"This is Father John. May I help you?"

George Braun left his house and stomped angrily to the old Hudson parked in the driveway. It wasn't enough that he worked all day to put food on the table. Now he had

to drive all the way to the store to get goddamned cat food.
Cat food, of all things.

The newest addition to the Braun household, a half-
grown tomcat, had shown up uninvited three weeks earlier
while George was at work. Millie discovered the animal
at the back door when she was taking the garbage out. The
cat, employing the same strategy its kind has employed
for thousands of years, rubbed back and forth against her
ankles and meowed piteously. It was a sucker ploy that
should have been obvious to anyone the least bit familiar
with the ways of cats and men. Millie fell for it anyway.
Within minutes the cat was lapping contentedly from a
saucer of milk and feeling vastly superior to the lesser
creatures he manipulated so skillfully.

Mildred named the animal Charlie Cat and ignored the
outraged protests from her husband when he discovered
the houseguest. The cat was staying and that was that. In
the face of his usually docile wife's adamant insistence
George reluctantly accepted the newcomer.

George was fuming as he backed the car out of the
driveway and into the street. A man should have control
in his own house. His father had always had control. The
old man had ruled his house, by God, up to the very end
. . . almost.

Gerhard Braun had been a huge man with a booming
voice and a thick, guttural accent. George couldn't remember a time when he hadn't hated the man, or a time
when he hadn't feared him.

When he thought of his father, which he did frequently,
George remembered a rundown farm in northern Penn-
sylvania that was home until he ran away when he was
sixteen. The farm had been the old man's domain, his
kingdom, and he had ruled it with an iron fist. George's
mother died when he was six and Gerhard raised the boy
alone according to the strict Germanic traditions he had
brought with him from the old country. A boy was supposed to work hard and respect his elders.

George drove slowly down Las Flores and tried to imagine how his father would have handled the problem of Charlie Cat and Mildred's obstinacy.

The razor strop would have been busy.

George felt a tingling in his groin as he thought about the heavy leather strap that had hung in the bathroom of the old farm. He pictured Millie screaming as the belt descended, slicing into her buttocks, across her breasts and legs. He saw her crawling to his feet, pleading with him to stop. His erection bulged painfully against the fabric of his pants as the images continued. He could almost feel the belt; he could hear the crack of the leather, rising and falling with murderous efficiency.

He rubbed himself with one hand and was sixteen years old again, sneaking quietly into the bathroom at four-thirty in the morning. He was taking the strop from its place on the wall and fondling the smooth leather. The house was quiet, the only sounds were the soft moans of pleasure coming from the excited teenager.

A huge hand smashes into the side of his head, knocking him to the floor, and the room is suddenly flooded with light.

"Verfluchter teufel," Gerhard shouts at the boy sprawling on the floor of the bathroom. He stoops and retrieves the leather strop where the boy has dropped it.

"You t'ink maybe I'm deaf? I don't hear you creeping around house?"

"Swish." The belt arcs through the air and across the boy's chest.

"You t'ink maybe I don't know you got devil in you?"

"Swish." The flesh across the boy's shoulder separates and blood flows.

"Verflixter bengel! You t'ink maybe I'm stupid?"

"Swish." Again and again the strap finds him as he crawls frantically on the bathroom floor in a futile search for escape. The boy screams and has an orgasm at the same time. The belt continues to rise and fall until the old farmer is exhausted and the boy is unconscious.

George's breathing was rapid and uneven when he pulled

into the parking lot of the market and stopped the car. He
sat in the car for several minutes to calm down while he
looked around the almost empty lot. The market and
the hardware store next to it would be closing in less than
half an hour. When he could do so without embarrassment, he got out of the car and locked the door. George
looked thoughtfully at the lights in the hardware store, and
an idea took shape. He was smiling broadly a moment
later when he trotted in the direction of the lights.

Marilyn watched through the kitchen window as Sean
kicked a volleyball to Michael in the backyard. She had
been surprised when Michael had come over and Sean had
asked her if they could go to the playground. Somehow
the request was too normal . . . too much like before the
accident.

"I'd rather you played in your own yard today where I
can keep an eye on you," Marilyn had answered. There
had been a surrealistic feeling about the exchange. Although her resolve to stand by her son had been made, she
was still uncertain about how to treat the boy. The shock
of seeing her baby earlier, avidly reading the morning paper, remained with her for the rest of the day.

As if he could see her thoughts, Sean had walked up to
his mother and said in a stage whisper, "For crying out
loud, Mom, I'm only eight years old." They had looked
at each other and both had burst into laughter.

That was all it took to break the tension. Marilyn
hummed cheerfully to herself as she turned from the window and began fixing supper. Everything was going to be
all right. Sean was her son and whatever it was that had
happened to him, she would adjust. They would adjust.
They were a family and they were going to work this thing
out together.

She remembered the scene when she had come out of
the bedroom that morning and found Sean in the kitchen.
She made a mental note to ask her son not to read the

paper while he ate his cereal in the morning . . . at least until she had time to get used to the idea.

George was also humming as he came into the house with his purchases in several bags. Millie hurried from the kitchen to take them from him, but he brushed past her and set them down on the counter next to the sink before turning and facing his wife.

"Okay, I bought the damn cat food. Now will you please see about feeding your husband?"

"Of course, George." Millie's tone was appeasing. "I'm sorry. Just let me put some food down for Charlie and I'll fix dinner."

"Never mind the damn cat. I'll feed the cat. You get some dinner going." Kiss a rat's ass, work all day, run errands all night. Was he supposed to cook his own meals, too?

"Okay, George." Millie turned obediently to the refrigerator and took out some hamburger as George opened a can of cat food and put it on a saucer. He hesitated and looked at Millie. "Here, give me a little of that." Millie was shocked to see her husband, who always professed a dislike of the cat, reach over and break off a bit of the hamburger that he separated with his fingers over the cat food. "Give the damn thing a treat," she heard him mutter.

He scooped something from the second bag and mixed it with the food in the saucer. Satisfied at last, he started to put the food down for the animal that was moving impatiently at his feet, but his sense of justice stopped him.

"Here, you feed him. Stupid animal doesn't like me anyway."

"Of course he does, dear." Millie started to argue but a warning look from her husband stilled her protest. "Okay, I'll give it to him." Millie took the saucer of food from her husband, and George walked into the living room with a contented smile.

He could have just bashed the damn thing's head in, of course. That would have been the quick solution. No. This way was better. No one and nothing pushed George Braun around. George felt that justice was being served as his wife set a plate of nutritious cat food, hamburger, and rat poison in front of her hungry pet.

CHAPTER FIVE

Father John

Jason's knock on the rectory door was answered almost immediately by a civil if less than cordial housekeeper. She led him down a hall to a large room containing a desk, several overstuffed chairs, and a sofa. She left with a curt "Wait here," and disappeared to find Father Cassidy. Jason felt ill at ease. No one had invited him to sit down and he remained standing, acutely aware that he was out of his element.

The room was cozy and dimly lit. Mahogany paneling covered three of the walls, adorned only by a large figure of Christ on one side and a statue in an alcove across from the desk that Jason assumed to be St. Anthony. The fourth wall was a floor-to-ceiling bookcase framing a large, draped window. The shelves of the bookcase sagged perceptibly under the weight of an odd mix of religious books with titles in English and Latin, along with more secular books. Leaning casually against a leather-bound set of Shakespeare's plays was a tattered copy of *Imitation of Christ* by Thomas à Kempis. On the shelf directly above that, Jason was surprised to see a three-volume set of *Blackstone's Commentaries* sharing space with *Confessions of Saint Augustine*. He was leafing idly through one of the *Commentaries* volumes when the sound of a door opening made him turn.

"Mr. Jeffries, I'm Father John." The priest strode into the room and Jason got his first look at Al's former partner.

The older man dwarfed the young attorney. At slightly

over six feet three inches and 260 pounds, Father John resembled a football linebacker in a roman collar, a role he had played with considerable distinction, though without the collar, over thirty years before.

"Al's been talking about you for years and now that we meet I have to admit you don't look anything like I pictured you." Father John held out a huge hand and Jason shifted *Blackstone* awkwardly to shake it.

"What kind of stories has he been telling you?" Jason had to smile in spite of himself.

"Let's just say I had a picture of something between Gladstone and William Jennings Bryan. You're much too young to fit that description."

"Al's been good to me." Jason acknowledged the compliment. "I've learned a lot from him. Do you see him often?"

"We stay in touch. For years we spent Saturday mornings together on the golf course, but I'm afraid age is catching up with us. Now we get together once in a while to talk about the good old days and try to remember what was so good about them." The priest laughed heartily and clapped Jason on the shoulder with his huge hand. Father John radiated energy and Jason doubted that age had slowed him very much.

"Father, I think I should tell you, I'm not a Catholic."

"That's all right. The same thing can be said about a lot of people. My commission is the same either way." The priest looked closely at the lawyer and his features became more serious as he observed the worry in Jason's eyes. "You said on the phone there was a problem with your son. Let's sit over here and perhaps you could tell me about it." Father John settled into one of the overstuffed armchairs and motioned Jason to the other.

For the second time that day Jason told the story of Sean's accident and the strange events that followed. Father John watched him intently as he talked, occasionally asking a question or pressing him for additional details on one point or another. Jason began to suspect that Al's former partner still had a lot of lawyer in him. Under the old priest's gentle probing, Jason remembered many details he had forgotten when he told the story to his partner just hours before. It took him almost thirty minutes to complete the narrative and when he finished, Jason leaned forward in the chair, searching the face of the cleric for any sign of skepticism or disbelief. Father John's expression revealed nothing, and after a moment of silence, Jason sat back again while he waited for the priest's reaction.

"When you ran around the house after the accident could you understand what Sean was saying?" Father John asked.

"Not at first. When I got closer to him I heard him say something like, 'Where did that goddamned Piper come from?' then he was screaming that his dog was dead. Everything happened so quickly. Father, I honestly can't remember his exact words. He may have screamed for Mugs first and then said something about the Piper. Is it important?"

"Probably not." The priest nodded thoughtfully before continuing. "He was speaking in English? That's what I'm asking."

"Of course." Jason answered. "I don't know what you're getting at. English is the only language Sean understands."

Father John ignored the lawyer's puzzled expression as he posed his next question. "When he had the seizure or later, when he talked with you and your wife about having these memories, did you notice any unusual activity in the room?"

"Unusual activity?"

"Smells, sounds, temperature changes?"

"Not that I recall."

"There was nothing happening that you would regard as supernatural? Furniture didn't fly around, the boy didn't speak in tongues or levitate or anything like that?"

"Absolutely not." Jason flushed angrily. "Please don't

humor me, Father. Everything I'm telling you is absolutely true.''

"I'm not doubting you.'' Father John regarded Jason with a serious expression. "Verified cases of possession are frequently accompanied by other supernatural, or unnatural, if you prefer, manifestations.''

"There was nothing like that at all.''

"Fascinating,'' Father John said almost to himself. "Truly fascinating.''

"I don't know that I could call it fascinating. Horrible perhaps, unbelievable certainly, but I have trouble with fascinating.''

"Forgive me, please.'' The priest looked chagrined. "I didn't realize how that would sound. What has occurred to me, though, is that there are some very positive aspects to this situation that you don't seem to be considering. For example, what is so horrible about having a son who may be the smartest ten-year-old in the world?''

"Eight-year-old,'' Jason corrected him. He thought about the question carefully before answering. "Put like that I guess there's nothing horrible about it if he's still Sean.''

"You said that your wife put the question to him directly last night. When she asked him who he was, what did he say?''

"He said he was Sean Jeffries.''

"Jason, let me tell you what I think about possession. First of all, as a priest of the Church I believe in God. It follows logically that I believe in the devil. It's impossible to look at the world around us without seeing a powerful force operating for good and beauty, just as it's impossible to deny the existence of another powerful and very real force that seems bent on promoting evil. The world is full of greed and lust and hate. I don't think man is the author of all of it.'' The priest hesitated and seemed to be ordering his thoughts. "I accept as a matter of faith that there is a real Lucifer who was second only to God in power and beauty and who thought himself the equal of God. I believe that for this sin of pride he was cast out of heaven into a pit of darkness and pain where he continues to wage war on God and mankind. Because I believe all of these things then I accept that demonic possession is theoretically possible.''

''Theoretically?''

''In practice, I have never encountered or heard about a case of possession that I didn't think could have had a purely natural explanation.''

''Then you don't believe Sean is possessed?'' It was more a statement than a question.

''That's correct and I have two reasons for not believing it. First, the phenomenon of demonic possession occurs so infrequently and is usually accompanied by such clear signs and manifestations, all of which are lacking here, that I just don't see the hand of the devil in this situation. Second, the effect appears to be a positive thing. It doesn't sound as though Sean is unhappy. You said that he sounded excited and even proud of his new knowledge. For some reason and in some way that we may never understand your son has become more intelligent than he used to be. This sounds more like a gift from God than an assault by the devil. In any case, I find it hard to credit the devil with a change that enriches a life.''

''Do you believe he was reincarnated?''

''No. I don't believe that either. I have no idea where these new memories of your boy's are coming from, but I'm intrigued. I'd like very much to have a chance to explore this further. May I see your son?''

''Would you like to come to the house?''

''Actually, I would prefer that you bring him here if that's possible.''

''I'll be glad to bring him by anytime that's convenient for you.''

''Good. Let's say Saturday, about one o'clock. Does that work for you?''

''Saturday is fine.''

''Excellent. I'm looking forward to meeting this extraordinary youngster of yours.'' The old priest sounded exuberant, as though Jason were doing him the favor.

"I just wish I shared your opinion that these changes in Sean were some kind of gifts from Heaven,'' Jason said unhappily.

Father John nodded without smiling. "Do you believe in God?''

"I suppose so. Frankly, I've never given the matter a lot of thought.''

"You should think about it some. You came in here with your belief in the devil pretty well established. Maybe your belief in God isn't as shaky as you think. There's something I'd like you to try.''

Jason looked up eagerly only to look down again as the priest continued.

"I'd like you to try praying over this.'' Father John saw the look of disappointment on Jason's face. "Now wait. Don't dismiss the idea that quickly. Open your mind and ask God for help.''

"How can I pray to a God I resent? What kind of a God turns boys into circus freaks? This is my son we're talking about. Whether this thing is a curse or a gift doesn't matter. We don't want it.''

"You don't want it. From what you've told me, your son doesn't seem to be unhappy about anything.''

"Okay, I don't want it then. I feel like Sean has become a pawn in some cosmic chess game.'' Jason shuddered and looked pleadingly at the priest. "I don't know what to do.''

"You need to open the channels of communication. Talk to God about it. Ask Him to help you understand your son and yourself. Nothing happens without a reason. Ask Him to show you the reason. You'll get your answers.''

"I'll try,'' Jason said without conviction.

"There's one more thing you can do.'' The priest smiled at the young lawyer. "When you get home tonight you find your boy and give him a hug. Tell him you love him.

That should relieve ninety percent of the anxiety you're feeling. Will you do that?''

"I certainly will." Jason rose and extended his hand. "Thank you."

Father John smiled warmly. "You're welcome, Jason. I'll be seeing both of you on Saturday."

"We'll be here."

The house on Canyon Drive was only ten minutes away from St. Anthony's. Jason maneuvered his car the short distance while fighting off the physical and emotional fatigue that hammered at his temples. Lights were on in the living room when he parked in the driveway, too weary to put the car in the garage.

Marilyn had the door open before he could locate the house key on his ring.

"Hi, sweetheart. I heard the car." She kissed him on the cheek and led him into the living room. "You look terrible. Sit down and I'll warm up some dinner for you. Would you like a drink?"

"No, thanks. I think I'll pass on dinner, too. I just want to sit here for a few minutes and then go to bed. Where's Sean?"

"He's over at Michael's. We gave up on you about an hour ago and ate dinner. I told him he could stay next door until eight-thirty so he should be home in a few minutes."

As if on cue, the back door slammed and a moment later they heard the refrigerator door open.

"Hey, Mom, are we out of Coke?"

Jason roused himself and called back, "You don't need any this close to bedtime. Come in here for a minute."

Sean hesitated in the doorway and Marilyn could see that he was nervous as he approached his father. Her maternal instincts were on full alert and though she wanted to remain in the living room she knew it was time to leave her husband and son by themselves.

"Well, if you don't want anything to eat I guess I'll run

down to the store and get some milk for tomorrow. I'll be back in a few minutes.'' She leaned over and kissed her husband again and then turned to the silent youngster standing in front of his father. ''And you want some Coke, right?''

''Yes, please,'' Sean replied in a small voice.

Marilyn got her keys from the kitchen table and stood in the middle of the room for a moment, listening. She couldn't hear anything from the living room. At last she went out the back door, trying to ignore her apprehension.

Sean and Jason faced each other silently for several seconds before Jason spoke. ''Come over here.''

The boy took several steps toward his father's chair.

''Come all the way over here,'' Jason repeated.

Sean advanced until he was standing directly in front of the chair, almost touching Jason's knees.

''May I talk to you?'' Jason's voice was soft.

''Sure.'' Sean could feel the emotion coming from his father but couldn't identify what it was. He was becoming increasingly nervous.

''Last night you told us that you remembered being an adult. Isn't that right?''

''Yes, sir.''

''Do you still remember all the things you told us about?''

''Ye-yes, sir.'' The boy stammered uncomfortably.

Jason put his hands on the boy's shoulders. ''Sometimes it's very hard to be an adult. Sometimes you make mistakes. Do you know what I'm talking about, Sean?''

''Not exactly.''

''I made a mistake. I want to tell you I'm sorry.''

''That's okay, Dad.'' The boy still wasn't sure what his father was talking about. He could tell Jason was upset and this made him even more nervous.

''I want you to know that I believe you. I believe you remember all the things you say you do. I don't understand any of it and maybe I never will. I don't think you do either. That doesn't matter. You and I together are going to try to find out how this happened and why it's happened. There's someone we're going to talk to Saturday who may help.'' Jason ran a hand through his hair and realized he was trembling. ''Anyway, I'm sorry. You're still my son and . . .''

His words were cut off by the impact as a relieved eight-year-old launched himself into his father's arms.

Marilyn deliberately took as long as she could getting the milk and Coke before rolling her cart to the checkout stand, and forty-five minutes had passed before she pulled into her driveway. She entered the house as she had left it, by the back door. She put away the milk and soda and strained to hear what was going on in the living room, but the house was silent. Finally, when she could stall no longer she opened the door that separated the kitchen from the dining room and headed for the front of the house, not knowing what she would find.

Marilyn saw her husband sitting where she had left him, his eyes closed, head back against the cushion, snoring gently. Sean was curled up on his lap with his head resting against Jason's chest. As she entered the room, Sean raised his head and gave her a warning look.

''Shhh. He's asleep.''

Saturday dawned foggy and overcast. Sean was awake and dressed by six-thirty. Jason had told him about Father John and he knew he was going to see the priest today, but this wasn't the reason for his excitement. Today they were going to pick up Mugs.

Sean poured some milk over his cereal and took it in the living room. He turned on the TV, and then switched it off when Channel 3 and Channel 12 both displayed test patterns. As Sean finished the cereal and raised the bowl to his lips to drink the last of the milk, he considered his options. He could try to find something to read. He could do nothing for thirty minutes until *Felix the Cat* came on at seven. He could wake his parents up and probably get yelled at, or he could go outside and walk around. Sean wiped the white mustache from his upper lip and carried the bowl into the kitchen. Moving quietly, he unlocked the back door and slipped out of the house.

The air was unseasonably cool and the lawns glistened with dew. The houses Sean passed on Canyon Drive were silent and peaceful. The boy wandered down the road with no destination in mind, enjoying the serenity of the morning. There was no traffic yet and Sean wished Mugs were with him.

Canyon Drive curved gently to the left and Sean turned to the right onto Arroyo Place. The houses were smaller now and closer together. As he passed some of them he sensed that at least one occupant was awake and moving around inside.

Sean was learning that the ability to "feel" the people around him involved more than just emotions. He discovered that people radiated an aura and that each aura was as distinctive and unique as a fingerprint. Some people were soft and wavy; some were loud and energetic. The words were poor approximations of what he felt, and he was often frustrated at his inability to find better words. Like a blind man attempting to describe a rainbow he has never seen, Sean was unable to define the things he could feel or verbalize, the subtle differences he recognized from one person to the next. He suspected the words didn't exist.

The boy had learned to control what came into his mind. The day in the hospital when he was barraged by the unwanted and painful feelings and fears of everyone who came near him had triggered its own defense. Without conscious effort on his part, Sean learned to erect a mental barrier that kept out most of the noise from other people. Unless he was preoccupied or deliberately relaxed his guard, he was able to shield his mind from the clamor around him. He couldn't explain how he did it any more than he could describe what he was blocking out. The defense wasn't perfect. Some of the buzz could still penetrate his shield but the level was bearable and Sean learned to "turn off" his mental ears. Just as one becomes deaf to background noises if they persist long enough, he could ignore the sensations that came into his head whenever he was around someone else.

The sun was beginning to burn off the morning fog as Sean paused at an intersection to get his bearings. He had been walking for twenty minutes now but didn't feel any need to begin heading back. The neighborhood was unfamiliar and he decided to go down the side street. Unless he was mistaken he ought to come out back on Canyon Drive.

A half-grown springer spaniel barked a challenge from the safety of its front yard and then, as though changing its mind, the dog trotted up to him with a friendly wag of its tail. Sean stroked the animal for several minutes before crossing Arroyo Place to the opposite corner. The spaniel, pleased at having found a pal to share the morning with, trotted next to him. The boy and his new friend turned left on Las Flores and began walking slowly toward Canyon Drive.

Someone emerged from a house midway down the block and climbed into an old Hudson parked in the driveway. Sean watched incuriously as the car backed out of the driveway and began moving toward him, slowly gathering speed. As the Hudson got closer, Sean began to feel the driver intruding into his mind. This was unlike anything he had felt before. Sean broke into a cold sweat as something oily and serpentine passed him in the car. The boy had only a momentary look at the driver, a thin scowling face blurred by the dirty windshield. The mental contact lasted longer and left Sean nauseous and shaking. The pleasant morning was suddenly ugly and threatening as he turned and began to retrace his steps. All that mattered was reaching home and safety as quickly as possible.

If Sean had looked behind him he might have seen a boy in old-fashioned clothes standing in front of the house

where the Hudson had been parked. The older boy was
dressed in the same outfit he had worn in the playground
at Puerta Grande when he had watched Sean and Michael
climbing Red Mountain. His eyes remained fixed on Sean's
back until the younger boy turned the corner and disappeared. Sean never looked back and never saw him.

George Braun had noticed the boy and the springer
spaniel as he passed them on Las Flores. The boy didn't
interest him but the dog, trotting next to the boy, brought
back memories of the animal that always used to follow
him when he was the boy's age.

He called it Thing. He was never sure what it was. It
looked something like a dog but the front legs were slightly
longer than the back legs, giving it a hyenalike appearance. Under its thick black fur, powerful muscles rippled
and surged when the creature moved. The head was narrow with gleaming, hypnotic yellow eyes that seemed able
to see into his soul. The snout was long, pointed, and full
of razor-sharp teeth in powerful jaws that looked like they
could snap a tree trunk. The creature must have weighed
more than a hundred pounds, but in spite of its size its
movements had a catlike quality that made George think
of a fox or perhaps a jackal. It was the only living creature
he had ever loved.

The first time he saw the animal, he was nine years old.
He had come home from school and tossed his books on
the bed then gone out the back door of the farmhouse and
was heading for the barn to pull down hay for the cows.
It was a cold November day. The sky was overcast. The
wind that was whipping at his clothing and lifting billows
of newly-fallen snow from the ground was too strong to
be called playful but not quite forceful enough to be called
angry. The boy put up his collar and hugged his coat more
tightly as he made his way across the yard through the
swirling powder. He was almost to the barn door when
he saw something a hundred yards away, at the edge of

the woods. His curiosity aroused, he hesitated and then changed direction. He walked past the barn, heading for the shape he had seen.

The animal was stretched out in the snow, watching without fear as George approached it. When the boy was ten feet away, the animal opened its jaws and yawned, revealing huge fangs. George stopped, torn between caution and a desire to get closer to the incredible beast. George could feel his heart beating rapidly as he took a hesitant step forward and then another. The creature watched calmly without moving as the boy's slow footsteps brought him closer and closer. Only five feet separated them. George was inching forward now, driven by a crazy desire to touch the monster, only too aware of what those deadly jaws could do to an arm or a leg . . . or a throat. Three feet. Two. The boy dropped slowly to his knees beside the thing and extended his hand. The animal's eyes narrowed and George froze, his fear once more gaining the upper hand. He remained paralyzed for only a moment and then his hand moved again until it was resting on the thing's side, his fingers burrowing into the luxurious black fur. The boy cried out as his mind and soul were filled with the dark power of the animal. An energy flowed from the beast that was stronger and darker and more beautiful than George had ever known in his life.

George saw the animal frequently in the days that followed. When he got home from school, Thing would be in the same spot at the edge of the wood behind the barn. When his chores were done, the boy would disappear into the woods for long walks with the dark beast. The creature would melt into the brush and while George couldn't see the animal or hear it, he learned to sense the energy and know when Thing was close, silently keeping pace with him. He began sneaking food out of the house for the animal. Thing always turned its nose up at these offerings.

George had never seen the creature eat anything and he
began to wonder if perhaps it didn't need food to live. It
was almost a month before George discovered the secret.

They had been hiking through the woods for several
hours. George saw a break in the trees ahead and as he
got closer, he was startled to see the Peppmuller's white-
washed outbuildings and weathered red barn. They had
come a lot farther than George realized. He turned and
began to retrace his steps when Thing suddenly appeared
in front of him, blocking his path.

The animal made soft growling noises deep in its throat.
Its lips curled back exposing yellowed, murderous fangs.
George gasped and took a step backward. The creature
advanced on him and George whimpered in terror. He
took another step backward and tripped over a tree root.
He fell with a crash and barely stifled his cry of fear.

The huge animal ignored the sprawled youngster. It
moved past him to stare into the clearing and then swiveled its massive head to stare over its shoulder in the direction they had come, the rumbling in its throat louder
now, sounding deadly and . . . thrilling. With a snarl, the
monster wheeled suddenly and disappeared into the underbrush.

George got to his feet, his sudden fear replaced by puz-
zlement at Thing's strange behavior. He approached the
break in the trees again and looked across the Peppmuller
fields. Everything seemed normal. The field was empty.
Most of the snow that blanketed the ground just a few
weeks before had now melted, leaving isolated dirty-white
patches amid the jumble and tangle of broken corn stalks.

He heard a noise behind him and turned his head. Something was coming through the woods in his direction.
George glanced around quickly, searching for a place to
hide, but before he could move, the underbrush parted and
he saw Billie Peppmuller's tangled red hair and freckled
face emerge through the heavy growth. The teenager

stopped in surprise at the sight of his schoolmate and then he scowled.

"Hey, Braun. What are you doing here?" Billie's voice was cold as he challenged the younger boy.

"Ain't none of your business, Billie. This ain't your land."

"About five feet in front of you it is my land and that makes it my business." The older boy held a pellet gun, which he waved threateningly in George's direction.

"Well, I'm not going that way so you don't need to worry none. I'm just walking with my dog and there ain't nothin' you can do about it."

"I don't see no dog, George," Billie continued, pointing the pellet gun at Braun, his dislike for the younger boy unconcealed. "I say you're hanging around lookin' for something to steal, that's what I say."

"I ain't no thief, Billie. I didn't take your watch."

"Oh, yeah? Well, what was it doing in your pocket after lunch?" Billie sneered at George, his grip on the pellet gun tightening.

"I found it. It ain't got your name on it. How was I supposed to know it was yours?" George felt his face growing red as he remembered his embarrassment when Mrs. Kimble made him empty his pockets in front of the whole class and discovered the gold pocket watch. His stubborn insistence that he found the watch on the floor seemed only to increase her wrath. He really had found the watch, although it was in Billie's desk and not on the floor as he repeatedly claimed.

"You're a liar, too. I still don't see no dog." Billie suddenly realized he didn't know what to do. He wasn't sure he had enough nerve to shoot his classmate, even with a pellet gun. On the other hand, it seemed a shame to waste this opportunity to bloody his nose at least. He leaned the rifle against a tree and took two steps closer to George.

"If you don't see no dog it's because you're blind as well as stupid. There he is now." George pointed at a spot behind and to the right of the bigger boy. Billie turned his head in the direction of George's finger and gasped. The animal walking calmly in his direction was enormous.

"What kind of dog is that?" He asked in sudden respect, his animosity temporarily forgotten at the sight of the incredible beast that moved in front of him and then stopped as though politely waiting to be introduced.

"He's my dog, that's what kind of dog he is. If I tell him to, he'll rip you up."

Billie ignored the threat. "Can I pet him? Will he bite?"

"Not unless I tell him to. You can pet him if you want." George's pride in the animal momentarily outweighed his dislike of the bigger boy.

Billie extended his hand, palm down, fingers curled under to the thing standing in front of him. The creature gently opened its huge mouth and before Billie could pull away, it closed its jaws around the boy's hand. There was a crunching sound as the animal's fangs came together, crushing flesh and bone between them. Billie screamed in agony.

"Get him off. Make him let go, George . . . please," he sobbed.

"I think he's hungry, Billie. You shouldn't have tried to pet him." George giggled as the older boy's screams became a single, high-pitched, hysterical wail of pain and terror. Thing began backing toward the underbrush, dragging the struggling Billie with him. The animal seemed to be growing larger. George had never felt so powerful. He was rooted to the spot as he watched Thing. Suddenly, he understood what he was seeing. Thing was feeding. It wasn't meat that sustained the beast. It was fear. The creature was swelling as it gorged itself on the mortal terror of the boy it was dragging into the bushes.

George remained standing at the edge of the Peppmuller field for more than an hour. The screams coming from the shadows had become weak gurgling sobs and then ceased altogether. For the last fifteen minutes, the only sound he could hear was the crunching of bone and occasional ripping noise that made him think of flesh being torn from the carcass of some large animal. He looked at the ground where Billie had stood, threatening him with the pellet gun that still leaned against the tree trunk. Something didn't look right and George peered more closely at the drops of blood that were spattered over the wooden stock of the rifle. The moist earth had been churned by the bigger boy's frantic struggles to get away. George could see Billie's footprints and the furrow left when he fell forward and was dragged on his stomach into the bushes. His were the only footprints.

The huge animal that George could hear feeding had left no impression in the soft, moist earth.

Only when Thing emerged, sleek and beautiful, did George stir from the spot. Together, the boy and the magnificent animal began hiking back home.

George braked the Hudson for a stop sign and his eyes narrowed as he saw a boy in shorts waiting at the bus stop across the intersection. The boy was holding up a surfboard with one hand while the other was extended, thumb outstretched in an unmistakable appeal for a ride.

Robert Frascotti stood next to the bus stop, steadying his board with one hand while he jingled the change in the pocket of his shorts with the other. He had no idea how he was going to get to the beach.

"Dumb shit," he muttered angrily to himself. He should have known he couldn't take a nine-foot surfboard on the bus. He should have asked his brother to drive him. Larry was a royal pain in the ass but he had his license and a 1953 Chevy. Robert still had two years to go before he would be old enough to get his license.

He looked at the Timex on his wrist and groaned softly. It was already after seven. He was supposed to meet the guys at Will Rogers beach by eight o'clock. He wasn't going to make it now. No way.

Of course, he could go back home and wake Larry up.

Maybe he could still talk his brother into giving him a ride. For a moment, Robert was on the verge of picking up his board and walking back the two blocks to his house. Only the knowledge that Larry would charge him a heavy price kept him standing at the bus stop in an agony of indecision. His brother wasn't about to do him any favors unless he got something out of it. Robert would have to fill his brother's car with gas and probably wash and wax it every week for the next ten years. On top of that, he would have to put up with Larry all day at the beach. No. There had to be a better way.

The boy glanced nervously in the direction of his house and then looked up Canyon Drive. A car was approaching. He considered what he was about to do for an instant and then made up his mind. The car had stopped at the other side of the intersection when Robert stepped closer to the curb and stuck out his thumb.

The car, a 1950 Hudson, crossed the intersection then slowed and pulled to the curb. Robert scooped up his towel and managed to tuck the board under his arm before running to the station wagon.

"You going to the beach?" The driver had walked to the back of the car and was opening the tailgate.

"Yup. I'm sure glad you came along. They won't let me take my board on the bus."

"Glad I can help out. I'm going to the beach myself." The driver positioned the surfboard in the bed of the wagon and secured the tailgate with a short length of rope that he produced from his pocket. "It's going to be a good day for the beach."

Two minutes later, the Hudson pulled away from the curb with Robert in the front seat next to a smiling George Braun.

At twelve forty-five that afternoon, Jason and Sean climbed into the Cadillac and backed out of the garage.

"I thought we were going to pick up Mugs first," Sean complained.

"The vet is open until five. Don't worry, there's plenty of time. We'll pick him up right after we leave Father John."

"Are you going to come in with me?"

"Sure I am. He may want to talk to you alone, but I'll be right in the other room if he does."

"Why don't you get Mugs while I'm talking to Father John?"

"Because he'd have to wait alone in the car and I don't think that's a good idea. Remember, he's got a cast on and he's going to be all taped up so he won't be able to move around very well." Jason gave his son an affectionate glance and realized that even if the boy had a mental age of forty his emotional age was still only eight. Somehow this made things easier.

They parked in front of the church and were admitted by the same housekeeper who seemed no happier to have company now than she had been two nights before. She led Jason and his son to the same study and went to get Father John.

It was almost five minutes before the huge priest bustled in to join them. Sean used the time to make a circuit of the room, examining the figure of Christ, the statue of St. Anthony, and finally stopping at the bookcase to study the titles, unaware that he was imitating his father's steps of two nights before. Although he was absorbed in his task, Sean had no trouble recognizing the approach of Father John. The mental buzz that filled the room was vibrant and energetic as the old priest opened the door.

"I'm sorry I took so long. I was on the telephone and couldn't get away. I'll bet you're Sean." He extended his hand soberly to the eight-year-old, who accepted it with equal seriousness. "I'm Father John. Your father has told me a lot about you." Without waiting for a reply the priest turned to Jason and smiled a greeting. "I'm glad you could make it. Would either of you like some lemonade?"

"I would," Sean said quickly.

"None for me, thanks. We just had lunch and—"

"Nonsense. Nora just made a big pitcher, and if we don't drink it, her feelings are going to be hurt. Let me have her bring you some."

"Well, if it's no trouble." Jason didn't think Nora's feelings had been hurt since they executed Ma Barker but held his peace and accepted the offer with reluctant good grace.

"Good. Let me tell Nora. I'll be right back." Father John left the room and Sean felt the man's energy moving down the hall, growing weaker as he moved away from them. The study now seemed quiet and empty. Sean marveled at the strength of the aura that surrounded the priest. He was like a huge dynamo, filling the air with powerful vibrations. It wasn't unpleasant, just forceful. Sean liked him. He began to feel the current building as Father John returned down the hall toward them. A second later the door opened and the room was again flooded with energy.

"Refreshments will be here in a minute." The rector of St. Anthony's smiled at Sean before settling into the other armchair next to Jason. A short time later the door opened again and Nora entered bearing a large pitcher, three glasses, and a plate of cookies.

Jason and Father John made small talk until the pile of cookies was reduced to three and assorted crumbs. Sean was beginning to think they would spend the entire day talking law when the priest finally stood and brushed at a stray cookie crumb on his shirt.

"Why don't Sean and I carry these glasses back to Nora. I'll show him around a bit if that's all right with you." He looked at Jason.

"That will be fine. If you don't mind I'll look over your *Blackstone*."

"Make yourself at home. There's probably something on those shelves for just about any taste. We'll be back in a little while."

Father John carried two glasses and the pitcher and Sean took the nearly empty plate and his own glass out of the study and down the hall into a large kitchen. The housekeeper was busy loading clothes into an old-fashioned washing machine and paid no attention to them as they came in.

"How about another glass of lemonade?" Father John put the glasses on the counter next to the sink and looked at Sean inquiringly.

"Don't be giving that boy any more junk. You're going to make him sick." The housekeeper looked up from her task and glared balefully at the old priest. "You, boy, put that plate up on the sink before you drop it and break it."

Sean carefully placed the glass and plate where he had been directed and, without thinking about it, sent a small mental probe in the housekeeper's direction. He looked up quickly in startled surprise as he felt the gentleness of the woman begin to enter his mind. Her words, her tone, and her expression were all contradicted by the soft affection that radiated from her.

"Now if you don't want something out here go someplace else so a body can get some work done." Again the contradictory signals and Sean felt his confusion growing.

"Come on, Sean. We'll go out back to the garden where we won't be in the way." Father John led the boy out the back door into a fenced yard to a couple of aluminum lawn chairs sitting under a grape arbor.

"Don't mind Nora. She's a little cranky sometimes." The cleric settled himself into a lawn chair and Sean did the same. "She doesn't mean anything by it."

"Yes, she does." Sean contradicted the priest as he suddenly understood what he felt in the kitchen. "She was telling us she likes us."

The priest was momentarily taken aback. "You know, I think you're right. How did you know that?"

"I could feel it. It's like a buzzing sound but it's not a sound. It's a feeling. I can kind of hear it coming from people."

"How long have you been able to do this?"

"Just since last Wednesday. After the accident when I woke up in the hospital, I was feeling . . . . just whatever anyone else was feeling. I mean, I could feel whatever they felt.'' Sean looked at Father John and remembered that first day at St. Mary's. "A lot of hurt," he said. Father John saw the pain in his face and changed to a different subject.

"Your dad says you remember a lot of things and know a lot of things you didn't know before the accident. Would you tell me a little bit about that?"

Sean told the story matter-of-factly, with none of the nervousness that had characterized his telling of three nights previous. He talked for a long time and Father John found himself caught up in the tale of the stocky history teacher who always wanted to be somebody important. In spite of his determination to draw no conclusions, the priest found himself almost ready to believe that the memories were real. When the boy had finished, Father John posed a question.

"When you decided to become a history teacher was there a particular period that appealed to you?"

"Not really. It was all interesting. Russian history is fun. It's so different from European history. I mean, there is no common background in Russian history the way there is with American and European history. Medieval Europe is an interesting time and place."

"Just as a kind of test, let me ask you something from history. It's been a long time since I've been in school so I'll have to make this an easy one. What can you tell me about Henry the Eighth?"

"You're right. That's an easy one." Sean grinned at the priest. "He was an English monarch on the throne from about 1510 or 11 until just after 1545. I don't remember the exact dates. He broke away from the Catholic Church in 1527 when Clement the Seventh wouldn't, or actually couldn't, grant him an annulment from Catherine of Aragon. I suppose the Pope would have been happy enough to annul the marriage except that Charles the Fifth was the Holy Roman Emperor at the time and he was also Catherine's nephew. Charles was making noises like he wanted to invade the Vatican and make it part of the Empire. If Clement, in effect, threw Catherine to the wolves to satisfy Henry, Charles was probably going to use this as an excuse to invade the Vatican. Poor Clement was really between a rock and a hard place so he appointed—''

"That's enough." Father John raised his hand and Sean stopped in mid-sentence. The old priest and the young boy sat quietly under the grape arbor for several minutes before the priest spoke again.

"What does the name Thomas Hutchinson mean to you?"

Sean shook his head slowly. "Nothing. The name's familiar but . . . wait a minute, wasn't he a governor? Yeah, that's it. He was one of the colonial governors in the eighteenth century. I think it was . . . was it Virginia? I'm guessing."

"It was Massachusetts. What was the purpose of the Congress of Vienna?"

This time Sean answered at once. "It was the European conference held in Vienna to establish the territorial boundaries in Europe after the Napoleonic Wars. That was in 1814."

"Sean, do you have any idea why this has happened to you?"

"I don't know. I haven't really worried about why. It's overwhelming enough to know that it's happened. Why does there have to be a reason?"

"Most things that happen to us happen for a reason whether we know it or not. Do you have any idea whose memories you have?"

"I thought they were my own. They feel like they're mine."

"Who are . . . who were you then? Do you remember a name?"

Sean took a long time to answer. "I never thought about that till just now. I don't remember a name."

"Do you remember a time, then? Do you remember when you died in the airplane crash?"

This time Sean answered immediately. "Oh, yeah. It was in March. March of 1985."

A little voice in Father John's head warned him too late. There was no way now to recall the question or to forget the answer.

"I see." The silence stretched between them again as Father John pondered the ways of God and wondered why the memories of a forty-year-old man who would die twenty-six years in the future had been thrust upon a young boy. He stretched his hand out and placed it on the boy's shoulder. "I don't know why this has happened to you either, Sean. I hope though, that if you have any problem you'll come and talk to me about it. God seems to have blessed you with a very special and unusual gift and you'll have to learn to use it as He would want you to use it."

"There is one thing. Could I ask you a question?"

"Of course."

Sean told Father John about his walk that morning and the strange encounter on Las Flores. As Sean described the alien feeling of evil that had frightened him, he felt the priest's hand tighten briefly and then relax.

"Son, there are some things in the world we need to be afraid of."

"Was that one of them? What was it?"

"Sean, your father and I talked a little bit about possession the other evening. Do you know what that is?"

"Yes, sir. I think I do."

Father John smiled at the boy and continued. "I told him that I had never encountered a case of possession or heard about one that I didn't think could be explained in purely natural terms. I realize now that I left out a different kind of possession, a kind that probably occurs every day."

"There's more than one kind?"

"Oh, yes. Your father and I had been talking about a victim whose soul is taken over by force and without his consent. There is another kind and it's even more dangerous. That's the kind that involves a man or woman who knowingly and willingly invites evil into his heart. I think this might be the state of the soul you encountered this morning. Stay away from it, Sean. If you ever sense anything like this again, run as fast as you can in the other direction.''

''Would it hurt me?'' The boy looked uneasy.

''I don't know. Maybe. Don't take a chance. Just get away from it as quickly as you can. Okay?''

''Okay.'' The boy's voice was barely audible. ''I will.''

Father John looked at his watch and was surprised to see that almost two hours had passed since he and Sean had come into the backyard.

''I have to start hearing confession at three o'clock so we're going to have to end our talk for now. I want you to remember what I said and if you want to talk again I'm always here, okay?''

''Okay . . . Father.'' The word felt strange to Sean.

They returned to the study and Father John walked Jason and Sean to the door of the rectory.

''You go ahead and get in the car. I'll be right there,'' Jason told his son. He waited until Sean had climbed into the car and closed the door before turning to the priest.

''Well, what do you think?''

''I think that what has happened is the work of God and not the devil, if that helps any. As far as how or why . . . I have absolutely no idea.''

Jason looked troubled. ''What should we do?''

''Love him and pray. An answer will come.'' The priest knew his response was bringing little comfort to the lawyer and he wished he could offer more.

Father John Cassidy stood in the doorway of Saint Anthony's Rectory and watched the Cadillac disappear down the street. He sighed heavily. He had never encountered anything like this before and really didn't have any idea how it could have happened. He did believe that everything has a purpose even though that purpose might be hidden from the eyes of men. He felt a moment of fear for the small boy who had just left and prayed silently that the youngster would be strong.

Jason and Sean drove directly to the Highland Vista Animal Hospital. The place was crowded and Sean fidgeted impatiently while they waited for their turn. Almost thirty minutes passed before a female voice called, ''Jason Jeffries,'' and Sean wormed his way through the crowd of people to the counter. Five minutes later they emerged with Sean holding an ecstatic terrier carefully in his arms.

PART TWO

Coming Around

"The blazing evidence of immortality is our dissatisfaction with any other solution."

Journal entry of Ralph Waldo Emerson,
July 1855

CHAPTER SIX

Angela

From the *Vista Tribune*, Monday, August 22, 1958:

TRAGIC END TO SEARCH FOR MISSING BOY

Homosexual Murder Stuns Community

*The search for sixteen-year-old Robert Frascotti
came to a tragic end today when hikers in the Angeles National Forest discovered his head and torso
covered with leaves in a ravine near Crest Highway,
ten miles north of Los Angeles.*

*The gruesome discovery was made by Brian Mor-
row and Arturo Ramirez of Temple City, who were
backpacking in the area and who notified the Angeles
substation of the Sheriff's Department. The teenager's severed limbs were found several hours later
by sheriff's deputies searching an area on the other
side of Crest Highway.*

*The high school sophomore, reported missing Sun-
day morning by his parents, had been the object of
an intense search by law enforcement officers who
now believe he may have died at the hands of the
same killer responsible for the murder of fourteen
children and teenagers in the Southland since January of last year.*

*At a press conference held late this afternoon in
Highland Vista, Lt. Aaron Winslow of the Los Angeles County Sheriff's Department released a prelim-*

*inary report from the Coroner's Office indicating that
the boy had been sexually molested and tortured and
may have been murdered at another location before
being taken to the remote mountain area and dis-
membered.*

*Police have no leads at this time and are asking
the public's help in locating the killer. Anyone who
saw Robert Frascotti since he left home Saturday
morning or who has any information that might help
police trace his movements is asked to call Sergeant
Dale Henderson at the Angeles Sheriff's substation.*

Dust motes floated in the rays of afternoon sunlight
slanting through the open venetian blinds onto the bed and
the sleeping girl. Angela whimpered unhappily and tried
to recapture the dream that was slipping elusively into the
mist. It was no use. The dream was over. Angela opened
her eyes slowly and felt like shit. She put her feet on the
floor and held her head with both hands. The throbbing
headache was bad but worse was the churning in her stomach. She rose from the bed and stumbled toward the bathroom. Halfway across the room her stomach put her on
notice that it would brook no further delay and she ran the
last few feet to the toilet, barely making it before the heaves
convulsed her. Moments later she was slumped naked on
the floor, her arms wrapped around the toilet and her head
resting on the bowl, as though hugging some obscene
panda bear. The scene was reminiscent of a Norman
Rockwell tableau: a small slice of Americana to be pre-
served on the cover of an issue of the *Saturday Evening
Post*: "Little Girl with a Hangover."

Angela Loomis had acquired her curvaceous body from
her mother and her green eyes from a close friend of her
father's. It is doubtful that Randy Loomis ever suspected
the little girl wasn't his own nor would he have been un-
duly concerned if he had known. Angela's acting father
was a long-haul truck driver whose brief periods at home
were usually spent chugging suds at one or another of the

local gin mills. It was at one of these beer bars on the outskirts of El Paso that an ill-considered remark of Randy's regarding the sexual preference of three Mexican-American gentlemen down the bar from him—witnesses would later quote him more specifically as having referred to "fucking greaser faggots"—prompted one of them to take umbrage. He also took a blade only slightly less than seven inches long and slipped it through Randy's sternum. This effectively ended the discussion and left Angela's mother a widow.

Dorothy Loomis ("Call me Dolly. Would you like to buy a lady a drink?") was devastated for several minutes by the news of her husband's unexpected demise but was able to bounce back in time for happy hour at the Oaks. The Oaks was a friendly, caring kind of place, and the grieving widow with the incredible bust received numerous expressions of condolence that night, all of them from unattached males anxious to ease her sorrow and find out if that was all really her underneath the bra.

Nine-year-old Angela was unable to match her mother's calm acceptance of Randy's death. Although her father had usually been on the road and had never been particularly affectionate when he was home, the little girl felt as though a part of her had been ripped violently away leaving a gaping and painful wound. She knew her father had loved her very much because . . . because all parents love their children very much. She had been told this in school; she had read it somewhere, and in her heart she knew it was true. She never talked about it with her mother, who was usually drunk and maudlin or hung over and vicious. Her father had loved her and he was dead. It hurt.

Time passed. Angela began discovering her body when she was eleven and a half. By the time she was twelve it was obvious that she would be, physically at least, her mother's daughter.

If Angela's life was changing due to the chemical messages of puberty, her mother's was changing due to the chemical messages of amphetamines. Dolly loved a good time. One night at the Oaks she had such a good time that an ambulance had to be called. The coroner cited benzadrine and alcohol as the cause of death. Dorothy Loomis was cremated at the expense of the state of Texas and Angela Loomis became a ward of that state.

Had it not been for Ted and Vera Loomis, Angela might have spent the next six years in a series of foster homes. The discovery that she had an aunt and uncle living in San Diego came as a shock to the girl and a pleasant surprise to the great state of Texas. She was immediately dispatched to California to begin a new life with her only living relatives.

Angela lifted her head from the toilet bowl and rose unsteadily to her feet. She turned on the shower and stepped into the bathtub under the stream of lukewarm water. It felt good and she carefully lathered her body with an impossibly tiny wafer of soap from the soap dish. The water was soothing and the girl tilted her head back to let the warm stream run through her hair and over her face. She groped blindly for the shampoo as the water ran into her eyes and finally located the plastic bottle on the little rack hanging from the shower head. She worked the suds into her scalp with her fingers and luxuriated in the sensuous feeling of warm, soapy water flowing over her body.

She remained in the shower longer than usual. The warm jets of water that were rejuvenating her felt too good to leave. Thirty minutes later, when she emerged from the bathroom, the transformation was miraculous. The resilience of youth combined with the long shower had wrought a magical change. Gone was "Little Girl with a Hangover." In her place was an extraordinarily pretty sixteen-year-old girl who looked as though she would be more at home on the arm of some incredibly lucky high school quarterback than in a seedy little two-room apartment on Selma Avenue in Hollywood. Only a trained professional, a cop, a social worker, or a pimp might have detected the flaw in the prom queen image. There was a hardness about the girl, a wariness behind her eyes only barely concealed by her angelic face. The inner person lived behind a barrier that no high school jock would ever penetrate. The shield was a gift bestowed by the streets on those girls able to survive in them.

Angela walked across the room to the pile of clothes on the floor where she had left them the night before. She scooped them up and carried them to the tiny closet in the corner of the room, where she dumped them on the floor before going to the dresser and taking a pair of cutoff jeans from the drawer. She slipped them on and then rummaged deeper in the drawer. She found what she was looking for and took two twenty-dollar bills from the roll of ten that was hidden under the pile of folded panties. She set the two bills on top of the dresser while she opened another drawer and took out a T-shirt that was at least one size too small for her, emphasizing both her wares and her occupation. She slid her feet into a pair of sandals and pocketed the forty dollars on the dresser. Dressed at last, she returned to the bathroom and opened the medicine cabinet. She took a wax-paper-wrapped packet from the top shelf and removed a small white tablet from the alarmingly diminished stash. She rewrapped the three pills that remained and placed them carefully back on the shelf. Finding Eddie would have to be a priority tonight. It was time to restock. Angela swallowed the Dexedrine without bothering with water. She spent a few minutes straightening the bed before taking a heavy padlock from a table by the door. She let herself out of the apartment and pulled the door closed behind her and then shoved the hasp in and secured it with the padlock. She dropped the key into her purse and moved down the dark hallway with its cracked plaster and perpetual smell of urine to the open front door and the city at dusk. The Dexie was beginning to work. Angela felt pretty good.

The evening was pleasant, and George Braun rolled down the window on the driver's side as he turned onto the Pasadena Freeway on his way to Hollywood. Cool air moved through the car and back out the open window, sweeping away the stale odor of cigarette smoke. Any other time, the cool breeze might have felt good, but today George was in no mood to experience the joys of nature. As he gripped the steering wheel tightly, his face was distorted by a look of hatred. A copy of the *Vista Tribune* lay on the seat beside him, last year's school picture of Robert Frascotti smiling up at him from the front page in hideous accusation whenever George took his eyes from the road to glare at it.

What were they talking about? What did they mean: homosexual murder? George took his eyes from the traffic again and read the smaller headline in disgust.

He ought to find out who wrote the story. Weren't there laws that said you couldn't print lies like that? For a moment, George toyed with the idea of stopping at a pay phone and calling the *Tribune* just to set the record straight. Didn't they have to print both sides?

He wasn't no fuckin' queer. Sex had nothing to do with it. If they could have heard the way the kid screamed when he shoved it up his ass they would know why he did it. It was the fear that mattered. How could they put a headline like that in the paper . . . right on the front page where everyone would see it? As if he got his kicks having sex with little boys. Jesus Christ in a wheelbarrow, he wasn't like that. People who did things like that were sick. They were monsters.

He had been on his way home when he stopped and bought the paper. His eyes caught the picture as he climbed back into the car and he read the story through twice in shocked disbelief before his mind fully accepted the ghastly charge leveled against him. When he started the car and pulled away from the curb, he drove to the corner and around the block. He wasn't about to go home now. He was too furious. He was going to Hollywood.

Someone was going to pay for this.

* * *

Morris Kirby chuckled happily to himself as he drove down the Pasadena Freeway toward home. His right hand reached over and patted the briefcase on the seat next to him. He would show Myrna the application. It was the biggest whole life policy he had ever sold. A hundred-thousand-dollar policy and Blanchard was sixty-three years old. His commission was going to be over eight thousand dollars on this one case. What a day. He couldn't wait to get to the office tomorrow and start rubbing Mark's nose in it. He had said he was going to close the deal with the old man and, by God, he had done it.

A marker announced the approach of Avenue Forty-three. Kirby turned on his signal and began changing lanes. A horn blared and he swerved back to the left, heart pounding, as a Hudson station wagon in the slow lane moved alongside of him. He glanced to the right and had a momentary look at the other driver's face, thin-lipped and angry, before the wagon pulled ahead of him. The insurance man ventured an apologetic wave and then, checking this time to make sure the lane was clear, he began easing the Chevy to the right, behind the Hudson.

He noticed the smell first. The car was suddenly filled with the sweet putrid odor of rotting meat. That was when he heard the soft growl from the backseat. Startled, he looked into the rearview mirror and gasped in terror at the reflected image. In desperation, he yanked the steering wheel to the right and frantically pumped the brakes. The Chevy skidded sideways across the freeway shoulder before slamming into the concrete barrier on the Avenue Forty-three exit ramp. Kirby was out of the car and running before it stopped moving.

Myrna never did believe the story her husband told her. He was excited. He was tired. He had just closed the biggest deal of his professional career. The sun had been in his eyes. He was imagining things.

And after that first night, Morris Kirby never again spoke of the day he smelled the stench of death and looked in the rearview mirror to see a creature from hell in the backseat. It had a huge jackal head with gleaming, hate-filled yellow eyes above a narrow, pointed snout full of razor-sharp teeth. The monster was gripping something in its immense jaws—something that twisted and struggled in a desperate and futile effort to get away . . .

Something that had the face of Morris Kirby.

Angela lived with her aunt and uncle for four years. Life was a lot different from the way it had been in El Paso. There was always enough to eat. There were new clothes. There was even an allowance of five dollars a week, earned by doing the dishes and straightening the kitchen each evening after dinner. Ted and Vera enrolled their niece in a private school for girls in nearby El Cajon, where the girl was able to earn respectable if not brilliant grades despite the school's academic standards.

Angela spoke frequently of her father and seemed happiest when she could launch her uncle into tales of his childhood and the things he and his brother had done together. In fact, Ted and Randy had avoided each other as much as children who dislike each other can when they are forced to live under the same roof. Ted recognized that his brother's memory was special to the girl and so invented long, rambling, and totally apocryphal stories of their escapades as young boys, painting Randy with larger-than-life strokes. Angela believed them all.

The death of her mother didn't seem to bother her at all. She never talked about Dolly and quickly changed the subject if Ted or Vera mentioned her.

The happiest time of the day for Angela was also the most troubling. Each night after she climbed into bed, Ted would come into her room and tell her good night in a ritual as unvarying as the rising and setting of the sun. It was their special time. They would talk in hushed whispers of the events of the day or of tomorrow's plans. And each evening, as their special time would draw to a close, Ted would reach over and begin stroking her hair. He would tell her how much he and Vera loved her. He would take her in his arms and his powerful hands would move from her hair down her body, enfolding and caressing her. Angela would feel electric currents begin to flow through her as his hands would move, linger, then move again. If a hand seemed to linger too long against her breast or thigh, Angela would pretend not to notice. It always did. Finally, he would kiss her lovingly. Then he would leave.

Sometimes the girl dreamed about her uncle. In these dreams Ted would stroke her and she would take his hand and guide it to deep and secret places within her. She would awaken from these dreams with an odd mixture of exhilaration and shame and a resolve to put such thoughts from her mind. The resolve would last until bedtime when Ted would again come in to say good night and share their special time.

Angela walked six blocks south on Highland Avenue to Santa Monica Boulevard, where she turned right. Lights along the boulevard were beginning to blink on and traffic was heavy with late commuters and early revelers. Foot traffic was also picking up as the lights of the night began transforming the city into a place of magic and fun.

Angela's success at her chosen profession was entirely in the hands of the older women who worked the city's streets and bars. Their goodwill was of paramount importance. With only a few exceptions, all of Angela's clients had been referrals from Bonnie, Gina, or a few of the other working women. No pimp in his right mind was going to add underage jailbait to his string and, in spite of her impressive physical development, the girl still looked too young to patronize the bars and nightclubs along Sunset Strip. In the shadowy subculture of the streets, the threat of being rousted on a prostitution charge was the potential price of doing business. Compounding that with a charge of contributing to the delinquency of a minor was an unacceptable risk to most of the older women and all of the pimps. As a result, their association with the girl was at arm's length, consisting of cryptic messages left with answering services and an honor system of commission payment. For her part, Angela understood that alienating even one of the women who sent clients to her would result in the loss of new clients from all of them. She made a point of honoring her obligations within a day of earning a fee.

It was an arrangement that worked out to everyone's satisfaction. Angela was able to earn a living and her "agents" were able to supplement their income from johns with a taste for the younger stuff. Angela kept sixty percent of what she made and forty percent was paid as a finder's fee to the referring woman.

Angela could see the lights of Pronto Burger in the distance. Eddie would probably be there with Gina. If she was lucky she could score and be back home with the dexie before seven, which would leave her the rest of the night to make some money. This might be a very good night.

Vera's decision to enroll in a five-unit French class had nothing to do with her niece. She was a perennial student who had been taking classes at the community college for all of her married life.

It was on a Thursday evening two and a half weeks after the start of the semester that the bottom fell out of Angela's world. Vera had prepared a roast before leaving for class and left instructions with Angela to warm a vegetable and put the rolls in the oven at six o'clock. Since her uncle usually got home between six and six-fifteen, this left the girl almost an hour and she decided to use the time to shower and wash her hair.

She had just finished drying off when she heard Ted's pickup truck parking in the driveway. With an unladylike exclamation she wrapped the towel around her dripping hair and ran quickly to her bedroom, where she wrapped her bathrobe snugly around her damp body. When Ted came in the back door, Angela was busily laying out silverware on the dining room table.

"Hi, princess." Ted gave the girl a quick peck on his way to the kitchen sink, where he began washing his hands with liquid soap. "Mmmm, you smell good. Is that a new perfume?"

"Silly, that's shampoo. I wanted to have supper on the table for you but I took too long in the shower. I'm sorry."

"I'm glad dinner isn't ready yet. I think I'd like to have you fix me a drink while I take a quick shower and unwind a little bit."

"Okay. It will be waiting for you here when you get back." Angela gave her uncle a happy smile and turned to the refrigerator for ice cubes. When she turned back, her uncle had left the kitchen. A few moments later Angela heard the shower running, and after preparing his drink she opened a can of green beans and put them in a saucepan on the stove.

Ted emerged from the shower fifteen minutes later, barefoot and, like Angela, dressed only in a robe. He took the scotch and soda his niece offered him and drained half the glass with one swallow.

"What do you say, princess, how about having a drink with me?"

"Well . . . ." Angela hesitated and then laughed as her uncle mimed an exaggerated look of pleading. "I'll force myself to choke down just one."

Ted laughed, too, and Angela dodged around him as he grabbed playfully at her.

Ted swallowed the rest of his drink and offered her the empty glass. "While you're making yours how about a refill?" He leaned back against the counter and watched as his niece put ice cubes into the glasses and then poured a splash of scotch into each.

"Good grief, princess, at least put in enough to change the color of the soda." He grabbed the bottle out of the girl's hand and added a generous portion to each glass before slapping it back down on the counter.

"Boy, you are in a strange mood tonight." Angela looked at the two glasses and tried to ignore the misgivings beginning to form in the back of her mind. "If I drink that thing I'm going to be in no condition to finish dinner."

"Let dinner wait. Turn everything off and we'll warm it later. I don't feel hungry right now anyway. Come on. Let's go sit in the living room."

Angela looked at the uncle she loved, and for a dreamlike moment she seemed to be seeing a stranger. There was something different, some nameless threat in the air. Her shadowy misgivings quickly passed and the real world again intruded itself. This was her home. These were her . . . her parents . . . her family. There was nothing to be afraid of here. A rush of love and relief flowed through her and she obediently began turning down the oven and shutting off the gas under the green beans.

An hour later when Ted brought her a third drink, Angela was happily and drunkenly sitting on the couch with her feet tucked under her, all of her earlier fears long since forgotten.

"Ya know what?" Angela spoke slowly as Ted eased himself onto the couch beside her. "When Vera fines out the roast dried up she'sh gonna kill both of us."

"Easy, baby. There are more important things in the world than roasts." Ted seemed unaffected by the alcohol. "Come over here and be close to me." He put his arm around the unresisting girl and pulled her toward him on the couch.

Four miles away at San Diego Community College a phone was ringing in the language department. A student assistant answered on the third ring and a few minutes later hurried down the hall to Mr. Pliego's French class. Jean Pliego was having pains at twenty-minute intervals. What should she do? Martin Pliego dismissed his class two hours early to hurry home and assist his wife. By two

in the morning he was the proud father of a daughter that
he and Jean decided to name Rebecca.

. Vera Loomis left the school to drive home at seven-
ten P.M.

Through a haze of alcohol Angela felt the tingle begin
as Ted's fingers traced lightly over her body beneath the
robe. It felt so good to be caressed. No . . . no . . . NO!
It was *wrong*. Angela struggled to sit up but her uncle's
body was pinning her against the back of the couch. He
had moved one arm under her neck and was now moving
his other hand lovingly over her stomach and breasts.
Something black and foreboding had invaded the girl's
earlier euphoria. Her body arched hungrily against the
hand that was stroking and caressing her as though di-
vorced from her brain that cried out in revulsion.

She wanted to scream, to make him stop. She wanted
to be a little girl again. It was no use. Tears were coursing
down her cheeks as she stopped resisting and tried to close
her mind to what was happening. She could feel Ted's
fingers moving from her breasts to her stomach and then
farther down, gently but forcefully into those secret places
Angela had dreamed about. She didn't move as the pressure of her uncle's body eased slightly and she was aware
vaguely that he was fumbling with the belt of his robe.
She opened her eyes suddenly when she felt him press
against her, naked and hard. Something was happening to
his face. His features were dissolving and reforming in
front of her horrified eyes. It wasn't her uncle's face any
longer. It was her daddy. Angela was sobbing now. She
couldn't control her emotions, her body, or the images that
were shaping around her.

"Daddy. Please, Daddy. I love you. Please . . . *DON'T.*"

Angela whimpered with pain as Ted entered her suddenly and violently. The face of Randy Loomis began
changing again. The girl saw her father's features begin to
sag and melt as if they were burning. Her whimpers became screams as the skin on the face just inches from her

own began dripping, hot and sticky against her breasts and neck. An eye fell from its socket to bounce against her chin before dropping off the side of the couch and rolling across the floor. Angela screamed again and tried to twist away. The air seemed filled with the putrid stench of decaying flesh as she imagined the second eye popping from the leering death mask that panted hungrily above her. She shuddered, gagged, and vomited just as the front door opened and Vera walked in on them, filled with the news of her French teacher's new baby.

George got off the freeway at Sunset Boulevard near downtown Los Angeles and began heading west. The sun had dropped below the horizon and he switched on the Hudson's lights as he drove toward Hollywood. There weren't many pedestrians on the sidewalk. It was too early. The prostitutes and hustlers would be waking soon, opening bleary eyes and preparing for another night on the streets. In a few hours they would be lounging in doorways, standing in groups of twos and threes, exchanging bits of gossip and keeping a watchful eye out for the police. A few of the more aggressive ones might stick out a thumb and direct an inviting smile at the oncoming traffic on the boulevard.

Some would return home in the early hours with nothing to show for their efforts but a curious feeling of rejection. They would be back again tomorrow night to offer their bodies to anyone with the desire . . . and the price.

Some wouldn't return home for several days. These were the ones unlucky enough to be noticed by the police. They would be booked and some would be bailed out by pimps, or boyfriends, or girlfriends. Those that managed to get out of jail would leave Hollywood and begin working the San Fernando Valley or the East Los Angeles areas. Others, working without the protection of a "manager," would remain in jail until they went to court and were sentenced to a short probation. Then they'd be back on the street, earning a living the only way they knew how.

And at least one of them would meet George tonight. She . . . or he . . . would never go home again.

The animal wail of pain and shock from Vera paralyzed Ted and came at the same time that Angela was throwing up her lunch all over the couch. The young girl was the first to recover as horrible reality forced itself into her alcohol-shrouded brain. What had she done? *MY GOD . . . WHAT HAD SHE DONE?* She struggled from beneath her uncle's limp body and clutched at her robe, giving her aunt a beseeching look, imploring forgiveness. Vera stood motionless, her throat working convulsively, no longer screaming. Angela wiped her mouth with the back of her hand. She looked around the room like a trapped animal seeking escape. When she turned back to her aunt she gasped at Vera's look of hate. Angela moaned softly and ran from the room. No one moved to follow her.

Angela never learned what words passed between her aunt and uncle that night. She heard no voices as she huddled sobbing in the corner of her bedroom. It might have been an hour later that she thought she heard the front door open and close but no one came to punish or comfort her. She wanted to crawl to Vera and beg her forgiveness but couldn't bear the thought of facing her aunt or uncle. She wanted to take another shower. She felt dirty all over. She wanted to scrub her skin until it was raw and red. If only she could wash the guilt down the drain with the soap and water.

At three in the morning she stopped crying. The house, silent and dark, was filled with a malignant, accusing spirit. The home she had grown to love with its memories of laughter and fun now seemed oppressive and menacing, challenging her right to seek shelter beneath its roof or find protection within its walls. Angela began packing an overnight bag. When the bag was full she laid out a skirt and blouse on the bed and then let the robe slip from her shoulders. As if in a daze she walked naked into the bathroom and turned on the water. Fifteen minutes later she stepped from the shower and began to rub her already abused skin dry with a bath towel. She dressed without haste and went to the telephone in the kitchen. She had sixty-five dollars that she had saved from Christmas and birthday gifts. That would be enough to get her away. She didn't know where she would go. Anyplace would do. Someplace where no one would know her. Someplace where no one would know what she had done.

When the taxi arrived, Angela was in front of the house waiting. By four o'clock she was at the bus station, buying a one-way ticket to Los Angeles.

Angela shook her head angrily. It was a beautiful evening. She didn't intend to spoil it by thinking about San Diego. She didn't want to think about anything except the future. It was too nice just strolling along, enjoying the bustle and activity of the boulevard and dreaming about her someday to come.

George turned left on Highland Avenue, heading for Santa Monica Boulevard. Too late, he saw the boy in the jeans and T-shirt standing on the corner with his thumb in the air. He tried to stop but he was already past the preteen and there was no place to pull over. He made a right turn and circled the block. A red light on Highland delayed him and it was almost four minutes before he was again cruising slowly toward the corner where he had seen the hitchhiker. The boy was gone. Someone else had picked him up.

That was okay. There would be others.

Five minutes to eight. The light on the corner changed to red as Angela stepped off the curb and began to cross La Brea Avenue. The frantic squeal of brakes snapped her head up and brought her heart to her throat. The Pontiac fishtailed to the left as its tires clutched desperately for a purchase on the asphalt. It came to a halt only inches from the girl.

"My God! Are you all right?" A white-faced elderly

man stepped from the car, holding the door for support and panting heavily.

"I . . . I think so." Angela could feel the hammering of her own heart as she gripped the side of the car weakly. "You didn't hit me. I'm okay."

"Young lady, are you trying to get yourself killed?" The man's face began to turn red as relief turned shock into anger. "Why don't you watch where you're going?"

"I'm sorry. I know it was my fault. I wasn't paying attention." Angela took her hand from the fender of the car and for some inexplicable reason began to cry.

"Here now, there's no call for that." The driver looked uncomfortable and took an uncertain step toward the girl before stopping and wringing his hands in an unmistakable gesture of helplessness. "I shouldn't have yelled at you. I'm sorry. You sure you're all right?"

Angela managed a nod and then saw something in the distance that chilled her heart. A hundred yards away she could see a black and white, its twin rotary lights clearing a path through traffic as it headed in their direction. She turned and shoved her way through the small crowd of onlookers that had gathered around them, ignoring the protests of the driver.

"Miss, don't run off. Lady, come back. It's okay."

She broke into a half run for a block down La Brea, turning only once to see that the police car had pulled to a stop at the corner, red beacons on top revolving brightly. She angled to the left through a shopping center parking lot and lost sight of the intersection. Her heart was racing, her pulse throbbing in her temples. She slowed to a walk, gasping for breath, ignoring the curious looks she was getting from grocery-laden shoppers returning to their cars from the supermarket. It couldn't end like this. She couldn't go back. Not now. Angela turned left on Fifth Street and then right on Norwood Court. The bright street-lights and black storefronts of La Brea were replaced by neat little houses of stucco and wood. The only light on the street filtered through the curtains of windows she passed, warm orange and only barely bright enough to keep her from stumbling on the broken, uneven sidewalk. Ahead of her she could make out the lights of Sunset Boulevard traffic crossing the intersection with Norwood Court. Her breathing was returning to normal and she quickened her step, anxious to reach the haven of familiar ground. Behind her a car turned onto Norwood from Fifth Street and Angela froze, momentarily terrified.

Don't panic. Just walk down the street. Don't do anything to call attention to yourself. Angela forced herself to walk slower. She watched as her shadow appeared, long and skinny in front of her. The shadow began to shrink and become sharper as the car behind her got closer and closer. Just keep walking normally.

She heard the sound of the engine change pitch as the driver took his foot off the accelerator and slowed. She bit her lip to keep from crying out. One foot in front of the other. Don't look around. Just keep your eyes on the ground. I live right up the street. No, Officer, I'm just on my way home. See, that's my house right over there. No, I didn't see an accident. Oh, gosh, no. I wasn't anywhere near the boulevard tonight. I was right over there at that house. That one there. I was doing homework with my girlfriend.

It couldn't end like this.

The sound of the engine changed again and Angela felt weak with relief as the car, an old Hudson station wagon, passed her. The driver had his window down and Angela caught a brief glimpse of an older man with an expression that combined a scowl and a leer. The intensity of his look might have been unsettling if Angela hadn't been so consumed by relief. She felt lightheaded as she again increased her pace to cover Sunset Boulevard and safety. As she walked rapidly to reach the three blocks to the intersection she turned and looked behind her. Norwood Court was deserted. She didn't notice that George Braun had turned the Hudson right on Sunset and was doubling back to Fifth Street.

* * *

The beautiful animal was keeping him company now. It was alive and riding in the car with him, next to him, inside of him. George felt the icy calm descend on him, holding at bay the tendrils of fear that always rode with him on these nights, his own fear that heightened the pleasure he would soon experience. Mixed with the fear of discovery . . . of capture . . . was the feeling of incredible power. He controlled; he was the master.

He was on fire.

Angela turned the corner of Sunset Boulevard at last and collapsed on a bus-stop bench with a gasp of relief. She recognized the motel across the street and knew she was little more than six blocks from her own apartment. Maybe she would just get something to eat and then return home for a quick nap before calling the answering service at ten o'clock. She had had just about enough excitement for one evening. Lately her body seemed to be developing a tolerance for speed; the Dexedrine she had taken at five-thirty didn't seem to be doing her much good at eight-thirty. With the effects of the Dexie almost worn off, Angela felt weary, irritable, and vaguely depressed. She almost hoped there would be no message with the service. This would be a good night to stay home and sleep.

The station wagon was back. It turned onto Sunset and slowed as it had when it passed her on Norwood Court. Suddenly, Angela's professional instincts were aroused. She smiled and looked directly at the windshield, trying to put an invitation into her expression. The car slowed further and stopped in front of her. The side window began to roll down but the interior of the car was too dark for Angela to see any details of the man's face.

"Need a ride, missy?"

"Thanks." Angela reached for the door handle even as she leaned forward to try to get a better look at the driver through the partially open window. "It seems to take forever for the bus to get here. My name is Angela."

"I'm George." Angela could see him clearly now as she settled into the front seat of the station wagon. He looked old. He smiled at her and the girl had an illogical urge to shudder. Suddenly, this didn't seem like such a good idea after all. Still, a fee is a fee. She realized he was saying something else and forced her attention back to his words.

"I'm sorry. What did you say?"

"I said, what's a pretty miss like you doing in Hollywood?" His right hand snaked out and grabbed her thigh firmly. There was nothing gentle or subtle about him. Angela almost recoiled but forced herself to relax and moved a couple of inches closer to him.

"Are you a cop?" Angela had been told and believed the myth that a police officer had to identify himself as one if asked directly. She tried to stifle her revulsion and continued smiling invitingly but her words came out sounding cold and distant.

George Braun cackled with glee at the question and this time Angela did shudder. "No, little missy. I'm not a cop. I'm a producer. How about having a drink with me?"

"Well, I'd like to but . . . well, my rent is due and I'm trying to make a little money. You know what I mean?"

Braun cackled again and moved his hand farther up the girl's thigh. "Oh, I know exactly whatcha mean, missy. Old George Braun wasn't born yesterday. Nosirree. How much do ya charge?"

"A hundred and fifty an hour and a ride back." Angela added fifty dollars to her price and hoped Braun would pull to the curb and drop her off. Even at that price she wasn't sure it was worth it. Her voice remained cold and she used none of the finesse she would have employed had she been picked up by a human being.

George Braun seemed unfazed.

"Chump change. A hundred and fifty is nothing to old George. Shit, I spend more than that for lunch. Yer in luck, little missy. George Braun's gonna take you to his house and pleasure you up a bit." Again that throaty cackle and Angela wondered if she would be able to stand the feel of his flesh against hers.

As they talked George had gone around the block again and then turned west on Sunset. They were past the Strip now and were approaching a residential area with palatial Beverly Hills homes lining both sides of the street. Braun made a right turn onto a wide street that narrowed to a two-lane road within a few blocks of Sunset. They began to climb as George followed the deserted road higher and higher into the hills above Hollywood.

"Where are we going?" Angela spoke flatly, determined not to let Braun know the fear she was feeling.

"We're goin' to my house, little missy." The old man's voice was as devoid of warmth as her own. "We're goin' to my house," he repeated. "Old George Braun is gonna pleasure ya good."

Suddenly, Angela wanted desperately to be out of that car and away from the evil old man and his inane, vicious cackle. "Hey look, let's just forget the whole thing, okay? Take me back where you picked me up, okay? I don't want to go to your house." She heard the fear and was sure he did, too. Braun made no attempt to slow the car. Instead, he sped up as the twisting mountain road straightened out for several hundred feet in front of them.

"Okay, just drop me off here, then. I'll walk back." The darkened road and a four- or five-hour walk back to Hollywood would be a small price to pay to be away from the old man.

Braun looked over at her and leered tauntingly. "Don't you worry, little missy. Old George is going to take care of you real good. Real good. When I'm done with you, ya ain't gonna need to worry about no rent or nothin' like that. I'm gonna pleasure ya like you ain't never been pleasured before."

Angela knew a moment of sheer terror but timed her next move perfectly. As Braun slowed for a curve she suddenly yanked the door handle and rolled out onto the pavement with bone-jarring force. Ignoring the pain, she was on her feet and running down the road before Braun could stop the car. She heard the squeal of brakes and prayed he wouldn't come after her. For a moment she thought her prayer had been answered; then she heard an engine roar as Braun restarted the car. Moments later, he careened past her, and again came the squeal as he braked and the car slid sideways across the road in front of her, blocking her escape. Like a rabbit paralyzed by the gaze of a snake, Angela stood rooted to the pavement as the door of the car slowly opened and George Braun emerged and began walking toward her, a terrifying smile on his face.

"Not yet, little missy. Not yet. I gotta pleasure ya first." He was almost on top of her before her limbs would respond to her command and she twisted violently to the left, trying to escape. His arm shot out and grabbed a handful of her hair. He yanked it savagely, bringing tears of pain as well as fear to the girl's eyes.

"Don't run from old George Braun, little missy. I gotta do somethin' for ya, see?" She smelled the fetid odor of his breath and almost passed out.

"Please leave me alone. Please don't hurt me." She was sobbing now as George Braun put his other hand around her throat, his thumb massaging her neck with almost sensuous gentleness. He released her hair and now both hands were around her throat. Slowly he began to tighten his grip until Angela could no longer sob . . . or plead . . . or breathe. Angela kicked and fought but no force could break the grip of iron that was squeezing her life from her. As her struggles grew weaker and the world began to grow red and dim around her, a thought suddenly came to her. It couldn't end like this. Not now. She couldn't die at the hands of this monster in the Hollywood Hills. She had too much to live for. There was too much she wanted to do. It couldn't end this way . . .

But it did.

CHAPTER SEVEN

Dragonlady

Sean stood by the window and watched as the parade of new clothes, new, brightly colored bookbags, and new haircuts streamed into the schoolyard at Puerta Grande. Excited children were arriving for the first day of school. The procession that began at seven-fifteen would continue until the first bell rang at eight forty-five. The youngsters came singly and in groups, the older ones on foot, many of them in animated conversation with friends not seen all summer. The younger ones were dropped off in front of the schoolyard by relieved parents looking forward to a few hours of freedom.

The mood was festive. Next week some of the faces would be glum and some feet would drag as children made their daily pilgrimage to classes. By next week young minds would yearn for the return of summer and the freedom to play, explore, and just hang out. Today it was exciting to meet old friends, new teachers, and former rivals. Tomorrow old animosities would flare. Dislikes forgotten over the summer would be remembered and children would argue and fight the way they always have. Today, at least, a truce was declared. The greetings exchanged were friendly and exuberant. Four Eyes Bradley, who would spend the next nine months as an object of ridicule and scorn from childish peers, had a friendly smile and a wave for Toby Elliot, the class bully in the fifth grade who would initiate most of his torment but who today had a grin and cheerful wave of his own to give in return. Fat little Myrna Krebs was bussed affectionately by dozens of other little girls who would pointedly and cruelly ignore her for the rest of the school year. The first day of school was a happy time for all.

Or almost all.

Sean could feel the excitement and happiness in the air but didn't share it. In the weeks since his accident he had avoided crowds of people. Although his mental shield protected him from the day-to-day "noise" around him, the prospect of being exposed to the clamor of hundreds of pre-teens for six hours was frightening. He wouldn't be able to relax his guard for a minute. Sean wasn't certain he was equal to the task.

As he stood by the window, looking across the street, he could hear his mother cleaning up the breakfast dishes in the kitchen. He raised his voice to be heard over the running water as he turned from the window, "Hey, Mom, why don't they offer correspondence courses for third grade in California?"

"Wait a minute, honey. I'm almost done here."

Irritation registered on the boy's face. It upset him that his mother could sound so cheerful. She obviously didn't understand.

Marilyn turned off the faucet after prerinsing the last of the plates. She loaded the dishwasher with detergent before closing and latching the appliance door. There was a rumble as the machine came to life. She glanced at the kitchen clock and knew she had only a few minutes to pack her reluctant son off to his first day of school. She was aware of his concerns but didn't know how to resolve them.

Marilyn dried her hands on a towel and prepared herself for the argument she knew was coming.

Sean felt his mother enter the room before he heard her walk up behind him. He continued staring morosely out the living room window.

"Now, what were you saying?" Her voice still had that ring of cheer that annoyed him earlier and the boy frowned before answering.

"I said, why can't they offer a correspondence course for third grade?" He turned from the window and his face was glum.

"I don't know." Marilyn pretended to think about the question. "Maybe the subject matter is too technical."

"Yeah, right."

"Why don't you just relax and give it a chance? Who knows? It might even be fun."

"Mom, you have a curious idea of fun. I can feel it from here. Everybody's . . . everybody's . . . I don't know how to say it. They're radiating. I don't know how long I can keep it away. I'm going to drown out there."

"The day is going to come when you will have to go out in the world, son. What else can you do? Would you rather stay locked in your bedroom all day? Do you want us to bring your meals in to you and play with you and keep you company for the rest of your life while you hide in the closet or under the bed? If that's what you want to do, we'll sit down and talk about it. Somehow, I can't believe anyone as special as you would be satisfied with that kind of a life for very long."

Sean's anger and fear battled with the ridiculous image of him crawling under the bed to a tiny dinner table set for one. He couldn't help smiling.

"I guess the closet would be better. It's too dusty under the bed."

"That's more like it." Marilyn nodded toward the coffee table and the green book bag sitting in a heap where Sean had tossed it. "Grab your stuff and jump into the world. You'll be okay."

Sean tried a last desperate gambit.

"I don't need to go right now. You know what? I can remember how to do trigonometry. Why do I need to spend all day sitting at a desk in a third-grade classroom learning how to multiply? Why don't we just wait awhile and—and—I don't know." It sounded weak even to him, and his mother wasn't looking sympathetic anymore. "Look, why can't I get a job as a high school teacher and work my way through grammar school? The whole thing is ridiculous, Mom.'' Sean was laughing again, his final argument a victim of his own sense of humor.

"Come on, kid. Let's get to school. The worst that will happen is that you might get a little bored.''

"A whole lot bored, you mean,'' Sean said in a final attempt to avoid Puerta Grande.

"I don't think you're worried about being bored. I think you're still frightened of being with so many people. Am I right?''

"Yeah,'' Sean agreed reluctantly.

"Go to school. If it gets too bad just tell your teacher that you're sick and come back home. At least give it a try until we can make some other arrangements. It's only temporary, Sean. You know we've talked to Dr. Taylor. He thinks we'll be able to have you tested and get you placed in a higher grade. If worse comes to worst, we'll see about private tutoring.'' She put her arms around the boy and hugged him.

"I'll try.'' He sighed and turned to the coffee table where the book bag with pencils and notebooks awaited him. He picked it up and headed for the door before he remembered and ran back to kiss his mom good-bye. The boy went out the front door with all the enthusiasm of a Christian late for an appointment with a lion. Marilyn was shaking her head sadly when the door opened again and Sean's head reappeared.

"I'm going but just don't expect me to have a good time.'' He grinned at his mother and slammed the door. Marilyn smiled and looked out the window to see Sean running across the front yard toward Puerta Grande.

Hobie Anderson and Doug Thomas were both in Sean's class the year before and both were waiting for him near the front of the playground when he ran up.

"Hey, Sean, hurry up. You want to be late your first day?'' Doug chided the smaller boy.

"Are you ready for a year of Dragonlady?'' Hobie's

forehead was sweating even though the morning air was cool. Hobie's forehead was always sweating.

"I heard she was retiring and Mr. Platt was going to teach third grade this year." Doug looked at Sean, hoping for a confirmation of the rumor, and when none came he turned back to Hobie. "Well, anyway, that's what somebody said."

"Are you kidding? Dragonlady's never gonna retire. I'll bet she's been teaching for a hundred years." Of all the kids in the playground only Hobie seemed to share Sean's feelings about the first day back to school. He looked depressed as he wiped his hand across his forehead and continued in sorrowful tones, "We gotta put up with her all this year."

"Michael had her for third grade and he says she's not so bad." Sean tried to reassure his classmates.

"Well, Four Eyes had her too and he says she's a bitch." Doug rolled the word off his tongue casually and then looked smug as Hobie glanced around in panic to see if anyone else had heard the forbidden word. "I'd rather have Mr. Platt any day."

"Mrs. Farrell is okay." Sean felt guilty as he realized he had never called the teacher by name before, preferring the nickname by which she was universally known at Puerta Grande.

While the three friends were making their way to the side door to line up in front of their classroom, the object of their discussion was sitting in the small teachers' lounge off the lunchroom, bracing herself for the start of another school year.

Alice Farrell sipped her tea and tried to remember what it was like when she began her teaching career thirty-four years before. It had seemed so much simpler in those days. She had been so much happier then. Classes were better structured, the basics were stressed, and discipline was as much a part of the curriculum as arithmetic. The children were better behaved in those days. They were smarter.

Or were they? Was it the children who were different now or was the change in her? Alice wasn't sure. This has got to be my last year, she thought wearily, taking another sip of tea. If only I can make it through the year. If only there isn't another . . . incident.

She carried her cup to the sink and washed it out, dried it with a paper towel, and placed it in the small cupboard over the coffee maker. She went back to the table to get her purse and thought of Carl.

Life was so unfair. How could a man so robust and vigorous drop dead of a heart attack at fifty-nine? Alice had been alone for two years now and sometimes when she thought of her husband of thirty-one years she was convinced he was the lucky one. At least he didn't have to continue day after day trying to go through the motions of living. They had been happy, she and Carl. Now she was alone. Life wasn't fair.

She hadn't wept. She had handled all the details the way she knew Carl would have wanted her to, and she had been brave, the way she knew he would want her to be.

But sometimes, usually early in the morning, hours before the alarm would summon her to another day as bleak as the one before it and as empty as the one that would follow, sometimes she would awaken with an ache in her heart that threatened to overwhelm her. It was at these times that she wished she could follow her husband to heaven, hell, or oblivion. It didn't matter where.

The five-minute warning bell filled the room with its soft buzz. Alice Farrell looked up, startled. She hated that bell. School bells were supposed to sound like bells, not like the insipid bleating of anemic sheep. Things were so much different now. She gathered up her purse and then went to a shelf near the door and took down a large brass bell that she had brought with her to school on impulse almost a year before. Armed with this symbol of her authority, she left the room to round up this year's charges.

Doug, Hobie, and Sean were still commiserating near the side door when Sean saw Dragonlady emerge carrying a large brass bell. She scowled menacingly at the boys and then turned her attention to the playground. A quick look and *"CLANG . . . CLANG . . . CLANG"* The muted Klaxon from the speakers was drowned out by Dragonlady's harsher call. The first day of school was officially under way. Sean and his friends found themselves lined up to begin the third grade under the watchful eye of Dragonlady Farrell.

Ed Taylor faced Vernon Tibbs across the desk and smiled at the principal of Puerta Grande School with what he hoped was the proper note of subservience.

"Mr. Tibbs, I appreciate your reservations about testing the Jeffries boy at the beginning of the school year. I'm not here in the role of advocate. I'm here as a messenger. His parents want him tested. I said I'd talk to you."

"Rules, Doctor, are rules." Tibbs paused to give the psychologist time to absorb the full import of his words. "You are certainly aware that the district does placement testing in January. There are very good reasons for this policy. I don't know why I'm bothering to tell you this. You helped us work the system out six years ago. Why should we make an exception for one youngster?"

"Well, it's my belief that this is a special case. I know the family and—"

"We have over three hundred young people here. I pulled the boy's records after I got your memo, and I looked them over at great length. I fail to see any reason why we should waste our time and money giving him special consideration."

"I don't believe the boy's parents are asking for any special consideration. They would like us to make a small exception in terms of the timing. They don't want to wait until January for us to administer—"

"I won't permit it. Simply because his parents think he's a smart boy is no reason for us to deviate from our standard procedure. We have a lot of smart children at this school. Should we throw the rules out the window? Should we rewrite the rule book?''

''I'm not disagreeing with you. I'm only telling you that his father was pretty adamant about wanting him tested and placed immediately.''

Vernon Tibbs licked his mustache and considered the word *adamant*. A firm believer in rules and procedures, it pained him to think that a member of his staff would consider, however briefly, not following the System. On the other hand, Vernon Tibbs hated scenes. He had no wish to confront an irate parent making loud and unreasonable demands.

''Taylor, I'm expecting you to tell this boy's parents that we will make no exceptions at Puerta Grande. I don't want to be bothered again about the matter. We're going to treat the Jeffries boy the same way we treat every other youngster at this school, in a fair and even-handed manner. I'm certain you can understand why this is the only fair thing to do.''

''I was pretty sure that's what you would say.'' Ed rose to leave the office. ''I might add that I rather admire the stand you're taking. I have to admit that I was somewhat intimidated by the fact that the boy's father is a lawyer. My first inclination was to give in to his request and arrange for the testing. I guess that would have been the wrong decision.''

''His father is a lawyer?'' The first hint of doubt began to cloud Tibbs's expression.

''Oh, yes. He's with one of our more prestigious law firms. I think that probably bothered me more than it should have. You're absolutely right, of course. We have to treat all of our students equally. We have no business making special exceptions in cases like this.''

''Well, we certainly can't let the father's occupation influence our decision.'' Vernon squirmed uncomfortably in his chair. ''How, eh . . . adamant did he seem?''

''He was pretty insistent. He says that his son should be several grades further along and claims we've been neg-

ligent in not discovering this last year. When I indicated
that I didn't think you would budge from our established
procedures, he seemed very upset." Ed sat back down in
the chair opposite Tibbs and tried to keep from smiling.
It was time to start reeling him in.

"Why does every parent think his own kid is the best-
looking, the smartest, and the most deserving? We have
almost three hundred kids at Puerta Grande. Can you
imagine the chaos if we tried to make special cases out of
each one of them? We have to follow the system and treat
them all alike, don't you agree?"

"I've already told you I believe your decision is the best
and fairest all the way around. I should have told him just
what you told me: rules are rules. On the other hand, I
didn't see any major problem with the idea of bending a
little and in view of the possible fallout, well, I probably
would have chosen the path of least resistance and agreed
to test the boy. I realize now such a move would—"

"Wait a minute, Taylor. What fallout are you talking
about?"

"Oh, I'm sure it was just talk. The right thing to do is
just to tell him we will not make an except—"

"What was just talk? What fallout?"

"Oh, that. It wasn't anything really. Mr. Jeffries was
pretty upset. He told me that if we couldn't see our way
clear to testing his son and making whatever adjustments
were necessary, he would bring legal action against the
district for nonfeasance and negligence. Remember, Vernon, he's my neighbor and I know him fairly well. I'm
sure when he calms down . . ."

"Look, Doctor Taylor, don't you think you're being just
a little bit hasty?" Tibbs's complexion had taken on a
greenish cast. "I certainly didn't mean to imply that we
wouldn't cooperate with him. I was merely stating that it
is usually—not always, mind you—usually a bad policy to
deviate from the system."

"But you just said—"

"Let me finish, please." Tibbs paused to frame his next

statement and Ed suppressed a chuckle at the frantic retreat the administrator was making. "You of all people
should be aware that each and every one of the young
minds placed in our charge is special and important. I'm
really surprised at how inflexible you seem, Taylor. There
are times when a system, any system, has to take a backseat to a young person's individual need. Would you want
it on your conscience that one of our boys or girls failed
to achieve his or her full potential because of something
you did or did not do?" The principal of Puerta Grande
rapped impatiently on his desk with a pencil and waited
for the psychologist to acknowledge the wisdom of his
words. His face was returning to its normal, somewhat
pasty hue, and he frowned imperiously as Ed Taylor nodded in reply. Tibbs felt a small rush of pleasure and pride
at his own ability to resolve problems and avert disasters.
God, he was good.

"There are still a few problems, though." Ed began
thoughtfully as if he hadn't been the one to bring the request to Tibbs to start with. "The whole idea behind mid-
year testing is to allow us to measure those other qualities
besides intelligence that influence a child's growth and development. What if the boy lacks the social skills necessary to adjust to a classroom situation where he's the
youngest and probably the smallest one in the class? What
about the boy's maturity level? We need time to evaluate
these things as well as his intelligence. This is why we
have the policy." Ed could see doubt beginning to form
on Vernon's face and cursed himself for not quitting while
he was ahead. "I'm quite sure Jason will rethink his position and not take us to court and waste the time and
money involved in a—"

"That's enough, Taylor. I want the boy tested as soon
as possible." The mention of a lawsuit was enough to
stack the deck for Tibbs. He frowned and held the expression for just the correct length of time, then allowed his
face to relax into a forgiving, fatherly smile intended to
show the psychologist that he, Vernon Tibbs, was an un-

derstanding leader of men. "I believe you erred when you refused to accommodate this parent's very reasonable request. The boy was a student here last year, wasn't he? Surely we are able to talk to the boy's previous teacher and get some idea of his maturity and social skills. Even if he had just transferred to us I would think you'd have ways to measure these qualities. Isn't that right?"

"Well, I—"

"So, it's settled then. I want you to contact the boy's family and let them know what we're doing. After that, I want you to make all the arrangements and get back to me with the results. I want all this done as quickly as possible. Is that clear, Doctor Taylor?"

"Perfectly, sir. I apologize if I failed to handle the situation properly."

Tibbs flashed his condescending smile again to show the psychologist that anyone could make a mistake. Vernon Tibbs would find a way to save their asses and forgive them. "I accept your apology. In the future I would appreciate it if you would come to me for guidance before making important decisions. That's my job, you know. I have a better understanding of the impact of these decisions than you do. We must never forget the importance of our children. Occasionally we have to step outside the system when one of our little ones shows a special ability or a special need. I'm sure you know of my reputation in the district. It no doubt surprises you to learn that a man with my administrative skills can also be a warm and compassionate human being, but that is exactly what I am." Tibbs spread his hands apart in a self-deprecating gesture. "I will trust you with this little secret of mine, Doctor Taylor." The principal stood to signify the end of the interview and Ed Taylor rose from his chair. Vernon Tibbs was widely known throughout the district to be a pompous ass, a reputation Ed knew to be well deserved.

"Thank you, sir. I'll arrange everything and get back to you with the results."

"You're quite welcome, Taylor." The principal sat down

and busied himself with some papers as Ed turned and left
the office.

He closed the door behind him and strode down the
hall. He didn't quite make it to his own office before the
laughter began bubbling inside him. Four eighth graders
passed him in the hall and gave him curious looks before
exchanging furtive smiles. He was inside his office with
the door shut, still chuckling and wiping his eyes with a
handkerchief when he dialed Marilyn at home to tell her
the news.

Sean was scheduled for placement and intelligence testing one week from the following Saturday.

Sean looked at Mrs. Farrell in the front of the class and
thought of a predatory bird. The impression didn't last.
Mrs. Farrell proved to be very different from her reputation. The morning began with a fifteen-minute discussion
on the merits of not speaking unless spoken to. Shortly
after these instructions were handed out, Dragonlady had
pounced enthusiastically on a hapless boy in the front row
who had the audacity to chew gum in class. This had been
good for another ten-minute denunciation of gum-chewing.
When she was satisfied that each child understood the
seriousness of the offense and the danger that a stick of
gum posed to dental health, hygiene, and common eti-
quette, she finally allowed the unhappy boy to sit down
again to the snickers of his classmates. It was after nine
before she got around to the seating arrangement. Dragonlady Farrell liked her students arranged in alphabetical order, and she spent the next hour patiently sorting her boys
and girls and directing each one to a desk. Mrs. Farrell
treated each child with exaggerated courtesy. She repeated
each instruction at least three times, as if she were trying
to explain a difficult concept to a severely retarded four-
year-old. At some point during the second hour she suc-
ceeded in losing control of the class and Sean cringed with
embarrassed empathy as he listened to the whispering and
laughter around him. Dragonlady appeared not to notice.

By ten-thirty everyone was in his or her appointed seat. The morning was passing with excruciating slowness. Sean slumped in his chair and listened to Betty Somebody-or-Other relate the exciting things that happened to her over the summer. He looked again at Mrs. Farrell and wondered if yawning pointedly would hurt her feelings. He decided not to chance it.

Dragonlady had decided the children would stand and introduce themselves, then tell the class something about their summer vacations. Now she seemed to be following the endless narrative with every appearance of interest. After fifteen minutes of nonstop monologue, Betty had worked her way to the end of June and Sean estimated glumly that it would be almost lunchtime before she got to Independence Day.

Dragonlady wasn't listening to Betty at all. If she had been, she would have cut the girl off sometime earlier and moved on to the next student. Mrs. Farrell was reliving a nightmare.

It happened three weeks earlier. A faculty meeting had been scheduled to discuss changes planned for the coming school year, and Vernon Tibbs had made it clear that attendance was compulsory. Alice had arrived at the school at nine-thirty, half an hour before the conference was to begin. The maintenance man had unlocked the side doors and as she entered the building she marveled at the difference in the atmosphere of empty halls and deserted classrooms. It was so desolate without the chatter and bustle of boys and girls.

She went directly to the teachers' lounge and warmed a pot of water for the tea bag she had had the foresight to bring with her. Jack Hollaway came in while she was pouring the water into her cup and she nodded curtly at the young phys ed teacher. She didn't like Hollaway and he knew it, but he still smiled at her and returned her nod. She had gone to a table in the corner of the room and was sipping her tea slowly while the other teachers began arriving.

The strange thing was she felt good that morning. She had slept well the night before. She wasn't thinking about Carl. She was even surprised to find herself looking forward to the start of class three weeks from now. That's what made the episode so frightening and hard to understand.

The room was full. It was five minutes before ten. Ed Taylor walked in the door and she greeted him with a smile. When she heard the sound, she didn't realize at first that she was making it.

"Ticka . . . ticka . . ticka . . ticka . ticka . tickaticka-tickaticka."

Conversation in the lounge came to a halt as the rattling noise got louder and faster. Alice Farrell looked down and gasped as she saw the hand that was holding her teacup vibrating and shaking as though possessed by a life of its own. The teacup was beating a staccato rhythm against the saucer until suddenly the little plate shattered. Alice tried to open her hand and release the cup, but her fingers refused to let go of the handle. She was trembling and could feel tears coursing down her cheeks. Teachers were looking at her curiously and Ed Taylor started across the room in her direction. Alice wanted to scream that nothing was wrong. She was fine. But she couldn't stop shaking and she couldn't stop the tears that streamed from her eyes, eroding crooked trails of grief through her mascara.

"Alice, what's wrong?"

The question of the hour. What was wrong? Alice Farrell didn't know.

"I'll be okay," she whispered. She would have given anything to be someplace else—anywhere but here in full view of the entire faculty of Puerta Grande. "I have to leave. I think I'm going to be sick."

"Let me call a doctor." Ed Taylor still had his arm around her shoulders, supporting her, and she suddenly hated him for his concern. If only he weren't drawing attention to her plight, she could slip out the door unnoticed.

"No, please . . . that's all right. I'll just go home. I'm

all right.'' She got unsteadily to her feet and was relieved
to notice that the shaking of her limbs and body was easier
to conceal when she was standing.

"I've got to leave.'' She pulled away from Taylor and
almost ran from the lounge and out of the building to her
car.

Betty Whatsername was still talking as Sean picked up
a pencil from his desk and began doodling absently on a
sheet of notepaper. Something began to nibble at him.
Some memory from the past. He looked up as the little
girl on the other side of the room prattled on about staying
at her aunt's house in Glendora for the weekend—thank
God she had finally moved into July at least. She had said
something that triggered a memory. Interested for the first
time, Sean watched the girl and listened closely.

". . . And then my aunt Mary told my cousin that she
could come over to my house after that and she did too
when I came home and her name is Mary too and she
stayed for a week but that was after Uncle Peter took us
all to Marineland and we saw . . .''

At the sound of the name, Sean sat up in his seat. That
was it. The name.

When Father John asked him if he remembered a name,
he had answered truthfully that he didn't remember. It
never occurred to him to wonder about it. Later though,
after the question was asked, it had come back repeatedly
to haunt him. Who was he? He was sure he hadn't been
Sean. It seemed important to have a name to go with the
identity that was now so much a part of him. He had to
be somebody. Who was he, really? The boy slouched back
in his chair and picked up his newly sharpened pencil
again. He wrote the name "Peter" on the same piece of
notepaper he had been doodling on earlier. He wrote it
again right below where he had written it the first time.
He printed it in block letters and stared at it. So absorbed
was he in his task that he failed to notice when Betty
concluded her account of the summer, apparently deciding

that nothing of any significance happened after July seventh. He jerked his head up as Mrs. Farrell's angry voice suddenly filled the classroom.

"SEAN JEFFRIES!"

"Yes, ma'am?" Sean fumbled with his notebook and dropped his pencil to the floor as he got to his feet.

"In my classroom we try to be polite to each other. If it is your turn to speak we will listen to you and when someone else has the floor we expect you to be paying attention." Gone was the sweet-tempered, elderly woman who had been treating them like four-year-olds. In her place was the Dragonlady they had heard about and feared.

"Yes, ma'am." Sean felt his face burning as everyone looked at him and then gasped as a rush of emotion brutally assailed him from twenty-eight third graders. Although he had never felt this particular emotion secondhand before, his memories of fifteen years spent in front of a classroom made it easy to identify the cause. At the sound of Mrs. Farrell's voice, twenty-eight boys and girls had all felt a surge of adrenaline and a delicious mix of fear, interest, and anticipation as one of their own was singled out to face the wrath of the legendary Dragonlady. There was something chilling and pagan in the feeling: a throwback to the days of sacrificial offerings made to appease the angry gods. Sean, preoccupied with the riddle of his identity, had forgotten to keep his mental guard up and was momentarily stunned, like a boxer who has just taken a sucker punch.

"Is there something wrong?" Mrs. Farrell was able to make the transition from angry to solicitous without missing a beat. Sean wondered which was real and which was an act.

"No, ma'am."

"Well, please pay attention from now on. You may sit down." Suddenly, she didn't sound angry at all. Sean was startled and embarrassed at the pleading note he could hear in her voice.

Sean retrieved his pencil, which had rolled under his

desk, and sat back down. Dragonlady was indeed a peculiar duck. There was something about the woman that didn't ring true to him. Her moods kept changing. One minute she could be wrathful and impatient. A moment later the anger would disappear and she would be clucking over them like a mother hen protecting her brood.

She had turned her attention back to the seating chart on her desk and when she looked up, Sean had a strange feeling that the real Dragonlady Farrell hadn't come to school today. The woman in front of the class wasn't real; she was an actress playing a role she hadn't studied for.

"All right, be quiet, children. Hubert Anderson, please stand up and introduce yourself to your classmates."

Hobie Anderson stood up, red-faced and unhappy, and began stammering out his name and an obviously painful account of his summer vacation.

In spite of his nervousness, Hobie was determined to use just as much time as Betty Whatsername had used before him; she had set the pace. Sean looked to Dragonlady and saw the same look of rapt attention to the meandering discourse that he had seen when Betty had been talking, and he groaned inwardly. It was going to be a very long morning.

Careful this time to keep his guard up, Sean returned to his musings while keeping one ear on Hobie. So his name had been Peter. It didn't really make much difference, but Sean was glad to know. Did he have a last name? Sean chuckled to himself as the question popped into his head. Of course he had a last name. Did the question tell him something about what he had become?

Sean realized he was responding to the world around him on three levels. Part of him was eight years old and was behaving and thinking the way an eight-year-old would behave and think. Part of him was adult. Lately his favorite program on television was the evening news. His feelings were pure Peter as he thrilled to the events of a history he had taught for years unfolding in front of his eyes. It was like watching a dimly remembered movie for the sec-

ond time after reading the book. So many things he had
missed the first time around he noticed now. It didn't matter that he knew how the movie would turn out, at least
for the next quarter century. It was still exciting.

And the part of him that was analyzing which parts were
which? Sean suspected there had been a blending. Part of
him, maybe the best part, was a compound of Peter and
Sean. It wasn't a mix; it was a compound. The two per-
sonalities had combined and melded until the result was
neither Sean nor Peter but someone else, someone better.
Someone different from either personality alone.

In fact it was this third side, this blended personality
that would make the first day of school in the third grade
at Puerta Grande a memorable experience for everyone in
the class, including a lonely, burned-out Dragonlady.

A mile away from the school on Las Flores Avenue,
Millie Braun was searching for Charlie Cat. The animal
had been mysteriously absent for several weeks now and
she missed her pet. She called to him in the backyard,
always expecting to see the gray-and-white tomcat streak
from beneath a bush or leap from one of the lower branches
of the Chinese elm that had been growing on the same
spot for decades. There was no sign of the cat, and Millie
resolved to ask George junior if he had seen him. Her
brow furrowed as she thought of George junior. Where
was he? An uneasy malaise gripped her. The boy was
always off, gallivanting around the neighborhood. She
supposed that was typical of an eleven—no, wait a minute.
He was born in 1926. This was . . . let's see . . . Millie
had trouble keeping track of dates. Was it 1958? Of course,
it was. That means Georgie would be . . . oh, my gosh
. . . he was twelve years old now. She wiped her hands
on the apron she always wore and turned back to the house.
It was almost time to fix George senior's lunch. He always
drove home from the high school for lunch. He was such
a good husband. He was so patient and loving. But the
dear man would sometimes get just the teeniest bit upset
if his lunch wasn't ready when he got home.

As Millie started to open the back door she heard the side gate slam. That would be Georgie now. Millie felt a thrill of pleasure that she always felt when she thought about her son. He came around the corner of the house and then stopped and looked behind him as though waiting for someone. A moment later he was joined by a girl in a T-shirt and cutoff jeans. The girl looked a lot older than Georgie, and Millie peered closely at them as they stood by the corner of the house talking. Good grief! Millie pursed her lips in disapproval. It was shameful the way some parents allowed their children to dress. The girl was positively indecent. She would have to talk to Georgie about his choice of friends. Surely there were nice girls around that didn't dress like hussies.

The boy left the girl standing by the corner of the house as he came up to his mother and kissed her on the cheek. He was so tall for his age and so manly. She blinked and looked more closely at her son. There was something wrong. His outline was fuzzy and indistinct. She blinked again and for a moment it seemed as if she could see right through him. Her old eyes were giving out. It was time to get her glasses changed. George senior would complain but it had to be done. She took her son's hands in her own and faced him directly. That was better. His features were clear now.

"Have you seen Charlie Cat anywhere? He's wandered off, and I can't find him."

"Oh, sure. He's behind that bush." Georgie indicated a spot near the corner of the cedar fence where the ole-ander had grown tallest and Millie followed his gaze anxiously.

"He's back there?"

"He sure is. Stupid cat's been fighting again. He's asleep behind the oleander. Can't you see him?"

"These old eyes are giving out. I swear I can't seem to see anything anymore." Millie laughed and in her laugh was the stored-up anger, frustration, sorrow, and despair of fifty-five years. Her gray-blue eyes were as alert as ever as she approached the oleander and pushed the branches aside. Charlie Cat was there just like Georgie had said he was. He was sleeping . . . or . . .

"Oh, you poor baby," Millie gasped. She stared at the body of the cat that was curled into a ball in the dirt beneath the bush, its mouth open, lips drawn back into a mute snarl of outrage. In the weeks it had lain there, the maggots and weather had done their work. Part of the cat's upper lip was gone and one eye socket was empty. The body was bloated and the rancid odor of death hung over it. Millie's face registered shock for only the barest instant and then, as though a curtain had dropped over her mind, the expression faded and her eyes relaxed into their familiar laugh lines.

"You've been fighting again, you naughty kitty." She reached under the oleander and scooped up the stiff body of the cat. There was a quiet "slurp" as the moist earth beneath the bush released its prize, and then Millie was holding her pet close to her bosom and making little crooning noises.

"Momma?"

George junior stood next to her. He had a strange look on his face.

"Daddy wants to hurt Charlie. You can't let him hurt Charlie the way he hurt me." The boy's voice was urgent as he looked at his mother.

"Don't you talk about your father that way. Land sakes, you kids get the craziest ideas sometimes." She hugged the dead cat tighter. "Your father is a kind, generous, loving man. He wouldn't hurt a fly."

"He wants to hurt Charlie Cat," the boy insisted stubbornly. "He wanted to kill him just like he killed me. Don't let him do it, Momma." His image was fading again. Millie was so proud of him. He was so handsome, her twelve-year-old son . . . or was he thirteen? Let's see. He was twelve. Of course he was. A shadow passed over Millie's face. Something had happened when Georgie was twelve. She furrowed her brow and tried to remember what had happened. No memory came to her.

"Oh, phooey! You get into that house and get ready for lunch. Your dad will be home soon and you know he likes his lunch on time so he can get back to work by one o'clock. We'll have no more of this foolish talk."

What were they talking about? Millie couldn't remember. She relaxed her grip on the cat and looked nervously around the backyard. Where was George junior? He must be off gallivanting. She supposed that was typical behavior for a nine-year-old. No, wait now. George was eleven. No . . . he was twelve years old. How could she be so forgetful? She went into the house still holding the decaying body of the cat and hummed a cheerful little tune as her mood became suddenly lighthearted and happy. George would be home soon, wanting his lunch. She had work to do and couldn't spend all day nursing an aggressive tomcat who probably deserved every scratch on his body. Still, Charlie Cat was such a love. She walked through the house and into her bedroom, where she placed the body gently on a pillow at the head of the bed. He could sleep there until he felt better. A part of her was glad that George senior never came into her room. He really didn't like Charlie Cat although he was too kindhearted to ever say anything. She knew he would be upset if he saw the cat on the bed. He wouldn't complain, but the dear man would be upset. Better that he didn't know. Charlie Cat just needed a little rest and then he could go back outside.

She closed the bedroom door behind her and headed for the kitchen, where she opened a can of soup and poured it into a saucepan before putting sandwiches together for George senior's lunch. The soup was starting to bubble before it occurred to her to worry about Georgie. Where was that boy?

Oh, well. If he missed lunch he'd be here in time for dinner.

Isn't that just like a thirteen-year-old though? A shadow passed over her face and she paused, one hand holding an open mayonnaise jar and the other holding a dinner knife. He was thirteen, wasn't he? Let's see, this was 1958. Georgie was born in 1926 so . . . so, of course, he was twelve. Where was that little troublemaker? Millie peered out the kitchen window. No sign of her son. He was probably somewhere in the neighborhood, pestering people and getting into trouble. She wondered why George senior never seemed to pay attention to his son. Then the thought disappeared as quickly as it had come, and she stared at the open mayonnaise jar in her hand. Oh, goodness! The time was flying and George was going to be home any minute now. She was going to have to hurry. She spread the mayonnaise over the bread and then set it aside and began stirring the soup as she waited and listened for the sound of the station wagon pulling into the driveway.

Three seats in front of Sean, the boy who had gone to Hawaii with his parents sat down and the girl behind him began to stand up, but Dragonlady (Sean now thought of her as Dragonlady with none of the guilt he had felt earlier—the name fit) motioned her back to her seat.

"It's almost noon so we'll stop here until after lunch." She looked at the clock on the wall and, as though on cue, the school bell buzzed loudly. The room was filled with the sound of chairs scraping against the floor and the slam of desktops, when a stentorian voice brought all activity to a halt.

"I HAVE NOT GIVEN YOU PERMISSION TO LEAVE YOUR SEATS!"

There was complete silence as everyone in the classroom froze in place. This time Sean was ready. He had kept his mental shield firmly clamped ever since he had been jolted earlier that morning.

"All right, children. You are dismissed." Dragonlady stood motionless behind her desk as twenty-nine third graders paraded quietly and fearfully out of the classroom.

Sean hung back until most of his classmates were out the door. As he walked past his teacher, he sent a tiny

mental probe in her direction. He winced inwardly and
snapped his guard back into place almost at once. A minute later he was out the door and on his way home for
lunch.

When the last student was gone, Alice Farrell sat back
down and took a brown paper sack from the bottom desk
drawer. She would eat her lunch here. She still hadn't
recovered from that day three weeks earlier when she had
made a spectacle of herself. She was more comfortable in
the classroom anyway. This room or one like it had been
the center of her life for a great many years now.

As Alice Farrell nibbled on a ham sandwich, she
glanced down at the seating chart still in front of her on
the desk. This was the crop of third graders she would be
spending six hours a day with for the rest of the school
year. She was not yet able to connect many faces with
names, but that didn't matter. Within a week she would
know each of them. She would spend each day guiding
them, teaching them, loving them . . . and then . . .

The sandwich began to taste like cardboard. Alice forced
herself to complete the thought. These children would go
on and she would remain. Except that she wouldn't remain. Not this time. There would be no more children
after this class. This was the end of the line for her. And
what did any of it amount to? Alice had no fear of death,
but she was terrified of futility. These children would leave
her as the others had left her. They would leave her the
way Carl had left her and in the end . . .

In the end she would be alone. And there was no point
to any of it. No monuments would ever be put up in her
honor. No one would remember . . . or if anyone did remember, no one would care. She had accomplished nothing. Every time she looked in the mirror she saw a funeral.
The lines in her face were the tombstones of her unreal-
ized hopes, the graveside markers where her shattered
dreams were buried.

Less than a year to go. Nine more months and then she
would retire. And if anyone took an accounting of her life

they would find there was nothing on the bottom line. She added up to zero.

The sandwich fell from her numb fingers, leaving a mustard streak on the new skirt she had bought for this happy first day back to school. In the solitude of the empty classroom Alice "Dragonlady" Farrell wept.

By the time Sean got home, his mother had a hamburger and a pile of potato chips on a plate waiting for him. With uncharacteristic rudeness he brushed past her without a word and threw himself into the chair at the kitchen table.

"Hi to you, too." Marilyn could almost feel his frustration and thought she could understand some of what he must be going through. "Am I to assume from your sunny smile and cheerful disposition that we're having a good day?"

He looked at her and Marilyn saw the corners of his mouth twitch just a little bit. "I'm sorry, Mom." He looked down at his plate and then at his mother and now the twitch had grown into the full-blown smile she had hoped for. "Would you believe me if I told you it's a jungle out there?"

"I think your dad has mentioned that once or twice." She went to the refrigerator to get him a glass of milk and marveled at how normal it seemed to talk to the boy as she would to an adult. She set the milk in front of him and gave him a kiss on the top of his head. "I have some news that might cheer you up a little." She told him about Ed's phone call and his scheduled testing for a week from Saturday. As she had hoped, his face brightened at the news but then fell a moment later.

"I guess that means nothing is going to change for two weeks. Great. I've got a feeling it's going to be a fun two weeks."

"Can you last that long? Was it all that bad?"

"No. It wasn't as bad as I thought it would be. I can

probably hang on for a couple of weeks, but I'm not sure about Dragonlady.''

"Who?"

"Dragonlady. That's our teacher."

Marilyn looked disapproving. "You shouldn't call her that."

"Yeah, I know," Sean agreed. He took a huge bite of hamburger and chewed rapidly. "The name kind of fits, though," he said at last. "It's strange, but she is dragon-like. She makes me think of some big, friendly dragon that nobody likes because she looks so fierce."

"And everybody calls her Dragonlady?"

"Oh, not to her face, of course, but, yeah. The kids have called her that for years."

"But you like her."

"No, not exactly. It's just . . . I don't know. It seems like she's not real. It's like she's acting." He regarded his mother solemnly. "When I was leaving to come home for lunch, I kind of nudged her, you know?" He pointed to his forehead and Marilyn nodded uneasily. If Sean noticed his mother's discomfort at the reference to his strange ability he ignored it and continued speaking in a somber voice. "When the bell rang, everybody got up and she got upset because we didn't wait for her to tell us we could leave. She yelled at us and then, when we were leaving, she was just standing there behind the desk, glaring at us. I'm not sure what I expected when I tried to 'listen' to her. I suppose I thought she'd be angry or indignant or even frustrated. The funny thing is, she wasn't feeling any of those things." He stuffed the last of his hamburger into his mouth and chewed slowly.

"Don't put so much in your mouth. You're going to choke on it." Marilyn discovered she was interested in the story in spite of herself. She waited until he had swallowed the mouthful and taken a swallow of milk before asking the logical question.

"So what was she feeling?"

"She was sad."

Marilyn laughed at the serious way her son passed on this information. "She was sad? That's all?"

Sean still looked troubled. "It wasn't just that she was sad. It's how strong the feeling was. It was painful just to feel secondhand. I guess it was more than sad." He tipped up his glass and swallowed the last of his milk, then looked back at Marilyn. "I think I felt what someone feels when they don't want to live anymore," he said finally.

When the third grade class lined up outside the school after lunch, the Dragonlady who led them into the building wasn't the same Dragonlady they had spent the morning with. Before they even got inside, she had singled out one girl for talking in line and delivered a blistering lecture to the entire class on the subject of standing still and remaining quiet after the one o'clock bell rang. Mrs. Farrell had somehow become the Dragon they had feared, and suddenly the entire third grade class knew it. The children who followed her to their classroom were probably the best behaved students at Puerta Grande. No one talked or giggled in line. No one jostled or pushed. And in contrast to the mood of the morning, no one wanted to be there.

Sean couldn't resist. He waited until they were in their seats before sending another gentle probe in the direction of his teacher. What he felt made him gasp and frantically pull away. It was like putting a mental finger into a candle flame. Dragonlady's torment radiated out from her, filling the classroom with chaotic and conflicting emotions. Sean wasn't sure how much pain a person could take before reaching a breaking point, but he had no doubt that his teacher was on the verge of something very unpleasant.

And there wasn't anything he could do. He was going to have to sit quietly while something destroyed Alice Farrell. Not only was he powerless to help her, he was the only one in the room who knew what was happening.

If only he could get her out of the classroom and get word to Dr. Taylor. The psychologist would know what to do.

While Sean was thinking this, Dragonlady was running her finger down the seating chart. She found the name she was looking for and raised her eyes to the class.

"All right, children, we were about to hear from Deborah Campos when the bell rang. Deborah, stand up, please, and introduce yourself." Mrs. Farrell addressed the girl two seats in front of Sean.

The little girl blushed self-consciously and rose to her feet.

"My name is Debbie Campos and the thing—"

"Deborah," Dragonlady interrupted. The girl looked up, surprised. "Your name is Deborah, not Debbie. We do not use nicknames in this class."

Debbie looked confused. "But, it's not a nickname. Everybody calls me Debbie." She looked around quickly to see if anyone in the class would confirm that everybody called her Debbie.

"Your name is Deborah. Debbie is a shortened form of Deborah. I'll tell you children again: we do not use nicknames in my class. Now begin again, please."

"My name is Debbie!" The little girl had a stubborn look and Sean had a premonition of disaster as he looked from her to the angry Dragonlady.

"Everybody calls me Debbie. The thing I did this summer was—"

"*DEBORAH!* Your name is Deborah in this class and you will not contradict me again. Do you understand?"

"It is *not*—" Debbie's face was red and Sean knew she was about to start crying. The rest of the class watched the exchange in terrified silence and Sean knew if anyone was going to defuse the situation it would have to be him. He nudged his notebook and pencils off the left side of his desk. They fell with a small clatter to the floor next to him. He jumped from his seat to pick them up, deliberately knocking his desk a foot across the floor into the desk in front of him. The diversion worked. He was now the center of attention and the focus of Dragonlady's reproving glare. He tried to look sheepish and apologetic as he scooped his belongings together and returned them to the top of the desk. "Sorry, ma'am," he mumbled as he dragged his desk back to its original position and took his seat. There were several titters from the class that died away as Dragonlady glanced quickly around the room with venom in her eye.

"Nothing funny has happened. No one has permission to laugh." She waited until the classroom was silent. When she was satisfied that she had regained control, Mrs. Farrell turned her attention to Deborah. "Now, Deborah, you were going to introduce yourself to us properly. We're still waiting."

Crash! Sean's book bag and reader slid off the right side of his desk and onto the floor with a satisfying racket. Again the boy jumped to his feet, this time shoving his chair into the desk behind him with the backs of his knees. Even Mrs. Farrell's angry expression couldn't prevent the general laughter. Sean began walking down the aisle between the desks as though intending to come back up the next row and retrieve his book bag.

"Mr. Jeffries, I guess we know now who the class troublemaker is." The old woman gave Sean a look that belonged on the face of an impassioned prosecutor addressing a particularly nasty felon.

Sean brushed past Debbie and continued toward the front of the room.

"Mr. Jeffries, I didn't tell you to leave your seat. Return to your desk and sit down." Confusion registered briefly in her eyes when the boy continued to walk calmly down the aisle as though he hadn't heard. Behind him, Debbie had already decided that if Sean wasn't going to sit down then someone certainly should and she sat down, thankful not to be the center of attention.

Mrs. Farrell had been teaching elementary school for thirty-four years and in her entire career she had never before dealt with so brazen a mutiny. The boy approaching her desk had to be either deaf or crazy. That was the only explanation. She raised her ruler and brought it down with

a loud "SMACK" on the edge of her desk, hard enough
to break off inches seven through twelve and send them
flying into the air. The boy never batted an eye as he
reached the front of her desk and moved around it to confront her. Her heart was pounding and one hand went to
her throat as the boy stopped a mere three feet away and
spoke so softly that she had to strain to hear him.

"Could I talk to you for a minute, please?" He smiled
sweetly at her as though delivering an apple to a favorite
teacher.

"Young man, you do not leave your seat unless given
permission. Return to your desk at once."

The youngster made no move to obey. "It will only take
a minute. Could we go out in the hall, please?" The boy
continued to speak in that same low voice. All twenty-
eight children watched the drama being played out in front
of them with rapt attention.

"I'm telling you for the last time. Return to your seat."
Mrs. Farrell was angry; she was suddenly angrier than she
could ever remember being. It was all so unfair.

Sean felt the woman's fury wash over him, an emotional
acid bath, tingling and burning in his brain. This was going to be harder than he thought. He had to find a way to
calm the woman down.

"Mrs. Farrell, everything is all right. Will you please
come out in the hall and talk to me? It's important."

Dragonlady Farrell looked at the small boy standing in
front of her desk and felt threatened. Why was he dis-
rupting her class? Why was he preventing her from going
on with the afternoon lesson? The room seemed to be
closing in around her and she was having trouble breathing. She realized with horror that her hands were beginning to shake. Why couldn't everyone just leave her alone?
Nine more months and it would be over. Hadn't she paid her
dues? Didn't she deserve more than she had received? Her
reward for a third of a century of dedication: a troublemaker
determined to undermine her teaching and her life.

Why did Carl have to die?

For the first time in her many years of teaching Mrs. Farrell forgot where she was and who she was talking to.

"You little bastard, sit down . . . *I TOLD YOU TO SIT DOWN!*" There was a muffled gasp from the other children in the room. Sean was jolted by the intensity of her resentment, and he struggled to conceal his own anger at the unexpected assault. He reached over and put one hand on the woman's arm. The turmoil in her mind flowed into his brain with painful intensity but he maintained the contact as though trying to drain away the poison that was destroying her. The woman seemed to calm a little and Sean spoke again in the same low voice.

"Everything's going to be all right. Come on, let's go out in the hall for a few minutes. Please, Mrs. Farrell."

Dragonlady hesitated and Sean could feel her confusion and dismay as she realized what she had said. At last, she nodded and let him lead her to the door of the classroom. Just before they got there, Sean turned to face the silent class of third graders and someone from another time and place used his voice to speak.

"We are going to be right outside that door. Please stay in your seats and keep quiet while we're gone." He turned away and followed Alice Farrell into the hall, making sure to close the door behind them to the disappointment of twenty-eight curious boys and girls. No one in the class noticed that, as she left the classroom, Dragonlady's hands were trembling violently.

Hobie Anderson turned in his seat and looked at Doug Thomas, who was sitting three seats back and one row over. His face was serious as he whispered loudly to his friend, "He's gonna get it now." Hobie's forehead was sweating profusely.

Ed Taylor was running late. He should have been at the high school thirty minutes before. The session with Tibbs had taken longer than planned. After calling Marilyn he had spent the rest of the morning reviewing the six transcripts belonging to five boys and one girl who had been promoted into the eighth grade on "Academic Probation." All six children had come to his office that morning before beginning class. Ed had patiently explained to them the significance of their status and was able to get their commitment to work harder and improve their grades. He was confident that the girl and three of the boys would improve. He had some doubts about the fourth boy and was certain that the last boy would repeat the eighth grade next year.

The concept of academic probation was new at Puerta Grande. Ed had been the driving force that finally convinced the school board to implement the program on a trial basis. Two mothers whose children had the dubious honor of being the first participants in the program called to complain, and Ed took both calls. He was able to overcome their objections to the stigma of academic probation by agreeing to withdraw both children from the program. When he explained the alternative, both mothers decided they might have been just a bit hasty. They both agreed to come in and meet with Ed and to work with their child in the coming year.

It was already one-thirty in the afternoon when Ed tossed a stack of papers for filing into the basket, and grabbed his jacket from the back of his chair. He was about to open his office door when it suddenly opened from the other side. Sean Jeffries stumbled into the room looking panic-stricken.

"You've got to help her. I think she's dying." The boy grabbed Ed's arm and tugged desperately.

"Whoa, hold on. Who's dying? What's wrong?"

"It's Mrs. Farrell. She's just lying there on the floor. I don't know what's wrong with her. Help her, please." Sean was crying as he pulled urgently on Ed's sleeve.

Ed yanked his arm from the boy's grasp and ran from the office, heading for Alice Farrell's classroom. He slowed as he passed the administration counter and yelled to the startled switchboard operator to call an ambulance and then continued toward an intersecting hallway. As he

turned the corner he saw something slumped on the floor
at the end of the corridor.

When Sean walked in the back door, Marilyn could tell
something was seriously amiss. His face was pale and unsmiling. She waited for him to say something but the boy
only nodded in her direction before walking to his bedroom. Mugs, who had been asleep under the kitchen table,
looked up and then scrambled to his feet to follow his little
master.

It was all fine and good to give someone space to grow
but there were limits. She set aside the blouse she was
ironing and followed her son.

His bedroom door was closed and she knocked softly
before opening it and looking in. Sean was stretched out
on his bed, stroking Mugs.

"Hi." She took two steps into the room. "How was
your afternoon?"

"Okay, I guess," he answered in a monotone.

"Is something wrong?"

"No, nothing is . . . yes, something is wrong. Could I
just be alone for a little while?"

Marilyn took another step into the room. "Would you
like to talk about it?"

"If I wanted to talk about it I wouldn't have come in
here and shut the door. Would you leave me alone for a
little while . . . please?" Marilyn was taken aback by the
emptiness in her son's voice. She started to say something
but then backed slowly from the room instead. Sean remained in his room the rest of the afternoon and it wasn't
until Ed Taylor stopped by at five-thirty that Marilyn
learned of the events at Puerta Grande.

When Ed ran from his office, Sean remained behind
feeling guilty and sick over what he had done. The knowledge that he hadn't intended to hurt Mrs. Farrell brought
him little comfort. Somehow, in a way he didn't really
understand, he had done something to her. Maybe he had

killed her. Maybe they'd put him in jail. That possibility didn't bother him at all. He deserved to be in jail. He deserved to be locked up someplace where he couldn't hurt anyone else. He started to leave the office and stopped when he realized he didn't know where he was going. He couldn't go back to class and see Dragonlady being wheeled out on a gurney. He wouldn't be able to stand that. He couldn't go home. He would have to explain why he was back from school so early. He couldn't talk about it yet. Maybe later. Not now.

Sean left Ed Taylor's office and went out of the building by a side door. He continued walking aimlessly for ten minutes and was already four blocks from the school before he realized where his feet were leading him. There was someone he wanted very much to talk to.

CHAPTER EIGHT

Taking Control

The doorbell at the rectory chimed melodically and Nora got to her feet, her irritation obvious. If the housekeeper could be said to have a fault (and only the most foolhardy would ever say it to her face) it was an addiction to afternoon soap operas. Nora Moynahan arranged each day to leave herself free in the afternoon from one until two-thirty. This time was devoted to *Love of Life, Search for Tomorrow,* and *The Edge of Night*. A doorbell ringing during these hours was the last thing in the world she wanted to hear. With a sigh she got to her feet and turned off the television set. She had served four pastors at Saint Anthony's over the past thirty years and never once had she put her own pleasure above duty. She grumbled to herself as she made her way to the front door. Nora did not believe that being warm and fuzzy to every Tom, Dick, and Harriet was part of her duty. If anything, the opposite was true. Like an efficient secretary, Nora believed in protecting the pastor of St. Anthony's from the countless demands on his time and attention imposed by selfish parishioners. If someone didn't act as a buffer, the housekeeper firmly believed that Father John would be badgered to death within a month. Nora loved the old man and faulted him only for his inability to say no to anyone wanting a favor, or an ear, or a shoulder to lean on. Whenever possible Nora tried to say no for him.

The doorbell chimed a second time before she could get to it and her scowl deepened as she reached the entryway and turned the dead bolt. She opened the door and peered out.

"Yes? What is it?"

A small boy was standing on the front porch. Nora recognized him at once as the boy Father John had counseled several months before.

"May I see Father John, please?"

"Father John isn't here right now."

"Oh." The boy seemed to deflate at the news and Nora thought she saw tears beginning to form in his eyes. Her face relaxed and the scowl vanished as she opened the screen and beckoned the boy inside.

"I didn't say he wouldn't be right back. He's at the hospital. I expect he'll be driving up any minute now. Come in and have a glass of milk."

"I'd rather not . . . the milk, I mean. Could I just wait for him until he gets back, please?"

"Well, don't stand there on the porch letting the flies inside. Come in, boy." Nora opened the screen wider and Sean followed her into the rectory.

The housekeeper often resented the petty and unreasonable people who imposed on Father John, but she hadn't worked at St. Anthony's for thirty years without learning to recognize real pain when she saw it. This child obviously had a problem. Father John might be the one to do the counseling, but Nora knew a thing or two about children with problems. Cookies and milk was the answer. It was as basic as the Doctrine of Papal Infallibility or the Virgin Birth. Nora was convinced the world would be a better place if the nation's leaders had been given cookies and milk when they were children. When Nora made up her mind about something there were few who dared raise objections. Sean was no match for the formidable housekeeper, and in spite of his earlier refusal, when Father John came in fifteen minutes later, the boy had finished a big glass of milk and six cookies.

And he even felt a little better.

If Father John was surprised to see the boy sitting in the

rectory kitchen, wearing a milk mustache and facing a
plate of Oreos, he didn't show it. Instead, he shook hands
solemnly with the youngster and then took one of the
cookies and popped it into his mouth. He chewed without
a word and then glanced over his shoulder at Nora before
reaching for the plate and palming another cookie. He
swallowed and grinned at Sean. "I'm glad to see you,
Sean. Is this a social call or can I help you with something?"

"I need to talk to you, sir . . . Uh, Father."

"Okay. Let's go out back. It's beautiful out today, isn't
it?" Father John reached for another cookie, but this time
Nora saw the movement and scowled threateningly at him.
The priest pulled his hand back guiltily and started for the
back door. Sean stood and, remembering the last time
he had eaten Nora's cookies, he took his empty glass and
the plate to the sink while Nora looked on approvingly.

"Now, what's up?" They were seated in the same lawn
chairs under the same grape arbor they had occupied six
weeks before.

"I did a terrible thing." The boy turned a tortured face
to the huge priest. "I hurt somebody. I may have killed
her, I'm not sure." Tears began running down his cheeks
while Father John tried to keep his own dismay from
showing.

"Take it easy, son. Take as long as you need. Tell me
what happened."

"It was my teacher. I didn't mean to hurt her." Sean
told the priest about the first day at Puerta Grande and
about Dragonlady. "I just wanted to get her out of the
classroom. I didn't mean to hurt her. Honest."

"I believe you, Sean. Tell me what happened."

"I don't know what happened." The boy wailed. "I
was just trying to help her . . ."

Father John said nothing as Sean's words were choked
off. He recovered a moment later and gave the priest a
tearful smile. "I guess I'm not doing a very good job
telling the story, am I?"

"You're doing fine, son. Just take it easy and tell me what happened. Take as much time as you need." The priest reached over and put a hand on the boy's shoulder.

Sean wiped his eyes with his sleeve and took a deep breath.

"It was all my fault. I wanted to get Dragonlady out of the classroom. Something was terribly wrong with her. All I wanted was to get her out in the hall and somehow get word to Doctor Taylor. He's the school psychologist."

"What was wrong with her?"

"I'm not sure. She was hurting . . . she was radiating pain from in here." The boy pointed to his forehead. "I've never felt anything like that before. Even that day in the hospital after the accident, none of the feelings were this intense. I was afraid something was going to happen to her."

"And what did you do?"

"Well, I followed her out the door of the classroom and she turned around and looked at me. The pain was even stronger. She was saying something but all I could feel was this frantic, horrible energy coming from her. I didn't mean to do it. It just kind of happened all by itself. One minute I was standing there and she was talking. It hurt my head and I sort of . . . It was like I pushed the bad part back at her. In my head I . . . I shoved it away. All at once she was shaking all over and then she fell down. I called her and I shook her, but she didn't move. I couldn't feel anything coming from her and I got scared. I ran to Doctor Taylor's office and told him what happened. He ran to get help for Mrs. Farrell and I left and came here." Sean fell silent and waited for a response from Father John.

The priest took several seconds to digest this newest revelation, then he leaned forward in his chair.

"You say you 'pushed' the bad part away. How did you do that?"

"I don't know. It wasn't something I planned to do. It just happened. Do you remember I told you that I could feel things coming from people—emotions and things like that?'' The priest nodded and Sean continued. ''The only way I can describe it is I pushed the feeling away and back to her.''

''Sean, what can you feel coming from me right now?''

''It's not very loud.'' The boy concentrated on the feelings he was picking up from Father John. When he looked at the priest, he was frowning. ''I can tell you don't really believe me. You're curious and . . . you're worried, a little bit.''

''That's pretty good. That comes fairly close to the way I feel. It shows me you're perceptive. There's nothing abnormal or unusual about being able to tell what other people are feeling. Everyone can do it. Some people are just better at it than others. I don't believe you're lying, but I'm having a little trouble accepting the story exactly the way you've told it to me.''

''It's not empathy,'' Sean insisted. ''It's more than that. It's something I can feel. I'm telling the truth!''

''I want you to do something for me, okay?'' Father John regarded the boy closely.

''Okay. What it is?''

''This feeling that you say is coming from me, I want you to push it back at me.''

''No!'' Sean was horrified and Father John felt an irrational moment of doubt, which he quickly put out of his mind. He was too old to start believing in mind reading.

''Don't you realize what I did to Mrs. Farrell? Please. I can't do that.''

''Sean, you didn't do anything to Mrs. Farrell. You just think you did. I want to prove to you that you don't have to take the blame for what happened. Trust me and do the same thing now that you did at school. Nothing's going to happen.''

''Father, I can't.'' Sean's voice was pleading. ''I don't want to hurt you. Please, just believe me. I'm telling you the truth.''

''Sean, I want you to push whatever you feel back to

me." Father John's voice was stern and unyielding. "Do it!"

Their eyes locked and for a short while it seemed neither would back down. Then, slowly, Sean nodded and the priest relaxed and settled into the lawn chair, his hands still folded on his lap.

Sean's expression never changed. There was no twitch; there was no outward sign at all when he pushed the mental buzz at Father John.

The priest was totally unprepared when a huge mental sledgehammer smashed into his brain. His body went rigid in the lawn chair. As though from a great distance he heard the boy cry out and knew he was losing consciousness. He struggled to come back to the pleasant backyard and grape arbor, but something was pulling him deeper and deeper into the blackness. With a superhuman effort he clung to the sound of the boy calling to him and very slowly the shadows began to disperse. When he could open his eyes he saw the boy leaning over him, panic-stricken.

"Here now, I'm okay." Father John managed a weak smile and relief flooded the boy's face. "I want you to do me another favor."

"What's that?" Sean looked at Father John fearfully.

"If I ever ask you to do that again, don't do it, okay?" The priest was smiling, but Sean knew he was serious. "It was a little more than I expected."

"I promise. Do you believe me now?"

"You don't leave me a lot of choice. The demonstration was impressive, to say the least." Father John tried to get up and failed. He sank back into the chair and waved the boy away when he tried to help. "That's okay. Just give me a minute to get my legs working again." The priest looked thoughtfully at the anxious youngster. "I was wrong. What you just did puts a new perspective on everything. We'd better find out how your teacher is doing."

"You mean you think she might be okay?" Sean looked doubtfully at the priest.

"We won't know until we make a few phone calls but

let's hope for the best, shall we?'' Father John tried again
to stand up and this time accepted the boy's steady arm.

"Here.'' The priest gestured toward the side gate.
"Let's go out this way and in the other door. Nora will
have a fit if I walk in like this.''

The huge priest and the small boy left the yard through
the gate and returned to Father John's study without being
seen. When Father John closed the door of the study behind them he looked relieved.

The first phone call was to Puerta Grande. They were
able to learn only that Mrs. Farrell had been taken by
ambulance to Baylor Memorial Hospital. Father John
dialed Baylor while Sean perched on the edge of a chair
across from his, waiting impatiently for news.

The phone at Baylor rang six times before someone answered. Sean watched the priest anxiously for some clue,
but Father John kept his face impassive.

"Hello. This is Father Cassidy from St. Anthony's
Church. I wonder if you'd be good enough to page Rev-
erend Blackwell. I think he's . . . yes . . . that's the
one. . . . I'll be glad to.'' Father John cupped his hand
over the mouthpiece and looked at Sean. "He should be
able to learn more than I can over the telephone. I just
hope he still—'' The priest took his hand off the mouthpiece. "Yes, Bill? This is Father John. Listen, I need a
favor that only a pushy Baptist can do.'' Sean listened
while Father John gave the minister the patient's name and
a very edited account of her collapse at Puerta Grande.
When the priest hung up a few minutes later, he turned to
the boy and tried to sound hopeful. "Now we wait. Bill
should call back in a couple of minutes.''

"I hope she's okay. I didn't mean to—''

"I know you didn't. It was an accident. You'll have to
stop feeling sorry for yourself if we're going to figure out
how to keep this from happening again.''

"How can I keep it from happening when I didn't do it
on purpose the first time?'' Sean sounded defeated.

"The first time you didn't know you could hurt someone. Now you do. You're going to have to watch yourself closely from now on.''

"What if it happens accidentally like it did this time? How do I know I won't hurt somebody?''

"Son, you can choose not to do it. You're not to blame for what happened today. If it happens again you will be to blame.''

"Yes, sir.'' The boy's voice was flat and Father John knew he wasn't convinced.

"Sean, you're the only one who can control this thing. Don't you believe you have a choice?''

"I suppose so. It's just that . . . I don't know . . . I'm afraid, I guess.'' Sean looked unhappily at the priest, but before Father John could reply the telephone on his desk rang. The old man picked it up on the second ring and held up his other hand to silence Sean.

"St. Anthony's, this is Father John.'' There was a long silence and suddenly the priest's face split into a huge smile. Sean let out the breath he had held since the telephone rang.

"Thanks, Bill, I owe you one. What's that? Just tell her I'm someone who's been very concerned about her. Listen, thanks again for your help. I'll probably see you tomorrow.'' Father John listened for several minutes more and then thanked the minister again before replacing the receiver in its cradle and turning to the boy sitting across from him. "Well, whatever else that thing is you do, at least we know it's not fatal. Mrs. Farrell is in stable condition. She's awake and thinks she fainted.''

"But we know better, don't we?'' The momentary euphoria Sean had felt at the news evaporated quickly as he returned to the problem of what he had become. "What if she had a heart condition? What if I had been mad and maybe pushed a little harder? What if something is wrong with her right now that we don't know about yet?''

"And what if you had taken a gun and shot her? Sean, there are enough things to worry about in this world without inventing more. 'What if' is a miserable way to go through life. 'What if' leaves you unhappy about something that might have happened and didn't, or fearful of something that could happen but won't. You'll spend your life unhappy or fearful of things that exist only in your own mind. That isn't the way you want to live.''

"I suppose you're right. I just wish none of this had ever happened.'' The boy looked at the clock hanging on the wall behind Father John and climbed from the chair. "I think I should get back. I want to get home at three so there won't be any questions. I don't want to have to tell my mom what happened. Maybe later but not right away.''

Father John nodded slowly. "I understand, Sean. I'd like to do you a favor if you'll let me.'' He looked at the small boy kindly. "Why don't you let me call your dad and explain what happened?''

Sean saw the logic at once. "If I tell him he may not believe me . . . about the pushing part.''

"That's right. I think I can convince him.''

"I'd like that, Father. Thank you.''

"You're welcome, son.'' The priest stood and walked around the desk. He opened the door of the office for Sean but instead of leaving, the boy stood uncertainly in the middle of the room and finally moved to Father John's side. He looked into the priest's face and Father John understood the loneliness he saw there. He hugged the boy tightly and heard Sean's voice, muffled and small, "I wish I weren't so afraid.''

"Sean, when I was talking to your dad I told him his problems might be easier if he would pray over them.'' The priest disengaged the boy's arms from around his waist and looked at him. "This power of yours is a gift from God. Pray that He'll show you how to use it wisely. That will help. I promise you, son, you'll feel better.''

"Okay, Father.''

The boy and the priest went to the front door and Father John watched as Sean walked down the street and disappeared around the corner. He remembered standing in the same doorway not so long before and praying that the boy would be strong. The old priest smiled to himself. Somehow, he was sure that the boy would be strong enough to face whatever came his way. The boy was a fighter. He would pray for him. The priest smiled again as another thought came to him. Perhaps he should be praying for the rest of the world instead.

He closed the door and returned to his study. It was two forty-five when he picked up the phone and dialed a number he called at least once a week.

"Hi, Margaret . . . Father John. No, today I don't want to talk to Al. Is Jason there? Good. May I have a quick word with him?"

Ed's news didn't come as a complete surprise to Marilyn. She had known something was terribly wrong, and Ed's visit served only to provide the details. She was able to conceal her surprise and forced herself to lie to her neighbor when he asked her if Sean came home at one-thirty after leaving the school. Yes, he had come home and they had talked about Mrs. Farrell. But why had she collapsed? Ed lit a cigarette and thought before answering.

"I have an idea Alice Farrell has been skirting the edges of a breakdown for some time now." He told Marilyn about the incident in the faculty lounge just three weeks before. "We may never know exactly what triggered it this time. It could have been something she said; it could have been something Sean said or it could have just happened. It was time. The pressure inside her built up until . . ." The psychologist shrugged. "It's really too bad, you know. She gave her life to teaching. The timing was unfortunate. I hope Sean isn't blaming himself. It would have happened whether he had been there or not. I guess he must have done something to get into trouble. She had brought him into the hall for something when the breakdown occurred. Are you sure you wouldn't like me to talk to him? If nothing else I could try to reassure him that it wasn't his fault." Ed seemed concerned about the boy.

"Maybe later, Ed. I think we pretty much talked it out.

He was upset and he's in lying down right now. I think
we've gotten past the worst of it.'' Marilyn was ashamed
at the ease with which one lie followed another. Ed remained unconvinced but didn't press the issue. They talked
about other things for a few minutes and then the psychologist excused himself and left for home and dinner.
Marilyn sat in the rapidly darkening kitchen and felt the
hard knot of fear growing in her stomach. She was still
sitting there when Jason got home at six-thirty.

Jason entered Sean's bedroom without knocking. His
son was curled into a ball on the bed but his eyes were
open, and Jason went to the side of the bed and gently
touched his son's shoulder. ''I think we need to have a
talk. Would you come out in the living room, please?''
The boy rose wordlessly and followed his father from the
room.

''We're not blaming you for what happened after Mrs.
Farrell went out in the hall with you. I accept that it was
an accident. My question is: Why did you feel it was necessary for you disrupt the entire class just because you
thought your teacher was upset?'' Jason brushed a lock of
hair from his forehead and looked at his son impatiently.
''The three of us decided you would maintain a low profile. If we hadn't made that decision what would you have
done—placed a classified ad in the *Times*?''

''She wasn't just upset. She was being tortured. I
thought I could help.'' Sean's tone was defiant.

''And now she's in the hospital. Wouldn't it have been
better if you had just let her alone?'' The lawyer held up
his hand before Sean could object. ''I know, I know. It
was an accident. You're going to have to become responsible for your actions. Now we find out that if you're not
careful you can hurt someone or maybe even kill them.
Can't you see that this puts a tremendous responsibility on
your shoulders? What on earth possessed you?'' Jason
looked at the boy and waited for a reply.

"But when I did that, I didn't know; how was I supposed to know something like this could happen?"

"Okay." Jason's voice was more gentle now. "I'll accept that answer. So the question is, knowing what we know, where do we go from here?"

"That's what I spent all afternoon thinking about in my room." Sean answered listlessly.

"And what did you come up with?"

"Nothing. I don't know what to do." The boy shrugged sadly and the action seemed to infuriate Jason.

"It's about time you found out what to do. Let me tell you what you're going to do first. First, you will stop making everyone else's problems your own. Until you learn to control this power you have, you're not doing anyone a favor by interfering in their lives. Later on you can save the world. Right now concentrate on getting to be nine years old and leave saving the world to the rest of us. Do you understand?"

"Yes, sir." Sean bowed his head.

"Second, the next time something happens I want you to come and tell us. We love you, son. You don't ever have to feel ashamed or afraid to talk to us. Do you promise?"

"I promise."

"The last thing should be obvious." Jason paused and tried to find a way to describe the third thing. "Whatever it was you did to Mrs. Farrell . . . I want you to promise you won't ever do that to anyone again. Do you promise?"

This time Sean barely waited for the question. "I promise," he said emphatically.

"Shake on it." Jason extended his hand and smiled. As they shook hands, the boy made a silent vow to himself that, no matter what happened, he would never "push" at anyone again.

And, as sometimes happens with promises quickly made, Sean's vow remained unbroken for less than twenty-four hours.

* * *

Vernon Tibbs took his pipe from his jacket pocket and to Ed's annoyance began filling it. They were in Ed's office and the school bell had just announced the beginning of a new day of work and study.

"You say she had a spell—I guess that's what you'd call it—at the faculty meeting in August? Why wasn't I told about it then?" He struck a match and held it to the bowl while he looked expectantly at Ed.

"I don't think any of us thought that much about it. She said she was feeling ill and had to go home. And by the way, I do remember telling you that she got sick and had to leave."

"Hmmm." Tibbs grunted noncommittally. "There's a difference between getting sick and slipping your gears, wouldn't you agree?" He sucked on the pipe stem and was rewarded with a thick cloud of smoke that he blew in Ed's direction. "So how is she now? Is the old elevator stuck between floors or what?"

"Vernon, you have a very colorful way of describing other people's misfortune." Ed swallowed the rest of his anger with difficulty. The principal of Puerta Grande was an ass but at the same time if he chose to he could make Ed's life very difficult. "Alice will be in the hospital for the next day or two and then she will probably take a leave of absence. I talked with her yesterday afternoon at the hospital, and I have a feeling she isn't going to be back. I'd suggest you start looking for a replacement." Ed hoped Tibbs would take the hint and leave, but the principal continued sitting across from Ed's desk, sucking on his pipe and blowing the smoke into Ed's face.

"Well, that's too bad." Tibbs frowned and removed the pipe from his mouth. "I heard the Jeffries boy was with her when it happened. Isn't he the youngster we're going to be testing next week?"

"That's right. It was just coincidence that he was the one who happened to be with her. He was also the one who ran to get help. Fortunately, I was still in my office and . . . you know the rest of the story."

"Mmmm. Good for him. Well, I have work to do. The world must go on, eh? When you see Alice be sure to give her my best, won't you?" Tibbs blew a final cloud of blue smoke into the air before letting himself out. After the door closed Ed got up from his desk with a look of disgust and opened the window behind his chair to air out the office.

Toby Elliot was a singularly unattractive child. His puffy red face almost buried his little pig eyes. His dark, short-cropped hair began almost where his eyebrows left off at the expense of a forehead. He would have made an excellent poster boy for Planned Parenthood, or perhaps some large manufacturer of condoms if either wanted to use an aversion approach to marketing. In the savage world of grammar school with its heartless cruelty and rigid pecking order, Toby would have been the butt of jeers and ridicule were it not for the fact that he was also the largest boy in the school, this a result of both genetics and a bicycle accident when he was nine that broke his leg and kept him back for a year in the third grade. Unlike the book that can't be judged by its cover, Toby's appearance in many ways matched his personality. He was happiest when he found someone to torment. Other children at Puerta Grande either tried to avoid him or, in a few cases, joined the ranks of his followers who steadily abused the less fortunate or less well-connected children.

Toby had just learned something that bothered him a great deal. Some kid in the third grade had taken on Dragonlady and the bitch had to be hauled off in a meat wagon. The whole school was buzzing with the news. Toby had no love for Mrs. Farrell. He had suffered through nine months in the old bag's class two years earlier when he had to repeat the third grade. He had hated the old woman intensely. What troubled him now was not that someone had finally nailed her but rather that he hadn't been the one to do it. His pig eyes darted from Bobby Acuna to Phil Venables, seeking details.

"What did he do to her?"

"Nobody knows. I guess he musta hit her with something if she had to go to the hospital." Bobby practically glowed with pleasure at the attention he was getting from Toby. "I heard he almost killed her."

"Did the cops take him away?"

"Nah, he was here today. They say she's not coming back—ever."

"Well, he didn't hit her if the cops didn't take him away. You're a real shithead, ya know that? If ya hit a teacher they put you in jail. That's the only reason I never pasted the old broad myself." Toby glared at his ignorant lieutenant and then turned his attention to Phil. "Did you hear anything about it?"

"Sure. Everybody's talkin' about it. This little kid got pissed off and dragged her into the hall and WHAMO! They took her away in an ambulance."

"Somethin' don't sound right." Toby chewed thoughtfully on his lower lip and considered the possibilities. Bobby Acuna chose that moment to make a serious error in judgment.

"Well, I guess he wasn't afraid of going to jail." He started to laugh, but his amusement was cut short when Toby grabbed him by the shirtfront and yanked him roughly forward.

"Listen, piss ant, I never said I was afraid. I ain't afraid of nothin'."

"I know you ain't, Toby. I didn't mean it like that." The smaller boy cringed in dismay at his sudden fall from grace. "I never said you was scared."

"Well, you better not. Not if you know what's good for you." Toby released Bobby's shirt and turned back to Phil. "I had it all planned. I was gonna get her good. See, I'm too smart to do anything dumb like hitting a teacher. I was gonna do something else if she ever got in my way."

"I'll bet she'da been sorry, huh Toby?" Phil wasn't about to make the same mistake Bobby had made.

"Hey, Toby." Bobby saw a way to redeem himself.

"That's the kid over there. Why don'tcha go over and ask him what he did?" Bobby pointed across the playground at a small blond boy in earnest conversation with Michael Taylor.

Toby's little pig eyes looked in the direction of Bobby's pointing finger and something very much like pleasure animated his puffy face.

"Why don't I go over and do just that?" The big fifth grader swung a leg over the bicycle he was holding and started across the playground with his two junior officers in pursuit.

Sean's second day in the third grade had passed without incident. The substitute teacher assigned to Mrs. Farrell's class seemed to know he would be around for a while and had approached his job with a no-nonsense spirit. The day had been a monumental bore, to be sure, but it helped a little that Sean liked Mr. Kaufman's style of teaching. The young teacher controlled the class without resorting to terror tactics and never talked down to the kids. It didn't help a lot but it was something.

The three o'clock buzzer was a welcome reprieve, and Sean was one of the first ones out the door. He felt a little bit of pride that he had made it through his first full day of third grade without a problem, and he paused outside the main door to watch the tumble of boys and girls pouring from the exit. He was one of them and at the same time he wasn't. A shadow of sadness passed over his face as he saw his classmates joyfully leaving the building. It was hard to be different. He wondered if he would ever have a friend, a real friend who would know him and like him the way he was.

As if in answer to his question he heard a voice call out behind him, "Hey, Sean, wait up." Michael Taylor ran up to him, breathless and grinning. "What's happening?"

"Hi, Michael." Sean returned the grin and felt better. "Hey, you want to come over and play some catch?"

"Okay. Let me go home and tell my mom I'm going to

be at your house. Hey, buddy, what did you do to Dragonlady?'' Michael faced his younger friend in awe. "Everybody's saying you had a fight with her and she had to
be taken to the hospital. What happened?''

"Everybody's wrong.'' Sean avoided his friend's eyes
as he brushed the question aside. "I didn't do anything.
Let's talk about something else, okay?'' Sean started
walking across the playground toward home.

"Okay.'' With a maturity that belied his ten years, Michael fell into step beside the younger boy and tried to
think of something else to talk about.

"How's the new teacher? I saw him at lunch.''

"He's okay. I—'' The rest of Sean's reply was cut off
by the *whoosh* of bicycle tires as Toby Elliot skidded to a
halt in front of them.

"Hey, kid, I wanna talk to you.'' He grinned wolfishly
at Sean and a moment later Phil Venables and Bobby
Acuna arrived and dismounted from their bikes behind
their leader. The three of them faced Sean and Michael,
cutting off their retreat.

"Hi, Toby.'' Michael greeted his classmate nervously.
"Whatcha doin'?''

"Get lost, Taylor. I wanna talk to your friend for a
minute.'' Toby never took his eyes from Sean as he
brushed Michael's greeting aside. Bobby, anxious to make
up for his earlier breach, moved around Toby and Sean to
take a position in front of Michael, confident that Phil
would back him up if things got physical.

"I wanna know what happened to Dragonlady.'' Toby
made the demand in an almost pleasant voice. "I hear you
did something to her.''

"She fainted, that's all. I didn't do anything to her.''
Sean faced the bigger boy calmly. "Come on, Michael.
Let's go.''

"You'll go when I tell you to go.'' Toby continued
blocking their way. "You didn't answer my question yet.''
Toby's blotched face and narrowed eyes made Sean think

of some feral animal. He felt a pang of fear, which was exactly what Toby intended.

"Leave him alone, Toby." Michael tried to defend his friend.

"Shut up, Taylor. This don't concern you." The school bully turned his attention back to Sean. "I don't believe you, kid. I wanna know what you did." Sean could feel the menace radiating from the fifth grader and struggled with his own anger.

"I told you, I didn't do anything. Let us go."

"Come on, Toby. Lay off, will ya?" Michael pleaded with his classmate.

"Keep out of it, Taylor." Phil grabbed Michael's arm and twisted it viciously behind his back. "You queer for him or something? I'm still waiting, kid." Toby had already decided that Sean hadn't done anything to Dragonlady, but he was having fun. He reached over and shoved the third grader, who stumbled backward into Bobby. He would have fallen but Bobby caught him and pushed him roughly forward to face Toby's merciless stare.

"You're an asshole, Toby," Michael shouted in a last effort to draw the older boy's attention away from his friend. "Oowww. Leggo my arm, you sonofabitch." Michael kicked out and managed to land one good one to Phil's leg before Bobby jumped into the fray and with Phil's help wrestled Michael to the ground.

Other kids, attracted by the possibility of a fight, began to gather around them. Several of the bigger boys in the crowd watched Toby with scorn, and the bully looked around quickly when someone muttered, "Why don't you pick on someone your own size?" No one had the courage to challenge Toby directly. A quick glare from the big fifth grader was enough to quell the mutterings.

It was pure coincidence that Ed Taylor chose that moment to look out his window. What he saw caused his face to flush with anger. His son was struggling on the ground while two of Puerta Grande's miniature Mafia held him down. Toby Elliot was confronting Sean Jeffries while a dozen other students looked on. Ed started to turn from the window to go out and intervene, but before he could move, Sean raised his arm and pointed at Toby. What happened next made the psychologist gasp.

Sean made his decision. He forced his anger back and concentrated all his attention on the bigger boy standing in his way, his promise to his father completely forgotten. His face was almost serene as he raised his arm and pointed a finger at Toby.

"Get out of my way, *NOW*!"

Some animal instinct warned the bully that something was wrong and he felt a moment of unease before a hammer smashed into his brain with the force of a high-caliber bullet. His knees trembled and then gave out and he collapsed on the ground, arms and legs jerking spastically. Spittle and mucus oozed from his mouth and nose. Phil and Bobby released Michael and looked at their fallen leader, first in amazement and then in fear. Someone in the crowd gleefully called attention to the ultimate humiliation any fifth grader can ever face.

"Jeez, look at that. He's peeing his pants."

Across the playground, another boy watched Sean. He stood alone near the swings, where he had stood months before, watching Sean and Michael climb Red Mountain. He still wore the knee socks and knickers, the heavy plaid shirt buttoned all the way up, and the paperboy cap. He was smiling as he turned away from the swings and began walking toward the chain-link fence in back of the playground. By the time Ed Taylor came out of the building, the boy in the old-fashioned clothes had disappeared.

"Would you boys like to tell me what you were doing?" Sean, Michael, and Toby Elliot were seated in Ed Taylor's office. Phil and Bobby had fled in terror before Ed reached the playground.

"I wasn't doin' nothin'." Toby sniffled defensively. He had been conscious though groggy when Ed reached the crowd of children. Ed had taken him to the bathroom and cleaned him up as best he could before bringing all three boys to his office. "I was just asking the little kid about Mrs. Farrell and he hit me."

"I didn't hit you." Sean contradicted Toby and the older boy shrank back in fear. "Nothing happened." He looked at Michael for support.

"Why were you fighting with those other boys, Michael?" Ed addressed his son.

"We were just fooling around. Honest, Dad."

Ed sighed in frustration. There was little to be gained by prolonging this session any further. He shrugged in defeat and addressed Toby, trying to keep the distaste from showing on his face. "Are you okay to get home? I can drive you if you'd like."

"That's okay. Can I go now?" Toby made no attempt to hide his eagerness to leave.

"You can go." Ed noted grimly that the big fifth grader made a wide circle around Sean as he left the office. He waited until Toby had closed the door behind him before speaking again to his son. "Michael, I want you to go home. I'll talk to you later." Michael and Sean rose together and Ed waved Sean back to his seat. "Not you. I want to talk to you, Sean." The boy looked around unhappily, as though seeking an avenue of escape, but obediently returned to his seat. Michael hesitated, then reluctantly left the office without his friend. Ed stared thoughtfully at the boy sitting across from him, then picked up the telephone and dialed a number. He smiled at Sean while he waited for Marilyn to answer. The boy fidgeted nervously in his chair and avoided Ed's eyes.

"Hi, Marilyn. This is Ed." The psychologist leaned back in his chair and looked up at the ceiling. "Listen, Sean is with me. I want to talk to him about those tests

he's going to be taking, so he'll be a little late, okay?'' He
paused and Sean could hear his mother answer though
he couldn't make out the words. ''No, there's no problem.
Everything is fine.'' Again the pause. ''He'll be home in
about thirty minutes. No. I just didn't want you to worry.
Okay. He'll be along soon.'' Another pause and then Ed
slowly hung up the telephone and turned his attention back
to Sean.

''You know I'm your friend, don't you?'' He leaned
forward in his chair while the boy nodded wordlessly. ''I
want you to do something for me.''

''What's that?'' Sean felt his pulse quicken as he remembered when Father John had used almost the same
words.

''There's something going on here that I don't understand. Your dad tells me one day that he wants you to take
placement tests. Something happens to Alice Farrell and
you're the only one around. Half an hour ago I look out
the window and see you do something. What, I don't
know, but something. I want you to level with me. What
happened out there?'' Ed watched his neighbor's son
closely and waited for a reply. Could his imagination be
working overtime? Was it possible the youngster in front
of him was just a very normal, very bright third grader?
The psychologist almost regretted saying anything and then
he remembered the Elliot boy. Whatever Sean had done
to Toby was enough to terrify the fifth grader. In some
way that he didn't yet understand, Ed believed there was
a connection between Toby Elliot and Alice Farrell.

Sean was squirming unhappily in his chair. ''I don't
know what you mean.''

''Sure you do. What happened on the playground?''

The boy shrugged and said nothing.

''I'm waiting, Sean,'' Ed insisted firmly.

''I'm not supposed to talk about it,'' the boy finally said
in a low voice.

''Sean, whatever you tell me in here will remain in here,
just between us . . . okay?''

The conflict was plain to read on the small boy's face. Ed waited patiently, watching Sean struggle with his indecision.

An hour and a half later the psychologist and the third grader left Puerta Grande. Ed was numb. Even more incredible than the story Sean had told was the psychologist's reaction to it. In spite of reason, logic, common sense, and sanity, in spite of every instinct that cried out in protest, Ed believed the boy.

The news of Toby's humiliation was all over the school by the time the first bell rang on Wednesday morning. The story was told and retold during the day. Even the faculty talked about the incident in wonder. Most assumed that the tiny third grader had bested the older boy in a fistfight, and Ed Taylor said nothing to correct the impression. Those who had watched the whole thing weren't quite sure what it was they had seen. By lunchtime Sean was the school hero. Few believed Toby's story that he had been jumped from behind and even these few noticed that the big fifth grader did nothing to even the score and in fact, distanced himself from Sean on the playground. Like a lottery winner whose name appears in the daily paper, Sean discovered that he had more friends than he had ever thought possible. The boy enjoyed all the attention although he refused to talk about any details of the fight. This refusal only added to the mystique of his reputation and for the remaining week and a half at Puerta Grande, the boy was surrounded by young admirers.

Ed watched with some apprehension as his neighbor's boy became an overnight celebrity. Ed felt almost as much for the youngster as he did for his own son, and he worried that Sean would change in some negative way. He considered talking to Jason about the problem but felt that would be a betrayal of a trust. He had promised Sean that what passed between them would remain private, and there was no way he could talk to Jason without revealing what he already knew. Instead, he concentrated on gathering the materials he would need a week from Saturday. Ed planned far more than a placement test for the little boy. He was determined to learn the real limits of Sean's ability.

The day was overcast and drizzly as Sean dressed quietly in the semidarkness. Since it was Saturday, his mom and dad wouldn't be up for hours. Sean had slept poorly and awakened frequently during the night, each time looking at the clock to see if it was time to get up. Today was the day. He was due at Puerta Grande at nine o'clock. He left his bedroom after dutifully making his bed, a task made more difficult by Mugs's insistence on supervising the entire operation from the middle of the bedspread.

"Come on, Mugs," Sean whispered quietly to the terrier and closed his bedroom door behind them. The boy and dog tiptoed through the house and into the kitchen, where Sean fixed himself a huge bowl of cereal. He poured a generous amount of milk over the flakes and was chewing contentedly when the overhead light suddenly went on.

"Goodness, you're certainly up early."

"Hi, Mom. I gotta get ready to find out how smart I am." Sean scooped another spoonful of cornflakes into his mouth, then pointed at his mother with the empty spoon. "Whateryamphh?"

"Don't talk with your mouth full, Sean." Marilyn went to the refrigerator and took a dozen eggs out and set them on the counter. "Would you like some scrambled eggs?" She cracked two eggs into a small bowl without waiting for an answer.

Sean swallowed a mouthful of cereal and tried again. "What are *you* doing up so early?"

Marilyn looked at her son and smiled. "I've got to get ready to find out how smart you are." She turned back to the bowl in front of her and began beating the eggs with a fork. "Are you nervous?"

"No." Sean paused and decided that wasn't entirely true. "I'm not worried about how I'll do. I just want to find out what's going to happen after they grade those tests.

You know what's neat?'' The boy stopped with his spoon poised halfway between the bowl and his mouth. "I can do anything I want to do. I can be anything I want to be."

"That's always been true, Sean." Marilyn poured the eggs into a small frying pan and began stirring them.

"I suppose it was but, I don't know, it's different now."

"How is it different?" Marilyn asked.

"Look at the head start I've got. Do you realize I could finish medical school by the time I'm twelve? I could have law school behind me when I'm fifteen. There's no limit to what I could accomplish."

"Do you want to be a doctor?"

"Oh, I don't know. That's not the point. I could be if I wanted to. That's what I'm saying."

"Fortunately you still have a little time left. First we have to get you past the third grade. After that, it would be nice if you gave your dad a little time to earn the tuition for all these schools you plan to attend. Eventually, after you've gone to law school and medical school, you can decide what you want to do with your life. I just hope it's going to be something that pays a lot, because your dad and I will probably need money by then."

Sean looked at his mother seriously. "I think I've already decided. I know what I want to do with my life."

"What's that?"

"I want to deliver pizzas."

Jason was up by eight-thirty and took Sean across the street to Puerta Grande. Ed was waiting for them when they arrived and by five after nine that morning Sean was beginning the first of many tests he would take that day. At Ed's direction, Marilyn had packed her son a lunch, and it was almost four-thirty before the exhausted boy returned home.

Ed corrected each exam as Sean finished it. Any doubts he may have had about the boy's intelligence were quickly dispelled as the numbers and percentages began to paint a surprising picture. After Sean completed the last of the tests and had left, Ed gathered up the stack of papers and brought them to his office. He locked them in his desk and prepared to leave the building by the side door. The maintenance man gave him a surly nod when Ed told him they were through and he could lock up the building. The district's contract with the union required that a maintenance employee be present whenever the property was being used for school business, and someone had been sent over from the high school to spend the day at Puerta Grande.

George Braun found the key he was looking for and secured the doors of the school. He pocketed the keys and turned toward the station wagon parked in the empty lot, grumbling to himself about the loss of a Saturday. Of course, he could have refused the overtime. He almost had. It was only the knowledge that Tom Washington would come in if he didn't that persuaded George to give up part of his weekend. No nigger was going to take away his bread and butter. He had the seniority; he'd work the overtime.

Braun settled himself behind the wheel of the Hudson and started the engine. It wheezed and sputtered for several seconds and then died. Goddamn fuel pump! Goddamn car! Just about the time you're getting caught up, just about the time there's a couple of bucks left over, that's when something else breaks down. George pounded the steering wheel with his fist and then forced himself to relax. He turned the key again and this time the engine responded. He sat in the car letting it warm up and thought about trading it in. He could get something a little newer, something a little more comfortable. Kiss a rat's ass, he certainly deserved something better.

A thought intruded and George frowned. His trips to Hollywood were becoming more frequent. There was always the possibility someone would remember the Hudson. It was time to get rid of it. He'd be better off with a different car. Monday he would look into it.

* * *

Ed Taylor came in the back door and kissed his wife before acknowledging the question in her eyes.

"You want to know how it went."

"Well, I'm curious."

"On most of the tests I gave him he's off the scale. His scores on the college entrance exam put him in the eighty-fifth percentile. He was telling the truth."

"God!"

"There's something I had better do. I'll be right back." The psychologist turned and left the kitchen. He went directly to the room that served as an office in the back of the house and removed a dog-eared book of phone numbers from the desk drawer. He searched quickly through the Ts. When he found the number he was looking for he picked up the telephone and dialed Vernon Tibbs at home.

CHAPTER NINE

The Thing

George Braun took a gulp of lukewarm coffee from the Styrofoam cup on his desk and looked over the work orders for the day. The hot-water valve in the second floor boys' room needed replacing again. Someone had broken the window in the biology lab. Braun chuckled as he pictured Carruthers pissing all over himself about that one. Let the old fag have kittens. George tucked the slip on the bottom of the stack and continued sorting through the others. Mrs. Lambert wanted someone to replace two burned-out fluorescent bulbs in Home Economics. The loudspeaker system was still mute and inoperative on the west side of the third floor. George put the loudspeaker complaint in his shirt pocket and started to toss the other slips into the basket, then changed his mind and looked through them again. He located Carruthers's lab window and put the blue requisition into his desk drawer. If Carruthers asked he could always tell him that Washington lost it. He shuffled through the remaining orders and found the hot-water valve on the second floor. Braun took a stub of a pencil from his desk and wrote "DO FIRST" on the face of the work order, then initialed it and slipped it on Tom Washington's clipboard. He fanned the remaining orders one last time before tossing the remaining chits into the basket and leaving the maintenance office.

The building was quiet as Braun made his way down the hall to the first-floor storage closet. Washington, who always arrived before seven, was late today and George assumed he was the only one in the building. He unlocked the closet with his master key and bent over to get two fluorescent bulbs out of the box on the floor when he heard footsteps and voices approaching. There was something familiar about one of the voices that raised the hairs on the back of his neck. He waited, half concealed behind the closet door until the footsteps passed, and then he peered cautiously down the hall after the receding figures. He recognized the psychologist immediately. The boy looked like the same kid who had been at Puerta Grande last Saturday. It was the man next to Taylor that Braun had heard speaking and George looked curiously at the back of his head. He was taller than the psychologist. Why did he seem so familiar?

The tall man chose that moment to turn his head to say something to Taylor and Braun got a look at his profile. It was that smart-ass attorney, the one he had almost punched in the mouth three months before. The maintenance man's eyes fairly glowed with hatred, and the boy walking between the two men suddenly cringed and looked behind him. Their eyes met for an instant and then the two men and the boy rounded the corner and were gone.

George relocked the closet and mulled over what he had seen. What was Jeffries doing here? Could it have anything to do with him? And who was the boy? The brat must be his son. Braun was sure it was also the same kid Ed Taylor had been testing at the grammar school. But what did it mean? George didn't know but he was going to keep his eyes open. Jeffries was on his list. He had a score to settle with that sonofabitch. George never forgot that kind of a debt. Who could say? Maybe an opportunity would come along sooner than he expected. Stranger things had happened. Old George was going to keep his eyes and ears open, by God.

He cackled mirthfully and headed for the cargo elevator to change some light bulbs on the second floor.

It was just after seven on that Monday morning when Ed and Jason pulled into the high school parking lot with

Sean in the backseat. They had taken Jason's car. Ed explained they would be meeting with Tibbs, who could give him a ride back to Puerta Grande.

Over the weekend Ed had spoken with Tibbs and with Marjorie Clauson, the principal of the high school, and they had arranged a meeting for this morning. The psychologist had Sean's test results in his briefcase. As the three of them entered the building he tried to prepare his neighbor for the objections they would have to overcome.

"Marjorie is going to be the obstacle this morning. If we can win her over we've won the war."

"I thought you told me that Tibbs was the one with the 'system' compulsion?"

"That's true enough. Vernon is probably afraid to eat a TV dinner without having the set turned on, but he's going to do whatever he thinks you want him to do. Remember, I've built you up as an angry F. Lee Bailey all set to make an example out of him and the district. He's running scared right now. It's Marjorie we're going to have to convince. She's a sharp old bird and doesn't get intimidated." The psychologist nodded to himself and glanced over at Jason. "I wouldn't use that kind of an approach on her anyway. Marjorie is an educator. Tibbs is just a fool."

"Why is there any question about what to do with Sean? If he can do the work required of a high school student, why not just put him in high school? What's the problem?"

"It seems simple enough, doesn't it?" Ed agreed. "Too bad it really isn't that easy."

"But why not? Isn't that the whole point of aptitude testing? Put Sean at whatever grade level he qualifies for and we'll go from there."

"Like I said, it isn't that easy. Marjorie is going to probably argue against that solution because she's concerned about Sean's total development. If the papers in my briefcase have any validity, then Sean could start attending college tomorrow and never have a problem—at least not an academic problem. Sitting in a grammar school classroom for the past year when he was a second grader must have been torture for him.'' Ed paused to see if Jason would offer to tell him what really happened to Sean. The lawyer said nothing, and after a moment Ed continued. ''Our job in the schools isn't just to teach kids to read and write. We also have to teach other things that you don't see listed on a report card. Things like socialization skills, an ability to work with others, a sense of responsibility and maturity—all these things are taught in the classroom and on the playground. It isn't always the staff that does the teaching either. It's the kids themselves who teach each other every day. The fact that Sean can pass a college entrance exam based on his knowledge of math and English says nothing about how he'll get along with the other freshmen in his class, nor does it tell us that he will be happy going to college. College freshmen don't usually act like eight-year-olds in spite of the way it sometimes looks to their professors. If Sean is put into this environment, then when can he be a little boy? If he's forced to grow up at this kind of an accelerated pace, then when and how are we going to give him back his childhood?''

Jason looked at his friend and Ed could tell from the lawyer's face that he had made his point. ''I never thought about it that way. What do we do in the case of someone like Sean?''

''That's what we're all meeting this morning to find out. I thought you ought to know that there aren't any pat answers. There may not even be any right answers.''

Sean was trailing behind the two adults, only half listening to their conversation when something dark and threatening slammed without warning into his mind. He winced and stumbled. His father and Ed continued talking without noticing the boy's distress as Sean tried to erect a barrier against the thing that was roiling and writhing in his head. He tried to push it back but it didn't push. The presence seemed to weaken as they continued walking and Sean realized it was coming from behind them. He turned his head and saw an older man in overalls looking at them

from a doorway. Again he tried to dislodge the horror
from his brain and this time was able to feel the thing
slipping away, clawing for a hold and resisting but losing
the battle as Sean concentrated all his efforts on ripping
his mind free. They were almost to the end of the hallway
and Sean put all his energy into one last push. Suddenly
the Thing was outside him. His eyes met those of the man
in the doorway and he felt sick and frightened as he felt
the dark Thing circling and nibbling at his mental defense,
looking for a way back in. A moment later they turned the
corner and the Thing was gone, leaving Sean weak and
trembling. He hurried to catch up with Jason and Ed. The
psychologist reached for his key as Sean put his hand into
his father's. Jason looked down at his son in surprise.

"Good grief, Sean. What's the matter? You look white
as a sheet."

"Just nervous, I guess." The boy continued holding
Jason's hand until Ed opened the door and ushered them
inside to wait for Vernon Tibbs and Marjorie Clauson.

The two school principals arrived together at seven-
thirty. Even if Ed had not briefed Jason about Tibbs, the
lawyer would have disliked the principal of Puerta Grande
almost immediately. Jason found him an obsequious,
fawning little man and wondered how he had managed to
become the principal of even a grammar school. Marjorie
Clauson, on the other hand, was a completely different
story. Smartly dressed and as tall as Jason, she appeared
to be in her early fifties. She radiated warmth and humor
while the introductions were made, but there was no question who the commanding presence at the meeting would
be. Jason shook hands with the high school principal and
felt the way he sometimes did when he was pitted against
a competent adversary in the courtroom. The only thing
wrong with the courtroom analogy, he realized, was that
Marjorie Clauson was more than opposing counsel; she
was also the judge and jury.

"Good morning, Sean. I'm Mrs. Clauson." The woman

extended her hand, and Jason was pleased to see that Sean stood up to shake hands. "I've been hearing quite a few things about you this weekend. I'm pleased to meet you."

"Thank you." Sean looked embarrassed and sat back down when Marjorie released his hand.

"Would anyone like some coffee before we begin?" She looked at Jason as she walked to a chair at the head of the conference table.

"Please. That sounds pretty good." The attorney accepted her offer after seeing Ed nodding his agreement.

"That's okay, Marjorie. I'll call down." The psychologist stood up and began walking to the telephone on a table near the window but stopped and turned around as Mrs. Clauson spoke to him.

"Ed, would you mind calling Janice in my office and see if she can come up here?" She turned back to Jason. "I thought Janice could take Sean to the cafeteria for a little while so the four of us can go over a few things and decide on the kind of approach we want to take."

Jason had expected this and had his answer ready. "I'd like to make a request. The things that we are going to be talking about will have an effect on Sean's entire life. I believe, and in fact, the reason I'm here, is to convince you that he has the intelligence and maturity to understand what we're talking about. I would like to ask that he be allowed to stay and hear the reasoning behind whatever decision we reach."

"Quite out of the question." Tibbs looked shocked at this affront to propriety.

Mrs. Clauson gave Ed Taylor a questioning look. "I guess I don't have a problem with that. Ed, what's your feeling?"

"Fine with me. I agree with Jason. Sean ought to be able to hear not only what we decide but why we've decided it as well."

"Vernon, what about you?"

The principal of Puerta Grande, realizing he stood

alone, did a quick turnabout. "I have no objection. None at all." He smiled affably at the lawyer.

"Thank you." Jason gave his son a wink that went unnoticed by the others as he prepared to wait for the next round. Two points for our team, he thought, but it's going to be a long game.

Moments later a pot of coffee was wheeled into the conference room and the meeting got under way.

Tom Washington took the clipboard from the wall of the maintenance office and then turned to the remaining unassigned work orders in the large incoming basket on Braun's desk. He went through them slowly and extracted three more to put with the one George had given him as a priority. The rest could wait until after lunch. He shoved the four blue requisitions into his pocket and left the office feeling a little disappointed that the old man wasn't around. One of the things that made the day enjoyable was needling the bastard. Nothing too obvious. Nothing the racist half-wit could write him up for. Just little digs every once in a while to keep the old fool stirred up. A month ago he had hit the jackpot when he mentioned casually that his son was engaged to a white girl who was studying at UCLA. Braun hadn't said a word but his ears had turned a brilliant shade of red, and it was all Tom could do to keep from busting up. Last week he had let it slip that he was looking to buy a house up near Puerta Grande. Braun had muttered something and stalked out of the office to the black man's delight. The truth was that Tom was quite content in his home in Pasadena and both his children were girls. He had told his wife about the game, but the humor had been lost on her. She didn't understand how Tom could bear to work with the old fool. It didn't bother Tom at all. He liked to say that every black family ought to have a racist as a house pet. He had suggested this one time to Mr. Carruthers and the biologist had come back with the idea that they would make good laboratory animals. They were plentiful, they bred well in captivity, and they were impossible to get attached to. Tom had cracked up.

Washington took the stairs down to the school basement where plumbing supplies were stored and whistled cheerfully as he put two pipe wrenches and a new valve in a large toolbox. Maybe today he'd say he found a house he liked. Another idea came to him. Maybe he'd ask George to loan him the down payment . . . just to see what he'd say.

"I still have a problem with his age." Mrs. Clauson directed her words to Ed Taylor. "I just don't believe a twelfth-grade class of seventeen- and eighteen-year-olds is an appropriate environment for an eight-year-old, regardless of his academic level."

"On the other hand, Marjorie, a third-grade classroom is hardly appropriate for a boy who scored in the eighty-fifth percentile on his College Boards," Ed insisted calmly.

"I agree with you. The best place for Sean would be in a school that specializes in working with gifted children. Unfortunately, the closest one that I know of is in Colorado."

"Have you considered relocating?" Vernon made his contribution to the discussion.

"Mr. Tibbs, I'm a lawyer," Jason answered patiently. "It's not practical for me to think about uprooting my family, leaving an established practice, and moving to another state where I would have to take the bar exam all over again just to get a job as an associate at a third my present salary."

Tibbs nodded quickly, and glanced around the table, embarrassed.

"I think it might help if we recognize that whatever we decide to do, it will be wrong. At least it's going to be something less than an optimum solution. It's equally clear that we have to do something." Ed folded his hands on the table in front of him. "Marjorie, it looks like the ball is in your court. This is your school. You've heard the arguments. What's your decision?''

The high school principal didn't hesitate. ''I think that I've made the only decision possible under the circumstances.'' She looked from Ed to Jason and continued. ''I will accept your son into this school as a freshman.'' She ignored the groan from the end of the table where Sean was seated. ''During the course of this school year we'll watch him closely. We'll see how he gets along with the other students and with members of the faculty. At the end of the school year we'll sit down again and see if another adjustment is in order.'' She gave Jason an apologetic look. ''I'm afraid that's the best I can do for him right now.''

''That seems completely fair to me, Mrs. Clauson.'' Jason smiled his thanks while Vernon Tibbs let out a relieved sigh. ''When should he begin class?''

Marjorie looked at her watch before answering. ''Why don't you bring him in tomorrow morning. Vernon, would you please send his records over from Puerta Grande? Ed, could you stop by my office this afternoon and we'll lay out some kind of a program for him?''

''Certainly.'' Both men answered together. Marjorie stood and extended her hand across the table to Jason.

''Mr. Jeffries, if you have any questions about Sean's progress, please feel free to call me. We're looking forward to having him at Highland Vista.''

Jason thanked her and shook hands with Vernon Tibbs before leading his son out of the conference room. A few minutes later he and Sean were walking across the high school parking lot toward the white Cadillac.

''It's not so terrible, Sean. It just means maybe you'll be fourteen before you're a famous brain surgeon.''

''Yeah but, Dad, a freshman?'' Sean said unhappily.

''One step at a time, son. That's the secret of getting by in this world. You're making progress. Just keep going one step at a time.''

Sean was momentarily distracted by an unpleasant sensation: Very faintly, he could feel that the dark Thing was back. It was almost an echo, floating with the boy as he walked beside his father, dim and only half heard, promising to come again. Sean climbed into the car and didn't say a word the entire way home.

From his vantage on the third floor, George Braun had a full view of the parking lot and the football field beyond. He had a ladder braced against the wall and had climbed down to retrieve a pair of wire cutters that had fallen from the top rung he was using as a shelf. As he started to climb back up the ladder he glanced out the window and saw Jeffries and his brat walking across the parking lot. He kept watching the pair until the Cadillac drove away.

His time was coming. Something told him it was.

"Whadya mean, a hundred bucks? I paid nine hundred dollars for this car." George glared at the dapper salesman leaning against the passenger door of the Hudson. "This car is in perfect condition."

"Mr. Braun, I have two cars on the lot right now that are four years newer and I'm selling them for three hundred each. I may have to spend more money just to have this thing hauled off. Nineteen-fifty Hudsons aren't selling these days."

Braun did some mental arithmetic and reluctantly gave in. "So, I can have the Ford for two hundred fifty, then?"

The salesman nodded and smiled.

"And I get a one-year warranty, right?"

"That's on the power train, Mr. Braun." The salesman nodded and smiled.

"Okay, write up the papers." George slowly counted out twelve twenty-dollar bills and one ten and placed them in the salesman's hand, accepting in return a small ring with two keys on it. Only after the salesman had a firm grip on the currency did he look at his pigeon and pretend to remember something.

"Oh, yes." The salesman shoved the wad of bills into

his pocket. "There is, of course, the charge for tax and license."

George didn't get to work until almost eight-thirty on Tuesday. The goddamn car wouldn't start when he left the house at six-thirty and it took him almost two hours to get a mechanic with a tow truck to give him a jump start. He maneuvered the black Ford sedan into a parking stall an hour and a half late and twenty-five dollars poorer. He was in a foul humor when he walked into the maintenance office and saw Tom Washington sorting through the work orders for the day.

"Whatcha doing, boy?"

"What does it look like I'm doing, boss man. I'm looking to see what needs fixing today." Washington grinned at Braun and held the stack of work orders out to him. "Sorry if I'm stepping on your toes, boss man. You didn't call to tell me you'd be late."

"Well, I'm here now. I'll take care of those." George grabbed the stack of requisitions from Washington and tossed them on his desk. "I assign jobs around here, Washington. Don't ever forget it." George glared angrily at the grinning black face in front of him and wondered to himself why the nigger always made him so uneasy. Every once in a while he got a feeling. He wasn't even sure what the feeling was. It was just a feeling.

"Hey, boss man, did you see a work order from Carruthers in Bio? I ran into him yesterday and he told me he sent one down."

"You saw what we got. Did you see one from Carruthers?" He gave the black man an indignant look. "You think I hide them someplace? You think I throw them away?"

"Nope. Just checking."

"Tell the old fairy to send another one down and we'll take care of his problem, whatever it is."

"No need, boss man. I took care of it already." Tom gave George one of his best "house-nigger" grins, and

Braun wondered if Washington was mocking him in some way.

"I told you not to call me that, boy. You don't watch your mouth, I'm gonna write you up for insubordination. What do you mean, you took care of it already?"

"It was just a broken window." Tom answered seriously, realizing he had pushed the old man as far as he could without creating some unnecessary problems for himself. "I put a new pane in yesterday afternoon."

"Goddamn it, Tom, we're not supposed to do a job without a chit. You know that."

"Hey, cool off. It took me all of thirty minutes. What's the big deal?"

"The big deal . . . listen, boy, I assign the jobs around here. You only do the work I give you to do—nothing else. And I don't do anything without a work order." Braun threw up his hands in disgust and strode around his desk to drop into the broken swivel chair. "Have Carruthers write up another chit and sign it off so I can turn it in. As long as you've been here you should know how we do things."

"Well, it still didn't take more than half an hour," Washington insisted. "I know, I know. From now on I won't do anything unless I have a requisition."

"You're damned right you won't." Braun sorted through the day's work orders for a moment and then looked up in annoyance at the man still standing in front of his desk. "You got anything to do?"

"Yeah. The Eagles play Pasadena on Friday. We got an assembly at two o'clock. I'm gonna have to set up the bleachers. Mr. Dolan's first period PE class is gonna help." He turned and started out, then remembered something and turned back. "You hear about the new kid?" Tom didn't usually share current events with his dour supervisor, but this news was too astonishing to keep to himself.

"What new kid?" Braun showed little interest as he continued sorting through the work orders on his desk.

"They got some little kid . . . nine . . . maybe ten years old gonna be starting here today. Seems the kid's some kind of a genius. Doc Taylor was talking to Carruthers about him and Carruthers told me. The kid's from Puerta Grande and he's supposed to be one of those child prodigies or something. He'll be taking bio from Carruthers."

George looked up and regarded his assistant intently. "He's starting today? That what you heard?"

"That's what Carruthers said."

"His name Jeffries, by any chance?" Braun asked. Tom hesitated. There was something hungry in the old man's expression.

"I don't know what the kid's name is. Carruthers just said some little kid would be starting school today." Tom wondered what Braun had heard. "That's all I know."

"Well, it ain't no skin off my nose." Braun turned his attention back to the papers on his desk. "Shake a leg, Washington. Go do some work."

Tom suddenly grinned as he remembered something else. "Hey, George?"

Braun looked up again and gave him a raised eyebrow.

"You give any thought to that little matter I asked you about yesterday? You know . . ." He rubbed his forefinger and thumb together in the universal sign for currency. "Do you think you're gonna be able to loan me a couple of thousand so's I can get that house I told you about?"

"Hell, no, I ain't loaning you no money. You don't get your ass to work you ain't gonna have a paycheck much longer." The old man glared at Washington, who grinned and delivered a mock salute. "Yes, suh, boss man." He was out the door before he could see George's reaction.

Smart-ass bastard. Braun fumed silently for a moment and then opened the drawer of his desk and took out Carruthers's work order. He ripped it into small pieces and dropped them into the wastebasket before turning his attention again to the pile of repair chits on his desk. He selected a handful to work on before lunch, then set the others aside.

So, Jeffries's kid was going to be coming to Highland Vista. How nice. The expression on Braun's face at that moment would have frightened even Tom Washington.

A few miles away on Las Flores Drive, Millie Braun was peering through the curtains of her bedroom window. From this spot she could see all the way to Canyon Drive in one direction and to Arroyo Place in the other. The street was deserted. She let the curtains fall together, her usually cheerful face marred by a troubled, unhappy frown. She had a feeling that something was terribly wrong but couldn't put her finger on the source of her distress. Part of it was Georgie, she decided. She hadn't seen the boy in almost a week. It always bothered her when the little rascal stayed out all night. She would talk to him when she saw him again. He was too young to be carrying on that way. She peered around the small bedroom looking for anything out of place, anything that might be causing her heart to flutter with such foreboding. Everything was as it should be. Charlie Cat slept in his accustomed spot on the pillow at the head of the bed. There was nothing untoward or out of the ordinary in the room. Millie wrung her hands together unconsciously and left the bedroom, closing the door behind her as she always did.

Maybe a cup of coffee would make her feel better. That might be it. A good strong cup of coffee with a little milk and sugar would fix her right up. Her face brightened at the thought. She busied herself putting water on to boil and taking down a cup and saucer. When the water was hot she poured it over the instant coffee she had measured into the cup and added some milk and sugar. She carried it into the living room and set it carefully on an end table before dropping heavily into the armchair and closing her eyes. Her head was hurting. She removed her glasses and rubbed her eyes wearily. Maybe that was it. She was going to have to get new glasses. The headache she was feeling had become a regular visitor like an overly friendly neighbor who was always dropping in for a chat. It was eyestrain, she decided. For the past several weeks her eyes had been playing tricks on her. Every once in a while she would be engaged in something quite ordinary, like fixing dinner or talking to Georgie or playing with the cat in her bedroom, and for an instant everything would look so . . . so different.

Millie raised the cup to her lips and tentatively kissed the edge. Mmmm. Still too hot to drink. She replaced the cup on the end table and looked up when she thought she heard something outside. She cocked her head to the side and some of the sparkle returned to her eyes. Georgie was out back. She could hear him. She put her glasses back on and went to the kitchen window overlooking the backyard. There he was, the little rascal. She watched him fondly through the window as he scrambled in the branches of the Chinese elm. Such a little monkey, that one. Millie's expression changed to one of disapproval as she saw someone else in the tree with her son. That girl was back. Millie didn't think of herself as a prude but certainly there were limits. She tried not to be an unreasonable mother and didn't believe in telling the boy who he could hang around with. Just last week she had seen a movie on Channel 3 about a mother who had done just this to her young son and the boy had grown up to hate her. Millie knew better than to hold the boy too tight. Still, that girl out there looked so . . . so shameless. Millie turned from the window and went to the back door. She opened it and called through the screen, "Georgie, you come in here." She could hear the boy laughing, but he didn't answer her. She opened the screen and stepped into the backyard.

"Georgie, you climb down from there and come in this house." She waited for an answer and when none came, she walked directly under the tree and looked up into the branches. "Georgie," she called sharply. "I'm talking to you."

The branches rustled softly as though moved by the wind

and Millie saw her son, his face framed in leaves smiling down at her. She tried to stay angry with him but it was no use. All she could think about was how glad she was to see her son as he dropped lightly to the ground beside her.

"I heard you calling me, Momma," he said.

She tried to look severe and failed. She never had been able to discipline the boy, even when he was a baby. George senior always had to do that. She supposed that's what fathers were for. Sometimes she had worried that her husband was too demanding. Sometimes she had even been afraid he would hurt the boy, but . . . look at what a fine young man Georgie had become. Millie's depression had lifted and her headache was gone as she spoke gently to her son.

"Tell your friend she's going to have to go home now. You have to come in the house."

"I can't leave yet, Mrs. Braun." The girl was standing next to Georgie.

Millie felt confused. She hadn't seen the girl climb down from the tree. It was her eyes again. She promised herself she would call this afternoon and make an appointment to have her glasses changed. Having made that resolve, she felt better and even managed to smile politely at Georgie's friend. The girl had a pleasant face and voice. Millie decided she liked her. If only she weren't dressed so . . . so . . . shamelessly.

"Well, Georgie has to come in now." She looked at her son who remained standing motionless next to the girl and some nameless dread formed in her heart. Her tone was pleading as she repeated to the girl, "Georgie has to come in the house now."

"I can't come in the house, Momma."

"What nonsense. Of course you can come in the house. You live here."

"No, Momma. I don't live in the house. I've never been in the house."

"Georgie, how can you say that?" Millie was weeping

as she struggled against something that was trying to rise to the surface of her mind, something monstrous, something better left buried and forgotten.

"It's true, Momma. I can't come in the house. Not yet. Daddy won't let me come in." The boy looked sadly at his mother.

"Well, that's ridiculous." Millie tried to smile at the boy through her tears. "I'll talk to your father. He'll let you come in. Please, Georgie. Come inside. I'll fix you a hot lunch. Your friend can come in, too. Please, Georgie."

"He wants to hurt you, Momma. He wants to hurt you the way he hurt Charlie. Go look at Charlie, Momma."

"Don't talk that way about your father, Georgie. Please, he loves us, Georgie. Please don't say those things."

"Go look at Charlie, Momma. Go see what he did to Charlie." The boy's voice was insistent. "I don't know if I can stop him, Momma."

The boy's outline shimmered and Millie tried to wipe the tears from her eyes. It didn't help. A voice inside whispered to her, a voice that was soft and accusing. There's nothing wrong with your eyes, it said. The voice gloated and taunted. Your son . . . your beautiful, tall, manly son is . . .

"NOOOOO." Millie screamed and tried to push the voice away, to beat it back down into whatever hell had spawned it. She clutched at the tree to keep from falling. Her eyes were closed tightly to block out the image of her beautiful child dissolving in front of her. It wasn't true. None of it was true. Georgie was . . . Georgie was. . . .

When she opened her eyes she was alone in the backyard. Her face, puffy and tearstained, gradually cleared as she turned her head slowly to search for her son. She could have sworn she had heard him playing out here, yet there was no sign of the boy.

With an exasperated sigh Millie turned back to the house. She was definitely going to have a word with her son when she saw him. .

She staggered and almost fell. Goodness, what was wrong with her? She raised her arm and put her wrist against her forehead. It was hot. Could she be coming down with something? Millie didn't know why she seemed to tire so easily lately. The simplest little things these days wore her out. Maybe she would take a little nap. That was what she needed. A little nap would make everything all right.

The woman made her way wearily past the back door and through the house to her bedroom. Moving carefully to avoid disturbing the sleeping cat, she climbed onto the bed and lay back against the pillow. It felt so good just to close her eyes and drift without care or worry to that wonderful place between sleep and wakefulness. She wouldn't go to sleep. She would just rest her eyes for a few minutes . . .

Seconds later, Millie Braun was fast asleep and dreaming happily of her gentle, loving husband and her strong, healthy son.

Life had been so good to her.

CHAPTER TEN

The Threat

"Is something bothering you, Sean?" Jason took his eyes from the road long enough to glance at his son, who was sitting in the front seat next to him. "You're so quiet."

"Everything's fine." The boy continued staring at the houses they were passing on Canyon Drive.

"How's school going?"

"Okay."

"Just okay?"

"Well, all but Latin." Sean turned away from the window and looked at his father. "I didn't like Latin the first time I took it."

"If it makes you feel any better, I hated it, too. You need to take it if you're going to get into college."

"I know. I don't have to like it though."

"That's true." They rode in silence for a while, then Jason tried again.

"What else are you taking besides Latin?"

Sean thought for a moment. "General science, French, beginning algebra, and"—he frowned and sorted through the textbooks on the seat next to him—"oh yeah, biology."

"That sounds like a full load. Are you finding it any more interesting than Puerta Grande?"

"Of course. Anything is better than learning how to read again." Sean began piling books on his lap as Highland Vista came into view a block ahead of them. "What you're really asking me is how *I'm* doing. Right?"

Jason looked at the boy quickly and didn't know whether

to be annoyed or amused. He pulled the car to the curb in front of the school and chuckled softly. "I guess that's what I'm asking. How are *you* doing?"

"I'm doing okay. It's even kind of fun." Sean watched his father closely as he answered and debated whether to mention the . . . Thing. He finally decided not to, mostly because he wasn't sure how to explain it. "You don't need to worry," he said instead.

"I'm glad, son." Jason stopped the car and leaned over to give the boy a kiss when something in Sean's expression stopped him.

"Uh, Dad?" Sean pulled away from his father and looked around quickly. "Would it be okay if we . . . do you think we could . . . well . . ."

Jason laughed as he understood what the boy was trying to say.

"Would you rather we shook hands?"

"It's just that someone might think I'm a baby or something." Sean was blushing furiously.

"I understand. Here." Jason extended his hand and Sean took it gratefully. "Have a good day. I'll see you tonight."

"See you." The boy climbed from the car and watched as his father pulled away from the curb and headed down the street. He wished he could have found a way to tell him about the Thing.

Sean had felt the oily presence of the Thing four times since he began attending the high school three weeks before. The feeling was always weak and never lasted more than a few seconds, as though it was a long way off and moving away from him. Nonetheless, the contact had frightened him and he had concentrated all his attention on keeping his mental guard clamped tightly until he could sense that the Thing was gone. Whatever the Thing was, Sean was certain, it wasn't human. He remembered Father John's words: "If you ever sense anything like that again, run as fast as you can in the other direction." Easy enough

to say. Sean's fear was that he would meet the Thing someplace and not have anywhere to run. If the Thing got hold
of his mind, Sean wasn't sure he'd ever be able to get rid
of it.

He looked around as he felt a more pleasant sensation
approaching. Lamar Johnson was one of only five black
students at the high school and he had been the first person
to say hello to Sean on his first day of class. The two boys
were in the same homeroom and both had biology for
third period with Mr. Carruthers.

"Hi, Lamar." Sean smiled at his new friend.

"Hi, Jeffries. What are you standing out here for?" The
older boy smiled back. "You waiting for a bus?"

"Just thinking about something."

Sean fell into step beside Lamar and the two boys entered the building.

Sean's arrival had not gone unnoticed. Tom Washington
had been raising the flag, one of his regular duties each
morning, when a white Cadillac had pulled to the curb
and the small boy had climbed out. Tom watched with
interest as Sean stood on the sidewalk looking lonely, or
scared, or both. He had seen him in the hall a few times
and found it incredible that someone that young could be
going to high school.

As the maintenance man watched, the boy was joined
by another student. Washington looked on approvingly as
Lamar Johnson joined the new boy and both of them
walked into the building. It was a good sign. Tom knew
Lamar Johnson's name as well as those of the other four
black students in the school. He also knew that they saw
the same graffiti on the walls that he did. It saddened him.
He was glad his own daughters went to an all-black school
in Pasadena. He tried to imagine his little girls, so beautiful and so trusting, confronted with "niggers go back
to Africa." The thought sickened him. It was bad enough
that adults were so quick to hate and destroy each other.

At least the children should be spared. The children shouldn't be forced to drink from the same cup of poison.

Tom had learned how to cope with the world the way it was, but he wanted something better for the children, for *their* future. White or black, his own or someone else's, it didn't matter. The children mattered.

Maybe the boy Tom had seen emerge from the big white Cadillac hadn't learned how to hate yet. Tom hoped that was it.

The burly maintenance man heard the bell ringing inside the building and realized he was still holding the flagpole rope in his hand. There was work to be done. Tom suddenly remembered something else he had heard about the new kid. It was funny the way rumors got started. Tom had been talking to a sophomore who had assured him in a hushed whisper that the little kid was able to read minds. The sixteen-year-old insisted that his little brother went to Puerta Grande and everyone at the grammar school knew about it. Tom hadn't believed it for a minute, but thought it might be fun to try to get Braun to swallow it. Tom Washington was smiling to himself as he gave the rope five quick wraps around the cleat on the flagpole and then started walking back toward the main doors of the high school.

Inside the school, Sean and Lamar were sitting next to each other in homeroom, listening to Mrs. Levine read an announcement about an upcoming meeting of the chess club. Sean listened with one ear while he riffled through the pages of his Latin book for his homework. It wasn't there. His agitation increased as he went through his other textbooks without finding the paper he had worked on painstakingly for an hour last night. He groaned as he realized he must have left it on the little desk in his bedroom. Latin was his first class. There wasn't time to do it again. Great.

"What did you lose?" Lamar whispered next to him.

"I must have left my homework at the house," Sean answered unhappily. "I can't find it."

"Tough luck." Lamar looked sympathetically at the younger boy. "Who do you have?"

"Mr. Martin. First period."

"I wish I could help but I've got Canti." He looked at the Latin book on Sean's desk and continued. "We don't even use the same book."

"That's okay. It's my own fault. Thanks anyway." Sean gave up the search and began stacking the books in a pile to carry to Mr. Martin's class. A moment later the bell rang announcing the end of homeroom, and Sean stood along with thirty-two other students and tried to load his books under his arm. It was a difficult job, but he finally managed. With some trepidation, he left to face Mr. Martin without homework.

Had he not been so preoccupied as he walked to class he would have sensed the approach sooner. He was turning a corner to get to the stairway when the Thing slammed into his head with the force of a locomotive.

George Braun stood in the doorway of the basement storage closet and tried to locate the projector. Mrs. Simmons wanted to show a film in her first-period history class, and George had been instructed to bring the projector to room 105 before the first-period bell. He was already late and he couldn't find the goddamned thing. He took two steps into the closet and something in the back caught his eye. There it was. George wrestled the big rag barrel out of the way and rolled the Bell & Howell from the back of the closet on its aluminum stand. He pushed it into the hallway and then turned out the light in the closet and closed and locked the door. He wheeled the projector to the elevator and pushed the call button. The car took forever to arrive as it always did when he was in a hurry. George was furious by the time the elevator doors opened. He shoved the projector into the car and slammed the button for the first floor. If goddamned Washington hadn't hidden the goddamned projector he would have had it in Mrs. Simmons's classroom on time. That was what he planned to tell Mrs. Simmons if she had any smart-ass remarks to make, goddamn it!

The car lurched to a stop and the doors opened. George pushed the projector ahead of him into the hallway on the first floor and made his way to the end of the corridor, steering the projector ahead of him on its stainless steel casters. He was about to turn the corner when Sean Jeffries suddenly appeared in front of him, almost bumping into the cart.

"Watch where you're going, kid," Braun snarled. He started to push the projector around the boy, only to stop abruptly and stare at Sean's look of shock and fear.

"What's the matter with you?" George asked in a surprised voice. The boy's mouth was opening and closing like some kinda goddamned fish. He had dropped his books and they were scattered on the floor in front of him. Braun was torn between confusion and amusement as the youngster pawed the air in front of him as though trying to push something away. He had backed into the wall and was gasping for breath.

"What did you do to him?" a voice behind him asked accusingly. George looked around and discovered a crowd of students had begun to gather.

"I ain't done nothin' to him," George said defensively. "The kid is a loony-tune. I didn't even say nothin' to him."

"You're a liar." The boy who had spoken earlier pointed at Sean, who was cringing against the wall in terror. "You did something or he wouldn't be acting like that."

George clenched his fists and turned to face the youth. The boy was both bigger than he was and more muscular. George relaxed slowly and promised himself he would remember that face. No one called George Braun a liar.

"I told you, I ain't done nothin' to the little bastard. The kid's crazy." He glared defiantly at his accuser, who looked uncertainly from Braun to the boy cowering against the wall.

The Thing filled his mind. It was too powerful to push away. Sean felt like he was drowning in a sea of writhing tentacles. It was reptilian and evil . . . and ancient. It was incredibly, unbelievably ancient. The boy didn't see George or the crowd that was gathering. All he was aware of was the presence that threatened to consume him. The Thing was a monstrous weight in his head that was pushing him deeper and deeper toward oblivion.

Sean's tongue was hanging from his mouth and he was panting like a dog as he struggled to get away from the presence that was burying him. From some far corner of his mind that still remained his own, a voice called out to him urgently, "If you ever sense anything like that again, run as fast as you can." Sean tried to make sense out of the words, but they seemed to be in a foreign language. "Run, Sean. Run as fast as you can." Again the warning voice, weaker now. Sean felt himself slipping closer to the abyss that yawned hungrily, waiting for him.

"Run . . . Run, Sean. Run!"

For the briefest moment the fog seemed to clear and the boy was looking down a dark tube at a tiny spot of light that offered salvation. If only he could reach it. With a strangled cry, the boy staggered toward the light, forcing his unwilling limbs to move and carry him closer and closer to the end of the tube. With each step, his head seemed to clear a little more; the monstrous weight that was burying him became lighter. Sean could hear human voices behind him. His legs were moving faster. A door loomed in front of him, and he pushed it open and stumbled through the emergency fire exit and out of the building. The presence was outside his head now, sniffing and circling. Sean could feel the Thing's anger and frustration. He commanded his trembling legs to move faster. He didn't stop until the school was almost a mile behind him.

* * *

George Braun entered the maintenance office, dropped into the swivel chair, and tried to make sense out of the scene he had just witnessed. He was so distracted that it took several minutes for him to notice Tom Washington sitting at the small work table in the corner, eating his sandwich.

"It ain't lunchtime. What are you doing in here?" The words that should have come out challenging and angry came out almost conversational.

Washington raised the hand that held a partially eaten ham and cheese sandwich and pointed to the clock hanging behind Braun's desk on the wall.

"Break time," he answered simply.

George looked behind him and confirmed that it was nine-thirty. He turned back to his desk and ignored Washington as he tried to reconstruct everything that happened from the moment he first saw the Jeffries kid until the crazy brat went out the fire exit. He'd be asked questions. He wanted to have his answers ready.

"Hey, boss man, you seen a ghost or something? You look awful."

"Ain't no concern of yours, Washington. You just tend to your business and I'll tend to mine, okay?"

"Just askin'. Don't be so touchy." The younger man grinned without sympathy at his supervisor and remembered the rumor he had heard about the new kid. He hesitated, almost deciding it was too ridiculous to mention, when Braun suddenly leaned forward and spoke in a pleasant voice.

"You hear any more from Carruthers about that new kid?"

The coincidence startled Washington. He looked at Braun curiously. "Why you so interested in the kid?"

"I ain't interested." Braun looked away from Washington before contradicting himself. "I was wondering. That's all."

"As a matter of fact, I did hear something else but it's too crazy to believe." Tom put the remainder of his sandwich back in the brown sack and put the bag on the shelf next to his toolbox. He pretended to have forgotten the question and turned as though heading out the door to go back to work.

"What did you hear?" Again Tom was surprised by the eagerness in Braun's voice. He turned back to the desk and faced the old man.

"Well, it's just a rumor. I wonder how these crazy stories get started. One of the kids told me his brother goes to Puerta Grande, you know?" He waited for a response and George nodded impatiently. "It seems everyone at the grammar school believes the little kid can read minds. Can you beat that?" Tom laughed to show his disdain for anyone foolish enough to believe such a story while he watched Braun closely for a reaction. "Pretty crazy, huh?"

"Yeah." Braun laughed and Tom had an odd feeling the laughter was forced. "That's pretty crazy." The old man stood up and went to the file cabinet. "Yeah. It sure is crazy," he mumbled to himself. He opened a drawer in the cabinet, peered inside, and then closed it without taking anything out. He seemed distracted and Tom's curiosity grew. When Braun glanced at him again, he looked surprised to see Washington still in the office.

"Get to work, boy. You don't get paid to stand around in here," he said.

"Sure, George." Tom was so intrigued by the old man's reaction he forgot to be flippant. He turned and left the office.

George didn't have long to ponder this latest bit of news. No sooner had Washington closed the door behind him than the phone in the maintenance office began ringing. George picked up the receiver and mumbled into it. He paled and said something, then hung up. It was time to answer questions.

"If you didn't do anything to him, then what did happen?" Marjorie Clauson's angry tone made it clear to George that she didn't believe in his innocence.

the morning you're supposed to stay here until classes
over. If you feel sick again I want you to go to the
ool nurse or one of your teachers. Is that clear?''
''Yes, ma'am.'' Sean struggled to adjust the books un-
r his arm and at a nod from Mrs. Clauson, scurried from
e room with almost comic haste.

The principal continued to sit, looking thoughtfully at
spot halfway up the wall across from her desk, wonder-
g if she would ever know what happened. One thing was
rtain: She was going to be keeping a close eye on George
raun from now on. There was something about the man
at she really didn't like.

She placed the folder that held the academic records and
st results of Sean Jeffries into her outgoing basket to be
filed by her secretary, and turned her attention to other
atters.

Sean kept his guard firmly in place all afternoon, but
hen the three o'clock bell rang he left the building with-
t having sensed the Thing anywhere in the building. As
walked through the double doors of the school and
wn the steps, he saw his mom's Buick parked at the curb
d broke into a run.

One reason Sean was spared another meeting with his
mesis was that George Braun remained sitting at his
k for the rest of the day. He was still seething when
three o'clock bell rang and the building began to empty
students and faculty. To be called a liar twice in one
was almost more than he could stand. To be insulted
not be able to do anything about it was even worse.
d it was all that brat's fault. Tom Washington came in
office several times during the afternoon to get work
rs or tools from his tool kit, but very wisely said noth-
and never stayed more than a minute or two. At four
ock Tom went home and George began locking the
rs of the building. When he had completed his final
of the day he went to the time clock and punched out.

''I keep telling you, I don't know what happened,'' he
insisted. ''I was walking down the hall, see. I had the
projector for Simm—Mrs. Simmons. This kid comes barg-
ing around the corner and has some kind of a fit. I didn't
do nothin'. Anybody says I did is a liar.''

Mrs. Clauson's eyes never left Braun's face as she waited
for him to continue, and the maintenance man fidgeted
nervously. ''Ain't no more I can tell you. I didn't do anything.'' George began to feel angry at the unfairness of
his situation. The bitch had no right to jump on him. He
almost wished he had smacked the kid. If he'd known he
was going to be blamed anyway . . .

''That will be all, Braun.'' The principal dismissed him
and George heard the scorn in her voice. Only the knowledge that he'd lose his job kept him from coming around
the desk and teaching her a thing or two about respect.
Nobody talked to George Braun that way and got away
with it. As he turned to leave the office he added a new
name to the list of those who would someday pay a heavy
price for trying to push George around. He had almost
reached the door when Mrs. Clauson spoke again.

''One more thing, Braun.''

George halted but didn't turn.

''The most serious accusation that can be leveled against
one of our employees is the charge of physically mistreat-
ing a student at this school.''

''I'm telling you, I didn't do anythin','' George shot
back angrily.

''I hope that's true.'' Mrs. Clauson's expression told
him that she didn't believe it was. ''I just want you to
know that I intend to investigate the matter and find out
exactly what happened. If I learn that someone at Highland Vista is responsible for injuring one of my students,
that person will be looking for another job within the hour
and possibly facing criminal charges as well. You understand that, don't you?''

George was so mad he couldn't answer. His ears were

a brilliant shade of red as he turned back to the door and stormed out of the office.

Sean's footsteps slowed and then stopped. He looked around and considered his options. His head was clear now; the Thing was long gone.

He didn't want to go home. How could he explain what happened? He could see himself now, telling his mother about the monster at school that was trying to eat him. Even Father John would have trouble believing this one. Besides, it was his own fault. If he hadn't been thinking about his forgotten Latin homework, he would have kept his guard up and the Thing couldn't have gotten into his mind. The boy shook his head sadly and wondered if his life was going to be a long series of disasters, one after another. That's the way it had been ever since the accident. Why couldn't he go to school, become rich and famous, and live happily ever after the way they did in stories? Was that so terribly much to ask? He had to go back. There was no other way. Whatever the Thing was that prowled the halls of Highland Vista, it wasn't going to chase him off. Already the boy was beginning to feel ashamed of running away. He'd have to think of a way to explain leaving school and skipping his first-period class. He'd get in trouble about that. It couldn't be helped. He would try to stay out of the Thing's way, but he was going back.

Some of Sean's newly-found courage left him as he began retracing his steps. He remembered the way it felt to have the Thing inside his head and stopped in his tracks. What if he wasn't strong enough to keep the Thing out? He almost decided to go home and take his chances with his parents, but he remembered Father John's admonition: " 'What if' leaves you either unhappy about something that might have happened and didn't or fearful of something that could happen but won't. That isn't the way you want to live.''

It wasn't the way Sean wanted to live. He forced himself

not to think about the Thing as he started wa toward Highland Vista and his second period

"You say you felt sick?" Mrs. Clauson ask
"That's right. I felt kind of dizzy and so I j around for a while.'' Sean looked earnestly a school principal and tried to put conviction into He could tell she didn't believe him.

"How were you sick? Were you just dizzy have an upset stomach or what?'' Her voice wa

"Just dizzy. I feel fine now.'' The boy glance at the pile of books on her desk that he recogni own, recovered from the hallway floor. "Could now?''

Mrs. Clauson sighed and wished someone her what was going on.

"Do you get sick like this very often?''
"No, ma'am.''
"Did anyone do anything to you? Did any you?''
"No, ma'am.''
"Are you afraid of anything? Are you afraid what happened?''
"No, ma'am. Nothing happened except that and went outside to walk around. That's all.''

Marjorie Clauson didn't believe a word of didn't think he was going to tell her any more already told her. She gestured toward the bo stacked on a corner of her desk, and Sean k angry.

"Take your books and go back to class. W this later.'' She watched as the boy reached and knew they probably wouldn't talk about ever was bothering the youngster wasn't som willing to talk about. She couldn't shake t he was frightened.

"Before you leave, I want you to unde can't come and go as you please. When yo

He was still muttering angrily to himself as he strode across the parking lot to the black Ford. His mood did not improve when he turned his key in the ignition and nothing happened. It was forty-five minutes later before the tow truck arrived to give him another jump start.

"So, tell me about your day," Marilyn prompted.

"What do you want to know?"

"Did you have fun?" She pulled around a station wagon that was angled into the curb and waved to the young mother behind the wheel. "What did you do all day?"

"It was okay."

"What did you do?"

"I did school stuff. What do you think?" Sean glanced at his mother and then was sorry he snapped at her. "Nothing much happened that's worth talking about."

"You know, Sean, sometimes it's very hard to talk to you." She looked at the boy, then turned her eyes back to the road and drove the rest of the way home in silence.

It was three A.M. and the house on Las Flores was dark. A bread truck lumbered past on its way to a supermarket with a load of cakes, pies, pastries, and breads for the shoppers who would want them later in the day. A dog barked at the sound of the truck and another dog a block away joined in.

Inside the house everyone slept. Millie's sleep was deep and dreamless. Her husband in the other room tossed fitfully and muttered aloud as dreams and images chased each other through his head. Something was nagging him in his sleep, something he had seen, or heard, something he had overlooked. Braun rolled onto his back and opened his eyes. He stared at the ceiling in the dark room and tried to remember the dream that woke him up. There had been a warning in the dream. He gave up finally and turned on his side, trying to go back to sleep. The alarm wouldn't go off for another three-and-a-half hours. He wondered sleepily if the car would start. The thought jolted him to full wakefulness. He opened his eyes again and fumed silently at the misfortunes that were always being thrust on him. If he was late for work, Tom Washington would pick over the day's requisitions and take the easy ones before George even had a chance to see them. Goddamned nigger with his smart mouth and mocking air. He was going to get to work on time one way or the other. If the goddamned car wouldn't start, he'd walk. This decision made, George settled back against the pillow and closed his eyes again.

Another thought came to him just as sleep was about to claim him. Something Washington had said about the kid . . .

With a strangled gasp, George sat bolt upright in bed as his heart pounded in his chest. Washington had said the kid could read minds. That was impossible.

Or was it?

How else could he explain the reaction when the brat almost bumped into him in the hallway? How else could he explain the fear he had seen all over the kid's face, the terror when he had run out the fire exit. That had to be the answer. The kid could see into his head.

George felt as though a hole were opening up under his feet. The kid *KNEW WHAT HE'D DONE*!

Had the brat told anybody yet? He felt sweat beginning to form on his forehead and wiped it away with trembling fingers. Even if he had told somebody, how would he prove it? George felt his panic subside. Nobody could prove anything. That's what mattered.

Or could they?

George got out of bed and went into the kitchen, where he put on a pot of water for coffee. There would be no more sleep for him tonight. He had to figure out what to do. He had been so busy thinking about his run-in with the Clauson bitch that he had forgotten all about Washington's news. Well, he remembered it now. He was going to have to do something about it—but what?

By the time George finished his fourth cup of coffee it

was five-thirty and the sky was beginning to brighten. He put his cup into the sink and returned to the bedroom, where he dressed slowly.

He was going to have to kill the brat.

George was climbing into the Ford by six o'clock. It was important to get to school before anyone else. He held his breath as he turned the key and felt perversely irritated when the car started smoothly and immediately. He let the engine idle for a minute, then shifted into reverse and backed out of the driveway. A few minutes later he was turning into the deserted staff parking lot at Highland Vista.

The problem was how to do it. It was too risky to do anything there at school. He would have to snatch the kid and take him somewhere else. That meant finding the boy alone and keeping him quiet, or unconscious, long enough to get him into the car and away from the school. He had to do all this without arousing any suspicions. When the brat disappeared, people were going to remember yesterday's episode in the hall. That was okay. Let them remember. He hadn't done a thing. All the same, he couldn't afford to have anything else connect him with the boy in people's minds. He needed a plan.

George unlocked the front doors with his master key and let himself in the building. He made his way down the hall to the administration office and opened that door with the same key. The sun had climbed above the horizon and the room was bright enough to see without turning on any lights. The maintenance man went to the file cabinets that occupied the entire south wall. He cursed when he realized they were locked. He didn't have a key for the file cabinets. He went through each of the desks, being careful to put everything back in place before searching the next one. He came up empty-handed. George began to perspire as he looked at the clock and saw that ten minutes had already passed. He looked around the telephone switchboard and then searched the desks a second time. Still no key.

The goddamn key had to be somewhere. He leaned against the counter that separated the office workers from students during the day and tried to think. If he didn't get into the file his job was going to be a lot harder. Maybe even impossible.

The answer was so obvious, George kicked himself for not thinking of it sooner. Clauson had to have a key. He walked across the room and unlocked the door of the principal's office with his master key.

There were two file cabinets in her office, but George ignored these and went directly to her desk and tried the drawer.

It was locked.

Braun snarled furiously under his breath and sat down in the principal's chair. He had to think. The key had to be here. He needed to remain calm. George closed his eyes and placed his head against the headrest. He sat that way for several minutes before lifting his head and looking at the oak clock hanging on the wall. It was six-thirty. Time was running out. Washington would be punching in at seven. He wouldn't have any reason to come up here, but if he saw George's car he might wonder why Braun wasn't in the maintenance office. He might even start looking for him. It wouldn't do to be found in here, going through desks or file cabinets. If he didn't find the key soon he wouldn't have time to use it anyway.

George got to his feet and was about to leave the office when his eye fell on a stack of folders in a basket on Mrs. Clauson's desk. He lifted the pile and began looking through them without expecting to find anything of much interest. He almost cried out with joy when the file he was looking for proved to be in the middle of the stack.

While Braun was sitting behind Mrs. Clauson's desk, rapidly copying Sean Jeffries's class schedule into a small notebook, Tom Washington was leaving his house for another day at Highland Vista. He was tired. Thursdays were always hard. He was taking evening classes at Cal State on Wednesday nights and he never got home before ten-thirty. He yawned sleepily as he opened the garage door. In spite of the difficult schedule it was going to be worth it. One more semester and he'd have his B.A. He didn't plan on being a janitor for the rest of his life.

Tom started his car and smiled as he wondered if Braun would be able to start the Ford. Life had a way of evening things out. He completely approved of any bad luck that might go Braun's way. The old bastard deserved it.

There were better things to think about. The morning air was pleasant and the sun was shining. Despite his sleepiness, Tom felt good. Estelle had remained in bed this morning; she was still going through the morning sickness phase. Tom secretly hoped this one would be a boy. Little girls were beautiful and Tom loved his daughters, but every man wants a son to carry on his name.

His mood was buoyant when he got to the school. He took his usual parking spot and noticed that Braun was already here. He walked over to the Ford and smiled when he saw the old fool had left his window open again. Just one more bright spot in what promised to be a fine day. Tom reached through the window on the driver's side and turned on the Ford's headlights, just like he had done for three mornings in a row.

Yes, sir, it was going to be a great day.

Sean's ride to school in the morning with Jason was as quiet as the ride home with his mom the previous afternoon. Jason tried a couple of times to draw the boy out and finally swung the car over to the curb and parked. Sean looked at him in surprise.

"Okay, son, let's stop playing games. What's bothering you?"

"Why do you think something's bothering me?" the boy asked evasively.

"Come on, Sean. Don't insult my intelligence. You've been moping around for days. Your mother and I are lucky

if we can get a civil word out of you. I thought you promised to come and talk to us if you had a problem."

"It's not anything you can help me with," Sean said
finally.

"Why not let me be the judge of that? Is it school?"

"Not exactly."

"Well, what then?" Jason pressed.

Sean turned away from his father and stared out the
window uncomfortably.

"There's something . . . something at school. I don't
know what it is. I ran into it a couple of times. It's . . ."
The boy's voice trailed off.

"Are you talking about some*thing* or some*one*?"

"I—I'm not sure." The boy turned back and faced his
father. "Dad, will you do me a favor, please?"

"What's that?"

"Will you let me work this out by myself? Please? I
know it's hard to accept but . . . I have to do this myself."

"Nonsense. You're eight years old. You don't have to
work anything out by yourself. That's why your mother
and I are here."

"You know that's not true." Sean looked at his father
sadly. "I used to be eight years old. Now I don't know
what I am."

"It wouldn't matter if you were eighty. Taking care of
you is still our job, your mother's and mine. Why not let
us help?"

"There isn't anything you can do." Sean's face was
troubled as he tried to find a way to explain the Thing to
his father. "Do you remember when we went to the high
school the first time?"

"The time we went with Ed and we talked to Mrs.
Clauson?"

"Yeah."

"Yes, I remember."

"When we went in the school we walked right past the
Thing and you didn't even know it was there." The boy

turned back to the window as if the matter were settled. "I'm the only one who can feel it."

"What is it? This . . . this thing?"

"I don't know."

"But you're afraid of it?"

This time the boy took longer to answer.

"I don't know."

Neither spoke for a moment and then Jason restarted the car. His concern was mingled with irritation as he glanced over at the boy. "I'm certainly glad we had this informative discussion, son," he said sarcastically.

"Don't you see, Dad? That's why I didn't come to you before. I don't know how to describe it. I don't know what it is. Just trust me for a little while."

Jason didn't answer and they were both quiet for the rest of the ride. The car was idling next to the curb in front of Highland Vista before Sean made a last attempt to get his father to understand.

"I'm not trying to be a problem."

"Then talk to me. What's going on?"

"Please give me just a little more time. Let me try to handle it by myself and if I can't I promise to tell you about it," Sean pleaded.

"How much time is a little?" Jason asked.

"Give me a week. Just one week, okay?"

Jason shook his head and surrendered.

"One week, that's all. If we don't have our happy, good-natured child back in seven days, you'll let us try to resolve this thing for you . . . whatever it is. Is that what you're saying?"

Sean nodded.

"Well, if that's the best you can do I guess it will have to be enough." The lawyer smiled at his son without humor and put out his hand. "Shake on it."

"Thanks, Dad." Sean took his father's hand and then started to open the door.

"Sean."

"Yeah?" The boy looked back.

"One week. That's all."

"One week. I promise."

As his father disappeared around the corner the young boy standing on the sidewalk in front of the high school felt more alone than he ever had in his life.

When Tom Washington got to the maintenance office, George was sitting behind the desk looking through a small notebook. He slipped the book into his desk drawer as the black man came into the room, and Tom was astounded to see a cheerful smile on his face.

"How long you worked here, boy?"

"About five years, now, I guess. Why?"

"You should know enough about how we work to be able to sort these." George tossed the day's requisitions, neatly paper-clipped together, to his surprised assistant. "I gotta take care of something in the basement today."

Washington was too surprised to answer. The old man guarded the work orders with the zeal of a jealous lover. It was a mark of his office and status.

"You okay, George?"

"I'm fine. I just think it's time you took a little responsibility. Something wrong with that?"

"I'm surprised, that's all."

"If you don't think you can do it, give them back and I'll go through them." Braun's smile turned into a sneer as he held out his hand for the requisitions.

"I'll do it. No problem, George." Something was wrong. Tom didn't know what Braun was up to, but he had worked with the bastard too long not to smell a rat when George let go of one of his status symbols.

"Leave anything you can't handle on my desk and I'll take care of it." As if the old man felt that further explanation was called for he added, "Clauson wants me to do something for her first thing this morning." He took the notebook he had been looking at when Tom walked in and shoved it into his baggy coverall pocket. "Sit back here if you want." He pointed to his swivel chair and Tom's mouth dropped open. Two symbols relinquished on the same day.

"You gonna stand there gaping like a fish or you gonna get to work?" George stepped from around the desk and scowled.

"I'll take care of everything. Go ahead and do whatever you have to do." Tom moved to the chair Braun had just vacated and sat down behind the desk. Braun looked at him and Tom thought he saw an expression of resentment flicker across his face, then it passed and George smiled. The smile looked out of place. George never smiled. Tom was even more certain the old fool had something up his sleeve. But what?

"I'll be checking back." Braun turned and walked from the office, leaving a very perplexed Tom Washington to organize the day's activities.

George went quickly to the basement and began his preparations. A plan had begun to form. He was pleased with the way he had handled his assistant. Tom was so impressed with being in charge he wouldn't be wondering what George was up to. Letting him sit in the chair was a brilliant move. Let him get his rocks off pretending to be boss. It was only for one day. Tomorrow things would be back to normal.

Almost back to normal. Tomorrow Highland Vista would be short one troublesome little brat.

In the maintenance office Tom sorted quickly through the requisitions and pulled several to take care of right away. It was Thursday so he'd have to start the lawn this afternoon. None of the work orders were urgent or marked for priority treatment. That meant Tom had only one priority facing him. He was going to find out what George Braun was up to.

CHAPTER ELEVEN

The Attack

The five-minute warning bell was ringing by the time Sean got to his locker and found the envelope taped to the door. He ripped it open and read the memo from the guidance office. "Meet me in Room 131 at sixth period to talk about yesterday." Ed Taylor's name was typed below the one-line instruction. Sean refolded the paper and stuffed it into his pocket. The one thing he didn't want to talk about was yesterday. The psychologist wouldn't be put off as easily as Mrs. Clauson had been. The boy's face was gloomy as he made his way to his homeroom.

George Braun took a folded canvas laundry bag from the supply closet and shook it open. He held it up in front of him and estimated it would be big enough. He refolded the bag and placed it on the table next to the two lengths of clothesline he had already cut.

Room 131 was an excellent choice. It was used in the morning but was empty all afternoon. It was at the end of a corridor and right next to a fire exit that opened into the parking lot. On the other side of the classroom was a girls' rest room and then a language lab that would also be empty at that hour. If the brat made any noise it wasn't likely that anyone would hear him.

He still needed a way to keep him quiet until he got him out of the building and into the car. George walked across the basement to the cage where plumbing supplies were kept and unlocked the door. He selected an eight-inch riser from a box of miscellaneous sprinkler parts and slipped it into his pocket. This just might be easier than he had thought.

Tom Washington had just finished mopping the floor of the locker room in the gym when the bell rang to announce lunch. He dumped the dirty water into a utility sink and shoved the empty bucket against the wall with the mop in it. He left the gym and strode down the hallway on his way to the maintenance office. He glanced down an intersecting hallway and saw Braun working on a door handle at the end of the corridor. His curiosity aroused, Tom continued walking until he was past the intersection and then stopped and retraced his steps. Very cautiously, he peered around the corner and watched the old man remove the handle from the door. His curiosity increased as he saw George turn the handle around and begin attaching it again. He chewed his lower lip thoughtfully, then continued walking to the maintenance office. The old man didn't do any work during lunch hours. By the time the last echoes of the lunch bell died away, he was usually halfway across the parking lot to his car. Why would he be working five minutes after the bell? And why was he reversing the knobs on the doors? That didn't make sense.

The doors of the classrooms locked automatically when they closed, but fire laws required them to be unlocked from the inside. Unless he was mistaken, George was installing them backward. That meant anyone could walk in whether the door was closed or not. Once inside, if they didn't have a key, they wouldn't get back out again. That didn't make any sense at all.

One-thirty arrived much too quickly for Sean. Twenty-five minutes from now when the sixth-period bell sounded he was going to have to go to 131 to face Dr. Taylor. He still had no idea what he would say. *If only everyone would leave him alone.*

Sean had worried about the upcoming interview from the moment he read the memo from the guidance office.

The only good thing that happened all day was that something didn't happen. The Thing hadn't come near him.
Sean had kept his mental shield in place since getting out
of the Cadillac this morning, but there was no sign of the
monster. The boy decided to be grateful for that. He'd
figure out something to tell Dr. Taylor when the time came
. . . or he'd just tell him that he couldn't tell him anything.
Maybe he'd understand.

The boy reached into his pocket and took out the folded
piece of paper. He opened it and reread the single line.
The written word conveys so little information. He won-
dered if Ed was angry or curious or just doing his job.
Maybe Mrs. Clauson told the psychologist to talk to him.
She hadn't believed his story about feeling sick.

Sean looked at the clock again. One-forty. Fifteen more
minutes. He folded the memo and slipped it between the
pages of his algebra book, then, with an effort, he forced
his attention back to the blackboard and solving quadratic
equations by completing the square.

Braun stood in the doorway of the empty cafeteria and
looked up and down the hall. He could see the corridor
that Sean would have to go down to get to his "interview." It was almost time. The canvas bag and the rope
were stashed under one of the desks in 131. He could feel
the tingle of anticipation and fear that always came to him
at times like this. Before long the dangerous part would
be over and the threat of exposure gone forever. Just like
his unsuspecting victim sitting upstairs in Mr. Fremont's
algebra class, Braun found himself looking at the clock
every few minutes, and he concentrated on relaxing. In
just a few more minutes it would be finished. George
couldn't help feeling a certain glow of pride at the clev-
erness of his plan. It was so simple, so foolproof. The
beauty of the whole thing was that he would also be settling a score with that smart-ass lawyer. How much more
could he ask? Two birds with one stone. Braun's usually
sour expression was replaced by a wide grin that threat-

ened to split his face in two. Nobody pushed old George
around. He knew how to get even.

When the bell rang, Sean had already gathered his books
together and was one of the first to rise. There was no use
postponing it. Doctor Taylor would either understand or
he wouldn't. In either case, Sean couldn't tell him about
the Thing. He left the classroom feeling almost relieved
that the waiting was over.

From his vantage at the entrance to the cafeteria, George
watched the halls fill with students hurrying to their sixth-
period classes. No more than two minutes after the bell
he saw the small blond boy turn the corner and start down
the hall toward 131. He waited another minute before
starting after him. By the time he rounded the corner,
there was no sign of the kid. He cackled happily to himself
and walked more slowly, savoring the moment.

Sean reached the classroom at the end of the hall and
was mildly surprised to find both doors closed. He tried
the knob and hesitated when it turned easily and the door
opened. That wasn't right. Sean tried to identify what
seemed out of place, the odd, ''What's wrong with this
picture'' sensation. After a moment the feeling passed and
the boy entered the room and took a seat at a desk in the
front row to wait for Ed Taylor. Behind him the door swung
closed with a firm *cachunk.*

Doctor Taylor was his friend. Maybe he should try to
tell the psychologist about the Thing. Sean knew that he
needed an ally. There had to be someone he could tell
who would believe him and not think he had gone off the
deep end. The boy almost decided to share his secret until
he tried to imagine how he would describe the experience.
He didn't know what it was or why it seemed so predatory.
His heart sank as he heard the doorknob turning and realized there was no way he could talk about the monster
that haunted him.

"Hi, Doctor Taylor. I . . ." The smile of greeting that appeared on his face as he turned his head to the door faltered and disappeared. The boy froze in terror as he came face-to-face with the Thing.

Braun allowed the door to swing closed behind him and stood facing Sean. He could smell the terror radiating from the boy. He felt powerful and in control as he leaned casually against the wall, determined to extract every bit of enjoyment possible from what he was about to do.

"So we meet again, huh, kid?"

Sean felt the Thing hammering at his barrier and it took all of his attention and energy to keep his shield in place. His voice came out in a shaky whisper. "Who are you?"

George laughed. "You know who I am, kid. I'm a friend of your father's. But you already know a lot more than that." The maintenance man took a step forward and sneered at the terrified boy. "Don't you?"

"Leave me alone."

George laughed again. "You and me got something to talk about, kid. You don't mind talking to old George, do you? That wouldn't be very friendly after all the trouble I've gone to setting up this little get-together?" He took three more steps in the boy's direction and was rewarded by the sight of tears running down the boy's cheeks.

"I've never done anything to you. Go away and leave me alone." The kid's voice was so hoarse that George barely understood him. Too bad he couldn't drag this out a little longer, but any minute the kid might start screaming. No point in taking any unnecessary chances. Almost with regret, George reached into his pocket and withdrew the steel riser. He raised it above his head as he took the last four steps to the side of the trembling youngster.

It was all Sean could do to keep the Thing out of his head. It circled and gnawed at him in a frenzy of hate, powerful and ravenous. He didn't realize until the last minute that the attack would be physical as well as mental.

The threat from this new quarter distracted him for a fraction of a second. It was enough. Sean barely had time to feel the Thing lunge into his mind and wrap its tentacles around him before the steel pipe crashed into the side of his head.

Braun looked at the body on the floor with disgust. The damned kid was bleeding like a stuck hog. He hurried to the other side of the room and took the laundry bag from its hiding place. He returned and pulled it over the boy's head before tying the boy's hands and feet securely with the two lengths of clothesline. He pulled a rag from his coveralls and used it to gag the boy. Better to be safe. The kid was probably going to be dead before he got him to the car, but there was no point in taking any chances. When the boy was finally trussed and gagged, George pulled the canvas bag over the rest of his body and managed to get it closed. He tried lifting the bag and staggered under the weight. Damn kid was heavy. He set it down and looked around the room. He'd have to do something about the blood. That was stupid. He should have known the kid would bleed all over everything. Kiss a rat's ass, why couldn't anything go right? George opened the door with his key and peered cautiously around the corner. The hallway was deserted. He stepped through the door and realized as it closed behind him that there was a drawback to having the handles reversed. Anyone could walk in and discover the bag . . . and the blood. Well, he'd have to take that chance. He walked purposefully to the end of the hall and turned right. Fortunately there was a utility closet next to the cafeteria. Braun could feel his heartbeat slowing to normal as he opened the door of the closet and filled a bucket with water. He dropped a brush and a couple of rags into the water and then rolled the whole thing into the corridor.

While George cleaned room 131, Tom Washington was on the third floor, talking to Mr. Carruthers. The portly biology teacher was showing a film on DNA to his sixth-period class, and after watching it four times that day was thankful to have something else to do. They stood in the hall with the door of the biology lab propped open behind them. The voice of the narrator could be heard describing the process of heterozygosis, and the two men spoke in hushed tones.

"I still don't think I've gotten used to it." The teacher was talking about the newest addition to his class. "I've heard about kids like that before but I never thought I'd be teaching one. Just talking to him is an experience. He's a tiny adult."

Tom nodded and changed the subject. "Speaking of strange, I saw something today that has to take the prize for unusual. This afternoon, right after the lunch bell, I'm walking back to the office to get something to eat and I see the old man. He doesn't see me and I watch him for a few minutes. The bastard's not only working during lunch, he's also turning the doorknobs around in 131 so's they open from the outside. That make any sense to you?"

The teacher thought about the question. "You've got to be mistaken. The doors have to open from the inside. It's the law."

"I'm telling you what I saw," Tom said.

"They must have been backwards to start with. Maybe he was turning them around the right way."

"If they were backwards I think we would've heard about it before now. This is the fifth week of the semester."

"That is strange." Carruthers looked into the darkened lab at the thirty-five freshmen watching the film with varying degrees of interest. The movie still had at least fifteen minutes to run. He turned back to the maintenance man and gestured in the direction of the stairs. "Let's go take a look. You want to?"

"Sure. You got time?"

"Plenty. Let's see what's up," Carruthers said. He began walking to the stairway and Tom followed. The maintenance man would have wondered at Carruthers's interest, but he had a good idea what the teacher was thinking. Braun and Carruthers had had frequent run-ins over the years, and the feud between them was common knowledge at Highland Vista. Tom was sure the teacher would tell Clauson if he found out Braun had knowingly violated the fire laws. Washington smiled to himself. This day kept getting better.

"You're right, Tom." Carruthers held the door of 131 open and looked into the room. "That's exactly what he did but damned if I can think of any reason." Carruthers saw something inside and said to Tom, "Hold this door for me. Somebody forgot his books."

"Just pull the desk over here. We'll prop it open." Tom wanted to see if anything in the room would explain Braun's unusual behavior. He held the door while Carruthers dragged the desk over and propped it in the door-. way. The two men entered the classroom. Everything looked normal. Tom hadn't expected to find anything but still felt disappointed that there wasn't something in the room they could use against the old man. As Carruthers picked up the textbooks from the front desk, Tom walked over to the window. Something moved in the parking lot and he suddenly called to the teacher excitedly.

"Hey, Pete, come here a minute."

"What is it?"

"Come here quick. Take a look."

Carruthers hurried to the window and looked where Washington was pointing. George Braun was struggling across the parking lot with a laundry sack over his shoulder. While the two men watched, the old man opened the trunk of his car and heaved his burden inside before slamming it closed and walking back slowly toward the school.

"Bingo." Tom clapped his friend on the shoulder. "I told you the old bastard was up to something. What do you want to bet he didn't want anyone to see him put that sack in his car? What do you think?"

"I'll be damned." Carruthers breathed softly. "You think he's stealing something?"

"What else? That didn't look like his lunch he was carrying. Let's get out of here before he comes back."

Carruthers nodded and the two men turned away from the window. Tom held the door open while Carruthers slid the desk back in its place. As they walked up the stairs to the third floor, the teacher tried to think of some way to use what they had seen. It would be easier if he knew exactly what they *had* seen. Braun had reversed the doorknobs of a classroom on the first floor and had carried a bag of . . . of something and stashed it in the trunk of his car. Should they go to Clauson? As much as the teacher hated to admit it, there could well be an innocent explanation for Braun's actions.

"Hey, Pete, I don't know if we should say anything about this yet or not."

Carruthers gave Tom a startled look.

"For Chrissake, why not? If the bastard's ripping us off let's hang him out to dry."

"I just think we ought to know more before we say anything."

"Tom, since when have you two been friends? You know damn well you'd love to see him thrown out on his ass. Why did you show me the doorknob if you didn't want me to do something about it?"

Washington knew a moment of self-loathing and wouldn't meet the teacher's gaze.

"Look, it's easy enough for you. If we go to Clauson and it turns out to be something innocent, you come back to your classroom and that's the end of it. It's not so simple for me. I have to work for him. I just want to be sure of what we have before we say anything."

That possibility had occurred to Carruthers also. He could understand Tom's reluctance although he didn't share it. If they accused him of something and it proved groundless, the racist had a hundred different ways he could retaliate. With two kids and a third on the way, Tom wasn't in any position to risk losing his job. The teacher nodded slowly. "What do you think we should do, then?"

Washington sighed. "Nothing right now. Let me keep an eye on him, I guess. If he's up to something I'll know about it pretty soon. Let me get some hard evidence and I'll go to Clauson with you."

"I don't know, Tom." Carruthers frowned. "I think we have a responsibility to the school. Look, I can tell Clauson about the laundry bag without involving you. I'll just say I was alone when I saw him through the window."

Washington shook his head unhappily.

"No, that wouldn't be right. If you're going to say something then I should be there, too. Otherwise it's just your word against his." He looked at the teacher for the first time since they had climbed the stairs and was ashamed of his fears. "If you want to bring it to Mrs. Clauson, I'll go with you."

"I think we should. Don't you?"

"I suppose so." Tom grinned ruefully. "I can always find another job, I guess."

"I think it will be someone else in the unemployment line. Don't worry. I have another class after this. Let's plan on seeing her tomorrow morning. I have an open period at ten. Meet me up here and we'll go down together. Okay?"

"Okay, Pete."

There were still five minutes left to the film when they reached the lab. The two men talked briefly and then Tom excused himself and headed for the storage shed behind the school. He still had the lawn to mow.

Braun reentered the building through the back doors just as the sixth-period bell rang to mark the end of the school day. He threaded his way through the stream of teenagers who were pouring out of classrooms on both sides of the hallway. He was lightheaded with the glow of success as he made his way back to 131. He had the kid and nobody had seen a thing. He got to the end of the corridor and opened the door, expecting to see the kid's books where he had left them fifteen minutes before. They were gone. His heart skipped a beat as he stepped into the room and let the door close behind him. He checked the floor under the desks. The books had disappeared. George told himself to stay calm as he thought about the implications. Okay, somebody came in and picked up the books. That didn't change anything. No one could connect him with the kid just because a few textbooks showed up in a deserted classroom. He had still pulled it off. Some of his initial panic drained away and he remembered the next thing he had to do. Taking a screwdriver from his overalls he began removing the doorknob.

Marilyn drummed her fingers on the steering wheel and began to get annoyed. Sean was usually one of the first to leave the building. It was almost twenty minutes after three and there was no sign of him yet. He could have come out and told her if he was going to be delayed. Marilyn wasn't happy with some of the changes she was observing in her son. She would give him five more minutes and then she was going in after him.

So much had changed in such a short time. What do you do with a young son who thinks he knows more than you do? How do you cope with a boy like that when you know he might be right? Where was the line between loving concern and overprotection? Marilyn wasn't sure. It was hard to let go but even harder to be pushed away. She didn't ask him about school anymore. He didn't want to talk about school. He didn't seem to want to talk about anything anymore. Since he began attending Highland Vista her son had become an eight-year-old recluse. When they got home in the afternoon, Sean went directly to his room and studied until dinnertime. After dinner he watched TV until bedtime and the next morning the whole routine began all over again. He seemed depressed and preoccupied much of the time, but when she tried to talk to him he either denied that anything was wrong or refused to say anything at all. He was as stubborn as his father.

Marilyn was torn between concern for her son and resentment of his attitude. Today, as she sat in the hot car waiting for the boy to emerge from the high school, resentment outweighed concern.

She looked at the clock on the dashboard. Three-thirty. She wasn't going to wait any longer. With an angry shake of her head Marilyn got out of the Buick and locked the car. She was going to have a talk with that boy about courtesy. And he'd better have a good reason for not being in front half an hour earlier. She began climbing the stairs to the front doors of the school. Her patience was exhausted.

"If he was in the building I'm sure he would have heard the page." The young woman behind the counter in the administration office looked at Marilyn and tried to decide what to do next. "Could he have walked home with one of his friends?"

Marilyn shook her head. Her son could be inconsiderate but he wouldn't deliberately leave her waiting at Highland Vista while he walked home. "No, he's got to be here somewhere."

"Let me check with his homeroom teacher." The girl went to the row of file cabinets against the wall and opened one of the drawers. Her fingers walked through the folders until she found the one she wanted. She pulled it out and brought it to the counter, where she opened it in front of Marilyn.

"He has Mrs. Levine for homeroom. Let me page her and see if she can tell us anything."

They were waiting for Mrs. Levine to arrive when a portly, middle-aged man came in and approached the secretary.

"Janice, you'd better hang on to these." He handed a stack of textbooks across the counter to the girl. "Somebody's going to be looking for them. I found them in one of the classrooms."

"Thank you, Mr. Carruthers." Janice took the books from the teacher, who smiled pleasantly at Marilyn before leaving the office. The girl put the books on a long shelf in the back of the room. As she returned to Marilyn the door opened again and a severe-looking woman in her thirties came in and approached the counter.

"Did you call me, Janice?"

"Yes, I did, Mrs. Levine. This is Mrs. Jeffries. Sean Jeffries's mother." She nodded in Marilyn's direction. "Sean was supposed to meet her out front and he hasn't shown up yet. I thought you might have some idea where he might be."

"Mrs. Jeffries"—the teacher held out her hand—"I'm Mrs. Levine." They shook hands and the teacher's face was less severe-looking when she smiled at Marilyn. "You can't find Sean?"

"That's right. He always meets me out front after school. Today he didn't show up. I was hoping you might have some idea where he is."

"As a matter of fact, your son didn't come back to homeroom this afternoon. We always take attendance in the morning and afternoon to be sure our kids don't leave in the middle of the day. Sean wasn't there."

"That can't be." A tiny fear began to stir inside Marilyn. "He wouldn't leave without saying something to somebody. He knew I'd be here to pick him up."

"Janice, get Mrs. Clauson, please." The homeroom teacher nodded in the direction of the principal's office, then gave Marilyn a reassuring look. "Don't worry, Mrs. Jeffries. This happens all the time. He probably took off with one of his friends."

"I can't believe he would leave when he knew I was coming to pick him up. That's not like Sean." Marilyn could tell that Mrs. Levine didn't share her belief. She was beginning to feel like a character in an early fifties horror movie who knows something is wrong but is unable to convince anybody else. She was about to insist again that Sean was somewhere in the building when they were interrupted by the arrival of a well-dressed woman with an air of authority.

"Mrs. Jeffries, I'm Marjorie Clauson. Could I talk to you in my office for a moment?"

"Do you really think that's necessary? I just want to find my son."

"This won't take long. Something happened yesterday that you should know about. It may even shed some light on where to look for your boy now."

Marilyn hesitated then allowed the principal to lead her through the swinging gates and into the office in the back of the administration department.

"Sit down, won't you?" Mrs. Clauson indicated a comfortable-looking chair in front of her desk.

Marilyn shook her head and remained standing. "If you don't mind, I just want to know where my son is. If there's something you want to talk to me about perhaps we could take it up some other time, after I find Sean."

"I understand your concern, Mrs. Jeffries," the principal replied gently. "I think you ought to know that we've been having a little trouble keeping Sean in school."

"What do you mean?"

"Yesterday he left the building and didn't show up for his first- or second-period classes."

"I can't believe it," Marilyn said. She took the chair she had refused earlier and looked at Mrs. Clauson with surprise. "Where did he go?"

"When I talked to him about it he said he just walked around."

"Why would he do something like that?"

"I was hoping you might be able to tell me."

"Didn't you ask him why he left the school?"

"Of course I did. He said he felt sick and went out to get some fresh air."

"You say that like you don't believe he was telling the truth."

"He may have been sick but I think there was more to it. I had a feeling that something frightened him. I've been working with children for a long time. I can recognize a very scared youngster when I see one."

"I don't know what to say. Sean didn't mention any kind of problem." Marilyn didn't add that he hardly ever talked about anything since Highland Vista. "Did he give you any clue at all? Did he say anything else that made you think he was afraid?"

"Not directly, but there were witnesses—several other students and the maintenance man. Your son appeared to be terrified of something. He seemed to have an attack of some kind, almost a seizure." Marjorie Clauson tried to phrase her next question as tactfully as she could. "Mrs. Jeffries, does your son have any medical or—or perhaps emotional problems we should know about?"

Marilyn felt the room closing in around her and tried to conceal her dismay from Mrs. Clauson.

"Certainly not. Sean is a perfectly normal boy. I have no idea what could be wrong."

"Mrs. Jeffries, I don't mean this in a disparaging way, but your son is most certainly not a normal boy. One look at his aptitude test scores will show you that. Is it possible that—"

There was a knock and the door opened. It was the secretary, who cast a worried look at Marilyn before speaking.

"Mrs. Clauson, may I see you out here for a second?"

Marjorie Clauson gave the girl an irritated look and turned back to Marilyn. "Would you excuse me for a moment? I'll be right back." She stepped out of the office and Marilyn could hear the murmur of voices through the open door. When Mrs. Clauson returned she had a slip of paper in her hand and a strange look on her face.

"Janice has some books outside that were left in an empty classroom."

"I was here when one of the teachers brought them in." Marilyn wondered why they were talking about lost textbooks.

"She was going through them to see if she could find out who they belong to. They're Sean's."

Marilyn felt the icy hand of fear grip her heart. She stared numbly at the principal of Highland Vista.

"There's more." Mrs. Clauson held the slip of paper out to Marilyn, who took it with trembling fingers.

"It's a note from the head of our counseling office to Sean. The only thing wrong is that Doctor Taylor doesn't come to the high school on Thursdays. He spends all day at Puerta Grande."

Marilyn tried to understand what Mrs. Clauson was telling her but the principal wasn't making any sense. Something about Ed's not coming to the high school today. Of course he came to the high school if he had an appointment with Sean.

"Mrs. Jeffries, are you okay?" Marilyn hadn't noticed when Mrs. Clauson came around the desk to stand next to her with a look of concern on her face.

"Yes, I'm okay. I'm sorry. Did Sean see Ed this afternoon?"

"I assume Sean went to the appointment. He wasn't in his sixth-period class." Mrs. Clauson paused and seemed to be having trouble finding the words to continue. She and her husband lived next door to Stan and Meg Frascotti, and her mind kept returning to a mangled body in the Angeles Forest that looked like it had been torn apart by a monstrous animal. She prayed silently that the anxious mother next to her wouldn't notice something in her face or expression and remember a newspaper headline from two months before.

"Well, Doctor Taylor must know where Sean is. Can't you telephone him at the grammar school and see if Sean got a ride home with him?"

"Mrs. Jeffries, we've already done that. When Janice discovered the note and knew we were trying to find your son, she called Doctor Taylor at Puerta Grande before she came in here. He didn't write that note. No one from our counseling office wrote that note."

"But . . . what does that mean? What are you saying?"

Marjorie Clauson looked at the fearful woman sitting in

her office and wished she didn't have to speak the words
out loud, but her voice was steady as she lifted the telephone and paused with the receiver halfway to her ear.

"I'm afraid it means that it's time to call the police,"
she said.

It was four o'clock. Braun paced back and forth in the
maintenance office. Where was Washington? Any other
day he would have been down here thirty minutes earlier,
signing off the paperwork for the day and cleaning up to
go home. George never left the building until everyone
was gone without saying something to Washington. This
was the wrong time to do anything unusual, anything out
of the ordinary that someone might remember later and
mention to the police. Braun couldn't leave until he was
sure Washington would stay late and lock the building after everyone else went home.

There was still a lot to do. He was going to have to
dispose of the body somehow. He had already decided to
drive out to the desert and burn it. He had to be careful.
This wasn't like some bimbo or faggot in Hollywood that
nobody cared about anyway. It wasn't like the surfer two
months ago. This was too close to home. The brat went
to Highland Vista. Even worse, there was that episode
yesterday, still fresh in everyone's mind.

He was going to be a lot safer if the body was never
found, but there was no way to guarantee that. He hadn't
expected anyone to find the Frascotti bastard and forty-
eight hours later the kid was on the front page of the paper. At least he could make sure they would never be able
to identify the body. It was a lot of trouble but it had to
be done. There was a five-gallon can of gasoline in the
garage at home. That ought to be enough to do the job. If
anyone found the pieces and managed to fit them all back
together, it still wouldn't tell them anything.

Braun fumed impatiently and looked at his watch. It
was two minutes after four, a minute and a half later than

the last time he had looked at it. Where was that god-damned Washington?

Jason was having a bad day. A client file was spread across his desk; he had to be ready for court in the morning and he couldn't concentrate. His mind kept returning to this morning's conversation with Sean. For the third time he tried to force his attention back to the volume in front of him.

"The major underlying principle applying to a judicial foreclosure is that the surplus represents the remnant of the equity of redemption available to valid liens vacated by such foreclosure."

He shouldn't have let Sean go to school. He should have forced the boy to share the problem, whatever it was. He WASN'T an adult. Regardless of what he knew, what he thought he remembered, he was a little boy.

The lawyer sighed and tried again.

"The major underlying principle applying to . . ."

The buzz of the intercom seemed unnaturally loud. He jabbed the call button, unable to keep the irritation from his voice. "Yes, Margaret."

"I'm sorry, Jason. It's Marilyn on the phone. She says it's an emergency."

"Thank you." Jason released the button and picked up the telephone. "Hi, sweetheart. Listen, I'm up to my neck here. What's up?" There was no change in the lawyer's expression as he listened to his wife, but his hand on the receiver tightened until the knuckles were white. "Okay, here's what I want you to do. Call Linda. Tell her to go to our house and make sure he hasn't come back. Stay where you are and wait for me. I'll be there in fifteen minutes. Has anyone called the police?" There was a pause and then he nodded into the telephone. "Good. Wait for me there, okay? I'm leaving right now."

It took all of Jason's self-control to keep his face impassive as he left his office and told Margaret he would be gone for the rest of the day. The effort was wasted. His secretary knew him too well to not recognize the fear in his eyes.

Millie Braun finished putting the folded towels away and shut the closet door. She hurried back to the ironing board that was set up in front of the TV to avoid missing the end of *The Price Is Right*. It was her favorite program although she never tried to guess any of the prices. George bought everything they needed and Millie had no idea what things cost anymore. She watched the game show religiously because she thought Bill Cullen was the cutest man she had ever seen.

She was too late. The credits were already scrolling up the screen when she came into the living room. She watched for a minute, relishing the ease with which she could read the names with her new glasses. Everything was so clear and sharp. She should have had her eyes checked a long time ago. That must have been why she had been having those terrible headaches.

Millie reached over to the TV and turned the selector to Channel 3. It was time for Jack Bailey to turn some lucky woman into a "queen for a day." Millie liked to imagine herself sitting in front of the TV cameras, dressed in mink and wearing a crown as she graciously accepted the gifts and prizes Jack Bailey gave away every weekday at four o'clock. She almost always watched *Queen for a Day* before turning the set off and beginning dinner.

Millie took one of George's shirts from the laundry basket and stretched it over the ironing board. She was reaching for the iron when she thought she heard a noise in the backyard. She stood motionless with the iron in her hand, listening, but the volume on the TV was too high for her to be sure if there was something out there or not. She carefully replaced the hot iron on its little metal plate on the end of the board and turned the volume down. Yes, she definitely heard someone. There it was again. Georgie was calling her. She could hear him clearly now.

Millie wiped her hands absently on her apron and went

to the kitchen. Her son was standing at the foot of the three steps leading up to the back door as she opened the screen and stood in the doorway.

"Land sakes, boy, what do you want? I've got to finish ironing and get dinner started." She smiled affectionately at Georgie even as she scolded him.

"Momma, it's going to be soon now. Please help me."

"What are you talking about, Georgie? What's going to be soon? I don't have time to play with you right now. Come in the house and get cleaned up. We're having a nice dinner tonight and I want you to eat with us for a change."

"I can't come in the house, Momma. Not yet. Soon. I'll come in tonight. We'll all come in tonight."

"What do you mean?" Millie looked at her boy's unsmiling face and felt a chill. "Who's coming in?"

"All of us, Momma. We're not going to let him hurt you. All of us will be here, but you have to help, Momma. Please help us," the boy pleaded.

Millie peered closely at her son. What was wrong with him? Where did he get the crazy ideas he came up with? She started to laugh but something in Georgie's face stopped her. He was upset about . . . about what? Millie didn't know, but this was no time for laughter.

"How can I help, Georgie?"

"You have to tell us we can come in the house. Please, Momma. May we come in?" There was an urgent note in Georgie's voice.

"What a question." Millie relaxed and she laughed again—a thin, nervous sound that lacked humor. "Of course you can come in the house. This is your house, too."

"Can all of us come in, Momma?" Georgie pressed.

Millie hesitated and then consented. "I don't know who you're talking about but if it's that important to you then go ahead and bring your friends over. Your father and I won't mind."

"We can *all* come in the house, Momma?" Georgie repeated his question.

"You can all come in the house, okay? Now get cleaned up and . . . get cleaned up . . ."

Millie looked around the empty backyard and could see nothing. She must have imagined the noise out here. She closed the back door and returned to the living room and picked up the iron. She would have to hurry now. It was almost time to begin fixing supper.

CHAPTER TWELVE

The Last Day

Braun's distress was evident when Tom Washington finally walked into the office at four forty-five.

"Where the hell have you been?" He snarled.

"It's Thursday, in case you forgot. We do the lawn on Thursdays." He spoke without his usual bantering tone. To his surprise, George seemed not to notice.

"I want you to stay and lock up tonight. I got an appointment at five and I got to get out of here."

"Sure, George. Take off." Washington moved to the workbench and began signing off work orders with his back to Braun, who looked at him curiously.

"Something wrong with you?"

For once, Tom didn't feel like putting up with his shit. "If you've got to leave, then get going. Ain't nothing wrong with me. I'm not in the mood for a hassle, okay?" Washington continued going through the requisitions spread in front of him.

Braun's eyes narrowed. He swallowed the angry retort that sprang to his lips before it could escape. He had more important things to do today. Tomorrow he would have a little talk with Washington about respect.

"Just you be sure all the lights are out and everything is locked up before you leave, understand?"

"Of course I do. You going to leave or not?" Washington said. There was no response from George. Tom signed off the last of the chits and gathered them together before speaking softly. "What was in the bag,

George?'' When the old man still didn't reply, Tom looked up.

The office was empty. Braun had already left.

It began to seem to George that Lady Luck had abandoned him. His first surprise came when he turned the key in the Ford and nothing happened. The urge to scream in frustration and outrage was almost overpowering.

He had to remain calm. This was only a minor setback. It wasn't a disaster. He would call the tow truck and get a jump start. By now he had the phone number memorized.

His second shock came just moments later when he walked up to the administration counter to use the telephone and saw the two cops standing in Mrs. Clauson's office. What the hell were they doing here? George pretended to look for a phone number in his wallet as he strained to hear what they were saying, but he was too far away and their voices were pitched too low for him to make out words. When he couldn't stall any longer he stuffed his wallet in his pocket and picked up the telephone on the counter. The girl at the switchboard gave him a questioning look and he nodded to her for an outside line. Any hope he might have had of learning why the police were there vanished when the principal's door was closed by someone he couldn't see. He listened to the phone ringing at the garage and fumed impatiently. It seemed to take forever before someone finally answered. He explained what he needed and gave the address to the dispatcher at Westside Tow & Body Shop, then hung up and left the office in a state of extreme agitation.

Tom climbed the stairs to the third floor shortly before five-thirty and began securing the building. He moved down the main hall, trying doors and checking the rest rooms to be sure they were empty. When he reached the electrical panel next to the stairs, he opened it and switched off all but the emergency lights before descending to the next level. He made another careful circuit of

the second floor and then turned off those lights as well.
There was no one on the upper two floors. He wasn't
expecting to find anyone on the first floor either and was
surprised when he entered the front office and saw Marjorie Clauson talking to a man and woman he didn't recognize.

"Excuse me. I didn't know anybody was still working.
I'll come back later."

"That's okay, Mr. Washington. Go ahead and leave if
you want to. I'm going to be here a few more minutes. I
can lock up when I finish," Mrs. Clauson said.

Washington nodded. He thought of Braun's peculiar behavior and frowned. Maybe running into the principal was
a stroke of good fortune. Perhaps if he could talk to her
unofficially . . . maybe she would understand the awkward
position he was in. It might be just the kind of insurance
he needed in case Braun's actions had an explanation and
the bastard decided to make things rough for him.

"Any chance I might talk to you for a minute?" He
regretted the question almost immediately when the woman
sighed and shook her head impatiently.

"Tom, I'm pretty busy right now. If it's not important
could you come by my office tomorrow during the day?"
For the first time the maintenance man noticed how worn
and tired she looked.

"That's okay, it can wait. I'll be leaving then unless
you need something."

"Good night, Mr. Washington."

"Good night, Mrs. Clauson." He left the administration office and locked the rest of the doors on the ground
floor before letting himself out of the building and heading
across the parking lot. It was probably just as well he
hadn't been able to say anything. Carruthers was right. It
would be better to wait until they could go to her together.

He was almost at his car when he spotted the tow truck
parked in front of Braun's Ford. The sight warmed his
heart and as he drove out of the parking lot he was humming cheerfully.

* * *

It was a quarter to six before George was able to leave the high school. As he drove past the front of the building he saw something that made his blood run cold. Jason Jeffries was leaving the high school with Mrs. Clauson and another woman. How could they have missed the brat so soon? Braun's worst fears were confirmed. That's why the police had been there. Kiss a rat's ass. He had expected the police to be poking around and asking questions, but not until tomorrow. Why were they involved already?

This was no time to get rattled. Braun thought back over each detail of the afternoon. He hadn't made any mistakes. He hadn't slipped up. There was absolutely nothing that would connect him in anyone's mind with the kid in his trunk.

Unless the kid had blabbed already. Unless the kid had already shot off his mouth to somebody.

That was impossible. If anyone suspected him of anything he would have known by now.

Another thought came to him and he gripped the steering wheel tighter. What started as a suspicion seemed more and more likely. What if none of it was true? What if the little bastard didn't know anything? He was driving around with the body of a kid in the trunk of his car; the police were already snooping around, and he had done it all because Washington told him the brat could read minds. Worse than being suckered, he had suckered himself.

The more he thought about it, the more convinced he became. George felt ridiculous. How could he have been crazy enough to believe anything that damn nigger said? It wasn't as if he didn't know about colored people. They were superstitious. You could take the shine out of Africa but you never got Africa out of the shine.

That put everything in a new light. If the kid didn't know anything then he couldn't have said anything. That meant that George was home free. What was he worrying about? Braun laughed savagely as he turned into the driveway of his house on Las Flores and got out of the car to open the garage door. It was in the bag. He chuckled at his own pun, then remembered the boy's reaction in the hallway yesterday afternoon. His amusement vanished and suddenly the fear was back, black and threatening. The kid had looked at him and something had terrified him. He practically had a fit right there in the hall. What could that mean except . . . except . . .

George parked in the garage and closed the door from the inside before opening the trunk and lifting out the canvas sack. He carried it to the front of the garage and dropped it on the floor. The sweat that bathed him wasn't entirely due to the temperature or his exertions. He crossed the garage and heaved the red five-gallon gas can. Wouldn't you know it? The can was empty. Another hitch. One more thing gone wrong. Maybe he should just bury the kid in his backyard and be done with it.

He had to calm down. He had to think. Okay, so he would have to buy gas. He'd go out after supper and fill the car and the gas can. Everything was still all right. This was no time to do anything stupid. He would stick with the original plan. In spite of his jitters, he felt the familiar tingle of anticipation and a stirring in his groin. When he finished he would burn what was left. Nothing else was going to go wrong. He was on the homestretch.

George leaned against the car and took a deep breath. There wasn't anything to worry about. He was jumping at phantoms. Tomorrow he would be safe—the kid would be dead, and everything would be back to normal. He took another deep breath and began to feel a little better. When his trembling stopped he opened the garage door and then locked it behind him. The kid was probably dead but there was no point in taking any chances. He stood for a moment in the driveway, mentally reviewing everything he had done, looking for any detail or oversight that might put him at risk. He couldn't think of anything, and some of his former confidence began to return. Everything was going according to plan. After one last look behind him

to be sure the padlock on the garage was snapped shut,
George entered his house through the front door to have
dinner.

"It looks like we're going to have to find him by our-
selves," Jason said as he stood with Marilyn in front of
the high school. "Take the Buick and work your way east
on Jackson. Go down about a mile or so and then start
doubling back on Eureka. Drive up and down the side
streets. He's probably walking on the sidewalk, but check
all the driveways and side yards. I'll go west in the Cadillac and do the same thing between here and Canyon
Drive. Is Linda watching for him at the house?"

"She promised me she would stay by our phone until
we got back."

"Good. If you find him, go to the closest pay phone
and call the house. If you don't find him, call anyway
about six o'clock. I'll do the same thing. If we don't have
any luck by seven, we'll meet at the house and I'll try the
police again."

"Jason, he didn't just wander off. Something's happened to him. I can feel it. What are we going to do?"
There was an edge of hysteria in Marilyn's voice.

"I just told you what we're going to do." He spoke
sharply and Marilyn reacted as if she had been slapped.
Jason continued in a more gentle tone. "Don't fall apart
on me now, honey. I need you too much and Sean needs
you. Okay?"

Marilyn nodded.

"We're going to find him. Just keep believing that.
We're going to find him and before the night is over he's
going to be sleeping in his own bed at home."

Marilyn nodded again and walked around to the driver's
side of the Buick. Jason watched her start the car and pull
slowly away from the curb to head east on Jackson Street.
He was going to have to tell her about the conversation in
the car this morning on the way to school. Sean had been
afraid of someone or something at Highland Vista. He

should have demanded that his son tell him the whole story this morning. He should have refused to allow Sean to return to school until the boy told him exactly what was frightening him. Now it was too late.

Jason pushed the thought out of his mind. It wasn't too late. They were going to find the boy and before the night was over Sean would be sleeping in his own bed.

Millie Braun scraped her husband's plate over the garbage bag and shook her head sadly. The dear man had hardly touched his dinner. Now he was off taking care of some errand or other. He worked so hard to provide a good home. She worried about him when he didn't eat properly.

Millie looked up and peered anxiously around the room. She couldn't shake the curious feeling that someone was watching her. Since early this afternoon she had been haunted by an uncomfortable sense of another presence in the house but, except for Charlie Cat, she had been alone all day. Even Georgie had remained absent, no doubt playing with his friends somewhere. The kitchen was empty. Millie shivered before turning back to the supper dishes. She filled the sink with warm, soapy water and put the plates in to soak before picking up the big carving knife from the counter. She had cooked a ham for dinner and most of it remained uneaten. She would slice it up and put it in the refrigerator. It would make good sandwiches for George when he came home for lunch next week. She was humming as she carved out the bone and cut the meat into thick slabs. She stacked the ham slices on a plate and covered them with wax paper before setting the knife aside and turning back to the dishes. Suddenly, she heard Georgie's soft voice behind her. It startled her and the plate she was holding fell and smashed as she whirled around in panic.

"Oh, my Lord, don't ever sneak up on me that way." Millie clutched her chest and scowled angrily at her son. "You scared me to death." She pointed an accusing finger at the broken plate. "Look what you made me do. If you're here for dinner, you're too late. You know what time we eat. You'll just have to go hungry tonight." Millie regarded the boy sternly. She would fix him a snack after the dishes were done, but she wasn't about to tell him that. Not yet. Let the little scalawag think he had missed out. It served him right for scaring her that way.

"It's time, Momma." Georgie stood in front of his mother. "We're all here now. You have to help us."

"What are you talking about, Georgie? It's time for what?" Millie gave her son a perplexed look. "Who's here?"

"In the garage, Momma. Go look."

"I don't have time for foolishness. I've got to get these dishes cleaned up. Go watch some television while I finish up in here." She could never stay mad at the boy for long and added quickly, "If you're real good then I'll fix you a ham sandwich when I'm done, okay?"

Georgie made no move to obey. Millie frowned and started to walk around him to get the broom and dustpan to pick up the broken pieces on the floor. She stopped when he clutched her arm and spoke in a low, urgent voice.

"You have to look in the garage, Momma."

"What's in the garage, Georgie? What do you want me to see?" She began drying her hands on her apron and her mouth trembled as something clammy and terrifying gripped her heart for absolutely no reason. "I don't want to go out there, Georgie. What do you want me to see? Just tell me."

"You have to go to the garage, Momma," Georgie insisted, and Millie heard the sadness in his voice. She closed her eyes and struggled with the dread that filled her.

When she opened her eyes Georgie was gone and she was alone again. She moved with uncertain steps to the drawer where they kept the key to the back door of the garage. Strange pictures formed and vanished in her brain as she picked up the key and moved slowly to the screen door and then out into the backyard. She gasped as her mind suddenly filled with the image of a boy hanging from a ceiling joist in a tiny apartment somewhere . . . somewhere. It was so real. She could see the body turning as the breeze caressed it. Now she could see the face, puffed and swollen, the mouth working soundlessly, trying to form words, trying to speak to her. Oh, my God! No! *NO!* It was Georgie.

Millie fell to her knees on the gravel path. She uttered little choking cries and her eyes bulged as arms and legs pushed against the pebbles and stones in a macabre imitation of a swimmer fighting to remain afloat in a deadly riptide.

"I'm in the garage, Momma. You've got to help me." The dead boy raised his head and Millie's eyes, those brilliant gray-blue eyes that were her most impressive feature, became dead and vacant as the abused, disfigured face of her son smiled with loving sadness at her, driving away the last remaining vestige of her sanity.

George was ten miles away, driving west on Broadway and looking for a gas station. He passed a Standard and two Shells without slowing. The brand was unimportant. It was the station itself that mattered.

He should have waited longer before leaving the house. Most people were home eating dinner or settling back for an evening of television and relaxation. This wasn't a time when service stations did a peak business. If it were an hour earlier or an hour later . . .

The station he was looking for appeared suddenly on his right. It was a Texaco with two islands and at least four cars lined up waiting for the one beleaguered attendant to fill them with gasoline. A hastily scrawled sign announcing "GAS WAR" was propped next to the curb. George turned into the lot and rolled to a gentle stop to wait his turn. The pump jockey was so busy he would never be able to remember filling a five-gallon gas can and a black Ford sedan for a thin, middle-aged man with gray hair. Braun turned the engine off and a thin-lipped smile of pleasure twisted his face.

* * *

Officer Phil D'Angelo ignored the urge to light a cigarette as he glanced at the notes he had taken. He looked back at Jason and shook his head.

"Mr. Jeffries, this isn't much to go on. Sean told you there was something at the school he didn't want to talk to you about. What are we supposed to do with that?"

"Or someone."

"Did he say it was a person or a thing?"

"I don't know. I mean, he didn't say. But he was frightened."

"Yes, sir. I'll pass it on but you're really not telling us anything that's going to do us much good. We're doing all we can, believe me."

"I'm telling you our son didn't run away. I'm having a lot of trouble understanding why the police are doing so little to help us find him. What do we have to do before you people will take this seriously?"

D'Angelo understood the lawyer's anger and wondered if his own reaction would be the same if their positions were reversed.

"Sir, we *are* taking it seriously. We have officers contacting all the names you gave us at the high school. A Frequency Two was broadcast just after five o'clock. All the units in the area have your son's description. If he's on the street someone is going to spot him and pick him up. According to the report you gave us this afternoon, this wouldn't be the first time he's wandered away. The policy of the Sheriff's Department—"

"I know about your policy. I also know that Sean didn't wander off. Something's happened to him and we need help."

"Yes, sir. You didn't let me finish. I was going to say, the policy of the Sheriff's Department ordinarily is to wait twenty-four hours and see if the child comes home on his own. Believe me, in most cases that's exactly what happens—"

"But Sean—"

"Please. Let me finish." D'Angelo hesitated, knowing that any reference to the Frascotti boy would alarm the attorney more than reassure him. "Our policy for the past several months has been to involve the detectives immediately whenever any child is reported missing in this area. Wait and see if one of our guys picks him up tonight. Nine times out of ten these kids come back home on their own."

Jeffries's look combined pain and apology. "I'm sorry, Officer. I just feel so powerless. Isn't there something we could be doing? I mean, instead of just waiting here."

"We're doing everything that can be done." The young cop shook his head sadly, realizing Jeffries knew full well why every missing-child report in Highland Vista was treated seriously.

The lawyer turned briefly to his wife, who was standing behind him, and then faced D'Angelo again. "If you don't mind, my wife and I will spend the rest of tonight driving around and we'll call you again in the morning."

"And you'll call us if you find him?"

"Of course."

"Wouldn't you be better off staying here so we can reach you if one of our cars spots him?"

"Someone will be here to answer the phone and we'll check back at intervals," Jason said. "If you find him we'll know within half an hour of your call."

D'Angelo shrugged and put the pad he was holding back in his shirt pocket, then buttoned the flap down before speaking again. "I know another officer was by earlier to pick up a picture of Sean, but do you, by any chance, have another one that I could take with me?"

"I'll get it," Marilyn said, and left the room quickly. She was back in a minute with a wallet-size color photo. She handed it to the policeman, who glanced at it without a word and then put it into his other shirt pocket.

Five minutes later Officer D'Angelo was guiding his patrol car down Canyon Drive and thinking about Sean Jeffries. He hadn't needed the picture. His only reason for requesting it had been to give the parents a small dose of hope. Maybe it would help them to believe he was keeping a special eye open for the missing little boy. By tomorrow there would be one in his mailbox at work, compliments of the department. If his worst fears were confirmed, he wouldn't even need that. The whole town would be getting a photograph of Sean Jeffries, compliments of the *Vista Tribune*.

Phil D'Angelo had been a cop for eleven years. He hadn't been the brightest cadet to go through the academy, but he was a good patrol officer. His success was due to his street sense and his instincts.

And tonight those instincts were telling him that the Frequency Two broadcast about Sean Jeffries involved more than an angry or adventurous boy running away from home. D'Angelo had a feeling it involved a lot more.

The form on the gravel path began to stir. The woman opened lifeless eyes and pushed herself to a sitting position. She cut her hands on her glasses that lay shattered on the stones, but as she got to her feet and hobbled slowly to the back door of the garage, only one thought existed for her; only one compulsion drove her. She must get to Georgie before her husband did. He would hurt the boy again unless she stopped him. Millie unlocked the door with the key she still clutched in her hand and turned the knob.

They hardly ever used the back entrance to the garage. The door was warped and moisture-swollen and refused to budge when she pushed against it. She shoved harder. It moved a few inches and then stuck again. She began beating against the rotting wood with her fists. A high-pitched, keening wail was coming from her throat as she pummeled the last barrier separating her from her son. The door moved another inch, froze, and then slammed against the wall with a crash as Millie stumbled into the darkened garage.

She groped along the wall until she found a switch, and suddenly the garage was flooded with light.

Her tormented wail became a series of moans that grew softer and then died away altogether. The woman looked confused and shuffled in large, seemingly aimless circles for several moments as though she had already forgotten her mission. All at once she stopped and cocked her head as if listening to someone. She looked to the back of the garage and then started forward, her movements purposeful once again. She bent over the canvas bag on the floor and began working on the knot in the drawstrings with bleeding, arthritic fingers.

Phil D'Angelo drove the patrol car into the faculty parking lot of the high school and parked in the shadows next to the building. He turned his lights off and flipped the toggle switch to turn on the outside radio speakers. As he took the heavy black flashlight from the seat beside him and emerged from the car, he wondered what he was doing there. He had no idea what he expected to find. Nevertheless, he made a slow circuit of the grounds, playing his light into corners and under fire escapes. The search produced nothing and D'Angelo got back in the car and lit a forbidden cigarette that he produced from a pack concealed under the seat. The department had recently decreed that its officers were not to smoke while in uniform, a rule D'Angelo obeyed occasionally and ignored the rest of the time. He inhaled deeply and listened to the crackle of the radio that was now coming through the inside speakers again.

He left the door of the patrol car open while he smoked and thought about the missing boy. Only when the glowing coal had burned down within a quarter inch of his lips did he toss the butt on the ground and shut the door. He started to reach for the key and then changed his mind and picked up the microphone instead.

"Three-six, Dispatch."

"Dispatch, bye."

"I have a Frequency Two on a juvenile male Caucasian, Sean Jeffries. Is the code still active?"

"Affirmative, Three-six."

"Requesting FI still open."

"Stand by, Three-six."

"FI" stood for "Find and Interview" and referred to a list of people sought for questioning about a criminal suspect or a missing person. While D'Angelo waited for the dispatcher to check the case file, he stretched and was about to reach under the seat for another cigarette when the radio crackled to life again.

"Three-six, Dispatch."

"Three-six, bye."

"One open FI."

"Stand by, Dispatch."

D'Angelo flipped on the interior light and yanked the pad and pen from his shirt pocket.

"Ready to copy."

"Lamar Johnson, male Negro, fourteen years old. Address is one-seven-three-one Las Flores in Highland Vista, described as a friend. No phone response as of eighteen hundred hours. Do you want a phone number, Digger?"

"Negative, Sally." The policeman smiled at the dispatcher's use of the nickname as he put the pen back in his shirt pocket. "Three-six clear."

"Dispatch clear."

The young cop put back the microphone and reached for the ignition. The car roared to life and Phil "Digger" D'Angelo pulled slowly away from the high school and made a wide circle in the faculty parking lot to get back to exit and to an address on Las Flores Avenue.

Georgie was heavy, almost too heavy for the woman to lift. She managed to get him out of the bag and drag him to the back door of the garage before she had to stop and rest. While she waited to catch her breath, she untied the boy's hands and feet. It had taken all her strength to get

him this far. It was going to be even harder to get him
over the step and across the path to the house. She was
panting and would have liked to wait longer, but she knew
her husband would be back any minute. She had to hide
him where George wouldn't find him. She ignored the
pains that shot up her back and arms and the rapid beating
of her heart as she half lifted, half dragged her son over
the single step in the doorway and out of the garage. She
didn't put her burden down until she was across the yard
and in front of the kitchen door.

The first thing Sean became conscious of was pain. If
he could have viewed himself from a distance and seen
with his soul, he might have been intrigued and astounded.
He might even have thought to himself, ''How beautiful it
is,'' and laughed with delighted, childish pleasure at the
brilliant colors that emanated from his body like a miniature aurora borealis.

But Sean's pain was too overwhelming. It wrapped him
and surrounded him like a tapestry made of blue-white
shafts that pulsed in rhythm with the throbbing in his head,
of thirsty, deep-brown sheets of burnt ochre, surging and
rippling from his parched, dry throat, of yellow-and-orange
banners, waving and fluttering and becoming flame-red
tongues of agony as blood rushed back into limbs too long
denied. He opened his eyes or at least thought he did.
Only his left eye opened; his right was cemented closed
by a hard coating of crusted blood. An image floated over
him and the boy blinked and concentrated on forcing the
picture into focus. The vision remained blurred and mys-
terious. Through his pain he could feel himself being
dragged across a hard, abrasive surface. He tried to remember where he was and understand what was happening to him. Fragments of memories came and with them
came sorrow. Mugs was dead. He had crashed into the
runway. He was chasing a tennis ball and lost control of
the airplane and crashed into the end of the runway. Mom

and Dad were going to be mad at him. He shouldn't have
. . . shouldn't . . . sh . . .

The rest of the boy's thought was lost as he drifted
peacefully back over the line into unconsciousness.

Terror is a shy creature. Like a skittish animal of the
woodland, it cloaks itself in darkness and shadow and seldom ventures into the man-made world of electric lights,
automobiles, safety razors, and mortgage payments. Other
passions have been captured and domesticated. Anger
comes close to every man on occasion and then disappears
again with the ease and frequency of the household cat.
Fear is an emotional beast of burden that, like a plow
horse or a donkey, can be trained to aid the powerful in
bending the weak and helpless to their will. Even Love,
that most exalted of emotions, has been from the earliest
days a welcome and familiar visitor, its arrival bringing
pleasure and excitement and its departure causing sadness
and often despair.

Only Terror refused to cohabit with man. Only Terror
remained aloof, not willing to be examined and studied,
not willing to be dissected and analyzed.

And that's odd because it takes so little to summon Terror. Sometimes it requires nothing more than a light shining through a crack underneath a door.

George knew something was wrong the minute he pulled
the Ford into the driveway. Even with the car's headlights
on he could see the light coming from under the garage
door. He knew a moment of gut-wrenching, heart-stopping
terror that paralyzed him with its intensity. The moment
passed leaving Braun trembling and weak. He turned off
the engine and clutched the keys tightly as he got out of
the car. How could this be? The brat couldn't have gotten
loose. Goddamn it, he should have been dead by now. The
old man's hand was shaking and he had trouble getting
the key in the padlock. After what seemed an eternity, the
lock sprang open and he ripped it off and tossed it on the

ground behind him. He slammed back the bolt and raised the heavy door.

The single bulb in the fixture mounted on the wall provided ample light for him to see the empty laundry bag and the open back door. His eyes darted frantically around the garage, into corners and up to the overhead beams. There were no hiding places. The kid was gone.

Braun looked at the open back door again and saw something on the floor next to the step. He walked across the garage and stooped to pick it up. It was one of the kid's shoes. For the first time since he had seen the light shining under the garage door a rational thought formed in his mind.

The kid hadn't escaped. Someone had taken him out of the sack and dragged him away. And George knew who that someone had to be.

Phil D'Angelo parked against the curb in front of a small frame house on Las Flores. Someone was home. There were lights on and the garage door was open. He climbed from the car and began walking up to the front door when he noticed the brass numbers over the doorbell. He frowned and took the pad from his pocket and looked at the address he had copied. This was the wrong house. He wanted the house next door. He snapped the pad shut and began walking to the Johnson home. He was pleased to see that a car was parked in the driveway and lights were on inside.

The first thing George noticed when he entered the kitchen through the back door was the smell of gas. The second thing he noticed was Millie. In spite of his panic, the sight of his wife's bruises and her angry expression startled him, and for a moment all he could do was look at her in shocked silence.

"Stay away from him, George. Leave my baby alone," Millie said in a flat voice.

"Where is he, Millie?"

"You've done enough to him. Leave him alone."

"Goddamn it, where is he?" George advanced on his wife but the fear he expected to see didn't appear. Instead, she glared defiance at him.

"Last chance, Millie. Where's the brat?" George was now standing so close to his wife that she had to take a step back to look into his face.

"George, go kiss a rat's ass," she said.

He slapped her as hard as he could. He knocked her backward, but she was able to grab hold of the counter and remain upright. When she turned back to her husband with the same challenging look, he started to raise his arm for a second blow but changed his mind.

"Never mind. I'll find him myself. Then I'll come back and deal with you." He turned away from Millie and started through the doorway into the living room when he heard the shrill laughter behind him. He whirled around just in time to deflect the carving knife in Millie's hand as she launched herself at him. He screamed as the blade sliced into his shoulder and tried to shove her away, but she seemed to possess the strength of ten men. He grabbed for the knife and managed to knock it from her hand just before he fell backward under the rain of blows and kicks she was delivering. She slammed on top of him and clawed at his face as he twisted and struggled in a desperate effort to get away. She was a wildcat. One of her fingernails ripped a gash near his eye and George let out a bellow of rage. He struck out blindly and his fist smashed into Millie's face. He could feel the cartilage break and saw blood pour from her nose, but Millie didn't seem to notice as she continued to flail and scratch at his eyes. He delivered another blow to her face. This time his aim was better and she was knocked over on her back. Before she could recover, George was on top of her and now it was his turn to do the punishing. Again and again he pounded her head and body with his good arm until she was limp and unresisting beneath him. When he finally staggered to his feet, Millie's features were bloody and unrecognizable.

"Filthy bitch," he hissed and gently touched the side of his face with the back of his good hand where she had gouged him. So much of her blood covered him that he couldn't tell if his face was bleeding or not. He delivered a kick to the still body on the floor and would have done more but he suddenly remembered he had more pressing business. He would deal with her later. Five gallons of gasoline would have to be enough for two bodies. First he had to bind up his shoulder, then he would find the kid and finish him off. He would deal with Millie after the brat was dead. George straightened up and coughed. The smell of gas was much stronger now. Part of his mind warned him of danger from a new quarter, but the warning was drowned out by the churning in his gut that meant his beloved was ravenous . . . and impatient. First things first. He would take care of the kid, then he'd come back to take care of Millie. He began walking toward the bathroom to find something to staunch the flow of blood from his shoulder.

Sean moaned softly and opened his eyes. His face was damp and cool where Millie had sponged away the dried blood while he slept. His head was still throbbing and his thirst was a physical pain. In the distance he could hear people talking but couldn't understand the words. The voices were far away and muted like the sound of the wind in the leaves or the buzzing of insects on a hot summer day. He closed his eyes and wished the voices would go away. Instead, they got louder and more urgent. Now he could hear his name and Sean opened his eyes again. The room was full of people. He turned his head and was startled to see a boy in old-fashioned clothes standing next to the bed.

"It's time." The boy's lips didn't move, but Sean heard the words clearly.

"Who are you?" he whispered.

"You know who I am. It's time for the circle to close. You must get up." The boy's features glowed and the bedroom shimmered in the blue light. Sean felt his strength returning as the light washed over him.

"But I don't know. Please. Tell me what I'm doing here. Who are you?" Suddenly, the most important thing in the world to Sean was learning who the boy in the old-fashioned clothes was. It was more important than the pain in his head or his thirst or even life itself.

"You know who I am. I'm the reason you have to close the circle. You're the reason the scales have to balance. It's time."

"That doesn't make any sense at all," Sean protested weakly. He fell back against the pillow and closed his eyes, then sensed a movement on the bed next to him and opened them again. A gray tomcat on the pillow next to him stretched with languid grace, then walked with haughty disdain to the edge of the bed and hopped to the floor.

Sean tried to sit up but the effort caused a blinding pain to shoot through his head and he fell back with a startled cry. Instantly, he felt a hand move under him and gently support and prop him forward. The pain seemed to flow out of his body and his eyes widened in surprise as he looked over and saw that the boy in the old-fashioned clothes was gone. A huge, heavyset man in overalls was standing next to the bed, helping him to sit up. Sean could smell the pleasant, earthy smell of manure and hay as the man leaned over him and smiled. He reminded Sean of the picture of Farmer Brown in one of the books his mother used to read to him when he was younger.

"Das Liebchen, gohen wir jetzt. We must go."

Sean's head felt like it was full of cobwebs as he tried to understand the strange words. The farmer seemed nice though, and Sean didn't resist as the man turned him around until his feet were dangling off the edge of the bed.

"Hurry. *Beeilen Sie sich, Liebchen.* You must wake up."

"Who are you?"

"The circle must close. Come. It is time."

More riddles. Sean began to wonder if anyone was going to give him a straight answer. He was dizzy and wanted to lie back down on the bed, but the hand behind his back continued pushing him forward until his feet were touching the floor. Only when Sean was fully upright did the pressure ease, and the boy suddenly found himself standing alone in the darkened bedroom. Where had the farmer gone? Where was the boy in the old-fashioned clothes? Did he dream them? The pain in his head returned when the farmer disappeared, and Sean winced as he took a hesitant step without help. He wasn't going to stay here any longer. One way or another he was going home. He tried another step and then another until he was at the foot of the bed. He was resting for the next leg of his journey when the bedroom door was suddenly opened. Sean could see a man outlined in the light from the hallway. Dad was here to take him home. He almost cried with relief as he took another step toward the shape standing in the doorway.

"Dad, my head hurts. I want to go home."

An instant later Sean knew he had made a mistake. He could feel the oily Presence nuzzling his mind, searching for a way inside.

The Thing was back—and It was hungry.

Celia Johnson put down the magazine she was reading and gave her husband a questioning look as the doorbell chimed. He shook his head before getting up from his chair and walking across the living room to the front door.

"Yes, may I help you?" Dr. Johnson said to someone on the porch, and Celia thought he sounded surprised. A moment later he stepped aside, and her eyes widened as a uniformed policeman stepped into the room.

George looked quickly around his wife's bedroom and the angry churning in the pit of his stomach intensified when he didn't see the boy. He was about to turn away and look for the kid in the backyard when he heard a dry, croaking voice come from the shadows at the foot of the bed.

"Dad, my head hurts. I want to go home."

He let out a deep breath and smiled as he saw the boy take a wobbly step in his direction.

"So, you're still alive," Braun hissed. "We'll have to see about that, won't we?" His smile broadened as he walked into the dark bedroom to complete what he had begun.

The woman on the floor twitched as the eerie glow filling the room began to grow brighter. The hum of machinery, or perhaps it was the sound of distant voices, became louder, more demanding, summoning the woman to her final task.

A leg moved. An arm jerked. Millie raised her head and opened sightless eyes. One hand groped across the floor and fingers closed around the handle of the knife. She rose to her feet and began walking back and forth with mechanical, uneven steps. Her head swiveled back and forth while her arms swung up and down with exaggerated, twitchy movements like a wooden doll in the hands of an amateur puppeteer rehearsing for a performance. As she paraded from one side of the room to the next in a grotesque parody of life, the sound of rattling could be heard coming from the kitchen. There was a creaking noise and then a loud crash as the back screen door flew open and slammed against the side of the house. Shapes began to form and weave around her, human shapes, childlike, transparent shapes, each vague and undefined but adding an infinitesimal bit of light to the room. Faster and faster they streamed in until the room was ablaze with an unearthly radiance. Each new arrival first came near the shambling figure that still marched around the room and then moved a short distance with her like invited guests who must greet their hostess.

* * *

Sean barely felt the hands closing around his throat as he concentrated all his attention on keeping the Thing at bay. Only when the light from the doorway began to grow dim and the room began to fade did he realize that he was going to die in this strange house for no reason that he could understand. That was when he heard the voice inside his head.

"Push it, Sean." The boy in the old-fashioned clothes was inside him, shouting to him. "We'll help you. Push it away."

Sean tried to push back against the Thing but his oxygen-starved brain refused to cooperate. He no longer felt his body straining and crying out for air. The bedroom had disappeared and he was . . . he is . . .

He is stretched out on a bed in a tiny bedroom. His heart is pounding as he masturbates for the first time. The door is opening and shame fills him as his father strides into the room.

He is kicking and struggling as his father wraps a lamp cord around his neck. He is being hoisted aloft and hanging by his neck from the ceiling. His lungs are screaming for air. He is dying . . .

He is walking on a sidewalk in the cool night air. He has worked hard and he is tired, but he must hurry. It is his daughter's birthday and he has promised to be home before she goes to bed. He has no warning before a steel pipe crashes into the back of his head. It rises and falls and from a great distance he knows that his face and head are being smashed and broken. He is dying . . .

He is feeling the hot sun on top of his head as he wraps the chain around the stump and climbs into the seat of his Waterloo Boy. He is shifting to the lowest forward gear and the tractor lurches forward on the soft earth. One of the huge back tires loses traction and begins spinning, throwing dirt and pebbles into the air. The other tire continues moving forward and the big machine tilts as the right side buries itself deeper and deeper in the soil. It topples and he is splashed by kerosene as the fuel tank splits when it strikes a boulder. His legs are pinned underneath the behemoth and he feels the agony of crushed limbs as he lies helpless on the ground. He closes his eyes and waits to die but a laugh echoes in his ears and he opens them again. His son stands over him. The boy says something and he closes his eyes once more, knowing he will get no help from the son who hates him. He hears the strike of a match and an instant later feels the searing flames roasting his flesh. He is burning. He is dying . . .

The bloody figure moved across the living room and entered the hallway, the sightless eyes looking neither right nor left. The hand that gripped the knife began to rise until it was poised in the air, and some trick of the light made the blade sparkle and gleam with a pulsing luminescence as though it possessed a life of its own.

The voices in his head could not be denied. Sean's eyes opened and through the fog that filled the room, he saw a gray snout and yellow, demonic eyes bending over him. Slathering fangs dripped hot, viscous saliva on his upturned face as a force began to gather and build inside him. He could feel the boy in the old-fashioned clothes, the man with the blond hair, the old farmer with the thick accent, loaning him strength and purpose. He felt something powerful and deadly take form and grow until he could no longer contain it. Summoning every bit of energy remaining in his soul, he pushed the force into the leering face above him.

George gasped and released the boy, who fell to the floor. His hands jerked and twitched and he took a faltering step backward. He heard laughter and clapped his hands over his ears in terror. He turned to the doorway and gasped in horror at the apparition that blocked his escape. The barely recognizable, disfigured face of his wife seemed to change expression as he watched and he thought she smiled lovingly at him just before her arm swung down and she buried the carving knife to its hilt in his chest.

The room seemed to buck and roll like a ship in rough seas and George staggered to the hall, where he held on to the wall for support. A numbness was spreading from the center of his chest outward to his arms and legs. He reached the end of the hall and stumbled on the carpet to fall with a crash into the living room. He coughed and blood spurted from his mouth and splashed on the floor. The living room glowed and sparkled as Braun looked up through pain-glazed eyes and saw people standing all around him. He tried to speak and could only gurgle weakly. He tried again and this time managed to choke out the words: "Call an ambulance. I'm hurt."

The room was swimming and fading in front of him. His eyes wouldn't stay focused. Why wasn't anyone helping him? Who were these people? He looked at them pleadingly. "Help me. Please. Somebody help me." A face swam close to his own and George realized with growing horror that he knew the man bending over him.

"Hey, George. How you doing? You remember me?" The face of Tom McCarthy appeared and then began collapsing and falling in on itself. "See what you did to me, George, ol' buddy?"

"You were supposed to take me back where you picked me up. That was our deal." A girl Braun didn't recognize spoke angrily.

"Verfluchter Kerl! Verwahrloster Kerl!" George felt a pain more intense than the knife in his chest as his father's voice rang in his ears. "You t'ink I don't know you've the devil in you?"

Braun choked as he tried to speak, and more blood erupted out of his nose and mouth. With an effort that called upon every reserve of strength he possessed, he

managed to prop himself up and turn his face to the old
man standing over him.

"I love you, Poppa," he was able to gasp before blackness closed over him.

Sean awoke on the floor of the bedroom. His throat burned
as he drew huge gulps of air into his tortured lungs. Every
part of him ached and he got to his feet slowly, his mind
blank. Only a nameless compulsion to get out, to find a place
of safety kept him moving toward the front of the house. He
got to the living room and leaned against the wall, his brain
hardly registering the carnage and blood around him. A voice
next to him brought his head around and he looked into the
eyes of the boy in the old-fashioned clothes.

"The circle is almost closed." He smiled wistfully at
Sean and his features seemed to grow transparent and dim.

"Who are you? Who are those other people?" Sean
gestured weakly to ghostlike figures that were barely vis-
ible around the body of George Braun, sprawled in the
middle of the floor. The rotten-egg odor of gas in the room
made him cough and his raw throat constricted with pain,
but he forced the words out anyway, his need to understand all of a sudden as great as his need to get away.

"You must go. There is more for you to do yet." The
image of the boy in the old-fashioned clothes had almost
disappeared now and only a faint outline remained.

"But who are you? I have to know. And who are the
others?" Sean cried out in desperation.

The image was gone. Sean was alone in the room with
the silent corpses of Millie and George Braun. He staggered the last few steps and was opening the front door
when he felt the others rushing into his mind. The boy in
the old-fashioned clothes, the old farmer, the man with
the blond hair, they were inside him, moving to fill him
like weary travelers returning home from a long journey,
their voices combining and blending with dozens of others
in a ghostly chorus that filled him with terror as he heard
the words and knew the answer to his question.

"We are who you were. You are who we are. We are one."

Phil D'Angelo emerged from the Johnson house and crossed the lawn to the patrol car. He hadn't learned a thing that wasn't already in the original report. He unlocked the car and climbed in, then reached under the seat for his cigarettes. He lit one and inhaled deeply, enjoying the harsh bite of the smoke in his throat. He took two more quick puffs then raised the microphone to his lips.

"Dispatch, Three-six."

"Dispatch, bye."

"I'm mobile again."

"Ten-four. Dispatch clear."

"Three-six clear."

He replaced the mike and was reaching for the ignition when he thought he saw a movement outside the car. He turned his head and glanced out the window. A moment later he was out of the car and sprinting toward the small figure that was staggering down the sidewalk. He didn't need to take the picture from his shirt to recognize the Jeffries boy.

Sean was semiconscious in the back of the patrol car. D'Angelo called for an ambulance and a backup unit, then he got out of the cruiser and unsnapped his service revolver. He was almost to the curb when there was a crash of breaking glass, and something hurtled through the front window of the house and landed catlike on the lawn. Instinct and training were faster than thought. D'Angelo had his .38 leveled and was crouched, ready to fire before his conscious mind registered the sight. The animal was immense. It turned a huge head and gave the policeman a look of such hatred that D'Angelo staggered back under the force of the gaze. Fear paralyzed him for an instant before his reflex took over and he emptied all six rounds into the creature.

The animal snarled . . . and was gone.

* * *

D'Angelo remained frozen, not believing the testimony of his eyes. It was gone. He couldn't have missed it. Not an animal that large. Not at this range.

He could hear the wail of sirens getting closer as he stood up cautiously and reloaded his service revolver. He stepped up on the curb and took a half dozen steps around the patrol car before dropping into a half crouch and searching the front of the darkened house. He could see nothing. He straightened up again, took two more steps, and was almost to the sidewalk when he was blown off his feet and over the hood of the car as the house in front of him disappeared with a roar and an explosion that shattered windows a block away.

CHAPTER THIRTEEN

The Days After

The most effective medication known to man is time, but some injuries require larger doses than others. A shattered body will often respond more quickly than a broken mind; an injured mind will heal more swiftly than a shattered soul.

Officer D'Angelo was treated for third-degree burns on his face and hands and for a broken shoulder that he suffered when he struck the pavement after being blown over the hood of the patrol car. He was released after three hours and promptly reassigned by the Sheriff's Department to eight weeks of light duty, a consequence of his injuries that he found much more painful than his broken shoulder.

Sean wasn't as lucky.

Either Jason or Marilyn remained with him continuously during his first two weeks in the hospital. They took turns watching over him while he slept. They talked to him when his eyes opened and he stared, without expression, into a reality that existed only for him.

And they held him when he screamed . . . which he did often in those first days.

Most afternoons, Father John would stop in for a few minutes to see the boy and give what comfort he could to Marilyn who stayed with Sean during the day. More often than not, Sean would sleep through these visits without being aware of them. If he did awaken while the priest was in the room, he would sometimes turn his head and look blankly at the priest and his mother, who would be speaking in hushed whispers next to his bed. When this happened, Marilyn sometimes thought she could see a glimmer of light, a faint reflection of her son behind the eyes that stared without seeing.

And then the light would blink out and she would die a little more.

After two weeks, the hospital staff decided they had done all they could for his physical injuries and the rest was up to someone else. They recommended that Sean be placed in a controlled environment at an institution that specialized in "Cases of This Kind." When Jason and Marilyn refused to consider the idea, the hospital reluctantly discharged the boy into the custody of his parents and the care of his God who, after all, was probably the Only Physician who could do him any good anyway.

And a strange thing happened.

Sean's improvement began as soon as the Cadillac pulled into the driveway of the house on Canyon Drive and a gray blur that was Mugs bounded up to the car. The boy got out before his parents had a chance to open the door for him. Jason and Marilyn watched their son and held their breath while Sean stood motionless, his eyes fixed on the small animal that was jumping up and down, trying desperately to leap into his arms.

And then the miracle happened.

While his parents watched, not daring to believe what they were seeing, the boy who had been away for two weeks suddenly came home. He reached down and scooped up his small pal and suddenly he was laughing as the terrier planted sloppy wet kisses all over his face. At the sound of the laughter, Jason and Marilyn exchanged looks and dared to hope.

But life didn't return to normal quickly. If the boy's soul and mind began healing when he returned home that day, it still took a long time before the process was complete.

For the first month that he was home, Sean spent most of his time in a place that only he could visit. The hope that his parents had felt when he responded to Mugs and seemed to recognize the little dog paled and evaporated as day after day went by with no improvement in their son's condition. He was docile and cooperative. He would go where he was led, he would do what he was told, and seemed to understand at least some of what was going on around him.

But he never talked. It seemed as if his soul were still held hostage somewhere. The boy wanted to hide and he had found a place that kept everyone else away.

They brought him to a psychiatrist who spent six weeks trying to locate the boy's hiding place. He failed. They brought him to another . . . and then another.

And then they brought him to a doctor in Santa Monica, a woman everyone said was the best in the state and maybe even in the country. Dr. Pariel's office was a parlor in the run-down house she had lived in for almost seventy years. As soon as the old woman opened the door and Marilyn saw what passed for a waiting room, she had second thoughts about trusting the ancient practitioner with her son's mental care. It was only the hour and a half drive she had already made that persuaded her to take a chance. When Dr. Pariel took Sean by the hand and led him into a room somewhere in the bowels of the tomb that passed for a house and office, Marilyn almost cried out, "No! I've changed my mind. Bring him back."

She said nothing, and that was Sean's salvation.

After two sessions with Dr. Pariel, Sean began to notice what was going on around him. After three months he was answering simple questions and responding to affection.

One night, six months after bringing her son to Dr. Pariel, Marilyn thought she heard someone crying. She got out of bed and went to Sean's room. She opened his door and went to the side of his bed.

"Baby, what's wrong?" She didn't expect an answer, and her words were spoken more to soothe and comfort than to communicate.

"MUGS! HE KILLED MY DOG! MOMMY, HE HIT MUGS!" The boy screamed at her.

She held him and reassured him and he was suddenly her son again. She turned on the light and called Mugs, who came out from under the bed with tousled hair and a put-upon expression. She was finally able to calm the boy and when he did go back to sleep, she stayed with him and sat by his bed until the sun came up the next morning.

Sean remained at home for two years before he was finally able to return to school . . . and to the third grade at Puerta Grande. When he finally did return, he was the oldest boy in the third-grade class.

No one at the grammar school seemed to remember Sean's reputation or the strange events of the first two weeks of class two years before. At least no one ever said anything about them to the quiet boy who always seemed to be with Michael (who now preferred to be called Mike) Taylor, when he wasn't in class. The only one who couldn't have forgotten was Toby Elliot. That didn't matter because Toby was no longer a student at Puerta Grande. Toby was at a place called Newhome, where the courts send children who display a penchant for stealing cars.

If any scars remained from the nightmare he had survived they were invisible to his family and friends. By the time Sean was fifteen and ready to begin high school, he was a very bright, quite normal, and reasonably happy young man.

It didn't take him long to learn his way around Highland Vista High School. He maintained a 4.0 grade-point average even after he started playing football in his sophomore year, and he had no difficulty being accepted into Stanford University after his graduation in 1969. He chose to major in history and seemed to have a special affinity for the subject that earned him the respect of his teachers and eventually a scholarship to Harvard Law School. In 1973 Jason and Marilyn drove their son to Los Angeles

International Airport, where he boarded a United flight to Boston on the first leg of his journey to Cambridge, Massachusetts, and the world of contracts, torts, chattels, and conveyances.

The field of law seemed to be a natural choice for Sean. Somehow, he seemed to have developed a sense of the fitness of things. A part of him that even he didn't fully understand seemed to be driven to fight for what he believed was right. It was almost a compulsion.

Sometimes he had dreams. They were strange dreams where people urged him and goaded him . . . and needed him. He wasn't sure if they were nightmares or not. They were just *strange* dreams that he wondered about for a while and then forgot.

In November of that same year he returned home for three days to attend the funeral of his father's partner. Al died in his sleep and Father John Cassidy celebrated the funeral mass at St. Anthony's on a rainy Friday morning. The old priest had tears in his eyes as he delivered the short eulogy to his friend and then was helped from the pulpit by Father McCullough, the youthful new pastor of St. Anthony's. He returned home for Christmas the following month and once again in February of 1974 when Father John followed Al Sutton to whatever reward awaits those who live a life of love and service to their fellow man. Sean asked for and was given permission to say a few words about the friend he had known all his life, and he was dry-eyed as he delivered the short tribute at graveside. It was only when the casket was lowered into the ground that his eyes filled with the tears he made no attempt to conceal.

In 1976 an established and prestigious law firm changed its name and became known as Jeffries and Jeffries. Sean worked hard and did well in his profession. Old-timers in the legal community remembered Jason's rise to prominence a quarter of a century earlier and were struck by the resemblance they were able to see in his son.

In 1980 Sean filed a personal injury lawsuit against an elementary-school teacher who lost control of her car in the rain and smashed into the side of his client's vehicle. Three months after filing he talked the girl's insurance company into an out-of-court settlement. It took six months longer for Sean to talk the girl into marrying him, but in the end he was successful and one sunny March morning in 1981 the office didn't open at eight o'clock. Both partners, an associate, three secretaries, and a receptionist had to attend a wedding.

Sean and Cindy spent hours picking out a name for their first daughter, who came along in late 1982. They finally settled on Theresa.

But when Cindy gave birth to their first son in 1984, Sean refused to discuss the matter. Cindy didn't like the name he insisted on but in the end she reluctantly agreed.

Sean's first son was named Peter.

EPILOGUE

1985

Sean parked his Fiat in the spot reserved for him on the fourth level of the parking structure and slowly climbed from the car. The day was warm and he was hot and tired as he waited for the elevator to take him to the fourteenth floor that was actually the thirteenth floor if you counted them, a concession to the superstitions of future tenants made by the architects who drew up the plans for the building.

He entered the law offices through the door that opened directly into his private office and spared him the need to walk through the reception area and the secretaries' desks. After closing the door behind him, Sean took off his jacket and hung it up in the closet then loosened his tie and opened the top button of his shirt. Instead of going to the big chair behind his desk, he sat down in one of the chairs in front of the desk that clients used when they came to his office. His face was troubled as he pulled the telephone across the desktop and prepared to make a phone call that was perhaps the ultimate in lunacy.

It was all because of the dream.

But wait. Maybe it wasn't only the dream. Maybe part of it was the dream but part of it was the strange feeling that it had all happened before, that he was reliving something he had lived through once before. It was more intense than déjà vu. It wasn't just a feeling. It was almost a memory.

And of course there was the dream. In the dream he was in an airplane waiting for the tower to give him clear-

ance to take off. The engine was idling and he was enjoying the feeling of power that he always (in the dream)
experienced when he was in his airplane.

Sean turned the digital clock on his desk and looked at
the time. It was twelve forty-five in the afternoon. It was
March twenty-third. For no reason Sean could put a finger
on, that date seemed to be important in some way to what
he was about to do. Not that any of it made any sense.

Even the dream itself seemed more detailed, more intense than dreams have any right to be. He would awaken
with the roar of the engine in his ears and the tense anticipation and pleasure of a flyer about to leave the earth
behind and soar to the heavens. Every detail of the dream
was as clearly and permanently imprinted on his brain as
the memory of his wife's body when he made love to her.
And overshadowing the dream was the urgent feeling that
something remained undone. He would get out of bed and
put on a robe, then sit in the living room, remembering.

In the dream he was Peter Marston, a high school
teacher flying a plane out of Meadows Field in Meadows,
Ohio. He was sitting in the plane waiting for clearance to
take off, but something was holding up the tower. He had
been sitting in the airplane for a long time. Something was
wrong. Something was supposed to happen that hadn't
happened yet. He couldn't get a clearance until something
happened.

He couldn't get a clearance until Sean Jeffries did something.

But what was the something?

It was lunacy, of course, but Sean had to be sure. He
opened his briefcase and took out a yellow legal pad and
put it in front of him, then took his pen from his shirt
pocket before lifting the phone receiver and punching
4-1-1 for Information. Old habits are hard to break, and
Sean always had a pen and paper handy when he picked
up the telephone.

"Operator Forty-one, what city please?"

"Area code for Meadows, Ohio, please."

"One moment, please."

Sean doodled absently on the pad while he waited for the operator to look up the area code then sat up as she came back on the line.

"That area code is 6-1-4," she said.

"Thank you."

Sean hung up the phone and then picked it up again. He knew that if he hesitated, if he let himself think about what he was doing, he would never make the phone call. As crazy as it seemed, he was driven to find out if Peter Marston was a real person or just a figment of an over-wrought imagination. This was the only way. He dialed Information in the 614 area code.

"6-1-4 Information. What city, please?"

"Meadows."

"What number, please?"

"Do you have a listing for Meadows Field? It would be a private airfield in Meadows."

"One moment, please."

Sean drew a half circle on the pad in front of him and then traced over it while he waited to find out if there was a Meadows Field in the town of Meadows, Ohio. A moment later the operator came back on the line.

"That number is 234-2340," she said.

"Thank you," Sean said in a shaky voice and hung up the telephone.

It's a dream. Nothing more. Sean rose from the chair and walked slowly to his usual seat behind the big desk. He sat down heavily and pulled the telephone over to him with one hand while he reached for the legal pad with the other. His hand was trembling as he lifted the receiver and began to dial the number in Meadows, Ohio.

The phone rang twice before someone picked up. Sean gripped the telephone receiver more tightly as a male voice came on the line.

"Meadows, may I help you?"

"Peter Marston, please," Sean said in a weak voice.

"Can you hold the line for just a minute? I think I saw

him come in, but he may have taken off already. Let me check.''

"That's fine. I'll wait,'' Sean said.

He continued tracing the half circle he had drawn on the pad of paper in front of him while he waited for someone who had never heard of him and who lived half a continent away to come back on the phone and tell him what remained to be done to give him peace of mind. While he waited he traced the half circle again and again until it stood out on the page in sharp contrast to the doodling and random shapes he had drawn earlier.

Suddenly, it didn't seem important anymore. There was no problem. This was nothing but nerves and superstition and coincidence. For the first time in several weeks, Sean felt at peace. He understood what was happening. A happy euphoria settled over the lawyer as he understood for the first time what was really bothering him.

His dad was retiring next month. Jason had already paid cash for a condo in Tahoe and was looking forward to at least six months with Marilyn to enjoy resort living before returning to Los Angeles to begin a life of leisure and idle after more than thirty years on the justice-system battlefield. Sean was frightened and insecure at the prospect of becoming the only Jeffries in the firm of Jeffries and Jeffries. That was all it was. The dream began to make sense to the lawyer as he held the phone to his ear and waited for Peter Marston to come on the line. Taking off in an airplane was like a new beginning. The feeling of something undone was just normal, human insecurity that was to be expected when he was faced with the total responsibility for the law firm that was to be his own. There were no mysteries. There was no supernatural meaning or import to any of it. He had read something about Peter Marston and his subconscious had filled in the gaps to create a dream that hinted at one thing but actually meant quite another.

With a smile of amusement at his own gullibility, Sean Jeffries hung up the telephone.

* * *

Almost three-thousand miles away Peter Marston was balancing precariously on a wing strut, struggling with a misplaced center of gravity as he tried to peer into the gas tank. That was when the phone call came in.

An instructor with the flight school had trotted up to Peter and told him he had a phone call inside. Peter had clambered awkwardly to the ground and returned to the FBO only to find the telephone line silent and dead.

No, the caller had not left a name. Yes, he had asked for Peter Marston.

No one had any idea who it might have been.

Peter returned to his airplane and finished his preflight. He climbed into the cockpit and buckled himself in securely before calling "Prop clear," in a loud voice out the window and starting the engine.

It was time to fly. It was time to be special and important.

It was time to begin a new adventure.

Sean looked blankly at the pad he had been doodling on. There was a half circle drawn on the bottom of the page and Sean looked at it for a long time before picking up a pencil from his desk and drawing a line that connected the two ends of the arc.

The circle was complete.